The Whale in the Cave

By Mike Avitabile

For Tate

"When the moon gets bored, it kills whales. Blue whales and fin whales and humpback, sperm and orca whales; centrifugal forces don't discriminate."

- Marina Keegan, *The Opposite of Loneliness*

One

"Do you know why you're here?"

I look away from the window, wincing when our eyes meet. It's not because I'm scared. It's just...that question was so deep, I wasn't expecting it.

"Do you mean...how do you mean? Like on a metaphysical level, do I know why I'm here? How I got here, what my purpose is? What my destiny is? Like that?"

He stares at me without any expression. I want to continue guessing. This could be a huge moment in my life! This might be the gateway to a new realization about myself. I could be on the verge of enlightenment here. This is huge. Maybe.

"I mean, no one has ever asked me this before. *Why* are you here? Or is it, why are *you* here? Is that what you mean? Why is it *me* that's here, in front of you, being asked this question? Like that?"

He just keeps staring at me, but really it's like he's staring through me.

"Okay. Well, you're asking me this, so obviously you think I know the answer. But I don't. I mean, do *you* know why you're here?"

I pause, and a smile cracks my lips apart. My mom always used to say that I had the perfect smile as a kid. I don't know if it was true, but it did give me the confidence to smile all the time. Even when it's not appropriate, I'm smiling. Funerals, sex, staring contests. You name it. I don't think there's a single picture of me where you can't see at least 14 of my teeth. So I keep smiling at this guy, knowing that I absolutely nailed the answer to his question and ignoring the fact that I probably would be smiling if I bombed it too. He takes a deep breath before speaking.

"Can you tell me how you heard about us? About what we're doing here?"

"What do you mean? You guys mailed me the invitation and that packet of information. I hadn't even heard of Malibu Oaks before. I mean, I had heard of *Malibu*...everyone has. But not this place."

"The invitation came in the mail, addressed to you?"

"Yeah, it came in the mail. Like a week ago."

"Addressed to you?"

I shrug.

"Sure. I don't know. I left it at my apartment. By the way, nice digs you got me set up in! I wasn't expecting something that nice. You guys really over-delivered."

The guy sighs so forcefully that I can smell what he had for lunch. I turn my head away. Tuna sandwich.

"Well done, Tony," he mumbles.

"Oh, it's Luke," I correct him.

He looks up at me and starts staring right through me again. I smile and shrug. A hummingbird is hovering outside the window, and I watch it for a little while. Hummingbirds are so cool.

"Luke," he starts. "Did you read the packet before you came in here today?"

"You bet. Every word. Though I have to say..."

"Every word," he whispers, shaking his head as he stares into his lap.

"Why, was I not supposed to?"

He looks up sharply at me, then eyes me up and down.

"Do you feel confident that you'll be able to pass a standard employment drug test?"

"There's a drug test? Is it today? I mean, that's fine. That should be fine. I just didn't know."

"Do you even know why you are here?" he repeats.

Alright, man. No. I don't know. Maybe I should have read the packet more closely. I look around the room. It's relatively stark, but it still feels comfortable. There must be good Feng Shui; that always helps.

"Sorry, how do you mean?"

"Jesus," he mutters. "Take a seat over here."

He motions to the right side of the room. There are no chairs or couches or anything that you would normally expect to sit on.

"Over here?"

I point to the same side of the room where he had just motioned. I think he might be crazy. There's nowhere to sit. Not even a beanbag.

"Over here," he repeats.

A beanbag would be great right about now. In my mind it's a blue one. I like them under stuffed. The kind that I can just sink into as I shed my tension from the day. It doesn't matter that it's 2:00 pm and I haven't had a job in weeks. A man can get tense at any time of day, in any circumstance. It doesn't matter if he's working or married or possibly still high from the joint he lit when he woke up earlier that day. Or none of those things. They're just examples.

I'm looking around the room, and there's nothing for me to sit on. Just me and this guy with the impatient face, and I don't think he wants me to sit on that either.

"Okay."

I reluctantly take a seat on the floor. I'm near a large window. I feel stupid, and for once I'm not smiling; but then I remember how white my teeth are, and a smile spreads across my face again.

"I'll be back in a moment with your written examination materials."

"Okay."

He walks out a different door than the one that we had walked in a few minutes earlier. He comes back almost instantly and hands me a tablet.

"You will have twenty minutes to complete the examination."

"On this thing?"

He nods as he looks out the window and lets out a very audible sigh.

"Sorry, I just thought this was going to be *written* written. Is this an iPad?"

I look at the device, and I don't recognize the style and shape.

"It doesn't look like an iPad," I tell him. "But I'm sure I can figure out how to use it."

"Your twenty minutes have already begun," he adds quietly, refusing to break his stare out the window.

"Really? Okay. Okay. I'll get started then."

He doesn't look back at me again. He just keeps staring out the window. Maybe my answer to his question has made him start to question why *he* is here. Or why any of us are here at all. It is a pretty poignant question. I could spend at least twenty minutes staring out a window thinking about it, I know that.

"When you're done, set the tablet on the table and wait for me to return."

He turns around and walks out the door, leaving me alone in the room with the tablet and this weird exam. It's not what I'm expecting, but then again, I wasn't expecting anything. It's one of those cause-and-effect exams where each answer determines the next question that pops up, like a fucked up choose your own adventure story.

8. What is Kanye West?

    a. Egotist

    b. Talented

c. Too black

d. Trustworthy

Damn, ball so hard. I like Kanye as an artist, but I'm not really into the things he says when he isn't recording music. Have you heard him speak recently? It's not just what he says, it's how he says it. That said, I am impressed that he was able to create a fashion line by designing clothes for homeless people. Not everyone could do that.

I don't have any problem with his level of blackness, and I'm confused that this is one of the possible answers. A part of me wants to see what'll happen if I choose it, but I feel like it can't be the right answer, unless they're all racist here. And I don't want to work for a racist company. I also don't want to get the question wrong.

On the other hand, I have no idea if he's trustworthy. He seems to tell a lot of truths. Remember that time that he said George Bush doesn't care about black people? I think that's true. But he's also an artist, so maybe his statements are all just part of his act. I don't know. I'm torn. He's obviously an egotist, but I don't think that's my full opinion of him either. That leaves me with B. I tap the tablet, but it misreads my tap and selects C.

"What the hell! Hey, this thing just screwed up!"

I look around the empty room for some sympathy, but the walls don't offer me any.

"Wouldn't have happened on an iPad," I mumble.

9. What is your favorite Kanye West album?

a. One of the ones with the bear on the cover

b. The auto-tune one

c. Too black

d. The one with Jay-Z

Great. More Kanye questions. Can't we just leave the guy alone? I don't pay attention to which songs are on what album, so this one's harder for me to answer. I also don't know why "too black" is here for this question as well. He doesn't have an album by that name. This poorly concealed racism is starting to make me uncomfortable. I go with my gut. I choose D.

11. What is the worst thing that someone could do to you?

a. Lie

b. Be dishonest

c. Present false information at a critical time

d. Flee

I don't know. D. I'm just glad it has nothing to do with Kanye.

14. Are lakes better than rivers?

a. Yes

b. No

c. The ocean

d. Define better

A. But D is pretty tempting.

18. Should you believe everything that you are told from an authority figure?

    a. Yes

    b. No

    c. Yes

C. I guess. After this question, the exam ends abruptly. I look up, and the guy hasn't come back yet. It's just me and this tablet.

"I'm done," I announce, hoping that someone will hear me.

No one comes to check on me, so I just stand here for a few minutes, shifting my weight back and forth.

"I'm done," I repeat, a little louder this time.

Still nothing. I place the fake iPad on the ground where I'm sitting, and I stand up and brush myself off. Then I walk toward one of the doors on the far wall. Maybe the guy is deep in thought somewhere and forgot to come back. I'd believe it. I probably threw him for an existential loop.

It smells like flowers as I pass through the doorway. I think it's lilacs, though maybe it's lavender. Or maybe it's something else that's purple and starts with an L. There's a woman sitting behind a desk on the far side of the room. It doesn't look like this is her office. It just looks like a holding room that happens to have a desk in it. Despite that, she looks pretty comfortable sitting there. Probably more good Feng Shui.

"Hi," I say as I walk in. "Should I close the door behind me?"

"Oh! Hello there," she greets me, ignoring my question. "You finished early. Please have a seat."

There's an overstuffed chair on the other side of the desk where you would expect there to be a chair. She's leaning back in it, her arms running along her sides. Her hands are clasped together on her lap. I sit down on a chair in front of the desk, and I mimic her body position. I've heard that people feel powerful when you mimic them, and I like to empower women whenever I can.

"This room makes a lot more sense than the last room," I tell her.

"That's good. So, what's your name?" she says as she smiles.

"Luke. Nice to meet you."

"And you got an invite from us in the mail, yes?"

"That's right."

"And you just passed the exam in the other room?"

"Sure, I think so. How do you know? Does it tell you? I don't think it told me either way."

She raises her eyebrows.

"You don't know if you passed or not?"

"No, I passed. Definitely," I confirm.

Man, I really need this job. I can't have some stupid fake iPad test stand between me and an opportunity like this. A free apartment? In Malibu? Please.

"Good! That's good."

"Mmm-hmm."

"I'm sure you have plenty of questions already. But if you'll allow me, I'd like to explain to you why exactly we brought you here."

"Good, I'm glad you said that. That last guy—I mean, no offense if you guys are friends—but he wasn't very helpful. And that packet you guys sent out? Forget it."

"You didn't read the packet?" she asks.

Shit.

"No, I did. I did."

"OK, how about we start over? In front of you is a contract. In it, you will see that for all references to our company, we are referred to as *The Board*. This is the business entity that we use when hiring all our staff members."

"So, wait. This is not Malibu Oaks? The invitation said..."

"The invitation's not important. All you need to know is that all the people working for us here in the community are technically employed by The Board, okay?"

"Does it have quotes around it?"

"What? The Board? No."

The Board. Got it.

"Anyway, that is the name of the company on your paperwork, but for everyone else out there, we are Malibu Oaks, and you can refer to us as Malibu Oaks."

"Okay." I lean forward and lower my voice. "So who *does* work for Malibu Oaks then?"

"Please don't ask me this again," she sighs.

"Got it."

"You don't have to keep confirming you hear what I'm saying."

"Okay."

She raises her eyebrows again.

"I mean...alright."

"So, a little history lesson, shall we? Malibu Oaks was formed in the early 1920s. Droves of people from the East Coast were moving out west as the film industry was just starting to take off. As more and more people arrived, more and more wealth was being created, but the housing market was slow to catch up to all the demand. A few years before the great depression, a group of the wealthiest men in town got together and purchased this parcel of land that we're on today. It sat undeveloped until the end of World War II, but after just a few short years, it had become internationally known as the pinnacle of private community living."

"Really? I've never even heard of it before."

She chuckles.

"Well, it's world-renowned among, shall we say, the elite? In total the property is about 500 acres. All privately owned and unlike anything else in the world."

"I saw that there's a lake somewhere in the middle of everything? I thought that we have no fresh water. How does that work?"

"It's man-made. It all but dried up in the sixties. We had to bring in a professional rain dancer to get the lake back to boating levels again."

"For real?"

"It's all on Wikipedia. You can look it up."

"Why did they choose to buy land all the way over here by the beach and not in the valley near all the studios? It seems so inconvenient."

"Who doesn't love the sea air?" she asks blandly.

"That's it?"

"Luke, I think we're deviating from the topic at hand. What you need to understand is that the Malibu Oaks community has been here for a very, very long time. And it will continue to be here for a very long time. And it is our job to ensure that it can do this. Do you understand?"

"No, not really."

"Luke," she says, tapping a pen on her knee. "We would like to maintain our community and the company that manages it as long as we possibly can."

She crosses her right leg over her left. I attempt to do the same, but my balls get in the way and I squirm uncomfortably.

"OK. But isn't that the goal of every company? Like, who has a goal to exist only for a few more years and then to get run out of business? That seems like a pretty standard goal to me."

"Please let me continue. It is important to understand how we make our money. As you can imagine, living in a community like this does not come cheap."

"Sure. But don't rich people love spending their money?"

She shakes her head.

"There's a whole slew of funding sources that funnel into The Board. We have community fees, association fees, conservation fees, heritage society fees...the list goes on and on."

"OK. Sorry, what does this have to do with me? I thought this..."

"These fees are what keep us afloat!" she blurts out, her hands slamming against the edge of the desk as she lurches up out of her seat. "And we need them to continue to come in. That is, we need the residents to continue to pay them. And to do that, they have to perceive that there is an immense *value* in them paying these fees. Do you understand?"

"Sure, yeah. Value. Got it."

She slowly sits back down, though her eyes are still a bit frantic.

"That's why we've started this program here, the one you've been invited to join."

"Program? You mean, this job that I'm interviewing for?"

"Exactly. This job is a part of a brand new program, and it's *very* confidential. Understand? It is absolutely imperative that no one outside of The Board even knows about its existence."

"You got it. I can keep a secret."

"Good, Luke. That's what we like to hear. I mean, you can imagine the kind of situation we'd cause if the residents learned that we've been hiring actors to make their community seem better than it is. It would be devastating! Absolutely devastating."

She leans back in her chair and laughs softly.

"Sorry?"

Suddenly, the door behind me swings open, and the man from earlier storms over to the desk, stopping abruptly alongside me.

"Did I not tell you to wait in the other room until I returned?" he barks.

I look up at him, and he looks pretty upset, so I smile.

"I finished the test early, so I came in here. She was just telling me about..."

"Is something wrong?" the woman asks.

The guy doesn't say anything and, instead, nods his head to the corner of the room. She follows him over there. They're whispering like I can't hear them, but three can play at this game. I lean over in my chair and cup my hand to my ear. I still can't hear them. Oh well. The woman looks back at me a few times, shaking her head. The guy is doing the same thing. After a couple of minutes of whispering, they both walk back toward me.

"Luke," she croons, sliding back down into her chair and flashing a wide smile. "There's been a slight change of plans. Have you ever fancied yourself as a *secret* investigator?"

Two

As I open the door to my apartment, that stupid packet is sitting in plain sight on the counter. I don't waste any time. I grab it and plop myself down onto my couch. I've had this couch for longer than I can remember. I think it might have been a wedding present that someone gave to my parents; it's that old. But to me, this couch is home. It smells like home, that unmistakable aroma of some precious nostalgia that's tucked deep in my temporal lobe. I breathe in through my nose as I flip through the pages, trying to locate that memory, also trying to find where I left off. I don't believe in dog-earing pages. I do not like to deface property, and I refuse to let this be the peak of the slippery slope to a criminal life that I'm not cut out for.

I'll just start from the beginning. I'm reading every word of this fucking packet forwards and backwards. It still doesn't make any sense to me, especially when I read it backwards. That is a terrible way to try to understand something further. As a word of advice, you are better off reading something forwards twice than reading it forwards and backwards. I don't know who came up with this saying, but it is very misleading.

I kind of got the feeling earlier today that they were on the fence about hiring me, but it didn't seem to matter. By the end of the interview, they had offered me the job. I was told to expect a call the next day with the details about my training program. And all of this was before I even took a drug test. Unbelievable.

The packet is resting against my chest as I fall asleep on the couch. I dream that I'm a cube in a two-dimensional world.

It's tomorrow. I mean, it's today. Fuck. My phone is ringing.

"The hell?" I whisper.

I can't find my phone. My brain has a boot up time that's roughly equivalent to a 1996 Dell PC. My senses are not yet on board, and I can't determine where the sound is coming from. My phone eventually kicks over to voicemail, and the room goes silent.

"Hello?" I rasp.

I don't know who I'm talking to; there's nobody here.

"Be at the main office at 8:00 am tomorrow," the voicemail says.

I push myself upright, and I look into my kitchen and at a magnetic calendar hanging on the fridge. It was hanging there when I moved in. If the calendar is to be trusted, yesterday was a

Wednesday. So that means tomorrow is a Friday. I learned the days of the week at a young age and have not yet forgotten them.

"Who starts a new job on a Friday?" I ask my couch, patting it softly to let it know that I'm addressing it directly.

The couch doesn't respond. It's probably sleeping.

* * *

The training is in a different building than the one that I had visited for my exam and interview. I find this to be acceptable. I'm standing outside the training facility, looking in through a pair of conjoined glass doors. Inside is a large, open space that looks like a refurbished airport hangar, exposed beams and trusses and all kinds of cool looking shit lining the ceiling. The floors are, well, floors. I don't pay attention to the things on the ground as much. There's a simple-looking sign erected on a simple-looking easel that faces out to the steps of the building where I'm standing. It says HAPPIES and then has an arrow pointing to the right.

Over on the far side of the room is a group of about 12 to 15 people. They're all standing around talking to each other, but I can tell by their body language that none of them had met until this morning. Still, they're all smiling, and for the most part, they're a very attractive group of people. They've formed a sort of semi-circle, and I add myself on to the end of the chain.

"Hey. Happies!" I announce with mock enthusiasm.

"Happies!" one of the girls cheerfully responds back.

"Uh, you guys all just get here too?"

"Yes!"

"Yup!"

"Uh-huh!"

Whoa. Much more energy than I was prepared for. I mean, it's still early. Who can be that amped at 8AM? I thought they would all have boot-up times like a Dell PC from 1986 and I'd be the sharp one. Just kidding. Dell didn't make PCs in 1986. Learn your computer history.

"Have you ever started a job on a Friday?" I ask. "I sure haven't."

"If you can call this a job," one of the guys replies through his smile.

A few of them nod again. I already feel like I don't understand. I smile anyway.

"What do you mean?"

"Did you read the packet?" one of the girls asks.

"Yes. I did. I read the packet. Did anyone else find it to be completely useless?"

Before anyone responds, a man in a grey sweater vest comes over from the other side of the room and stands in the small opening of our crooked little semi-circle.

"Luke Balena?"

"Yeah?"

"There you are. Come on over here with me."

He motions to the other side of the room where two lonely-looking nerds are sitting at a small folding table.

"Me?"

He nods.

"Yeah, come on. We're about to get started."

"Sorry, I think you might have the wrong guy. Maybe you made a mistake? I think I'm supposed to be over here."

He produces a clipboard from somewhere even though I didn't see him carrying one before. Guys with sweater vests can do stuff like this, especially when it comes to clipboards. He runs his finger down a piece of paper and then nods again as he stops his hand a few inches down.

"Nope. Luke Balena. I've got you right here."

He turns the clipboard to me and shows me my name.

LUKE BALENA

Well, shit.

"Maybe there's been a mix-up? I'm pretty sure I'm supposed to be here with the HAPPY group."

I look at everyone else in the circle, and they all look back at me with blank faces. I don't know what I'm expecting them to do, but they're letting me down.

"Is Kanye too black?" he asks me.

I'm still looking at the group. There's a black guy that kind of looks like Donald Glover standing a couple of people over from me. He looks directly at me and raises his eyebrows. I turn my eyes away and look back at the sweater vest guy.

"Hmm?"

"When you took the exam, did you not tell us that Kanye West is 'too black'?"

Donald Glover keeps looking at me. I can't blame him. We're talking about race. People always pay attention when you talk about race.

"No."

"It says here you did."

He flips back the paper with all the names on it and produces what looks like a readout of my exam answers. He nods vigorously while staring down at the results.

"That fake iPad screwed up!" I exclaim. "I didn't pick that. I picked something else! And that guy who gave me the test wasn't even there to help me out!"

"Luke, there are no wrong answers here. It's fine. You picked what you picked. Now come on, let's go over here."

"I mean, even if I picked that as my answer, that's kind of misleading, isn't it? Those were *your* racist answers on there. I was just supposed to pick one that..."

"Felt the most right to you?" the black guy asks.

He has a slight smirk on his face, and the rest of the all-white group lets out an uneasy laugh. One guy laughs a little too loud, and I decide that he's the real racist, not me.

"I don't know, man. I didn't pick that. I like Kanye. I didn't even know that he was black. He's black? I had no idea."

The sweater vest guy taps me on the shoulder a few times and gives me a slight tug.

"Come on, Luke. We all know that Kanye is black."

"I had no idea," I reaffirm.

"It doesn't matter. This is, uh...this is what happens when you choose that answer. Alright? You come over here with us. OK?"

"Wait, I could have been one of these guys instead?" I implore him, but he's tugging my sleeve and I'm slowly shuffling alongside him. "For the same pay?"

I keep looking at the group, and I'm struggling with a sense of loss, which really makes no sense since I still don't know any of them or what they're here to do. But there's something shitty about being taken away from a bunch of people labeled HAPPIES. The sweater vest guy gives me another good tug, and I reluctantly begin to follow him over to the other group.

"Too black..." I hear the black guy mutter as we walk away.

"Alright, everybody," the sweater vest guy announces. "We found our missing man. He was trying to sneak off and be one of the happies."

My group—my new group—lets out a murmur of a laugh. I look back at the happies, and someone has produced a soccer ball out of nowhere. They're all taking turns trying to juggle it between themselves. My stomach sinks.

"As I said before, my name is Don. I'm going to be your trainer."

"Sorry, before you begin...how long is this going to last? And when will you describe what the job actually is?"

He smiles, but it seems like a fake smile. It looks nothing like the genuine smiles from the people in the other group.

"We'll be in here as long as we need to be. Longer if you keep asking questions!" he shouts, slapping his knee with an open hand.

His jokes. Already, I can't. He continues.

"So, this is an entirely new program here at Malibu Oaks. You—along with those guys and girls over there—are the second class we're bringing on board. And as you've already heard during your interview panel, confidentiality is absolutely paramount for your employment here to continue."

"Confidentiality about what?" one of the two nerds asks.

"Oh, m-manners," Don stammers. "Should we do a round of introductions before we begin?"

I shake my head, but they go on anyway and introduce themselves. I don't listen. Nerd One, Nerd Two. Who cares.

"So, uh...yes. Confidentiality," Don continues. "You see, Malibu Oaks is in the middle of a resident retention, uh, crisis. We've got people moving out and renting their places out a weekend at a time. Airbnb, that sort of thing. Full-time occupancy is down to somewhere around 60%. The owners, they're starting to question the dues and the association fees. If they're not living here, why do they have to pay them? That sort of thing. All the things that we're charging them for, they're asking, *Hey, what's in it for me?* In some cases, they're outright refusing to pay. It's becoming quite a problem for us here as we rely on those funds to run the community."

There's a noise across the room, and we all turn to look at it. Someone knocked over a glass with the soccer ball. No one seems to care. They're all smiling, laughing, moving around. It's nothing special, but it looks like fun. Meanwhile, my group is sitting down with a guy wearing a sweater vest. A guy named Don. I bet their trainer is going to be a guy named Rocco or Bear or Vin Diesel. Maybe not Vin Diesel, actually. He doesn't usually look that happy. But he does have a fun name.

"So, what are those guys supposed to be doing over there?" I ask.

"In a nutshell, they're actors. We're going to be paying them to act like happy residents that are enjoying the community, in hopes of subconsciously convincing the actual residents that there's value here that's worth all the fees we charge."

"You think they'll buy that?"

Don shrugs. "Well, I don't know. Would you question it? I know I wouldn't."

He has a point.

"Ugh," I moan. "Pretending to be enjoying yourself in paradise? Sounds like a *really* tough job."

"You'd be surprised. It actually takes a lot of patience and effort to constantly project happiness in everything that you do. Have you ever tried it?"

I shrug.

"It's not like you can just be yourself and do that naturally," he continues. "It takes practice. So that's what they'll be learning over there today. We've got an acting coach from one of the major studios coming in to prime them all up."

I look over at the happies and shake my head.

"Still sounds easy to me."

"Doesn't matter. You're a part of the *other* team, Luke! And we have just as important of a role as they do." He looks down at his clipboard for a few seconds. "In fact, you didn't hear this from me, but most of the senior management here agrees that the investigators are so vital to our mission that if you had to choose one group that had to go," he pauses as he lowers his voice to a whisper, "you'd choose *them*."

"We're investigators?" Nerd One asks. "Do we get badges and guns?"

"Great fucking question," I mumble.

"Yes! Great question! You will be getting a badge. No gun, unfortunately. It's not that kind of investigation. You see, we need you guys to just, uh, patrol the community. Yeah. To look out for any malicious behavior. Look out for people that aren't supposed to be here. That sort of thing."

He pauses and looks over his shoulder and out the large window that lines the back wall of the room.

"Why do you need investigators for that?" I ask.

I mean, seriously. This sounds stupid.

"Luke, where are you from?"

"Me? I live right down the street. At the place you guys gave me."

"No, I mean, where are you from? Where were you born, raised, where did you go to high school?"

"Oh, around here, kind of. I was born in Pomona, and then my family moved to Carlsbad when I was 3."

"A SoCal boy! Alright! Well, be that as it may, if you're not from L.A. proper, you might not know a thing or two about what really goes on here. These movie people can be pretty sordid."

"What are you talking about, like coke? They do that in San Diego too."

Don snorts a laugh, an apropos reaction in my opinion. I laugh too.

"Coke! Right. Luke, let's just say that you're going to see things here that you never thought you'd ever see, alright?"

"Then what? Like meth? You got Walter White living back here?"

Don rolls his eyes playfully.

"A lot of these residents, they are in fact celebrities. And...they're *wild*. Out of their mind wild. And they sometimes bring all their crazy friends here to stay with them. And then they never leave."

"So you want us to, what? Make sure no one is making a mess of this pretty little community you've got here? Find reasons for you guys to kick out all the crazy guests that stay too long?"

"Exactly," he pauses, rubbing his chin. "Yes. Exactly. But you're going to have to be discreet. Because if there's one thing that the residents expect from us, it's privacy. So you're going to have to be very hush-hush in your investigations. You can't let anyone know you're, uh, you know, *investigating*. You got it? Very discreet."

"OK. So let's say I get some juicy information. What do I do with it?"

"Oh, uh, you'll report it up to your manager. I think we have instructions for you..." he trails off as he searches through the pile of papers on the table. After a few moments, he gives up. "Well, it doesn't matter. We'll go over all this later today. For now, all you need to know is that your job is crucial to our success here. You can't let us down. You can't make *any* mistakes. Or the consequences could be disastrous."

I laugh. I can't help it.

"What's so funny? You don't think this is serious?"

I shake my head.

"Are you sure that you picked the right guy for this?"

* * *

This first day of training bears on for so long that I'm weaving in and out of consciousness. The clock on the wall in front of me lifts itself off the nail that it's hanging on and jumps down on the floor.

"Hey, Luke!" it whispers.

"Yeah?"

"Do you know when this day is going to end? I can't take this anymore!"

"Tell me about it. I feel like I've been here all day."

The clock just shakes its head. Then it rolls over to one of the open windows that looks out toward the ocean. It hops up on the windowsill and stares out longingly at the sea. I can totally empathize. A breeze comes in through the window, and I catch the scent of the salty sea air. It's so hard to be trapped in a room like this when you have olfactory reminders just smacking you in the face. The clock looks back at me, and I can see the sadness on its face, a tear running down past the 2 and streaking all the way to the 5.

Suddenly, the clock turns back toward the open window and shoves itself forward. It falls and crashes on the sidewalk a couple of floors beneath us, and the hollow sound of plastic on cement reverberates back through the window. I'm mortified. I look around, and all I see are cold-hearted bastards. No one even cares! They're just moving the training along like nothing even happened. I sit and stew for a few minutes. I'm sad as hell for that poor clock.

Eventually, I look up at the wall and realize that the clock is still there and that none of what I saw had happened. I should have known it was just in my head. I've seen talking clocks before, but I've never seen a suicidal talking clock. I mean, come on.

If I take one thing away from the whole day, it's that despite all of their chest thumping about how important this job is, it's actually ridiculously simple. All I have to do is walk around and try to find out facts about any people that I run into and then report them back to my boss. Oh, and I have to do it *discreetly*. That's it.

When training ends for the day, I ride my bike home and reunite with my couch for a few minutes. Then I roll up a hefty joint with some of the loud that I had brought with me when I moved here. I need to ease out the afternoon.

I like the self-contained nature of a J. When I use a pipe, I never know when to stop. A joint tells you exactly when to stop. Sometime around when this one gets down to the last few hits, I flip open my laptop and start looking at porn. Then I fall asleep, a gif illustrating the results of a penis enlargement pill looping endlessly a few inches from my face.

I wake up not knowing what time it is. Has it been five minutes or five hours? Ugh. I'm hungry. I find a bag with some snacks that I bought at Ralph's. I pull out a granola bar and some candies, and I lie flat on my back on the floor. I slowly start eating the granola bar first. I'm arching my back each time I take a bite and turning my head to the side each time I swallow. I fall asleep again, thinking about how differently music might have turned out if Jimi Hendrix hadn't died when he did.

* * *

The sun rises and slams me in the face with all of its glorious brightness, just like the sun thinks it should do. I'm not much of a fan of the morning time, and I especially don't like being woken up by the sun. That always has a way of putting me in a bad mood to start off the day. On the plus side, I totally forgot to set an alarm, and if the sun wasn't so aggressive, I might have been late for my second day on the job. It's yet another day of training. Training with Don.

The facility is full of the same people from the day before, and that makes sense to me. I don't know where else they would go or who else would be here instead. The group of happies now has a game of corn hole, and they're taking turns throwing the little beanbag thing at the board like a bunch of lucky assholes. The more I see them, the madder it makes me. Meanwhile, all I get to do is hang out with Nerd One and Nerd Two as Don rambles on and on and on.

Lunch is the only time where we all intermingle, and that's only because both groups share the same buffet line. I'm standing behind Nerd Two, just looking down at my shoes. It's better than trying to have a conversation with him. I see the black guy from yesterday walking toward me, so I turn around like a little coward. He bumps into my back with his lunch tray.

"Racist," he mutters.

I stiffen my back and keep staring down at my shoes. I start to tighten my hands on my tray. Slowly, I turn my head around. I look up at his face, and he's smiling.

"Just kidding, man. How you doing?"

"Not bad. Pretty bored."

He looks over my shoulder and back at my group. Don is standing with one foot propped up on the seat of a chair, his knee at a perfect 90° angle.

"What kind of stuff do they have you doing over there?" he asks, holding back a laugh.

I can't blame him. Don looks like a fucking tool and a half. That's 50% more tool than your standard variety tool. That's a lot of tool.

"I don't think I'm allowed to talk about it. Hey, you know I'm not racist, right?"

He raises one of his eyebrows.

"Really, I'm not. I didn't even choose that answer! That fake iPad was fucked up."

"That question was fucked up, is more like it."

"Yeah. But you know what?" I lower my voice to a whisper. "I bet those other two guys over there with me said the same thing. Like this guy here." I nod over my shoulder at Nerd Two, obliviously combing through a tray of potato salad. "So really, you should be calling them racists. Not me. I like Kanye."

"Dude," he starts. "I actually don't care."

"Yeah, but— "

"But if you really don't want to be called racist, you can probably just avoid the words *too black*, and I think you're like 90% there."

"That's fair. I'll keep that in mind."

The lunch line starts to move after Nerd Two finally gets whatever crap he decided he wanted to get. We shuffle along and pile food on our plates. When I finish, I look back and realize that I have nothing else to say, so I start walking away.

"Hang on," the guy shouts out.

I turn around. He's jogging toward me.

"Where are you eating?"

I shrug.

"Cool. Me too."

I'm staring at Don's back as we sit down at a table. If he turns around and sees me enjoying myself, he'll probably come over and drag me back to whatever boring shit we're going to talk about next.

"So today, we're learning about the *quintessential embodiment of peace*," the guy tells me as he unwraps his disposable utensil set.

"Is that right?"

"Yeah. What do you think of that?"

"I mean...it sounds better than what I'm doing."

"Right. But what do you think the quintessential embodiment of peace is?"

I rub my jaw and shrug.

"I don't know. Getting high?"

He smiles.

"My man!"

"Word."

Shit. Why did I say that? I don't normally say that. I can tell he's judging me.

"Uh, okay," I stammer. "So, you guys are supposed to try to act like you're high when you're out there doing whatever?"

"Act like? Fuck that. I am going to *be* high if this is my damned job."

"You lucky bastard," I mumble.

I look up at Don, and he's sharpening a pencil. I don't even know why. There aren't any papers anywhere near him. He's just that kind of a guy. I've only known him for 24 hours, and I already know exactly who he is. He's a guy that is always ready with a sharpened pencil. He will never be unprepared for a standardized test.

"I am going to be so fucking high, these motherfuckers won't have any clue that I'm getting paid by a goddamned shady housing association to be that fucking high, you know what I mean?"

"That is a lot of unnecessary swearing, but yes, I know what you mean," I say. "What's your name, by the way? I didn't catch it earlier."

"My name's Wolf."

"Hmm?"

"Wolf. Like the animal. Why, what's yours?"

"Luke. Just...Luke."

"That's right, Luke."

"What do you mean, Wolf?"

"What do you mean, what do you mean? That's my name. *Wolf*."

"You really are a lucky bastard. How is that your name?"

He laughs.

"It is a pretty cool name, right?"

"Yeah. *Pretty cool*."

This son of a bitch, he not only has the coolest job that I can imagine, but he also has the coolest name that I can imagine too. Not to mention that he's black, which makes him significantly cooler than me without even doing anything. The next thing he's going to tell me is that he's invincible and that his dad is the CEO of the company that makes Totino's Pizza Rolls. I don't ask him what his dad does in case I'm right. It'll be too devastating. I love those things. They are *my* quintessential embodiment of peace, baked at 425° for 10-11 minutes on a cookie sheet.

"Wolf," I repeat, unaware that I'm speaking until the word has left my lips. He looks up at me with his sandwich stuffed in his mouth.

"Yeah?"

"That's really your name? Like your *birth* name? You were born with that name, that's what you're telling me?"

"I know. I bet you never met a black dude named Wolf, right?"

I put my sandwich down and smile.

"You're black? I didn't even notice."

Three

We have Sunday off, but no one tells me. I show up to the training facility, and there is pretty much nothing here but a fake-looking plane. I wonder how they got it here? I guess I was right about it being an airport hangar, or at least something that's meant to look like one.

The tables that were used for the lunch buffet are still in the same position up against one of the walls. Other than that, you can't tell that it was used for anything other than what you'd use an airport hangar for, which I think is just storing planes.

I walk around for a while. There's nobody here, and all of the other adjacent administration buildings are locked up. There's a boat sailing across the lake not far from where I'm standing. I stop and watch as it skims the surface of the water. Have I been dreaming these past few days? Is this all just in my head?

Everything here does feel a little dreamlike and hazy, detached from reality. Or maybe I'm in another dream, and that dream is within my dream. Or maybe nothing is real. Whoa.

I leave the hangar and head back toward my apartment. I stop by a Redbox on the way to see if they have a copy of *Inception*, but they don't, so I just think about it instead of watching it. After a while, I start thinking about birds instead. They make more sense to me. There's no totem ending that I don't understand when it comes to birds.

Oh, to be a bird. Sometimes I watch birds flying in the sky, and I get jealous. Like really jealous. So free, so careless, so...able to fly. Fuck, I've always wanted to fly. Up, up, up, in the sky. What a beautiful thing. It must be nice to be a bird.

That said, I can't stand birds as pets or even as animals that I have to interact with. They are mostly terrible. Take pigeons, for example. Everybody hates pigeons. If I were a bird, I'd be embarrassed that I was even related to a pigeon.

Other birds aren't much better. Chickens taste good, but they can live for a period of time without a head. I can't trust that. Turkeys are tasty too, but they're also big assholes. A wild turkey will stop in the middle of the road and not give a shit if you're about to run it over. They also defy English pluralization rules, and that doesn't sit well with me. Parrots: shut up. Cockatiels: take the advice I gave to the parrots. Ostriches: fuck you. Don't even get me started on them. Falcons are cool. But where do they live? They might not be real.

But to *be* a bird, oh, that is very different than to be in a world with birds. To be a bird means that you can fly. For my whole life, I've dreamt about flying. Sometimes I succeed and soar through the sky. Other times I can't even get off the ground, but I know that I should be able to.

Oh well. All I can do is just marvel at the birds I see flying by and wish that I was one of them. Or all of them, maybe, like I can be a whole flock of birds as one entity. I think that's possible. Are a group of birds just a bunch of individual creatures with individual brains and thoughts and feelings? How do we really know? Maybe birds are all just one connected thing, like that Banyan tree in Maui. Somebody should look into this.

I bet that sometimes, a happy gets to be a birdwatcher. A hobbyist birdwatcher. Just a guy or a girl hanging out somewhere. Maybe it's in the forest, maybe it's at the beach. Don said in training the other day that over 50% of all their association fees go to maintaining the private beach, but I don't buy that. What does it take to maintain a beach? Doesn't the ocean do all the work for you anyway?

* * *

It's Monday now. I'm not sure how this happened or what I did with my Sunday other than think about birds. I go to the hangar again, but for the second day in a row there's nobody here. I'm starting to wonder if I'm losing my mind. I walk down the long hill that leads up to the main gates, and I take a walk by the beach, leaving my bike back at the hangar. It's a windy day, my hair flopping all over my head.

I've been walking for a few minutes. That's when I see him. It feels a little too coincidental that I'm coming across the only person that I somewhat know in the whole town, unless you count Don. And I don't count Don.

It's Wolf. He's sitting on a flat rock overlooking the ocean. The waves are fairly calm and quiet despite the fact that the wind is howling as it scrapes along the ground. It's a strange juxtaposition. I'm still a little high from the roach I snubbed out this morning, and it makes me wonder if The Board would ever try to control the tide. Is that even possible? Like if they barricaded a section of the ocean and created their own tide? Probably not. Besides, I'd imagine the moon still would have something to say about it.

"Hey," I say, since I'm greeting him.

"Sup, man," he says back to me.

This conversation's starting off pretty good.

"Did you ever want to be a bird?"

"What?"

Shit.

"Nothing. I mean, how's it going? What were you? Or are you. Are you something right now? What are you today?"

He smiles.

"Today is my day off."

"Oh cool, is it my day off too?" I ask.

He shrugs.

"I dunno. I'm not your boss. *Is it* your day off?"

I start to feel a little weird, like out-of-my-body weird.

"Do we know each other?"

He squints at me with a strange look, which doesn't make me feel any better.

"Not really," he replies.

"So we haven't met before?"

"No..." he starts slowly. "We've met before. Are you all right?"

"Yeah. I'm fine," I say quickly. "So, it's your day off? I didn't know that a happy gets a day off. Isn't the whole premise kind of like a day off?"

"Yeah. It is. But like, I'm not off. Today is just *my day off.* I think we all start this way."

He looks at me and gives me one of these nods that insinuate that I already understand what he's saying, but I don't.

"You mean, your assignment today is to have the day off?"

"Yeah."

"How is that not having a day off?"

"Because I don't get a day off. I am just...this is just me, being a guy with a day off. So like, this is *my day off.*"

"Why do you keep saying it that way?"

"I'm trying to *emphasize* what I'm saying to you without actually saying it."

"I don't get it."

"Alright." He pauses, realizing that he's speaking loud enough for people around us to possibly overhear. He leans in to me and lowers his voice to a loud whisper. "So, I don't get any days off. Right?"

"Okay."

"And my *job* is to be a different guy every day. Whatever The Board assigns me."

"Yep."

"Well, today, they assigned me the job of being a guy on his day off. Like I'm supposed to just sit here, walk around, and act like somebody who is just enjoying some time off. That's it."

"That's it?"

"That's it."

"Shut up."

He smiles again and shakes his head.

"Yeah. *My day off.*"

"That's bullshit! I mean, I guess I'm not working either. And I don't even know when or if I am going to be working. They didn't give me a number to call or anything."

"So what are you going to do? Just keep showing up at the training facility until someone's there?"

"Pretty much. Meanwhile, you're having *your day off.* Bullshit."

"Well, it has its ups and downs, you know?"

For some reason I'm comfortable enough to try to punch him in the arm, but when I swing, I miss and hit him sort of near the shoulder blade. Ugh. It's awkward. I start talking quickly again.

"Well, uh, yeah, whatever. Do you want to go do something? Or does that violate the terms of *having a day off?*"

"I don't know...but sure. What do you want to do?"

I think about it a bit before I reply. Even though I haven't said anything yet, we start walking away from the beach. I don't know where we're walking to or who started walking first.

"I want to be a bird," I say, as though this is a viable answer to his question.

Wolf looks at me and doesn't say anything right away. We walk a little while in silence.

"Do you want to get high and tell me about that some more?"

"Yes."

We go to Wolf's place so he can pick up a bowl and his canister. While we're there, he also grabs a sweatshirt, a loaf of homemade cinnamon raisin bread that he zips up in gallon-size plastic bag, and two bottles of water.

"That's a sweet routine you've got there."

I wave at all the things spread out across his kitchen table. He nods, placing each item in a backpack that's sitting on one of the chairs. He doesn't say anything. I look around at his apartment and measure it up against mine. Even though happies get to live *in* Malibu Oaks and I'm just at an apartment in regular old Malibu, we're both being put up by The Board, so I figure that he's a good comparative subject.

His place is very small—smaller than mine—and like mine, it has very few pieces of furniture. There's an absolute lack of décor. He's probably a minimalist. I respect that. I'd like to be a minimalist too, but it seems like a lot of work.

The ceilings are low. It's making the room seem smaller than it is. Off his kitchen, he has a balcony with a better view than the one that I have. You can see the ocean from inside the apartment. You can probably smell it if the door's open, but the door's not open.

"What's the deal with your place?" I ask.

"Apartment over a garage. Seems to be what all the happies get."

"Whose garage?"

He shrugs.

"Let's go," he beckons, already standing in the doorway with his backpack slung over his shoulder. "I want to hear about this whole bird thing."

A couple of miles in from the coast, the quaint little streets of the community unravel into a series of long, windy roads that ultimately turn into a bunch of dead ends. At the end of these dead ends is a collective of ancient oak trees that extend up the coastal mountain range and hug the water for miles in either direction. The trees are majestic and proud and made of wood and leaves like trees typically are.

We're out here to go on a hike. I'll take any chance I get to take a hike. That's what young people in Southern California do. It's a birthright. We get a guaranteed 330 days of sunshine, and we're damned sure we're going to use them. In fact, even though I went hiking just a couple of days before I got to Malibu, I have no problem going on another one so soon after. I can post it on Instagram, and my friends will get jealous about how awesome my life is. *Hiking twice in the same week? Luke's made it!*

When we reach the end of the road, Wolf parks his car and we get out. There's no trailhead. There's just a small, faded NO TRESPASSING sign and a weak, little wooden fence that we step over on our way into the shaded thicket of the trees.

"Does anybody even look at warning signs anymore?" he asks me.

"They're all just white noise to me."

"Same here. But even when I do see them, I usually just think that they're outdated. Or that they were never meant to be taken seriously. I think I discredit all signs that I see that look more than six months old."

"How old did that one look?" I ask.

"Old enough to ignore."

Where I'm from, the forest is a great place to get high. Part of it is because we don't have that much forest around us, so it's a bit of a novelty. But mostly it's because it's so full of magic and quirkiness and life, I'm never alone or scared. I'm not vulnerable or reckless or out of control. I'm loved. I'm embraced. When I want to get high, I'm breathing in something that grows from the ground, so it only feels natural that I'm surrounded by more of the same.

Of course, I have all these feelings because I like getting high in the forest, and I'm justifying my actions. But damn, it makes sense while it's happening. I just want to be here. Amongst these trees, amidst all this filtered light. I love the way that everything outside of the forest seems like it might not be happening at all once I get in here. Above all else, I appreciate its authenticity. The forest is here because it's always been here, because something else put it here. I don't know why or how or when, but I know that it's something whose covers I can't peek under, even if I try, or if I know a guy who knows a guy.

I read somewhere that some of these oak trees are over 500 years old. Way, way older than The Board, or the community, or whatever the community was doing before the community became the community. Rain dances. Whatever. I can feel the reality of it, its enormity and breadth, its significance. I know it isn't something that's here to make me feel a certain way.

I try explaining this to Wolf, but it doesn't come out with the same poetic eloquence that it has in my head. He just stares straight ahead and listens to everything I'm trying to say.

"I like the trees too, man."

"No. Yeah, I mean, no, I know. But that's not what I'm saying."

"I like trees. They're so there, you know? I like that. That's so, so..."

"Trees."

"Right."

"Can you get me that?"

I'm talking about the cinnamon raisin bread in the Ziploc bag.

"This?"

Wolf picks up a stick. He doesn't have a good grip on it, so it falls on the ground. He starts to laugh, and I do too.

"No. That."

I nod toward the bag again.

"This?"

He picks up another stick and starts laughing, harder than before.

"Stop it, man. I want that," I say again, and nod, again, as though I'm giving him additional information that is going to help him.

He picks up another stick. This happens probably another 60 times before I realize that I can reach the Ziploc bag from where I'm sitting without even having to stretch out that far. I have some trouble opening the zipper at first, but eventually I get in there.

"That's some good shit, huh?"

He has this proud smirk on his face.

"Yeah, it is. How'd you get it to turn out so perfectly?"

"Bread machine. My mom got it for me."

"Why?"

"To make bread. I like bread."

"Are you sure it wasn't because she wants you to travel back in time to before you were born?"

"I can make white bread with it, French bread, you name it."

"Maybe you're supposed to use it to prevent your dad from getting killed...before he can impregnate your mom..."

"I've got recipes for sourdough bread, whole wheat bread. Even spelt bread."

"...or whatever The Terminator was about. What was it about? Did I get it right?"

"I don't even know what a spelt is. But yeah, she wanted me to be able to make bread, man. Like *bread* bread."

"Oh, you said 'bread machine'? Not time machine?"

"Jesus Christ," he moans.

"Wait, it's not a bread machine?"

"No. What? It *is* a bread machine."

"Oh. Have you tried to make any bread with it?"

"I dunno, man. Making bread is hard."

"Does it come with any cool recipes for bread? Like a bread that turns into a cake or something."

"I don't think so."

"Bread is a weird word. Bread. Bread. Listen to it. Bread. *Bread*."

We go on like this for a while. In the forest, with the trees, it doesn't matter. I marvel at my hands for a while, and then I marvel at the forest floor. I flex and bend a pine needle until it splits in half, and then I find another one and do it again. And again. Wolf rips off a chunk of bread and chews it for what might be four years. I rip off a piece and swallow it so quickly that I immediately need water. I fumble with the cap on the bottle while coughing and laughing. Wolf could be more helpful, but he just sits there watching me.

I fall asleep leaning against a big trunk of a tree. I wake up sprawled out on the ground. All of the cinnamon raisin bread is gone, and Wolf's lying on his side, the empty bag beside him. The sun has set, and a cool blue haze is settling throughout the forest. Soon it'll be too dark for us to find our way out.

"Hey, wake up," I tell him, shaking his arm. "We've got to go."

I stand up and brush the leaves off the back of my shorts. Wolf turns the Ziploc bag upside down, his lazy eyes following the crumbs as they tumble out. We hike back out of the forest, not talking much, still in a stupor. When I see his car ahead, I feel relief.

"Hey," Wolf calls out, twenty feet ahead of me. "Was there barbed wire on this fence earlier when we came in?"

"No. I mean, I don't remember. But I guess so."

He shrugs and then cautiously swings his leg over a low point in the fence. I follow behind him and do the same. We get in his car, and as he starts to pull out, my eyes catch the NO TRESPASSING sign. It looks much newer than before, like someone replaced it while we were out there. I rub my eyes as we drive away.

"I think I'm still a little high," I murmur, resting my cheek against the window.

Four

"Hey, I'm Luke."

I smile so she can see my really white teeth, so she won't be alarmed or scared of me. She's just walking out of her place. I don't want to freak her out.

"Oh. Hey."

"Luke Balena."

It's my first day out in the field. I have no idea what I am doing. I just got a call this morning from someone who told me they needed me to work today. They told me to take down this number and call it every day to check in. It's pretty weird, but I guess it's better than never hearing from them again.

"Hi, Luke Balena."

"I'm new here," I say.

"That's cool. Where are you from?"

Don said that we shouldn't give too many real details. It makes the act harder and harder to maintain.

"Me? Carlsbad."

Shit.

"Ooh, pretty. I went there once for a party."

"That's impossible. No one parties in Carlsbad."

She laughs, and then it gets quiet. I don't know if I should start walking away or keep asking more questions. I didn't think this through hard enough, and I'm regretting that I started with such an attractive girl. I was just walking down the street when I saw her, so I figured I'd try to prod and ask a few questions, get my bearings.

"Oh, shit!" she whispers, then flashes a smile my way. "Forgot my keys."

We're standing near the door to an apartment that sits above a garage. It looks a lot like Wolf's place. There's a chance that she's a happy, but I can't just outright ask her. I've got to dig some more. She turns around and walks up the stairs, leaving the door open. I look in under the top of the doorframe and watch her climb the stairs. It's a nice view.

I'm talking about her ass. The girl has a nice ass. She isn't gone for too long before I hear her start to come down the stairs again.

"Still here?" she asks, this time with a nervous smile.

Shit, I'm a creeper.

"I, uh, I didn't get your name in return."

This job sucks. Get me out of here.

"It's Amy. Amy Percy."

"Oh. You rhyme. That's cool."

"Amy Percy?"

"Yeah. Your name. It rhymes."

She shakes her head.

"Not really. Just because it ends with the same letter doesn't mean it rhymes. I mean, technically it does. But not really. You know?"

"OK, yeah. You're right. Well, have a nice day!"

I turn around and walk away. That was going nowhere. She closes the door and locks it up, goes the opposite direction I'm going. I turn back a few times and watch her walking up the street. Then I head down to the lake and watch a boat doing laps around a string of buoys. When my shift ends, Wolf and I meet up for a beer at a bar on the east side of the PCH.

"What was her ass like?" he asks.

I raise my eyebrows and nod.

"Tight."

"How could you tell?"

"I'm referring to her overall ass, not her asshole."

"Oh. How was her— "

"Dude, what did I say? I didn't fuck her. I just thought she was cute. Didn't you see cute girls today while you were working?"

"Oh, fuck yeah. Like all day."

"Okay, there you go. And do you know the composition of any of their assholes?"

"That's for me to know and for you to find out."

I'm in mid-sip of my beer, and after he says this, I double down and gulp to finish off the bottle. I set it back down on the counter and slowly turn my head to look at him straight on.

"I don't want to find out."

"Suit yourself."

"Anyway, I might go back there in a couple of days and pretend that I just happened to be walking by again when she comes out. What do you think?"

He scoffs.

"Creepy."

"But I think she might be a happy," I tell him.

"Even if she is...look, that's probably the oldest trick in the book. Are you desperate or what?"

"Why's it desperate? How's there anything desperate about that? It's my job to investigate people. How does she know who I'm supposed to be checking on? If she's a happy, she's like a girl version of *you*. She doesn't know what it's like at all."

"Oh?"

"You don't realize this, but my job is a lot more complex than you think it is."

"Yeah, yeah. Think about it, man. If she's a happy, then fine. She gets what you're doing. But if not? You're just some stalker. She'll call the cops on you. I would, if I was a girl with a tight butthole."

"Potentially tight butthole," I clarify.

"Sorry, my friend, but if that's how you are planning on finding out, you may never know how tight that little thing is."

"So what, anyway? So what if she knows that I'm just going back to try to hit on her? I don't want her to *not* know that I'm interested. So that's fine too. Even though I think she'd still believe that I was just, you know, doing my job."

"No way. But I accept your point. Put your balls out there and see if she accepts. I like it."

I wince.

"Or whatever," he adds.

Something about the visual of me putting my balls anywhere makes me uncomfortable. I like my balls right where they usually are.

"So I'll just show up in a couple of days and be like, *Hey, I'm Luke*...and then do a big wink face, right...and then ask her if she's a happy. Seems easy."

Wolf has his hand up to try to flag down the bartender.

"Never gonna find out," he mumbles.

I reach over and finish the rest of his beer while he's not looking. My phone vibrates in my pocket, but when I check it, there's nothing on my home screen.

I look up from my phone, and the bar is blurry. I can't read any of the labels on the bottles. I look down at my beer; it's dancing in front of me.

"What the hell is this?"

Wolf's still facing away from me. He shrugs.

"Some IPA. You like it?"

The bottle keeps dancing. I've got to brace my hand on the bar so I don't topple off the stool. I shove my phone back in my pocket.

"It's strong."

He looks back at me, but I can't focus on his face. The edges of my vision are dark and creeping inward. I put my other hand on the bar to steady myself. Fuck, this is embarrassing. Everything goes black.

There's a flashlight in my eyes. Someone's holding them open with a gloved index finger. I can hear a man's voice, but it's all garbled like he's underwater. The flashlight goes away, and everything's black again. I can't feel my toes. Or my anything.

Then there's water. A shit ton of water, all on my lap, on my face. My hair's dripping. I shake it off and wipe my eyes. I can't believe I spilled my drink. Wait. What drink?

Then the flashlight is back. Someone pushes my ribcage with their foot. My body falls over, and my head slaps against the floor. Porcupines are performing a synchronized swim routine, and I'm the only spectator in the stands. I hate it when I have this dream. It's so fucking weird.

Wait. Why am I dreaming?

The flashlight pops back on and blinds me again.

"Luke. Get up."

My eyelids flutter open. I'm in a small, dark room. The walls and floor are made of smooth cement. It looks like a glamorous prison cell.

"The fuck?"

"Get up, shitbag."

"I am up."

"Not you, Balena. This guy."

I look to my left and see Wolf crumpled over in a heap.

"What the...did we get arrested? What did we do? Is he all right?"

I can't see the guy that's in the room with us because he's blocking out all the light with his body. Big motherfucker.

"Take a few minutes to get your shit together, and then you can come out and we'll talk through this."

The guy walks out, shutting the door behind him. I turn toward Wolf.

"Yo. You alive?"

He moans.

"The hell happened?"

"I have no idea. I think we got arrested. I don't know what for though. I can't remember anything. Can you?"

He shakes his head.

"You think we're done for?"

"Done for? Shit, man. You are not living up to your cool name. If we got arrested, I'm sure it's no big deal. Like a drunk in public charge or something."

He props himself up. He's leaning against one wall, and I'm leaning against the other.

"It's short for Wolfgang, you idiot. It's not like I'm supposed to be a fearless fucking wolf."

"Well, that's disappointing."

I stand up, and water tumbles off my lap, splashing onto my shoes.

"Let's go."

I nudge Wolf and help him to his feet. The door's unlocked, so I push it outward and walk into the room on the other side. It's an office. It looks like a principal's office. I've never been to the police station, so I don't know if they usually have a room like this, but it seems out of place.

There's a guy with a serious buzzcut sitting behind a desk. There are two chairs in front of it. He motions for us to sit down.

"Boys, I've been doing this a long time. A long, long time. I've seen a lot of things, as you can imagine."

I look over at Wolf to see his reaction. He's staring straight ahead, nodding. The buzzcut continues.

"Every now and then, I find out that a member of our staff hasn't followed directions. Explicit, clear directions. And then I'm forced to discipline them."

"Sorry," I interrupt, "but did you just say *discipline*? Where are we? Is this not a police station?"

The buzzcut leans back in his chair and flexes his biceps as he folds his hands together on top of his head. His arms are scary big, full of veins. I bet he does a hundred curls a day. And maybe another fifty angry preacher curls when no one's looking.

"Oh, I see. So you're the one with the problem with authority, is that right?"

He leans forward again.

"I'm just saying, like, it'd be nice to know how the hell we got here. Or where here is."

"Oh, is that right? Well, first of all, neither of you replied to confirm that you would meet here tonight. Did you read the message?"

"What message?"

"Don't fuck with me. Let me see your phones."

Wolf hands his over first. The buzzcut taps a few times and then frowns.

"Hmm."

"Alright, man. Sir. What's going on? Can you tell us what we did wrong? That would be a good start. Because I have no fucking clue. And I sure as hell didn't get any message."

"You have no clue," he repeats.

I look over at Wolf and try to gauge his reaction. He's still looking like he's in shock.

"That's right. So why don't you tell us what we've done? And then we'll tell you we won't do it again, and then we can all go home and watch some Netflix. Or PBS. Or whatever you do with your free time, whatever. You know?"

"Do you understand what the words 'no trespassing' mean?"

Wolf nods.

"Yes, sir."

I look over at him and shake my head.

"Mr. Balena, you don't know what 'no trespassing' means?"

"No, I do. I was just..."

"So you both know what those two words mean. Good. So then this should not come as a surprise that you are here with me right now. Because you know what you did, don't you?"

"We trespassed," Wolf recites obediently.

"Yes, you did. And you saw the sign, right?"

"Sign?" I ask.

"Listen," he says, leaning even closer to us, defying gravity by not falling right off his chair. "I want to get home. I'm sure you do too. So let's just all agree that you will read the signs the next time you see the signs, and you will follow what the signs say. Okay?"

Wolf agrees almost immediately.

"Mr. Balena, do you agree?"

"Sure. You got it. This is about the signs. I just have one question."

"What's that?" he asks.

"What signs are we talking about?"

"Listen, Balena. We all know what we're talking about. *Where* we're talking about. So cut the shit."

"Oh, is this about those trailheads? Where we went hiking the other day?"

He's just staring at me. No. He's trying to burn a hole right through me. These Board people really have a thing for doing this. It's good to know that I'm so stare-worthy. I had no idea.

He closes his eyes and shakes his head for a while. I look over at Wolf, and I shrug to see if he's as confused as I am, but he's just looking down at his feet. The guy finally lets out a deep, slow breath. His buzzcut is motionless like a good buzzcut should be.

"If you see a sign, you're not supposed to be there. That's all there is to it. Is that clear?"

"You got it," I say, pushing myself out of my chair. "Thanks for the talk."

"I don't want to see you boys in here again, understood?"

I laugh.

"Heard that."

I walk toward the door, irritated and confused. We shuttle through a series of nondescript hallways and arrive at an exit door that looks like it might sound an alarm if we use it. I push the handle anyway. Nothing happens, and we walk outside. We're somewhere near the beach. I'm guessing this is another one of the administration buildings.

"Who the fuck was that guy? He's not a fucking police officer."

"I think he's just some guy in an office that works for The Board?"

"I don't get it. Did they kidnap us?"

"I think our beers were spiked. It hit me right when I saw you rolling off your stool. I don't remember anything after that until they started kicking me in that room."

We walk along the sidewalk in silence. I'm super confused. I don't even know if we're walking in the right direction.

"Your ancestors would be rolling in their graves, by the way," I tell him.

"Why?"

"Wolf?! You were, like, a pup back there."

"It comes from Wolfgang, dude."

"Whatever. A gang of wolves sounds even more fearless than a single wolf. I don't care what you say. You're supposed to be a tough as nails dude. And you were just Mr. Softy back there."

"My dad was a military guy. I, I don't know. I can't help it. I react very immediately to discipline. I hate getting in trouble."

"Yeah, I mean, no one likes getting in trouble. But most people don't clam up like you just did. They just take it in stride. Like, who cares? It's just some dude in an admin office. I bet he doesn't even have a secretary."

"Why does that matter?"

"It doesn't. That was probably sexist of me. Though a dude can be a secretary too. So I don't know now."

"Come on. Give me a break. That was a weird ass situation. Like, what do you think they're so uptight about behind that NO TRESPASSING sign? Did you see anything?"

"Nah, man, just trees. Who knows."

"Do you think they have cameras set up there? Like, how did they know it was us?"

"I'm guessing they do. How else would they know?"

We keep walking.

"This place, man," he laments. "They are more into their secret shit than I thought."

I shrug. The moon is somewhere up in the sky, looking down at us. I wonder if Wolf ever howls at it when he's alone. The sidewalk is uneven, and I'm doing my best to not step on the cracks. Up ahead is a little strip mall with a dispensary in the corner.

"Oh, snap. Hey, I'm gonna go in here. I'll see you tomorrow. Alright?"

"Wait!" he yells. "You're sure you don't have to work? I mean, I know *I* have the day off. But what about you?"

"They told me to call in. I'll just call when we're on the way. Worst case, we have to turn around and do it another day. Yeah?"

"Alright. Later man. I'll text you when I wake up."

I stand outside the dispensary and watch as Wolf eventually disappears around the corner up ahead. Then I walk in, and the pungent smell of bud immediately fills my nose. There's an attractive Asian girl behind the counter. She's wearing glasses. I don't usually like girls that wear glasses, but hers don't bother me.

"Hi. Welcome to Grace Dispensary."

"Hi. You're still open?"

She looks around and shrugs.

"Guess so."

"Cool. So, I'm new to Malibu. You guys don't have any special rules about medical cards here in L.A., do you? Like, what do you guys take for an ID? I just have the one I got from my doctor back home."

She holds out her hand as I walk closer to her.

"Let me see it."

I take my wallet out and give her my medical marijuana card. As I hand it over to her, I see a glimpse of the picture on my ID and smile as I remember how baked I was when they took it.

"It's legit. Still from California. I just moved here," I explain.

She examines the ID and then does some things behind the counter that I can't see. Her hands are moving a lot. Way more than I'm expecting for someone who's just verifying an identification card. After a few moments, she looks up and smiles.

"Well, welcome to our dispensary, Luke. I just need you to fill out this form, and we can get you on your way. And then the next time you come, you can just show your driver's license."

"Okay."

"It's cash only here."

"I know."

"You can't bring anyone in there with you unless they also are a member here."

"I know."

"Here you go," she says, pushing a clipboard across the counter.

I fill it out and push the clipboard back to her. There isn't that much to it; all of the questions are straightforward. It is certainly easier than the misleading test that The Board gave me.

"This way," the girl says, beckoning toward an open door in the back corner of the room.

I walk in, and the smell amplifies. It's like heaven. Oh fuck, it's better than heaven. I love the smell of the dispensary. Any dispensary. I really think that I missed my calling. I should be a marijuana farmer. Or maybe not a farmer. Maybe all I need to do is make just enough money to eventually open my own shop. Then I can sit amongst the sweetest perfume I've ever smelled. All day, every day.

The overhead lights are very dim, but the room still has ample light from the fluorescent strips that are shining on the rows of jars behind the glass case walls. I walk up to one of the cases and stare inside. There are a few other people roaming around, not saying much.

"What's good here?" I ask.

A girl walks over toward me and smiles. I smile back. This is what I do.

"What's not good here?" she replies.

"How much for an eighth?"

"Depends on the shelf. Our lower shelf goes for $40 for an eighth. Our mid-level shelf is $60. And the top shelf varies between $80 and $120."

"What do you go for?" I ask.

"I don't smoke."

"What?"

She shrugs.

"Never got into it."

"Then why do you work here?"

She looks around and smiles.

"It's just a job."

I frown. I mean, what the fuck? This is the best job that anyone can ever have. It's better than being a happy. Certainly better than my new job. It's better than being any fucking thing. To get to sit around with a bunch of weed all day is, hands down, the best job out there. No debate. Case closed. Bye bye.

"I'll take one of the mid shelf ones. What's good?"

"What's not good?" she repeats, but it sounds so hollow compared to the first time that she said it.

"I like strains that are more on the CBD side."

"So you want an Indica?"

"No, not necessarily. I like hybrids too. I just don't like the super high-THC ones. They're just too much for me."

"Gotcha. Well, this one is a pretty good compromise."

She points down at a jar, but I can't tell what she's pointing at because she's behind the counter and her hand is fully blocked. I don't know why she thinks I'd be able to see what she's pointing at. Maybe she doesn't know how solid objects work.

"Which one?"

"It's called Purple Cheese."

"No thanks," I say. "I'm lactose intolerant. What else do you have?"

She doesn't get my joke, or if she does, she decides that it isn't worth a laugh. She stares down at the case and scans the jars for a replacement.

"How about OG Ringo?"

"Sounds lame. What else?"

"Valentine X?"

"Too romantic."

She looks up at me and raises her eyebrows.

"Come on. Valentine X?" I ask. "I can't. I'm a single guy here. I just can't. Give me something else."

"How about Maui Bubble Gift?"

I think about it for a little while. I always liked Maui. I don't know a damn thing about the different strains and their lineages, but I figure with a three-part name, it is probably the grandson creation of some super strains from back in the day. Anything with the word "gift" in it is going to be just fine for me.

"I'll take it."

"That'll be $60," she says.

I hand over three twenties, and she pulls out a scale. In my old dispensary, they weigh the bud before you pay them. I guess they aren't as trusting here. It doesn't matter much to me. I'm going to pay either way. She packs up a little baggie and pushes it across the counter.

"Thanks," I say as I turn around and walk out the door.

The cute Asian girl is reading a book when I walk out. She looks up and smiles.

"Have a great day, Luke! Hope you enjoy what you picked up."

"I'm sure I will."

I think about asking her for her number, but then I think about shitting where I eat. Then I think about eating, so I make a stop at Ralph's before I go home.

I really want some Pizza Rolls. I march over to the freezer case. I swing one of the doors wide open and stand in front of it as I start searching the shelves.

"Pizza...Bagel Bites..."

I'm tracing my finger along the shelf, reading the labels aloud as I pass by each one.

"Pizza Rolls!"

I look up from my finger, and the shelf is completely empty. Everything else in the entire case is stocked to the very edge. It's the only thing that's missing.

"Motherfucker!"

I almost flag down a guy working here to ask him if they have any out back, but I stop myself short. I can't bring myself to ask him for such a trivial thing. It isn't trivial to me, but I know how it looks. You can't just ask the guy working at the store if they have more Pizza Rolls out back. Pizza Rolls are the kind of thing that you shrug off if they're out. They're not infant formula or medicine or respectable. They're little frozen calzones that some genius invented and that no one is actually supposed to ask for when they're not in stock.

But I still want them. Maybe I should ask anyway. What's the harm?

"Excuse me," I yell out as soon as I see a girl in a black Ralph's shirt down at the end of the freezer case. "Do you have any Pizza Rolls out back?"

The girl shakes her head and walks away. Not a word, like I'm scum. I knew it. I shouldn't have asked. But she could have at least checked. Unless she's Rainman out back memorizing boxes with her photographic memory on her lunch break. Stupid Malibu. The girls at the Ralph's in Carlsbad would all go back and check on it together, I bet. And then come back and carry it up to the register for me.

I'm standing here for way too long, just staring at the empty void in the freezer case. I get the feeling that someone from security here is watching me. I look up at the ceiling for the telltale signs of a surveillance camera, but I see none. No black orb, no actual camera. Just some white ceiling panels and some beams. If they don't have any cameras here, I wonder if they even have an automated inventory system that prevents sell-outs of things like this. If they don't, they should. I might have to talk to the manager.

I eventually give up and walk to a different aisle. I buy a box of macaroni and cheese because I rationalize that it's probably just as good, even though it isn't and I know it.

Five

Wolf pulls the car onto the dirt shoulder.

"Hello, this is Luke," I practice as the phone is dialing.

Someone picks up but doesn't say anything.

"Hello?" I ask.

"Who's this?"

"Hi, uh. This is Luke. Luke Balena."

"Call back tomorrow," the voice barks, then hangs up.

Wolf looks over at me as I slide my phone into my pocket. I shrug as I get back into his car.

"Guess I have the day off."

"Alright," he says as he buckles his seat belt again. "So, we're really going to do this?"

"Yep."

"Fuck."

I have what I consider to be a generally healthy fear of heights, and I don't feel bad about it. Most fears exist so that we don't hurt ourselves. A fear of heights makes sense because falling from a height will hurt you. It's pretty simple, and I think it's nothing to be embarrassed about. If you're afraid of heights, good for you. You're not incorrectly wired.

"Did you tell your parents?"

I haven't known him for long at all, but I think Wolf has a tendency to ask stupid shit like this.

"What? No. Did you?"

"No."

We're driving up a winding highway that cuts over a mountain pass. It zigs and zags enough that our short bursts of conversation fit pretty well in between the turns. A continuous conversation is kind of hard to have in this situation.

Wolf's not the best driver I've ever met. I'm doing my cautious parent impression, my right leg jamming into the floor in front of me, stepping on an imaginary brake pedal. It isn't working. Damned imaginary brake pedals.

"Do you know anyone who has done this before?"

"Yeah, I know a couple of people."

I start to think about who they are, and I can't come up with anyone other than an Algebra teacher that I had in high school.

"Who? Anyone good?"

"Nah. Just this math teacher I had once. Actually, a girl that I dated a while ago too."

"You dated your math teacher?"

Both windows in his car are down, and the wind is howling through our ears on practically every turn.

"No. A girl I dated skydived once. Skydove. Skydove?"

"Skydived," he confirms.

"And a math teacher I had in high school skydived too. They are two separate people. I did not date a math teacher."

"Math teacher, huh?"

"Yeah. She was pretty fat too. Like pushing 300. She made us watch the video in class. I think she broke her leg when she landed, now that I think of it."

"This place won't take anyone over 250lbs. You sure she was that fat?"

"Yeah, man. She was pretty big. I mean, maybe she was 250 on the dot, on her best day. Or maybe the rules at that place were different. It was a while ago. Maybe things have changed, like they realized that if you take a 300lb woman up in a plane, throw her out, and expect her to land, she might break her goddamned leg."

"That's pretty funny. Can you imagine being the guy strapped to her?"

"Oh, fuck. That would be scary as hell, man. I wonder if you're allowed to be like, *uh, no, I'll pass, thanks*, and give it to the next guy."

"It's got to be a pretty good story. You jumped out of a plane with a 300lb woman strapped to your junk, and when you landed, she snapped her leg in half."

"That's the extent of the story. I don't know if it'd be that good."

Wolf is smiling.

"It'd be good. I'd tell it."

"Yeah, you're right. I would too."

We're getting closer to the pass. On the other side, the road eventually straightens out.

"She made you watch the video in class?"

"Yeah. I think it took the whole class too. What a waste of time...how is that related to Algebra at all?"

"You took Algebra in high school? Are you retarded?"

"Algebra TWO."

"Ah. Not retarded."

"Nope."

"Don't you feel like your math teacher should have consulted with your physics teacher before jumping out of a plane?"

"Haha, yes. Yes, I think she should have done that. See, I would have been okay with watching that video in a physics class. At least it'd be a little more relevant."

"Right. Though I'm sure there is a math lesson in there, somewhere."

"Yeah, like don't be greater than 300lbs. Ever."

"If X is your weight, and X is greater than an offensive lineman, just...don't."

We reach the pass and begin winding downhill toward the valley floor that spreads out in the distance ahead of us. It'll be another 40 minutes before we get to the jump site. It is kind of a haul. But since we're jumping out of a plane for recreation, I think it's all right that we're taking a little longer to get there. It may actually be the last time I'll be in a car. But, statistically, I'm more likely to die in the car on the way to the airfield than in the plane itself.

Still, it's disarming. You never see a fantastic movie about a car crash. You don't read about car crash survivors. I think the stats are misleading. Planes are scary, and common sense prevails here.

The reality of what I am about to do doesn't really hit me until we get to the airfield itself. Tucked away in the far corner of the valley, near the ocean again, the jump site has their office on a rundown-looking airstrip. We pull up onto a gravel driveway, the rocks chut-chutting beneath our tires.

"Fuck, man. My stomach just dropped. We're actually doing this, huh?"

"Dude, you said exactly what I was thinking. It didn't really hit me until we got here."

"Well, good to know that we're thinking the same thing right before we're about to die."

We get out of the car and lock up some of our valuable things in the trunk, even though we really don't have much of anything with us. Then we make our way to the office.

When we get inside, we're greeted by this hot chick wearing a shirt that's way too low to be respectable. No complaints here. I like low shirts. Maybe this is part of the relaxation process here. First they confuse you with some cleavage, and then they have you sign your life away. Then it's too late for you to respectably back out, so they whisk you into the rundown staging area next door. There you'll get to watch a bunch of dudes that look like they might have woken up hungover, but there they are, rolling up the parachutes that will be used on the next set of jumpers.

"Are you guys here to jump?"

Wolf and I look at each other. As if we're walking in for any other reason. Maybe to see her as she leans behind the counter, the front of her shirt dropping down, showing off even more than I'm expecting. I'd have come here for that if it were advertised. Wolf nudges me, staring at exactly what I'm staring at.

"Yes," I say.

We begin filling out paper work. We're handing over credit cards and signing things.

"Okay. I'm also going to need to weigh each of you."

She gestures over toward a scale that's sitting in the corner of the room.

"This is the step that your math teacher girlfriend didn't have to take, right, Luke?"

I laugh. The girl with the boobs doesn't get it, but it's not like she's supposed to.

"Oh, your girlfriend is a math teacher? My sister is a math teacher too! Where does she teach? Are you guys from around here?"

"We're from over the hill. Malibu Oaks."

With these two little words, her eyes sparkle and open up larger than the neckline of her shirt. It really is an obscene shirt. I don't know why anyone other than a pervert would ever make something so revealing.

"You live in Malibu Oaks? I've never met anybody from there."

"I'm surprised you've even heard of it," I say.

"You must be doing all right for yourselves then."

"Yeah, we're doing all right," Wolf says. "Malibu isn't as expensive as you might think though. It's affordable, if you can find the right place."

Hashtag humblebrag.

"I don't know about that," she says skeptically.

"Nah. Trust me. It's not that bad. You should check it out sometime."

He flashes a smile. He's a good-looking guy, with a strong jaw line and some pretty cool black guy hair that a younger version of me would have been jealous of. I went through that white kid, wannabe rapper phase in high school. Yeah, that was me for a little bit. I always wanted to have hair that I could braid or put in cornrows, but when you look like me, that's not a good look. I actually got my mom to braid my hair once. I asked her if we could do it on the front stoop, but she outright refused and instead did it on a chair in the kitchen. I still think that's the main reason that it turned out so poorly.

After some more back and forth between Wolf and the girl, she leads me over to the scale. Her breasts are amazing, and I can't stop staring at them whenever she isn't looking. I'm finding it hard to pay attention to anything else until the numbers on the scale come back.

"Ah, sorry about that, Luke. Looks like you came in over our weight threshold. 204.8lbs. You're going to have to pay extra."

"What? Are you kidding me? I thought the weight limit was 250lbs.?"

"It is. But we have to charge an extra dollar for every pound over 200."

Wolf lets out a loud laugh.

"You stocky, little bastard! If only you had been to the gym this week, maybe you could have saved a few bucks!"

"Shut up, man. I went to the gym."

"Tell you what," the girl says, her boobs making me spiteful now that I'm the butt of a joke. "I'll round down to 204. So it'll only be four dollars extra."

"Wow, *thanks,*" I mumble. "Your generosity is almost as big as your..."

She looks up at me from the receipt she's writing out.

"...reputation for great skydiving."

Wolf slaps me on the shoulder.

"Right!" he yells out.

She shakes her head and finishes writing out the receipt. Wolf, of course, comes in at a sleek 178 lbs. Son of a bitch.

After we pay, she leads us into a little room behind the check-in area where we have to watch a safety and liability video, the kind of thing that probably scares some people off. But, since we already paid, there isn't much of a logical choice other than to go on and do what we came here to do.

The narrator in the video is a man in his mid-fifties, sitting behind a very plain-looking desk. He has a beard—that's an understatement—his beard is so long, the bottom of it rests on top of the desk. He looks terribly out of place sitting there. His arms are extended directly in front of his body, kind of like he's doing a zombie impression. His palms are flat on the desk, and he doesn't move during the entire presentation. I whisper to Wolf during the video to see if he notices it as well.

"What the fuck is up with that guy's posture? Look at his arms. Are they made of wood?"

"Look at his beard. Why is he behind that desk? Isn't he so out of place? I do not feel like I'm getting sound safety advice from this guy."

"Oh, you're definitely not. This dude doesn't know the first thing about skydiving safety. I think they must have landed on his farm during one of their jumps and damaged his property or something. And rather than reimburse him, they struck a deal."

"You're our new safety guru. Do this video."

"Keep your arms straight."

"Keep your beard in contact with the desk at all times."

"Don't blink."

"Ever."

The video ends, and we walk out of the room, a little less confident but a little happier. At least I am, until I see the girl again. Wolf looks like he wants to stop and chat some more, but I keep us moving along. Stupid boobs. They will cause the downfall of society one day. Just watch.

We have to wait for a while. Wolf and I are standing anxiously near the gate that separates the next set of jumpers from the families and next-ups. Eventually our names are called. Then someone writes them in dry erase marker on a white board, right next to some other guy's names. My guy's name is Joe. Wolf's paired with Ethan.

"I don't know how I feel about being strapped to an Ethan."

"Don't act like it's your first time."

He laughs. A few minutes later, the instructors stride through a door and stand in front of the board, figuring out who their next jumper is. Ethan and Wolf find each other. Ethan looks like a dude that knows how to skydive, though I don't know how to explain what that really means.

Joe kind of just looks like a regular dude. I tell myself that I'm okay with this, but I really want some guy with Oakleys and dyed blonde hair and maybe a barbed wire tattoo or a tribal or something. Something that signifies that he's super into skydiving and has been doing it for so long that he officially defies all future chances of him dying from a jump.

"We're gonna walk through some basic maneuvers on the ground to get you ready," he lets me know. "We'll do them again when we're in the air as well."

"When we're up there? Really?"

What if I'm terrible at them? We'll already be up there. It'll be too late. There should be a test beforehand, or at least some sort of check to make sure I'm not going to ruin our chances of survival. Who knows. I could be different. Maybe this is how I'm going to be different. I'll be the guy that accidentally kills the instructor in the air by doing the wrong thing. *Well, we never saw that happen until Luke Balena went out for his first jump.* I do not want to have a safety procedure named after me.

He helps me put the harness on. As soon as I step into it, I realize that it's not made of steel and titanium and Kevlar, but instead it's some kind of canvas and maybe aluminum. My expectation of how secure this would be was highly exaggerated.

"This is it?"

He nods. Not a man of many words, this Joe guy. The plane pulls up, and I looked over at Wolf.

"How you feeling?" he asks me.

"I would like to shit in my pants right now."

"Try to make it more than 4.8lbs. Maybe you can get a refund."

Our instructors lead us over to the plane, and we get in.

"This is it?" I ask again.

Joe nods again. Of course he fucking does.

Have you ever been in a metal sleeping bag that's flying through the sky? That is about how large this plane is. I can touch both sides and the top, all at the same time. I can count the rivets that secure the pieces of the hull together. I thought I knew what flying felt like before I got in this plane. I was wrong. This is a totally different experience. The plane is erratic. I can't trust it. It shoots up five feet and then immediately drops down fifteen. It kicks over to the left and then kicks even more to the left, and then it slams back to the right. It is basically the wind's bitch. It doesn't give a shit that there are people in here.

I look over at Wolf, and he has that regretful but stoic look on his face that most people probably have when they're on a tiny plane, strapped to some stranger, sitting on his lap. The next seven minutes of my life can be best summarized by quoting an original poem of mine that I wrote to commemorate the experience. It is titled, "Oh Shit, Oh Fuck, What the Fuck, Oh Shit."

Oh Shit, Oh Fuck, What the Fuck, Oh Shit

by Luke Balena

Oh shit. Oh shit oh shit oh shit!
Shit!
Oh fuck! Fuck fuck fuck what the fuck!

Shit! Oh shit!

Parachute parachute parachute

Oh shit.

Shit!

Joe you motherfucker

Joe what the fuck!

Oh fuck!

I bet you're nodding right now, you fucking idiot

Oh so NOW you have Oakleys on?

My balls hurt

Gravity

Oh fuck!

Actually this isn't that bad

Oh fuck!

Shit!

Well, alright.

Fuck!

Fuck!

Okay whew.

Fucking Joe. What the fuck.

It's probably not going to win the Nobel Prize for Literature, but you never know. I didn't actually submit it yet. Wolf lands a few seconds after me. His guy releases him, and he heads toward me. We give each other a huge, earnest hug.

"Fuck, man."

"I know, right?"

We exchange a few more exchanges that probably sound exactly the same. Then we load into a little van and drive back to the office. I feel dizzy and nauseous and alive. After we're back and we get our little certificates and whatever other bullshit we have to do in the office, we stumble out to the car. We're just sitting here. The keys are nowhere near the ignition. Wolf opens the moon roof, and we recline our seats all the way back, staring up into the sky that we just fell through.

"That was the most real thing that I've done in a long time," Wolf declares. "Maybe as long as I can remember."

"That's perfect. That's exactly right."

That is, in a way, the genesis of why we decided to go skydiving in the first place. That, and a baggie of some super potent bud that led to me filling out a form on the skydiving company's website. We wanted to *feel* something. I've only even known about The Board for a couple of weeks now, but it's already got me thinking. If the residents of Malibu Oaks are none the wiser, I keep asking myself, what other fake things could be happening that I don't know about? I just want to know that I'm not having the wool pulled over my eyes.

"You can't fake that shit."

I think about it for a while.

"You can't, can you?" I ask.

He shakes his head.

"How would you?"

"The Board can't control gravity," I state, though I say it partially as a question.

"Nope."

"The Board can't put a NO TRESPASSING sign around the fucking sky either. It's too big. And obviously, no one can own the sky."

"Nope."

"The sky is...like, look at it."

I point my finger up through the moon roof and wave it around a bit.

"Mmm-hmm."

"It's enormous. It's...it's infinite. You can't control infinity."

"Of course not," he confirms. "That's its infinite nature."

I change my voice into a high-pitched little whine, pretending to be the sky as I gesture up through the moon roof alongside his hand.

"You can't deal with my infinite nature, can you?"

Wolf copies the voice I'm doing.

"The Board can't deal with my infinite nature!"

We both laugh.

"There's no way, man," he decides. "The sky is very much a real and untouched frontier. It's safe. No one is fucking with it."

We sit here for a while, our hands dangling up toward the sky, defying the very gravity that just sent us shooting down toward the ground. It's good to know that we have another anchor we can fasten ourselves to. In a world that has less and less of them, the sky is a pretty good thing to feel sure about. Clouds drift by overhead, and we just lie here in his car, staring up at them as they slowly creep along.

"Unless, of course, up is really down and down is really up."

I look over at him and sigh.

"What the fuck, man?"

Six

"Hi, this is Luke Balena."

"Yes?"

"Is, uh...I'm just calling to see if you need me to come in to work today?"

A loud rustling sound pulses through the phone, and I hear some faint voices talking behind it. I can't make out what they're saying.

"Hello?"

"Luke?" a voice finally returns.

"Yes. Luke Balena. I'm an investigator."

"Yes, Luke. We'll need you today. There's been some, uh, suspicious activity. We're going to need you to gather some intel."

"OK, so..."

The call ends. It's kind of weird the way they do business here. They rarely give me any concrete direction. It makes the job a lot easier, but at the same time, I feel like I can't possibly be doing what they need me to do. I'm just guessing every time I'm out there.

It's balmy and there's no breeze today. I'm sweaty. For some reason, I decided to wear jean shorts. I don't know why. I have some kind of ass chafing going on now that I don't want to acknowledge, so I'm walking a little bit slower now.

I talk to a couple down by the lake, and they tell me about a regatta they sailed in last summer. I make a note to look up the word *regatta*. I talk to an old lady who's watering a flowerbed in front of her house. I make a note that she's possibly unconcerned about the drought and the impact it has on the lake. I help a gardener pick up some lawn clippings that spilled out into the street. He's all alone with a miserable-looking job, so I figure it's cool if I help him. After all, I'm supposed to be discreet. Good Samaritans are very discreet.

The rest of the morning passes, and as I'm wandering around, I realize that I'm coming up on Amy Percy's apartment. I stop to try to remember how long ago I was here. I can't tell if it'll be creepy or just a coincidence that we're running into each other. I'm standing in front of her apartment for a while. The calendar in my brain is very hazy. Then something overtakes me, and I decide to knock on her door.

No answer.

I wait for about 20 seconds, and then I knock again.

No answer.

Oh well.

Since I have some free time, I send Wolf a message to see what he's up to. I sit down on Amy's front steps and wait for Wolf to reply. The three dots spring up pretty quickly, so I keep my phone on and wait for his response.

At the Farmers Market. Near the beach. U free? Come down

I get up off the steps and brush off the back of my shorts before walking down the sidewalk. I have a weird feeling that someone's behind me, so I turn around quickly to look.

No one's there.

I look up at Amy Percy's apartment and see the curtains slightly move in front of the main window that looks down onto the street. The sun's shining bright overhead. I can't tell if the windows are cracked open, but for a moment, I wonder if she's up there and just ignoring me because she sees that it's me. I squint and put my hand over my eyes to try to see better, but I can't make anything out. Fuck it. I'll stop being paranoid.

* * *

Every Wednesday and Saturday, Malibu Oaks has its own private Farmers Market. It's just like any other Farmers Market, except you can only shop here if you live in Malibu Oaks. I spot Wolf at a table near the end of the right row.

"Welcome to my world!"

"Hey, yeah. Nice world you've got here. You're like a regular soccer mom."

"Correction: I am selling local, artisan honeycomb to the soccer moms."

"Where'd you get it from?" I ask.

"It was here when I showed up today. My job is just to man the table and explain the exclusive nature of this honeycomb to anyone who stops by here."

"Exclusive honeycomb," I repeat. "That's great."

"Next week's will be a little better."

"What is it? Organic patchouli?"

"Extreme exploration gear."

"Okay, Bear Grylls. Who buys that at a Farmers Market? I thought it was all just fruits and vegetables and occasional hippie clothing."

He shakes his head.

"That's the point. It's so out there, it seems exclusive. Doesn't it?"

"I guess."

"You should see some of these things. It's not just some tents and canteens and shit. It's some serious *man* shit. Like rappelling and spelunking gear, crazy ass knives, compasses that are controlled by satellites, waterproof headlamps..."

"Sometimes I don't mind my job."

"Just because you're not a man like me, don't knock the explorer gear. It's legit."

"Noted. So I tried going to that girl's house today."

"Tight butthole girl?"

"I really hope we get a new nickname for her. It's starting to feel weird."

"Oh, it'll feel *really* weird when you find out."

"Yes, her. She wasn't home."

He nods.

"So, that's it?"

"Yeah."

"I don't know how you can knock my Farmers Market, man. That was the lamest story you could have possibly told me. *I went to see a girl, and guess what, she wasn't there.*"

"Enjoy your fucking honeycomb. I'm out."

He waves as he smiles. I look back at him and his stupid, little table that he's standing behind. A group of older women are waiting for us to stop talking. Once I leave, I turn around and see them approaching his booth like I hadn't even been there. Vultures. Honeycomb-loving fucking vultures.

I take my lunch break while I'm over here. I'll start up again when I get bored. There's no real set time for when I'm supposed to finish. I just have to call in to my supervisor and report everything that I learned. When I do it is largely up to me, as long as I get it done. I imagine that it's kind of like being a postman, but I don't know if they have a set time to finish things. I read that Bukowski book once. It didn't seem like they had any rules that really mattered. But then again, that was like 60 years ago and he was a drunk.

I buy a sandwich from a little cart with a man behind it, because buying it from a cart without a man behind it would be weird. I eye the guy selling it to me for a little while, but he looks harmless. Or maybe that's how he's trying to look. I can't tell.

Fuck it. I walk down to the beach and sit down in an empty Adirondack chair that just happens to be there. I'm eating the hell out of my sandwich and watching people wander up and down the beach. Crumbs are flying everywhere and IDGAF. My eyes shift from one person to the next, trying to see if I can spot any happies amongst the crowd.

A Caribbean-looking guy with dyed blond hair is doing cartwheels down near the water, walking along with a little dog. Every now and then, he approaches a couple and talks to them for a little while. Most times they walk away after a few seconds. He seems like a typical beach drug dealer to me, but as I continue to watch him, I can't figure out what his deal is. Would The Board employ a drug dealer as a happy? I can't see why not, but it also seems a little strange. You don't usually *hire* known criminals.

He keeps cartwheeling while his dog trots behind him. I haven't spent much time at the beach until now, so I'm not really sure what to make of it. Maybe this is what he always does. Eventually, he walks close enough to me that I can wave him down.

"What's up, man?" I ask.

"How you doing, bruddah?"

"Good, good. What's good? Whatcha got?"

He eyes me up and down and then gives me the nod of approval. There's no way I look like a cop, so why's he looking me up and down? Is he a happy? Or just a regular dude? A happy that's assigned to be a dealer wouldn't be afraid of getting caught, so he wouldn't have to do the once over on someone like me. But then again, why would a real dealer even be here?

"I been looking for this couple that told me to meet dem here today. They said they wanted a few joints, so I got dem and rolled dem up for dem. But then they didn't show."

"So you're just doing cartwheels to pass the time."

He smiles.

"Yeah, man. Love the cartwheels."

"How much were you gonna sell them for?"

He eyes me up and down really quick.

"Twenty."

"How many?"

"Four. Fat ones. Baseball bats, bruddah."

"Good shit?"

"Da best."

His lack of hesitation makes me nod.

"I can do twenty."

He reaches into his pocket and pulls out a plastic bag. He tosses it onto my lap, and it lands on top of what is left of my sandwich.

"Oh, my bad."

I look down at the joints, and they're pretty thick, just the way I like them. Just the way most people like them. I pull out a twenty from my wallet and hold it low in my hand. He reaches over and gives me a little high five handshake thing where he pats me on the shoulder, taking the bill as he moves away.

"Enjoy dem!"

He exits by doing a few cartwheels, heading back down toward the ocean. His dog follows him. When he reaches the water, he yells back to me.

"And if that couple come back, tell dem I was looking for dem!"

As I'm nodding, I pull out my phone and send a picture of the baggie to Wolf. He's responding within seconds. The dude is super on top of his messaging game.

This thing closes at 6. Don't finish them all without me!

I don't have a lighter on me, so I'm going to have to wait until later anyway. I look at my watch. It's some time. Who cares. The cartwheel dude is still flipping around down by the water. He's actually very good at them. I still can't figure out his deal. I get up and brush the heap of crumbs off my lap, carefully checking my surroundings to ensure that no one sees how embarrassingly messy I am. There's no one around, so I try doing my own cartwheel. I topple over before I can even remotely come close to landing on my feet, and I get a bunch of sand down my underwear. Just like I intended.

I look out at the ocean and see a little splash off in the distance. I don't know why, but it makes me smile. I get up and brush off most of the sand, and I head back toward town.

* * *

Wolf is knocking on the door to my apartment. His knock has a weird pattern that I'm trying to not overanalyze.

"Sup, homey."

He walks in and plops down on my couch. I pull out a couple of the bats, and we puff through them, saving the other two for another day. I'm superiorly stoned by the end of it. I write something down on a piece of scrap paper about trying to find that blond Caribbean guy and his dog to get some more of what he is selling. There's something about how cheap it is that's making the high that much better. I can feel the conflicting notions churn against each other in my brain. I'm at the intersection of practicality and whimsy. I must have made a wrong turn sometime when we were smoking the first joint. I hardly ever go anywhere near practicality.

"Let's go out somewhere once this dies down a little," Wolf says.

He's slumped against the back of my couch, so sunk in that he looks like he isn't actually going to be able to get up again.

"The night is young."

"The night has no age. The night isn't a person."

He's right. But so am I. Or at least I'm not wrong. It's just a phrase, and I'm not the one who made it up in the first place, so I can't possibly be wrong about it. The night itself—if it has an age—would be a young night. It is like 8:30 or 9:00.

"Semantics. I can go out."

"Where?"

I point my finger at him and hold it out for a while.

"Your idea. You decide."

We don't move for a while. I think I eat a half of a bag of pretzels without saying another word. I'm just listening to the sound of my molars crunching away. My mouth is half-full and in mid-chew when I finally begin speaking again.

"I've been living here for like three weeks now."

"Yeah. Me too."

"The whole time I've been here, I haven't been able to buy Pizza Rolls at the store."

"What store?"

"Any store. Doesn't matter. They're always out."

"Tragedy."

I get up from the chair and pace around the room.

"It is! I love those things. Jesus, the more I even think or talk about them, the sadder I am that I don't have any right now. It's ridiculous."

"Fight on, brother."

He's so sunk into the couch that I'm not sure if he still has two arms or if the couch has swallowed one of them. He isn't moving, so I can't actually know for sure. I haven't fed my couch in a long time, so it wouldn't be unjustified if it's a little hungry.

"This is a city that has *so* much money. So much money! Even the Ralph's is practically a work of art. Can't they spend some of that money and invest it in a, you know, like a better inventory management system or something?"

"For your Pizza Roll conundrum?"

"Yeah, that and, like, anything else that they're short on. It's simple inventory management."

"You should run for office on this platform."

"Simple inventory management!"

I'm still pacing, but I can't feel my legs.

"What do you know about inventory?"

I grab a handful of pretzels and shove them in my mouth.

"Me? Nothing."

"You never worked in a store?"

"No. But whatever. Just because it's not my job or expertise, it doesn't mean that I can't have an opinion about it. This is shit!"

"Be the change you want to see in the world."

My hands are on my hips and I'm nodding.

"I want my world to have Pizza Rolls."

"Shout it from the mountaintops, man. Go wild. Let 'em know."

I sit back down and shove another handful of pretzels in my mouth.

"I don't even know why I'm eating these things."

"I think we need to go out."

"You. Pick a place."

"Air."

"No. I haven't been, but I've heard that it sucks."

"I've heard good things."

"Yeah, OK. Me too. But I want to believe that it sucks. The name just sucks..."

"Hey man, you told me to pick. So I picked."

He's right, so I don't fight it.

"Air," I repeat.

"Just wipe all that pretzel shit off your shirt before we go. You look like a homeless guy that fell asleep under a family of pigeons."

I look down at my shirt and laugh. That's a completely accurate description. I brush a pile of pretzel debris onto the floor. If I had a maid, she'd be coming tomorrow. But I don't. Wolf stands up, and I confirm that both of his arms are still intact. The couch burps.

"Inventory management," I mumble.

* * *

Air is one of the many pretentious and overpriced rooftop bars in Malibu. Whoever runs the place does a good job maintaining its lavish and impressive ambiance. It's on the roof of a seven-story hotel that sits right on one of the most popular beaches, but I don't remember its name. I don't remember any of the beaches' names, and I'm OK with that. Why does a beach deserve a name anyway? It's just the place where the ocean finally gives up. If you named every location where I gave up on something, you'd run out of names *really* quick.

When you exit the elevator and walk out onto the roof, the first thing that you see is a long, straight pathway lined with flames. The path opens up to a large rectangle, with skylights from the hotel below running down the center and rows of couches flanking each side. There's only one bar that's set way in the back, framed perfectly against the ocean, and if you time it right, the setting sun. If you time it poorly, you're basically just a blind guy trying to order a drink from a shadow.

Wolf walks in with a subtle swagger that isn't quite like he owns the place, but more like he knows someone who used to own it and who sold it and made a ton of money, and the reason he knows him is because they were secret business partners, so in actuality, he made a ton of money too. Swagger like that.

"We missed the sunset."

We're standing behind an unorganized group of people all waiting to order drinks.

"No shit. It's like 10 something."

"It is?"

"You high motherfucker."

"Where did you get this weed from again?"

"Just some random dude on the beach down by the Farmers Market. I've never seen him before."

"Is he a happy?"

I shrug.

"What's a happy?" a girl asks.

I snap my head around to see who's asking the question. Wolf keeps staring at me and doesn't turn or move. I make eye contact with her.

"A happy is...um...oh, it's kind of like a slang term we use," I say as I bob my head toward Wolf. "Me and this guy."

"Slang for what?"

Slang for what. Slang for what? I can't think. Who is this girl anyway? She's just someone behind us in this mob of a line for the bar. I have my head turned around, and I'm looking over my shoulder at her. I can't really see her too well, so I turn my body around some more.

"Oh."

That's all I say for a little while. She has a hell of a body, and it's throwing me off. I'm staring down at her breasts for longer than I should be, but my reactions are slow and I can't help it. I'm still high too.

"Oh?" she repeats.

Wolf is silent. Stupid Wolf. The one time since I met him that he isn't saying something.

"It's slang for like, a, uh...you know."

She waits for me to continue.

"I dunno, man," I mumble. "Like a dealer that only sells uppers or something."

"A happy?"

My face is flushed and beads of sweat are forming above my brow. Waves of body heat are radiating inside of my shirt. They're pulsing out through my collar. It all happens in an instant, and suddenly I'm traveling down a heat death spiral. Wolf must be zoning out, or maybe he's intentionally letting me crash and burn. Whatever he's doing, it has nothing to do with talking.

"OK. Whoa. This interrogation is too intense for me. I don't even have a drink yet."

The girl smiles. I turn around and face the bar, a little rattled. It's not that I don't know how to talk to girls. I have game. Hi I'm Luke blah blah blah let's go to my place. I'm usually pretty good at this stuff. I'm just uncomfortable that someone has already potentially learned about The Board from me. I sure as shit don't want to slip up. I'm still new to this whole thing. And I just *know* that there will be some buzzcut waiting to fuck me in the ear again if this girl finds out. All because I'm high and talking to silent fucking Wolf at stupid fucking Air.

But wait. I don't actually know if she's on the outside or not. It's not like our conversation was very substantive. She might be one of us and she's just fucking with me. Or she's not, and she's just a regular person trying to make conversation. I'm tapping my foot as I stare ahead at the bar.

"A happy..." she repeats.

I cringe. Then I turn around again.

"Just me and this guy," I repeat. "Just some slang."

She shakes her head.

"Nah. I can tell that you're lying. I know what a happy is."

I turn and look at Wolf. I can't tell if he's alive. He's staring right at me, but his eyes are motionless and so is the rest of his body.

"Motherfucker," I whisper, before turning back to look at the girl. "Look, it's what I said. Just some slang. Me and this guy."

"No," she says, leaning forward toward me. "I know what a happy *really* is."

"Okay. Whatever you say."

She continues to look at me straight in the eyes, and then she reaches forward with the back of her hand and taps the fly of my pants.

"That's a happy," she states.

Then she smiles one of those girl smiles where she bites her lip. I can't stand it when real girls smile like that. That's only supposed to happen in the sexy movies.

"No. That was my dick," I correct her.

"The real question," she continues, completely unfazed. "Is whether or not you're both gay or if it's just you?"

My anxiety about accidentally leaking anything about The Board is diminishing, but now I really just need the bar line to clear so I can get my fucking drink. This chick is kind of crazy.

"Sorry. Not gay. Also, no clue what you're talking about."

"Oh, so it's him?!" she exclaims, turning to Wolf. "I was wrong!"

"Him?" I ask. "Yeah. He's the gay one. Meanwhile, in case you didn't notice, you just tapped my dick for no reason. Just wanted to point that out."

She shrugs.

"A happy is a happy," she says plainly.

"Sorry, are you suggesting that a penis is referred to as a happy? I don't get it."

"What's not to get? You're the one who was going on and on about some guy on the beach and his big dick."

"What?"

"You said, 'Hey, I bought some weed from that guy on the beach. He has a huge dick. Which one of us should try to fuck him?'"

I look at Wolf and frown.

"I didn't say that."

"You said, 'Which one of us should try to suck his dick? His huge dick?' And then this guy," she says, slapping Wolf on the shoulder. "He just nods. Which is why I'm figuring that you're the gay one. But I guess I'm *wrong*."

She does some air quotes when she says the word *wrong*. Air quotes at fucking Air. I hate this place. Kill me.

"Do you have a name?" I ask her.

"I do. And I'll have a gin and tonic."

She nods her head and signals for me to turn around. The line in front of us has cleared, and the bartender is looking our way. Better late than never.

Seven

Fucking girls. I mean, no offense to any girls I know. I just don't understand them. And when they try to fuck with my head in weird ways with weird questions and then use assertively factual statements about things that did not happen, I don't understand that either. It makes me very unhappy about them as an entire gender. Again, no offense to any girls I know. I mean, some offense. Just the right amount.

It's hard to tell if this girl—who hasn't even told me her name yet—is going to be someone meaningful in my life or just one of those easy come, easy go girls. Maybe she isn't going to resonate in my life any more than the nutritional information section on a bag of chips that I refuse to look at while I plow through the entire thing.

She has a name, and eventually she tells me what it is. Amy. Of course it is. Malibu must be full of them. And like Amy Percy, the status of her butthole is also unknown. I buy her a few drinks, and we talk and dance and do the mating ritual shit that I insist I'm actually decent at doing. My eyes get blurry. Then my brain gets blurry too. I think it starts raining. I remember running under an awning, peeling off my soaked shirt and...

Where am I? I can't remember. Did someone fuck with my drink again? No. I held it tight all night.

I've had some blurs that I can remember, and they're pretty shitty memories that I actually wish I could just erase. Blurs should be forgotten. Blurs are nature's way of telling you that what you're doing is so smashed together and fucked up in your head that it doesn't really register with you. Blurs are the way you know that you're doing too much of a substance, any substance. Blurs are the best barometers for quitting time. I don't know what a Gaussian blur is, but it sounds like a really intense kind of blur that maybe involves a Frenchman, and I don't want anything to do with that. Okay, maybe once. But only if it ends quickly.

A clap of thunder snaps me into focus. Fuck, where am I? She's in a bed. I must be in an apartment. Maybe it's her apartment. I know it's not my bed. I have a big white comforter, and this bed just has a thin, little bed sheet. I'm not a savage.

Oh.

The comforter is on the floor. I'm kicking it away from me while I'm going down on her, my face buried in between her legs. The muscle in the back of my tongue—I remember that it's called the styloglossus—it's getting sore from all the exertion. I keep going, my styloglossus be damned.

She comes. She's loud. I haven't met my neighbors yet, but as long as she doesn't yell out my name, they might not know it's coming from my place.

"Luke!"

Well, never mind.

She comes again. Or maybe it's fake the second time. I can't tell. Also, I don't care. I can't tell the difference anyway. When people fake things, it's hard to know if anything they do is real. I'm drawing an allegory to my current situation. Happiness at Malibu Oaks is just one big female orgasm.

After she's done, I climb up on top of her and slide in. I'm not wearing a condom.

Oops.

Sometimes I do this. Blame it on the blur.

I mean, she's wet and I'm ready. I'd be an idiot to go searching around in my nightstand drawer for some terrible human invention that ruins the very reason I do the damn thing in the first place. She might give up if I take too long. Fuck that.

Don't get me wrong. I'll pull out before I come.

But still. We, meaning people, we have sex for a purpose. For one, single purpose. To make a little Luke Jr. or whatever your name's version of that would be. All the fake practice before we do it for real is just pretense. It's an act, a masquerade. It's a fantasy that we all actively participate in. In actuality, we fuck because we're animals that are supposed to fuck. All animals fuck. Humans just pretend that we're doing it because we enjoy it.

Don't get me wrong. I'll pull out before I come.

Wait. I already said that.

Don't get me wrong. I like having sex. And this chick has a body that's just out of control. Full breasts and a tight ass. Flat, little belly. Pretty face too, with full lips and crystal blue eyes. I'm marveling at her body while I'm pumping away. I'm smiling. Because I like having sex. I do.

I just don't think that we're honest with ourselves about *why* we're having so much sex. Humans and dolphins are supposedly the only creatures that have sex for pleasure. I don't believe this. And I don't mean that I think other creatures are out there secretly fucking for fun. I mean that I think we don't do it for fun either. We tell ourselves that it's fun. We feel great while we are doing it. We enjoy it. We come...but every time we fuck and it doesn't result in a pregnancy, we're just failing the biological program that we're all programmed with. We're only here to recreate. Procreate. Procrastinate.

That last word doesn't fit in. Blame it on the blur, part two: the remix.

So here we are. Us and dolphins. The last of the great fuckers.

Maybe that's why we humans have so many problems in the world. And maybe that's why dolphins need the tuna companies to fish with dolphin-safe lines or wires or nets or whatever other tuna fishing practices exist out there. Maybe it's because we're evil for fucking for fun. Or is it worse? Maybe it's because we're condemned for pretending that we're enjoying fucking when in fact we do it because we're programmed to do it. I don't know. I don't decide these things. I just fuck random girls without a condom and then try to justify my behavior afterward.

She falls asleep in my bed. I can't sleep right away, but I'm not sober enough to do anything else, so I try to count how many times the ceiling fan revolves each minute. I keep losing track because a minute is a long time when you're drunk. I look over at her, and the breeze from the fan is gently playing with her hair. My comforter is lonely down there on the ground, but I'm too stuck in place to drag it up onto my bed again.

Wait. This is my place, right?

I look around and think about shrugging, but I don't do it. You can't shrug while lying down. That's ridiculous.

My mind won't slow down. Is The Board going to be upset with me for having a girl over at my place? I didn't hear anything about it in my training. Does the packet say that anywhere? I don't know. Maybe The Board can kiss my ass. A dude needs to get some, just like plants need water and dolphins need safe waters and tuna needs to be on my sandwich with some mayo and pickles. Or maybe without the pickles. It just depends on the mood. Grilled cheese is also a suitable alternative.

Eventually I pass out and dream about missing a flight, over and over and over. I wake up with my hard-on poking up through the sheets and out into the stale, sex-scented air of the room. The fan turned off at some point, and now it smells like someone left a piece of steak out in the sun all day and then stuck it in a dark cupboard for the weekend. I look over at her, and she's still asleep. And she's breathing. This is good. It means that I didn't accidentally kill her.

A little while later, she wakes up. My hard-on has gone away, but my dick is still lying out there in the open. I don't care.

"Hey," she says.

It actually sounds kind of sweet, but I don't think that she's a sweet girl.

"How are you doing?" I ask.

I actually sound kind of sweet too, but I don't think that I'm a sweet guy.

She smiles and stares into my eyes. It's funny the barriers that we knock down once we allow ourselves to put our body parts inside of each other. Twelve hours earlier, I probably couldn't have looked at her straight in the eyes for much longer than I could look at the sun. Now I'm just staring back like I'm Stevie Wonder and she's something that won't make this sentence less offensive than it already is.

"What time is it?"

I nod over to the clock on my nightstand. I can't see what time it is, but she can. She sighs.

"I should probably go."

I don't fight it. I'm not sure if I'm supposed to resist like I actually want her to stick around. Her words just float around in the air around us. Even the words are thinking, *it kind of stinks in here.* I look around the room, hoping that some random noise interrupts the awkward silence.

"Gimme your number?" she asks.

I reach over to the nightstand and grab her phone to enter it.

"Phone on the nightstand?"

"I get comfortable *real* quick."

"I see."

"My dad was Tom Petty."

I sit up.

"What?"

"Okay. I'm gonna go."

And then she basically leaves. Well, she puts some of her clothes on, and I watch her like a creepy pervert while she's doing it. Then she smiles, and I look away. Then she puts the rest of her clothes on. Then she leaves.

I don't trust this girl at all, so I can only assume that Tom Petty wasn't actually her dad, but a part of me is wondering if it's the one meaningful thing she's said to me since I met her. In some completely unfair way, I can almost justify her strange behavior as being normal behavior for a girl raised by a famous musician. Maybe I just made Tom Petty's daughter come. Twice. Or maybe I made some random girl fake two orgasms. These are the polar opposites on the Punnett Square of my evening. I go back to sleep so I can see if I ever make the flight I kept missing in my dream.

* * *

"Hi, this is Luke Balena."

"Yes?"

"Do I work today?"

"You said this is Luke?"

"Yes. Luke Balena. I'm an investigator."

"Yeah, um...we're OK today. You can have the day off."

"Really?"

"Yes."

"So...I just call again tomorrow?"

The call ends. Since I don't know anyone in town other than Wolf and the girl that just left my place, I text him to see where he is. It's not like I can text her. That would be creepy. He doesn't reply, so I assume that he's busy doing some kind of happy shit. Selling more honeycomb. Who knows.

I'm at a loss for what to do. I wander around my place for a while, opening and closing windows, playing music, wasting time. Checking my phone more often than necessary. Wiping little smudges off things. Straightening out stuff. It's interminable. I sit down on my couch and close my eyes. I think about my parents. They still live in Carlsbad. They're still together, still going strong. They're actually still into each other too.

I don't visit them that often, but when I do, they seem like they're happy to see me but at the same time slightly casual about the whole thing. For most of my life, I've considered my parents like my guardians but not really like people that actually feel that invested in me. I think it's reciprocal. I think that's where I get it from. I'm just a son that they had that they hope won't fuck up miserably, so every time they see me and realize I'm not doing that, they're relieved. I guess that's all you can ask for as a parent. If you ask for anything more, you're setting yourself up for potential disappointment. Especially if your son is me.

Back in Carlsbad, I was the guy that no one thought would ever leave town. But I was also the guy that no one ever thought they'd see again after I graduated high school. And it was mostly true, on both fronts.

I'd see people at Ralph's when I'd go back to visit, and all I could do was try to avoid them. I didn't want to deal with the awkwardness of a forced interaction with someone who assumed that they'd never have to see me again.

And what could we possibly have to say to each other these days? It's not like I could tell them about my job. And it's not like anyone would believe that I live in Malibu. So I'd have to be vague. Or lie. And they'd probably have weird shit that they want to hide too, like kids that they had when they were way too young, or an expensive coke habit, or a job so close to their parents' house that they decided to never move out on their own.

Yeah, sometimes it's better when you just avoid people. Sometimes there isn't anything more that you need to say. So you duck down the frozen food aisle, open the freezer case, and hide yourself until the cart passes by you. If you're lucky, you pick the Pizza Roll case and grab a bag or two to take with you. If you're unlucky, it's frozen yogurt. Or Lean Cuisines.

I open my eyes and give my mom a call. I figure she might like to hear from me. It's been a little while. The phone rings only a couple of times before she answers.

"Hello?"

"Hey, mom, it's Luke."

Then we talk about shit. Meaningless shit. Who cares. The message here is that I am not a total piece of garbage.

We hang up. I'm bored. I take a shit. I think about calling my dad, but that would be overkill. Then Wolf texts me back.

Just finished, had an early shift. Meet at the beach?

Perfect timing. I think about smoking before I leave. I debate it for too long. The joints—the ones that I got from the Caribbean guy—they're already rolled up, and I'm tumbling them through my hands. He did such a good job rolling them, there's not a speck that's fallen out. And I've been tumbling them pretty good. Fuck it. I put them down and walk outside. I'm not going to smoke.

Then I walk back inside. I'm gonna smoke. Then I change my mind. These decisions are hard. I pace around my apartment. I sit back down on my couch while holding one of the joints in my left hand and my lighter in my right. Then I put it down again. Fuck.

I make a compromise with myself. I won't smoke now, but I'll bring one of the joints with me. I don't know why this takes so much evaluation. Thankfully no one is watching me.

* * *

"And then we all bought yachts."

Wolf just shakes his head.

"That's it?"

"Yeah, that's it. What?"

"How can that be anyone's favorite opening line to a song?"

"Oh, alright! Not good enough? What's your favorite? The line from *You're So Vain*?"

We're walking along the beach like an old gay couple, bickering about stupid shit that neither of us cares about but that we're refusing to concede. He passes the joint back to me, and I take a puff.

"Doesn't that have a yacht in it as well?"

"Maybe all the best opening song lines all involve yachts. Why would that be a bad thing?"

"Have you ever even *been* on a yacht?"

I think back to the time that I had been on one, but I think it was just a scene out of a movie that I've planted in my consciousness. I usually get seasick, so I feel like I wouldn't have liked being on a yacht anyway.

"Do you even lift yachts, bro?"

Wolf shoves me. I lose my balance and nearly trip.

"So tell me about this girl you banged last night. You gonna see her again? How was it?"

"It was pretty good. I got her number, but I don't know if I'm going to call her. She was kind of crazy."

"Crazy how? Like she squeezed your balls a lot or something?"

"No, she wasn't one of those kind of girls. She knew how to handle my balls. I just mean, like...like she told me that she was Tom Petty's daughter. Isn't that weird?"

"Tom Petty didn't even have kids."

"Yes, he did. I looked it up."

"Oh."

"Neither are named Amy though."

"Okay. So that makes her crazy, or what?"

"I don't know. She was kind of fun. Just fucking weird. Like she said random, super offbeat shit, and it was way too abstract for me to follow."

"That's saying something."

"I know. Exactly."

We've been walking down the beach for a while. I'm picking up little shells and fragments of rocks, and Wolf's mostly just kicking the ones he sees. The storm that passed through last night dragged all kinds of shit from the bottom of the ocean out onto the beach. It looks like Poseidon is having the shittiest yard sale you've ever seen. Strands of kelp, dead jellyfish, condoms, driftwood, you name it. Up ahead, a crowd is gathered in a large semi-circle, their backs to us as we approach.

"What's that? Some kind of bonfire or something?"

"Nah. Malibu Oaks community guidelines don't allow open bonfires on the beach."

Wolf laughs.

"Of course they don't. So then what is it?"

"Beats me. Maybe they're all getting ready to board a yacht."

"Jesus, man, you and the fucking yachts today. I had no idea this was going to turn into a referendum on how Luke Balena feels about yachts."

"Look...what is it? Is it some kind of boat or something? Do you see that rounded line that's kind of tracing the top of all the people? What is that?"

"Not a yacht. It's too short."

We keep on walking, now ignoring the litter all around us as we fixate on the crowd and the mystery object they're all focused on. We're still at least a few minutes away, but neither of us really says anything until we get close enough to understand what we're walking toward.

"Oh, shit."

It's a whale. Not a huge blue whale or anything, but some sort of grey whale that's washed up on shore. It's on its side, looking sad as hell. I would be sad too if I were a whale that was stuck on the beach. I get sad sometimes, and I'm just a human being with a pretty decent life.

"Did you ever see the video of that beached whale that blew up right on the guy?" Wolf asks.

"Dude," I whisper, as I look around us. "Not now."

"Yeah, some guy was, like, harpooning open the belly of this beached whale. And I guess there was a crazy amount of pressure built up inside, maybe from the thing just laying out there all day. I don't know. But yeah, it just kind of exploded all over him. You should look it up."

There's a group of older women standing next to us. I can see them out of the side of my eye, silently judging us. I can't blame them. He's talking about an exploding whale video as we stand in front of this poor creature that's either dead or getting ready to die.

"I don't trust videos on the Internet anymore," I tell him, trying to change the subject. "Too many fakes."

I start to slowly walk away from him, encircling the group of people around the whale, looking for an opening to help me get a closer look.

"You know what else you can't trust?" Wolf continues. "I'll tell you. You can't trust anyone that puts up NO TRESPASSING signs in front of the empty forest."

"I've seen signs like that in other places. It's not that weird."

"But to have security cameras on it...and to, like, drug us and drag us in for questioning? What the hell do you think they have hiding back there?"

He has a good point. Somehow I had kind of forgotten about it. The fact that private property exists is obviously not a big deal, but usually you don't get interrogated about it.

"I don't know, man. They probably have some shady shit going on back there. Maybe marijuana farms or something."

"You think so?"

I shrug. The whale lets out a loud moan and everybody gasps.

"Shit. Is it dying?" I ask.

Wolf shakes his head. We continue to circle around the group. There really aren't any breaks in the long chain of people, or at least there are none that make sense for us to push into. It's actually kind of surprising how many people are just gathered around the poor thing. No wonder she's moaning. She's probably annoyed. I don't know for sure if it's a male or female, but I'm just assuming that since it got lost and ended up in the wrong place, it's probably a woman.

"So, a marijuana farm," Wolf continues. "That'd be tight. But it seems pretty risky for some housing board nerds, don't you think?"

"Alright, fine. I don't know. What I don't get is how that one road was the only one that we weren't supposed to go down. Doesn't the whole stretch of forest all connect back behind all those dead ends? What difference would it make if you just entered through a trailhead right down the road?"

"Maybe there's a river or cliff or something that prevents you from getting to whatever they're hiding. So they only need to block off that one dead-end path."

We find a clearing right behind a father standing alongside his two sons. They're young enough that we can see right over their heads. It puts us practically face-to-face with the whale. We're maybe five or six feet away.

"Damn."

Her head is on its side, and her one visible eye is wide open, staring straight at me. It's intoxicating. She looks bewildered, angry, sad, and anxious. She's encapsulating more emotion than

I thought an animal could portray. Probably more emotion than I can even portray. I'm hypnotized. I can't stop staring at that eye, that huge, beady eye. It doesn't blink, it doesn't move much, but it's still very much alive. She's still very alive. There's no doubt about it.

"I think she's staring right at me," I whisper.

"She's just staring, dude."

"Yeah...at me."

It's surreal. I feel like the whale and I share the same mind, like she knows what I'm thinking and I know what she's thinking. She stares at me, and I stare right back. Wolf starts to tug at my arm.

"She's just staring off into nothing."

"Do you think we can all get her back into the ocean?"

"No way. She's too big."

"I just feel this sense of responsibility. Like we're supposed to all help her get back on her way. Shouldn't we? I mean, we have to, right? Why isn't anyone doing anything?"

I look around at the crowd, and it stirs something inside me.

"Hey!" I shout. "Why isn't anyone helping her?!"

Some people look back at me and shrug. Most people don't even turn around; they just flat out ignore me. Wolf doesn't say anything, but I think he's shaking his head. I can't tell. I'm fixated on her eye.

"Come on, man. Let's get out of here. I see the Coast Guard coming."

"Really?"

"No, not really. I just don't want to be here when this thing dies. It's already sad enough. Let's go."

He tugs my arm some more, and I eventually start to slowly walk backwards, still staring at her as the group folds inward and closes the circle again. I shake my head to try to snap out of it.

"You all right?" Wolf asks.

I'm not. I feel shaken up. And surprised. I didn't know that I could care about anything so quickly. I feel like crying. Thankfully I have sunglasses on. I still have a reputation to maintain.

"I'm fine."

"It's just a whale, dude."

He doesn't get it. I don't either, but Wolf, he *really* doesn't get it.

"Look, how about we go find one of those trails that we *are* allowed down and see if it can lead us back over to that forbidden area?" he asks.

"And get drugged and thrown in the fake jail again? And have that buzzcut yell at us some more?"

"Let's just go see what happens. I'm sure it'll be fine. If we see a sign, we can turn around. Deal?"

"Why?"

He shoves me, and then smiles.

"Because I'm curious, dude. I just want to check it out."

"OK," I relent. "But just give me a minute. I...I need a minute."

"I'll go get my car. Just meet me over in the parking lot whenever you're ready."

Wolf starts saying something, but I tune him out. Then he walks away. The haunting eye of that poor whale is still just staring at me. Even though the crowd is blocking my view, I can feel it. We're connected. Or maybe I just need to cool it a bit on the drugs.

"Hey, you're Luke. Right?"

I flinch, thinking that it's one of the older ladies coming to give me a lecture. But wait, how would she know my name? I slowly look up, and the first thing that I see is her shoes. They're not older lady shoes. I relax as my head tilts up to see who it is.

"Hi."

I see her and immediately get flushed. Well, this is embarrassing. I mean, what the fuck? This is the second time in 24 hours that a girl is making me sweaty. Third, if you count the sex. The more I try to fight it, the worse it gets. My skin is bright red, and anyone within a hundred feet can see it.

"Is it Luke?" she asks again.

I nod.

"Yep. Amy, right?" I ask back, trying to act like I don't know exactly who she is.

Like I hadn't gone to her house like a creeper just the day before. Of all the people to see, of all the places to see her. Amy Percy. Amy with the potentially tight butthole. I'm paralyzed.

"I heard you yell back there about helping the whale. What a pity, right?"

"It's horrible," I mumble. "Is there anything we can do?"

She shakes her head.

"That whale probably weighs 15 or 20 tons."

"Shit. I just feel so bad. What a terrible way to die!"

She's looking down at me with deep understanding, like she gets exactly how I'm feeling. We don't say anything for a little while.

"So, uh..." I try to continue, changing the subject. "What do you do, you know, for work?"

She looks around. I don't know what she's looking for, but I start looking for it too.

"I'm a happy," she whispers.

I nod, knowingly. Or maybe it's just in my head because I can't feel my head nodding now. She takes a couple of steps back and then paces a little bit, crossing her arms and squinting in a weird kind of judgmental way.

"What?"

"Why did you come to my house yesterday?"

I'm startled. I try to hide it.

"Yesterday? I was just walking around. Did I pass your place?"

She raises an eyebrow.

"Nuh uh."

"No? Okay. Why did I go there then?"

"I asked you first."

I look up at her and pull my shoulders up in a big, intentional shrug.

"You're pretty?"

She laughs.

"You came to my house because you think I'm pretty?"

"More or less. I wanted to ask you out. I thought you were out of my league, so I tried to pretend like I was just there again coincidentally to, you know, feel it out."

"Feel it out?"

"Not in a weird way. Not like feel you out. I mean, not that I wouldn't want to feel you. I do. I mean, I would. Well, and I do. But I meant, like, feel out the situation. With you."

It isn't the best answer I've ever answered, but it's going to have to do. We both say nothing for a little while. Somehow it doesn't feel awkward anymore. My skin is cooling off a little bit. Or maybe I just can't feel it.

"So, you don't think this is weird?" she asks.

"What's weird?"

"You came to my house yesterday to try to *feel me out*. But you didn't see me. And then today, I run into you all the way over here at the beach?"

"Yeah. I guess that's a little weird."

"Why haven't I seen you here before?"

"Maybe you have."

"I don't think so."

"How would you know?"

"I'd know."

"I dunno. Until you met me, how would you know that you haven't already seen me a dozen times out here? That's totally possible. I'm not that recognizable. I blend right in."

"You're pretty recognizable. I spotted you as soon as I walked away from that crowd and saw you staring down at the ground."

"Alright. I dunno."

She shakes her head.

"No. This is weird."

"Okay. Sorry."

"Well, you know what they say. Everything happens for a reason. Right?"

I laugh.

"Sure. So then what's the reason you came over here to talk to me? Charity?"

"No. You just seem so...so caring. Everybody else wasn't doing anything but gawking at the poor thing, and here you are, genuinely concerned. It just got me. I don't know. I guess I'm a sucker for a guy with a big heart."

She smiles, and I smile back.

"Well, I'm just a sucker. So I guess that makes two of us."

Eight

Wolf drives us over to the closest trailhead to the restricted area and parks his car along the right side of the road, facing the dead end. I don't see any signs. No signs that say NO TRESPASSING and no signs that say FREE LEMONADE. Nothing. Not even a sign about parking. It's kind of weird.

"Where did they all go?"

Wolf looks at me and shrugs, but I don't think he knows what I'm even talking about.

We walk out onto the trailhead with me leading and Wolf a couple of steps behind. The ferns and low shrubs are still wet with dew, vestiges from the storm the night before. There are no whales anywhere on the trail, but damn if I don't keep thinking about her. We aren't more than a few minutes in when I pull out my last joint to get us lifted again. I don't exactly want to spend all day hiking, so I figure it's better to get down to business soon.

On my first pull, I suck in a little bud. I have to stop and spit it out. I pass the joint to Wolf, who then takes in too much on his first hit, coughing it out almost immediately. No matter how many times I've done it, coughing always makes me feel embarrassed, like I'm an amateur who doesn't know how to handle my shit. It's like someone who gags every time they take a shot. You can't respect a person who repeatedly does this.

We take turns puffing and passing. Occasionally I look around to see if anyone's approaching, but all I see are lush, green blobs scattered among the tree trunks, shooting straight and decisively toward the sky. When the joint is kicked, I toss it on the ground and snuff it out with my heel.

"What's the deal with your parents?" I ask Wolf.

"Still married. My dad's retired. My mom never worked."

"Never?"

"I don't think ever. Not that I knew of. She was just a mom and wife. Military, you know?"

"Yeah, makes sense. My parents both worked. They're still married too."

"I'm glad we had this talk, Luke."

"Oh yeah, me too."

The forest floor is uneven but not all that hilly. As far as hikes go, this one is pretty easy. I'm surprised at how few people we've seen. In fact, I don't think we've seen anybody, but I can't honestly say that I've been paying attention.

"Would you still smoke weed if it didn't smell the way it did?"

"You mean, like, it doesn't smell at all? Or it smells bad?"

Wolf turns and looks at me before answering.

"Smells bad."

I think it's starting to hit him. I must be a little bit behind.

"I don't know. Probably not. The smell is pretty important. It's like with food. They say that 90% of taste comes from smell. Don't quote me on that. Or ask me who 'they' are."

"Okay, no smell then. Would you still smoke?"

"Yeah, probably."

"What if it didn't make you high either?"

"What? You're asking me if I would still smoke if it didn't make me high and it also didn't smell?"

He nods.

"Yeah, would you still smoke if that was, you know, how it works?"

"No smell and no sensation, that's what you're saying? No, I don't think I would. It may as well be a fucking candy cigarette then. What a waste of time."

He nods some more. I turn around to see if anyone's walking behind us, and when I turn back, the green blobs blur and dazzle across my eyes.

"Ah, shit." That feeling of disconnectedness is spreading through my brain and body. "I'm feeling it."

"Oh, I've *been* feeling it."

"The blobs dazzle some more. They dance, they sway. They blob."

"What?"

Oops. I didn't realize that I was talking out loud.

"I'm feeling it," I repeat.

Anyone who hasn't been in the forest and under the influence of drugs is missing out. I don't mean to suggest that you go out and do this right now, because, well, no one should ever take advice from me. But if you're ever tempted or intrigued to experience a surreal rush of natural emotions, and by that, I mean emotions that are derived from nature, it's really top notch.

I've done all kinds of drugs that are supposed to make you feel all kinds of things. Some of them are cooler than others. Some of them are scarier. Some of them are more expensive. Hands down, getting high in the forest is at the top of my list, right ahead of day drinking in public but when nobody else around you knows it.

Both of these are better when you can share the experience with someone else. It doesn't have to be someone that you have sex with. It doesn't even have to be someone you're attracted to. It could be someone of the same sex. Or the opposite sex, if you're a homosexual. Or it could even be with an animal. But only if that animal can get high with you as well. If it can't, then it's not the same and it doesn't count. Also, don't have sex with the animal.

Sometimes you have to go on the record against certain things to make sure your legacy isn't tarnished by speculation after you're gone. I'm proud to say that I am definitively anti-bestiality.

"Do you think that the lower part of the tree is jealous of the upper part of the tree?" Wolf asks.

He's leaning up against one, rolling his head back and forth along the rough bark. He's probably scraping the skin on the back of his head, or at the very least he's letting some ants crawl around on him.

"I think trees are living in perfect harmony with themselves. I think the top of the tree loves its job, and the bottom of the tree loves its job too. It's like asking if a linebacker is jealous of a quarterback. Linebackers don't give a shit about that."

"I think there's tree apartheid."

"That's not a thing."

"Sometimes it is, I bet."

I shake my head, and he continues on.

"Well then, why else would some trees just fall over out of nowhere? You don't think it's because the lower part of the tree is revolting against the upper part?"

"I don't want to shoot down another man's idea, but that idea, dude, that idea is fucking horseshit. Trees don't just fall over out of nowhere. It's due to poor root systems and, you know, fatigue or something. Not *jealousy*."

"You say so. I still think it's a thing. Tree apartheid."

There's a joke in here somewhere. I know I can find it if I keep searching for it.

"Tree apartheid," he repeats.

Still searching. Hang on. Almost there.

Ah! Got it.

"Okay, Nelson Mangrove."

Nailed it.

Wolf continues to lean against the tree. He looks like he might not move again for a while, so I take off and walk farther along in the direction that we were heading before we stopped. After a minute or two, I look back and can no longer see him. I think about turning around and heading back, but instead, I just stand still for the better part of a minute. Or maybe twenty minutes.

A plane quietly roars 30,000 feet above us. When its sound trails off, I begin to hear something that sounds like a waterfall or a babbling brook. Or a regular brook.

"Hey, man. I think there's some water over here!" I shout in Wolf's direction.

I hear him yell something back, but I can't hear what he's saying. I walk in the direction of the sound of the water, but I still don't see anything that sounds like what I think I'm hearing. The ground is flat. It must just be a stream or maybe some local runoff from the storm that's pushing its way down through a pre-existing gulch.

Wolf yells something again, and although I still can't make out what he's saying, I can tell that he's closer than the last time. I'm still not going to wait for him. I keep walking toward the sound.

I'm closer now. It's definitely some source of water, but I still can't see it. At least I'm not just hallucinating. That's always a bummer. Or awesome. I trek farther and farther, closer to the source of the sound.

Eventually I see a slight depression in the ground up ahead of me, jutting along in a mostly straight line like a sort of makeshift creek. There's no trace of a creek bed or gulch. This thing isn't supposed to be here. Plants and stones are getting sloshed around by the water's unanticipated force, like someone turned on a fire hose a few hundred feet away. I come up to the edge of it. I look around, still confused. My hands are on my hips. Wolf comes up behind me and sticks one of his arms through the jug arm that I've created.

"Whew. Had to run to catch up to you!"

"Do you hear the water?"

"I was just making sure those trees were getting along with each other back there. Can't have any more divisions in the plant world. They need to stick together if they're gonna have any chance of making it."

"Doesn't it sound like there's more water than what you're seeing right here?"

He looks around.

"I see what you mean. I mean, I hear what you mean."

"Is it just the loud?"

"Nah. It's not. I can hear it too. It sounds a lot louder than...it sounds more like a waterfall than a creek or stream or whatever this is. Like I hear the creek noises, and then I hear that waterfall noise too. Do you hear that?"

"Exactly. Yes."

I start walking up along the left side of the creek. I'm trying to find where all the damned sound is coming from. Wolf starts to follow me, but then he turns and goes in the opposite direction. It doesn't make any sense to me. It's not like it sounds like Niagara Falls or anything. It's just like a decent-sized waterfall. But without any hills or cliffs or rock formations, I don't understand where the hell it is actually *falling* from. The noise is getting quieter as I head farther up the creek, so I turn around.

"Whoa," I hear Wolf exclaim.

He's about 150 feet away from me. I jog in his direction.

"What is it?"

He doesn't respond. I get within about fifteen feet of him. I ask again.

"What are you whoa-ing about?"

Then I see it.

I was right. The creek is in fact falling off a ledge and creating a waterfall, but now I know why I couldn't see it before. A few feet in front of Wolf's feet is a cavernous pit, a vertical cave shaft that's about ten feet in diameter. The stream is running over the edge and down into the hole below, splashing on what sounds like a bunch of rocks that are way, way deep down underground.

"Holy shit," I mutter.

Neither of us is willing to get too close to the edge, but to me, it sounds like it's crashing down at least 50 feet below us. Maybe even farther. The sound is loud, yet distant. I'm in awe. I've never seen anything like it in my life. Wolf looks over at me and smiles.

"I think we found out why we're not supposed to be here."

Nine

It isn't even an hour into my first date with Amy Percy, and she's already exceeding my expectations.

"You can spit it out. I won't be offended or anything."

She's shaking her head, but the frown that's spreading across her closed lips tells me that a part of her is considering it.

"Here, do you need a napkin or tissue or something?"

She's still shaking her head but hasn't swallowed yet. I can't tell what she's going to do.

"Not everyone likes the taste of it. I'm just glad you tried it. A lot of girls wouldn't."

With a big gulp, she swallows the contents in her mouth and squeezes her eyes shut as it travels down her throat.

"Damn," she gasps. "I was not expecting it to be so...so salty."

I shrug.

"Sometimes they're brinier, sometimes they're not as bad."

"Which kind were these?" she asks, pointing at the larger shells.

"Prince Edward Island."

"And these?"

"Kusshi."

"How do you know all this again?"

"I don't. I just listened to what the guy said when he brought it out. You know...when you were grimacing and looking away from the tray."

She laughs.

"Well, thank you for being there for me when I tried my first oyster. I won't forget it."

"They might grow on you. Or maybe not. It's just one of those things. Love it or hate it. I don't think many people are just meh on oysters."

"Good to know."

She's done up right now, her hair tied up in a braid that's wrapped around the side of her head. She doesn't have a flower behind her ear, but she looks like she'd be able to pull it off. Her white dress completes the angel ensemble as she sits across the table from me at lunch.

Yes, I chose a lunch date as my first date with her. No, I am not a bargain shopper. No, I don't collect coupons. Okay, yes, sometimes I collect coupons, but only when they're too valuable to just throw away like they aren't worth anything. Initially I didn't plan on having lunch; I was planning on just getting in my car and driving up into the mountains to visit a few wineries that I recently learned about. I had no idea that L.A. had wineries, and I thought that wine would be a nice, adult thing to consume on a first date. Taste a little, get a little buzzed, fondle each other, who knows? The day was young. Nothing like an aphrodisiac to set the mood right away.

But she was hungry. And only when she said it did I realize that I was too. So rather than get hammered on our first flight at our first winery, we diverted and took in some lunch at a seafood place just outside of town. Oysters became the replacement aphrodisiac. As long as there's an aphrodisiac, my plans are intact. When we finish eating, I pay the bill in cash and then we both jump in my car, not too full but as full as you probably should get on a first date.

"So you're off again today?" she asks, as the wind whips her hair over the headrest behind her.

"Yeah, it's crazy. Third day this week. They keep telling me they have nothing for me to do. So I'm like, *OK.*"

"That sucks. I'm sorry."

"Hmm? Why? It's pretty great to not work and still get paid for it."

"They're *paying* you to not work?"

"Yeah," I backtrack, realizing that maybe I'm not supposed to be telling anyone this. "I mean, I think so."

"Lucky dude."

I turn off the PCH, and we drive up one of those twisting canyon roads. It looks like all the others, lined with brush-like trees that poke out around the jagged rock walls that were probably blasted through just to make way for the road. And it's steep. We get up to Mulholland, and the road opens up. We turn left and pass a winery, but it isn't the one I was navigating to. Not that I know anything about wine. I know nothing at all. I just like the name of this other place better. Amy doesn't seem to care one way or the other.

We get to our destination, and I run around to her side of the car to open her door before she can. I was trying to look like a gentleman, but now I think I just look desperate. The girl can open her own door. It's not 1906.

"Hi, guys. Welcome. Two tastings?"

"Yes."

The woman behind the counter is in her mid-40s, I'm guessing, and she looks sturdy. Not in an unattractive way. I can see her being a catch for a guy that likes that type. She has a pretty face. Before she pours, I ask her if we can have some paper and pens.

"Taking notes?"

I nod as she pours. I look over at Amy and watch her smell the glass, tilt it back, swirl the wine around, and then pull it up to her lips. I do my best imitation of what I just saw. Then I push a pen over to Amy and raise my eyebrows with a nod, like, *Hey, write something down.* Then I write something down and cover it with my hand when I'm done.

"What'd you write?" I ask.

"I wrote...floral, hints of jasmine and peach. Maybe apricot. Plum."

"Shit."

She laughs.

"Why, what did you write? Same thing?"

"Yeah, almost."

I move my hand away from the paper to reveal mine.

pretty good

Amy bursts out laughing, and I do too. The woman behind the counter looks over from whatever she's doing down at the other end and smiles.

"Well, that's definitely one way to describe it."

"Yeah, you know...I didn't want to be too descriptive. I wanted to let the wine do the talking."

"Very wise," she says, pushing me slightly. It's an affectionate push that's barely noticeable. It's natural. Being with her just feels natural, right from the start.

The next wine is a gold medal-winning, new American oak estate Chardonnay. It's buttery, so I write down *buttery*. I think I'm getting better at this. The one after that is a Pinot Noir. I write down *fruity*. Then we have a Grenache. Then a Cab. Then a Syrah. I write down words for all these wines, but it doesn't matter. Despite the food from earlier, I'm already feeling it a little bit. I eat a few crackers from a little bowl on the counter before we take off to the next winery.

Things speed up in the way that scenes in a movie turn into a montage. There are snippets of emotions, flying bursts of color, laughter, smiles, touching, cool mountain air. Her face, radiant and happy. My hands, gripping the steering wheel as I'm driving back down the mountain at the end of the day. My eyes, focusing on not drifting too far across the center line by using my knuckles as guides. We get back to her place at the golden hour. I look into her eyes as I'm standing on her stoop, that same stoop that I'd visited just a few days earlier.

What a difference time can make. The who, what, where, and why of it are all the same. The when is the only thing that has changed.

I look into her eyes, and as the sun glows a deep orange and twinkles against the glass window on her front door, I give in to all the romance and I lean in to kiss her. I think that I have good instincts on when to and when not to try to lay on that first kiss. I don't think I've ever had a girl pull away from a kiss before, and this time is no different.

"Thank you," I say when we're done. "For today, not for the kiss. Though thank you for the kiss too."

"I had a great time."

"Me too. So we can do this again?"

"We'd better."

We say goodbye. When I get back home, I flop down on my couch and text her something short and sweet because I'm feeling those feelings that you feel when you just have a great first date. I fall asleep, and I don't dream. Or maybe I do. I don't know, sometimes it all happens so...

Shit. What day is it? The sun rose, so that means it's...ahh, fuck. I look around the room, wait, what room is this? Am I home? My eyes refocus.

Shit.

"Fell asleep on you again, huh?" I ask the couch.

All of a sudden, my phone jolts me upright with a ring volume way louder than I would have ever intentionally set.

"Hello?"

"Luke, it's Tony."

"I'm sorry? Who?"

"Tony. Your boss."

My boss's name is Tony?

"Uh, have we met?"

He sighs.

"We're meeting today, son. And you're late."

"Oh. Is it now? I mean, what time is it?"

"Just get here as soon as you can, OK?"

"You got it."

I throw some clothes on and squeeze some finishing cream into my palms, rubbing it through my hair for that just-out-of-couch look. Then I pedal as fast as I can to, wait, where am I going? I aim for the place where we had the training. Luckily, I'm right. I think.

There's a guy standing outside the big glass doors with his arms crossed. He's a broad-shouldered man, a real man of a man, with hairy forearms and dry elbows and a thick set of eyebrows. You can tell a lot about the virility of a man by his eyebrows. My grandfather taught me this.

"Come on in, Luke," he booms.

He walks in, and I follow behind him toward a little office that's tucked away in the back of the building.

"So, how are you liking it here?"

"Here in Malibu? Or here working for The Board?"

"Both. Either."

"I like it here. I mean, how can you not like it here? It's like paradise."

"It is paradise," he corrects me.

"Right. And the job is pretty good. I'm getting used to it for sure. So far I haven't really provided any good intel though."

Tony taps his pen on a clipboard that mysteriously appears out from under the table, or maybe it's been here the whole time and I'm just being dramatic.

"Yes, I saw that in your records here."

"Oh, you can tell that already?"

"Of course. We, uh, we have a whole team of people—data scientists, analysts, mathematicians—all looking at the data to try to identify trends and patterns."

"The data? What data?"

"The data you and the other investigators give us."

"What...OK. Hold on. You have a team of people looking through our data to identify patterns?"

"That's right."

"No way. How can that warrant a team of people? There's only three of us!"

He laughs.

"You'd be surprised."

Damn. Nerd One and Nerd Two must be really hauling ass out there.

"What kind of patterns are you looking for?"

"Well, let's see. If you were me, wouldn't you want to know the patterns related to the people we're investigating? Where they are when we find them? What they're doing? What side of the street they walk on?"

"Why would any of that matter though?"

He laughs again.

"That's why you're an investigator, Luke. Always asking questions."

"I don't mean to prod. I just don't get it."

"Well, regardless. An inquisitive mind is a, uh, a healthy thing. Or whatever that quote is. You know, the one..."

I don't know what he's talking about, and he doesn't ever finish his sentence.

"So these data scientists, they know that if someone is on the left side of the street, they are more likely to be, like, a bad guy or whatever?"

"It's actually the right side of the street. But yes. As an example, we're now aware that over 70% of our residents walk on the right side of the street."

"Hmm. Okay, good to know, I guess. I should always be looking on the right side then, right?"

"No, no no no. You just keep doing your job the way you were trained. I was using that as an *example*. We haven't made any official statements or modifications to our methods based on this data. Not yet. Besides, if you start focusing on the right side of the street and the other investigators start to do the same thing, what do you think will happen?"

"We'll find out more about them."

"No. No no no. They'll just start walking on the left side of the street. You see how that works?"

"Okay. So then what is the point of identifying a pattern if you're not going to utilize any of the information to improve the way you do things?"

"Big data. It's all about big data."

I start tuning him out after this. Big data. Big fucking deal. I think he's talking about it for another five minutes before he switches to some of the more procedural things that I'm not aware of, like how to officially report my hours worked or how to collect my paychecks. I start paying attention again, but now Tony's walking me toward the exit. Our meeting seems to be over.

"Have you been able to take advantage of our fitness center yet?"

I shake my head.

"It's a great facility. You should check it out. It's great for a quick workout, a stretch, you know, whatever you're into."

"I'm into snacking," I reply. "Competitive snacking, actually."

He looks me up and down and smiles.

"You're quite the character, Luke. Remind me...how did we, uh, find you?"

"I got the invitation in the mail. Came in. Interviewed. And boom. Here I am."

Tony shakes his head.

"Well, enjoy your snacking. Take advantage of that metabolism while you've still got it."

"Oh, I don't really have it already."

"Maybe you can find a snacking partner down at the gym."

I laugh.

"Maybe. Thanks, Tony. I'll see you around."

I walk out of the administration building and down the wide set of stairs. When I get to the bottom, I turn around and look up what I just walked down. I get a burst of motivation. Maybe it's the fitness center conversation, maybe it's just because I'm bored. I double back and sprint up the stairs as fast as I can, taking two at a time until I get to the top. Then I run back down and almost fall when I'm not even halfway down, my foot sliding off the edge of a step and catching on the next one. I make it to the bottom in one piece. I'm panting and I'm already sweaty.

"Fuck."

I look over across the street and see two girls giggling and staring at me.

"I'm just practicing for my next snacking competition!" I yell out, unsure of what I'm saying until it's already out of my mouth.

The girls look at each other and walk away without saying anything.

Ten

Wolf and I are down on the beach, practicing tying and untying ropes around a Jet Ski. This is Wolf's assignment today. He's playing the part of a guy that's just come in from a day of Jet Skiing. I'm playing the part of a guy crouched down by his side. Only one of us is getting paid for our efforts.

"Were you ever in Boy Scouts?" he asks, his hands flinging the rope around with such speed that I already know why he's asking me.

"I was in Cub Scouts for a little bit but never really made it beyond that. I played soccer."

"Those aren't interchangeable activities. You could do both. I played sports, and I was in Scouts."

"A black Boy Scout," I muse. "Where are you from again?"

"Oh, because I'm black, I can't be in the Boy Scouts? Get the fuck outta here."

"Okay, well, Boy Scouts was for losers, at least around here. All the kids in it were the unpopular kids at school. The black kids were too cool for Scouts."

Wolf scoffs.

"No way. By me, all the cool kids were in Scouts. *Definitely* the cool black kids were. The losers were the soccer bunnies."

I shake my head, and he continues to toss the rope over and under and through and with such velocity that I feel like he's just pretending to tie something, like he actually has no idea what he's doing. But then he slows to a stop, and there's this magnificent-looking knot that he's just cinched, and I wonder how the hell he still knows how to tie a knot like this. He notices me marveling at his work.

"As you can see, I got my knot-tying merit badge."

I get up and slap him on the back.

"As you can see, you are a huge nerd."

He steps back from the Jet Ski and places his hands on his hips. The machine is tied to a short stump that's in a line of five little stumps that lead down to the water. They look like logs that someone had just stuck in the sand and then forgotten about.

"So, now what?" I ask.

"Now we untie it, I take it out in the ocean, I tool around for ninety seconds, and then I come back and we tie it up again."

"For real?"

He nods.

"If you weren't here, I would probably just Jet Ski around for a little longer, but my assignment is pretty specific. I'm supposed to be tying and untying the Jet Ski on the beach."

"But if you're only out there for a couple of minutes, won't someone notice that you're just on this weird, endless loop? Going out to the ocean, coming back, tying it up, untying it, going back out. Isn't that going to be obvious?"

"Hey, I don't come up with the strategy, alright? I just do what they tell me to do. But to be honest, I think you're giving people too much credit. The average person isn't going to watch me do this over and over again. No one's going to notice. No one has the attention span to just sit there and watch me tie and untie these knots all afternoon."

"Not no one," I remind him. "You're looking at him."

"Even you are going to bail on me after a few cycles. Don't you have to get back to fighting crime or whatever the hell you do out there?"

"*Investigating.* And yes, I do. They actually need me today, but not until later."

"Sounds exciting."

We don't say anything to each other for a little while, and the sound of the waves lapping up against the shore starts to fill my ears. It's peaceful. I can see why people like the beach so much, even though it's never really been my thing. There's something nice about the rhythmic flow of it all. Swooosh. Crash. Hiss. Silence. Repeat.

"Do you think they got the whale back in the ocean?" I ask.

"What whale?"

I look at Wolf, and without any words, I let him know that I hate his guts. He smiles anyway.

"You know what whale," I say. "That poor girl. She made it back, right? Otherwise there'd be some kind of big deal about it. We'd have heard. It'd be on the news or Facebook or something. Right?"

He's untying the knot now, taking his time and slowly wiggling the rope free from each little hold that he had just placed it under.

"Yeah, sure. So, I forgot to tell you. I had a dream about that cave last night. Like it was calling out for me or something."

"Cave? What does that have to do with the whale!?" I shout.

"OK. Chill out. I don't know about that whale, alright? I'm sure it's fine."

"I hope so."

I look away from him and stare down at the wet sand.

"Anyway, man. My dream. So I went back to the forest, and I searched for it—the cave—but I couldn't find it. There was no stream, and I guess I didn't really pay attention to how we got there the last time, so I was searching and searching, but I couldn't find it. I actually never found it. I just wandered around the forest, feeling unsettled and disappointed, kind of anxious even. Like when am I gonna find this thing?"

"What do you think that means?"

He shrugs. One of the ends of the rope has come free, and it's dangling along the side of the Jet Ski.

"Maybe," I theorize. "You are deeply aware of a hole in your life. Something that's missing. A hole that you want to fill. And maybe the cave to you symbolizes that hole, but you can't find it, like you don't actually know what the hole is, but you can feel it, so you're searching for it. And since the water has run dry, and the water was what led you to it..."

I stare out at the seam between the ocean and the sky. A deep sadness overtakes me, but only for a moment.

"That's some deep shit, hombre. But I don't think I have a hole in my life. My life is pretty dope."

"Yeah, your life really isn't that bad," I agree. "But that's what I would say too if I was depressed and hiding it."

"I'm not fucking depressed, man. I think I was just intrigued by that cave. Have you ever seen anything like that before?"

"Hell no. There's nothing like that in Carlsbad. Not that I know of, at least."

"Dude, don't you guys have the Carlsbad Caverns or whatever?"

I shake my head.

"That's in New Mexico."

"Oh. Really?"

"Yeah."

"Well, whatever. I thought those kind of things were only in real Mexico and Thailand and shit. I didn't realize we had them here too. So I think that's why I was dreaming about it. I was just intrigued. I mean, after all, that's probably what The Board is trying to hide behind all those signs. I think there's something more to that cave than we realize."

"Like what? The cave is an underground marijuana laboratory?"

"You need to get over the marijuana farming idea. That ain't happening out there. Trust me."

"Says the guy that dreams about caves. You're a real credible source. What do you know?"

"I think there's something special about the cave. Like, what if it's some Ponce de Leon type shit? That's the fountain of youth guy."

I pretend like I already knew that.

"No way," I reply.

"Well, how would *you* know?"

"Relax, Wolfman. If you want to believe in a fairy tale, don't let me stop you."

"Well, then why's that hole calling out to me in my sleep if it's not something important?"

"I'm telling you, it's a symbol. For the hole in your life, man. You've got a hole in your heart."

"The fuck I do. I feel fine. I mean, I get it. The fountain of youth is kind of a crazy concept, but I'm, you know, I'm not a religious guy or anything, so I don't really have any beliefs when it comes to heaven, the afterlife, all that kind of stuff. So when I think about dying, it actually scares the hell out of me that it might be the last thing that I ever experience. Like what if there's nothing after we die?"

The waves continue lapping up along the shoreline, although it's not as though they have any other choice.

"I always kind of figured that might be the case," I reply. "I don't want to bank on anything other than the worst case scenario. That way, if I'm wrong, I'll be pleasantly surprised, but I'll never be disappointed. Not that it would matter anyway, if I was dead. It all kind of doesn't matter if you think about it."

"Well, that's why a fountain of youth would be so great. Then suddenly everything matters, you know? Because now you won't die, so now you have a guarantee that there's some sort of eternal place for you. It just happens to be here, like now."

"Maybe the hole in your heart is the lack of God's presence in your life."

"Shut up."

"*Jesus take the wheel...*"

"Shut up."

"Well, how would a fountain of youth work anyway, like, what are the rules?"

"What do you mean?"

"Okay, so you find this source of eternal life. You bathe in it or whatever. What does that do to you? Do you just never age?"

"Yeah, exactly. You stay that age from there on out."

"Are you immortal?"

"Yeah, I just said that. You don't age."

"No, like, can you still die? Just because you don't age, it doesn't mean that you can't die. You could still fall off a cliff or get shot in the head or six million other ways."

"Choose one," he finishes. "OK, point taken. But still. Then you can spend the rest of your life just being *really fucking careful* so that you don't fall off a cliff or get shot in the face or whatever. You just hang out at home and live forever."

"You realize that this is some science fiction, Twilight with sexy vampires kind of shit, right? There's no source of eternal life out there that could stop you from aging. Not down in some cave in the forest in Malibu and not up in that rainy Washington town with the sad girl. That's just...that's crazy, man."

"Well, then what is it? You don't think that cave is something more than just a hole in the ground?"

I think about it for a little while as I take a turn untying the rest of the knot. He's really jumbled it all together. I want to just pull a knife out and cut it open, but I don't have a knife...also, that would just be entirely counter to the reason we're out here in the first place.

"Do you remember when we were skydiving, or after we were skydiving, we were sitting in your car and we were talking about how real it was...how the whole thing just felt so real?"

"Yeah."

"Do you remember what you said that fucked it all up?"

Wolf shakes his head.

"You said something like, 'What if down was up and up was down?'"

He laughs.

"Oh, that. Yeah, I said that. What about it?"

"We never talked about it. What did you mean when you said that?"

"I meant, like...have you ever looked up at the sky and wondered if it was really the layer between us and the rest of the universe? Like, how do you know? What if it was the other way around, but we've been lied to all this time?"

"I take it back. I think we need some loud. This is not conversation material for two sober guys with a Jet Ski."

"No, for real. You've never thought about it? Like, the big dome above us, the sky up there...that's supposed to be between us and space, right? But what if it's the opposite? What if going up is actually going *inside* the Earth, and going down is going *out*."

"So Mars and Venus and all the other planets and all the other galaxies and all the other stars, they're all just inside of the middle of Earth?"

"Think about it, man. Have you ever seen what space looks like?"

"Uh, yeah. Who hasn't? They didn't teach you about space in Boy Scouts? You didn't get your astronomy merit badge?"

"No. You've seen *pictures* of space. And you've seen videos and whatever, but you've never seen it yourself."

"Dude. I've never seen the Pyramids, but I am pretty sure that they exist. Do you think that things only exist if you see them?"

He shakes his head and places his hands on the seat of the Jet Ski, leaning over and looking deep into my eyes like he wants to put his stuff inside me. I hope he doesn't try.

"Ever since I started working here, I don't know...I just assume that anything I'm told might not be true. Like, if all these people here think that I'm a real resident, just having fun with my fucking Jet Ski...and the whole thing is just one big sham to make a bunch of money for this stupid housing community...then why should I believe anything else that I've been told? Like that space is out there. What if space is just down in the ground instead? Why's one any more believable than the other?"

He's taking an extreme stance, but I get where he's coming from. I've started to lose my faith in so many other things around me too. It's hard to know what's real when nothing around you is real.

"Okay. Let me reset. Because I don't disagree with you there, I think that in some ways, anything is possible and something that we're told may just be a huge cover for a lie that we'll never know about."

"Exactly."

"But...I don't think that means that *literally* everything is upside down. I think that yeah, maybe some other things that we think are true are actually untrue. But I don't think that The Board—or anyone, for that matter—would be able to pull off such an elaborate lie. For all this time."

"That's probably what everyone would say about this stupid place, though. If you don't know the truth, how do you know what's real?"

"So you think that this cave is a portal to outer space. That's what you're telling me?"

"No, I'm not saying that. I mean, maybe. You're the one who brought it up! I wasn't saying anything about up and down and the cave. You brought it up."

"I brought it up because I wanted to say that just like what you said that day, your whole fountain of youth thing seems ridiculous. There are plausible scenarios that we might be unaware of, and then there's just straight up fiction. This is fiction."

"I don't know, man," he replies. "You might actually be on to something. Like...what if that cave is the way out of here? Like The Board knows it, and they're trying to hide it from everyone else. And this whole scam that they're pulling with the community, it's just a distraction from the real scam. The real scam is that the world is upside down and no one even knows it."

"I think you might be losing your mind. Maybe that's the hole that you're searching for. It's a hole in your brain."

The knot is undone. Wolf turns toward the ocean and begins to shove the Jet Ski toward the water.

"I'm going to take this thing out there for a little while. You gave me a lot to think about. I kinda want to just shoot along the waves and think. Cool?"

Jesus. He's taking this so seriously. He starts the engine up, and it begins sputtering water out of the exhaust.

"I didn't give you anything, man. I had nothing to do with this."

"I'll text you later," he says, revving the engine and speeding off into the oncoming tide.

* * *

I'm up by the lake, and it's mid-afternoon. The sun is already starting to make its way down toward the top of the tree line. I'm walking around aimlessly and trying to listen in on people whenever I can. No one's really talking all that much. Sometimes I forget what I'm supposed to be doing out here, and I just walk around, looking at all the expensive houses. When the sun has disappeared and all the people on the lake have gone into their houses to do whatever they do in there, I call up the main office and give them a few phony pieces of observation. Then I ride my bike home.

I haven't reached out to Amy in a couple of days. I'm feeling a little guilty for not paying much attention to her, so I send her a quick text. I like her, and there's no reason that I shouldn't be trying to talk to her some more. I'm just bad at this kind of stuff. I'm playing a poor man's version of hard to get.

She texts me back after a few minutes, and we start texting back and forth, eventually deciding to meet up for a drink later on tonight at a bar I've never heard of. I think about jerking off while I wait to meet up with her, but then I think about saving it instead. Maybe I'm getting ahead of myself. We're probably just going to grab a drink or two and get to know each other some more.

I got a haircut earlier in the week. It was my first haircut since I had moved into town. The guy was all right, and he did a pretty good job. But it was the kind of haircut that looked really good on the day that he cut it, but then by the next day, I couldn't get it to look the same again. And the day after and the day after, and at some point, it made me distrust the guy, like he knew what he was doing and this was just his way to get me to come back and pay him some more to do the same thing again.

I'm staring at my head in the mirror and tousling my hair back and forth with some styling product that he also sold me. It still doesn't look the way he made it look. I almost want to call him and ask him if he can do my hair before I go to the bar. I decide against it and put on a hat. Then I take the hat off and re-do my hair. I change my shirt four different times.

It's just one of those days. Sometimes you think you look good. Sometimes you have to change your shirt and take a hat on and off.

I walk into the bar, and she's already sitting up on a stool, leaning forward with her arms pressed together in front of her. I walk up behind her and put my hands over her eyes.

"That better be Luke, or I'm about to neuter you."

I let go and come around to her side.

"That was pretty effective."

She smiles.

"How's it going?"

How is it going? My only friend in the new town that I live in might have gone off the deep end, and now it's partially my fault that he thinks that the universe is upside down. I still don't even know how to do my job correctly. I'm making shit up just to close out the day. The whole world might be a farce, and we don't even know it. And then there's the whale. Ugh.

"I'm good," I reply. "How are you?"

"Good now."

I sit down next to her and flag down the bartender for a beer. I'd tell you what kind of beer I ordered, but I don't want to start a trend.

"I was beginning to think that you didn't want to see me again," she laments. "I hadn't heard from you for a couple of days."

"I was playing hard to get."

She laughs at my admission that I'm disguising as a joke. I laugh as well, feeling like I succeeded and won some little secret prize for being both honest and inoffensive. It rarely goes that way for me. I'm usually pretty honest. I am rarely inoffensive.

"Well, you failed. Because you texted me tonight, remember?"

"I did fail. I gave in. Also, if I'm being honest, I don't know that many people here yet, so I was just kind of looking for someone to keep me company."

I can see that she isn't as impressed with what I'm saying now, so I try to make it a bit more upbeat.

"I mean, not just someone. I wanted *you* to keep me company."

"Okay, Romeo."

"Really. I have like one friend, this guy I met on my first day here. He's a cool dude, but, you know, he's a dude. At some point you want to spend time with someone of the opposite sex. And basically, you're the only girl that I know here."

"You're just racking up the points with me here. You should keep it going."

"Well, just because you're the only girl that I know, it doesn't make you any less interesting to me. If I knew 25 girls here, I'd still want to spend time with you. Unless, you know, they were like 25 versions of you. Then I'd probably just want to hang out with all of them. All of you."

I smile.

"You're weird."

"Am I?"

"You're different."

She's drinking something clear in a short rocks glass. There's too much liquid for it to be vodka or gin on the rocks. Also, that would be alarming. That is a drink for an alcoholic. You need to mix that shit. So I'm hoping that she has some soda or tonic in there as well. I don't want to fall for this girl and then end up having arguments about why I have a lock on the cabinet with the mouthwash. I've seen those intervention shows. I know how it gets.

"You know who's different? This guy, my friend. I mean, I think I can call him my friend. I've really only known him for a few weeks now, but we spend most of our free time together. I think he doesn't have any friends either."

"What's so different about him?"

"Well, to start, his name is Wolf. And when he told me, I was like, are you kidding? That's such a cool name. Do you think that's a cool name?"

"Yeah, I guess so. For a guy."

"It would be a tough name for a girl, I agree. Maybe Wolfina would be all right. Anyway, this guy, Wolf, he's a good-looking guy. He's a happy...you know...well, of course you know. You're one too. So he's been recruited here for his looks and for his charisma. He's the kind of guy that you see having a good time, and it makes you want to have a good time too."

"A Malibu dream."

"Sure, exactly. So, he's cool. He's got a cool name. He's got a cool look. He's just an all-around solid guy."

"Are you trying to pitch him to me or something?"

"No. Sorry. So, earlier today, we're down by the beach, and he's tying and untying a Jet Ski to a series of little logs on the beach. Because, you know, of course that's what he's doing. And I'm there talking with him. And..."

Shit.

"And...what? He suddenly became *weird*?"

"Sorry. I just realized that there's a lot of back-story that you have no idea about, and without it, this story is pretty meaningless. Or at the very least, it'll be confusing. And I can't imagine why you would want to hear about this anyway. It's not compelling, like at all. I don't even know why I brought it up."

She leans over and puts her hand on my knee. I don't know why she does it, but I was taught to never question an unexpected gift, so I just stop talking and smile.

"I want to hear about it. Because...well, Luke...I've got nothing better to do either."

If she were texting me, the sentence would have had a smiley face at the end of it. So I tell her all the relevant details and probably a bunch of other details that just come out along the way. About the first time we went back in the forest. About getting drugged and dragged in for questioning. About going back and stumbling upon the cave. About everything I can think of that might matter for her to appreciate the story more.

If we're here to get to know each other, there's no harm in just being my rambling self. If she likes it, great. If she doesn't...I can change. She's too cute to let her pass me by because of some stupid personality traits of mine.

I talk and talk and talk, and eventually I have to order another beer. She orders a refill but doesn't explain what's in the glass, so at this point, I'm still dealing with a potential alcoholic.

"Upside down?" she asks me, her new drink coming out from seemingly nowhere and with no time for me to observe its preparation.

"Yeah. Like...you go down the cave, and that's the way you get out into space. And into the universe. Through...the ground."

"And you don't believe this."

"Believe it? I don't believe that *he* believes it! I mean, I get it. Being an actor can really fuck up your perspective on what is real. But this is some pre-Columbus, world-is-flat shit that I just can't get down with. Not even conceptually. It's crazy. I can't understand how he's even thinking straight when he says that he wants to climb down there and see if he ends up in another galaxy or whatever. I don't know. It just seems ridiculous to me."

"It is crazy. Though, can you imagine if he's right?"

I shake my head.

"Okay, look. I'll tell you what I told him. I don't have any weed on me. If you want to get into *this* conversation, you're gonna have to come back to my place."

She looks down into her glass.

"That's fine by me."

Eleven

When I was in junior high, I chased around a lot of girls. It didn't matter what they looked like because I liked all types. It didn't matter if they were smart or dumb or somewhere in between. It didn't matter if they had money, if they wore nice clothes, if they played sports, if they were in band. I liked girls.

At least back when I was in junior high, you could have a girlfriend, but it was different than having a girlfriend as an adult. You didn't really do anything together unless you were *really* serious, and that hardly ever happened to any junior high couple. There was always one couple that lasted a long time, like a year or something, but for the most part these relationships were all fleeting and transient. That's the way it's supposed to be when you're in junior high.

I had a girlfriend when I was in seventh grade. Let's say her name was Lisa. It wasn't Lisa. Her name was Jenn. But in an effort to protect her identity, let's call her Lisa and pretend that I didn't just mention her name was Jenn.

Lisa and I were boyfriend and girlfriend for about a week. We went to one of our school dances together, and we danced during all of the slow songs. In my school, the last song of the dance was always *Stairway to Heaven*. I don't know how that came about, and from what I've since learned, that isn't a common last song at middle schools across the country.

Anyway, it's a long song. And the couples that are dancing during the song are usually just waiting for the last 20 or 30 seconds so they can start making out. It's when most of my friends had their first kiss, during those last 30 seconds of *Stairway to Heaven*. It wasn't where I had my first kiss, but that was because Lisa broke up with me right before the song began. I sat on the bleachers and contemplated my life while Jimmy Page and Robert Plant wailed away. I wondered what I had done to turn her away.

I thought that my dancing earlier in the night was all pretty good. I talked to her friends for a while. I even spent a whole fucking dollar on a soda she wanted. I had invested some serious time and effort into this girl, and she just chewed me up and spit me out.

I was bitter for a little while. I told all my friends to avoid her, and I did my best to do the same. Summer break came, and we didn't see or speak to each other the entire time. When school started up again in the fall, I started to see her in the hallways, and I would do my best to avoid eye contact with her. If I saw her approaching, I would look down at the seam that the lockers made with the linoleum floor, brushing shoulders with the oncoming traffic.

Winter came, and Lisa's family moved into a brand new house at the end of my street. At that point, there was very little that I could do to avoid her. One day, I was out playing basketball with my brother, and she came walking by. She asked me if I wanted to go take a walk around the block with her. I told my brother to go inside, and then I started walking with her.

I couldn't resist. If there was an opportunity to be with a girl, I was probably going to take it. Even if she had already discarded me. Even if it was humiliating.

We walked down the street, and at the end of the street, there was an old horse trail. We walked down the trail for a while. I don't remember what we talked about. After we couldn't see the road anymore, we stopped and I leaned against a fallen down tree. Lisa stood in front of me and then moved in closer. She drew her arms around me in a hug and buried her face into my chest. I stared straight ahead and wondered what the hell was happening.

She looked up at me and leaned in to kiss me. I had already kissed a girl at that point, but I was still pretty new at it. I'm not sure that it started off so great, but after a little while, we got into a good rhythm and were making out pretty impressively for a couple of teenagers. Or at least it was impressive to me back then.

I think I might have run my hands up and down her shirt. I can't remember what I did. I just remember it was an amazing 15 minutes out there on that horse trail. I don't know why we stopped, but eventually we did. Then we walked back home, and she waved goodbye. As I walked up my driveway, I started smiling my huge, wide smile, like I had just made off with a fortune that I wasn't supposed to have.

I learned a lesson from that experience, but it didn't come until a week or so later. I was so excited about what had happened that I started to tell some of my friends. I told my guy friends, and I even told some girl friends. Word spread around school, and before I knew it, Lisa found out that I was telling people what we had done. She confronted me about it in the hallway one day.

"Why the hell are you telling everyone a *lie?*" she seethed.

"I'm not lying. I've only been telling people the truth," I said.

"No, you're a liar!"

I shook my head. Then she slapped me across the face. It was so loud that everyone in the hallway stopped what they were doing and went, *"Ohhhhhhh!"* She stormed off, and all I could do was laugh as everyone hooted and hollered out my name. When things calmed down and I walked into my next class, I started to wonder why she was so upset with me. I hadn't lied. *She* was the liar, calling me a liar.

A couple weeks later, my parents took our family to Vermont to visit my grandparents over winter break. One day when we had nothing else to do, my father and I went ice fishing. I told him all about what had happened with Lisa. We didn't have the kind of relationship where I would tell him this sort of stuff, but for whatever reason—maybe it was the sheer boredom of being on a frozen lake—I opened up and told him everything. About the making out and about the whole school finding out. About the slap. About all of it. He just sat there, nodding. Then he told me something that I've remembered ever since.

"There are things that you will do in life that you won't be able to tell people about," he said. "Because to tell people about it will ruin the secrecy of it, and the secrecy may be the only thing that held the whole thing together. It might even be the only reason that it ever happened. Sometimes there are things in life that guys like us will only get to experience if we keep our mouths shut. You shouldn't forget that."

I haven't forgotten it.

So, when Amy and I left the bar, I can't tell you what we did or where we went. I can't tell you if we smoked some weed at my apartment, or if we just went back to her place, or if we wandered down to the beach and fooled around. I can't tell you if she stayed the night. I can't tell you any of that because I still remember that slap. And I still remember what my dad taught me.

* * *

It's a couple of mornings later, around the time that Amy could theoretically be leaving my apartment. I sit up in my bed and stretch my arms wide like I'm a cartoon character that just woke up from a long sleep. It feels great. Morning stretches are some of the best that you can ever have. The sun's high and bright, and a sliver of light is beaming through a crack between two of my curtain panels. It casts on the floor like an imaginary line, separating me from the kitchen on the other side of the room.

I call up to see if I have to work.

"Hi, it's Luke."

"Day off," a voice snaps, then hangs up.

"The fuck?"

I make myself breakfast and take a cold shower. I like cold showers. They're the best wakeup call you could ever ask for. Just don't take one around a girl that hasn't seen your penis at full attention.

I text Wolf to see what he's up to. That dude is always working. I really got the better end of the deal here, now that I think about it. We meet up about an hour later, a few miles across town from where I live.

"You look like you work in the circus," I laugh.

Wolf's job for the day is to be one of those hippies that hangs out on the grass near the beach, holding two plastic sticks and twirling around one of those fancy batons with streamers on its ends.

"Dude. I was so annoyed when I showed up today. How the hell is *this* supposed to get me laid?"

"Can you appreciate the irony though? At least for me...this is great. You look ridiculous. I'm not even sure if I want to be hanging out with you right now."

He flips the baton up in the air and catches it gracefully as it careens down toward the ground.

"You're not bad though."

"Yeah. I've had a few hours to get the hang of it. Pretty soon I think I can compete with the pros."

"Or at the very least, you can get your baton license. As the first black batonist ever."

"I think I might complain to my manager."

"About what? My racism? I was just joking. That wasn't racist. It really wasn't."

"First of all, white people don't get to define what is or isn't racist. Okay? And anyway, no. I meant that someone else should do this shit. Or no one. I don't care. This is not enticing at all. I don't think anyone here is jealous of a guy with a baton. I think it's just making them laugh and be glad they're not me."

"Relax. It's not that bad. How much longer do you have?"

"Until four."

I look at my wrist and pretend that I have a watch.

"Don't forget to do your hair for your baton license picture. You don't want to have that whole windswept beach-goer style memorialized on a piece of plastic for the next few years."

"Just shut up, man."

"Alright. Well anyway, how have you been? I haven't seen you in a couple of days. Did you make a new friend or something?"

"Nah, man. Just been hanging out solo."

The baton twirls up in the sky, and we both stare at it, squinting out the sun as the stick dances overhead. It's another warm day, maybe the warmest it's been since I moved here. There's no breeze, or if there is, it must be blowing against our backs. The heat is stifling.

"I've been spending some time with Amy with the tight butthole."

"Oh yeah? So that first date worked out all right?"

"Yeah. It went really well."

"Did you find out?"

"Not the butt, no."

"What about the other parts?"

"Wolf, I'm a gentleman. I can't say."

He gives a quick thumbs up while still holding on to one of the baton sticks, losing focus and almost dropping it to the ground. I don't know what will happen if he does drop it. I guess he'll just pick it up and start again.

"When?"

"Recently. So what have you been doing then? The last time I saw you, you were riding off into the ocean on that Jet Ski."

"That fucking Jet Ski," he mumbles.

"Actually, I was thinking about it. How did your shift end? Did you leave the Jet Ski tied up and then you walked away, or did you just ride off into a hidden cove and park it somewhere that no one could see you and then swam all the way back?"

"What?"

"You know, like with an oxygen tank or something so people can't see you."

"What do you think this is? Seal Team Six? I tied it up and left it where I found it. There's no secret cove. Ain't no oxygen tanks."

"Well, how would I know? There could be."

"The only secret cove I know about is the one that we found in the forest. And," he looks around to see if anyone nearby is listening. "I went back a couple of times already to check it out."

"Really? It's a cave, by the way. Not a cove. You know that, right?"

Wolf stares at me.

"So that's what you've been doing?"

He nods.

"Remember how I told you about the Farmers Market this week that I had to work at?"

"Honeycomb?"

"No, that was last week. This week is the extreme exploration gear."

"Oh yeah. Your *man* gear. How was it?"

He sets the baton down on the ground and crosses the two sticks in an X in front of his body while resting them against his chest.

"I was able to nab a couple of things that we can use to explore down there."

"We? I'm not going down in the cave. I don't care how many North Face jackets you've got."

"You really know nothing about the outdoors, do you?"

"I told you, I wasn't in the Boy Scouts. I played soccer."

"They're not mutually exclusive," he reminds me.

"So what did you get then? Some carabineers?"

"Ah ha! So you do know something after all!"

"Just carabineers. They're those rock climbing clip things, right?"

"Yeah yeah, don't pretend like you don't know. White people always know about camping shit. I got some of those for sure. And a bunch of high tensile rope for rappelling. I got some rock climbing boots that kinda look—hey, you're gonna like this—they look like soccer cleats."

"Okay."

"Flares. I got tons of flares."

"In case you get a flat tire, sure."

"I also got some body harnesses. Oh, and these crazy waterproof headlamps for underwater spelunking. They've got a battery life that can last up to a few days."

"Spelunking?"

Wolf sighs.

"Exploring caves, dude."

"That's not a word. How did you make off with all this stuff?"

"I just told them that I wanted to familiarize myself with the gear so I could sell it better."

"But your job isn't to sell the gear. It's just to sell the residents that the money they're spending to live here is worthwhile."

"Whatever, company man. They were like *yeah sure, take whatever you like, mate.* There were a bunch of Australians there, for some reason. I don't know. Maybe they're really into caves over there."

"Sounds like you're really into caves over here, bro."

"Don't you want to see what's down there? I don't get it. What if I'm right? You know, I was thinking about it the other day after we talked about it, and I don't see any reason why it couldn't actually be a path out into the rest of the universe. I mean, think about it. How would you know if it wasn't true?"

"I think that you've been spending too much time flipping this stick around. I think you need to read a science magazine or something. Maybe hang out with some normal people like me for a little while."

"Normal like you, huh? Got it. Come with me later today then, prove me wrong. What time are you working until?"

"I'm off today."

I look around to see what other happies are around us. Just the thought of work is making me vigilant, but I don't really know what I'm vigilant for. There's a guy selling ice cream and hot dogs from a cart. There are a few people walking their dogs. And then there's one guy walking his hot dog. I don't know what that's about, so I quickly look away.

"Come help me out, at least. You don't have to go down in the cave. You can just hang out at the top and make sure nothing goes wrong."

"I dunno, man. I was going to hang out with Amy later today; she's off today as well."

"Come on. Hang out with her at night. I can't be out too late anyway. I've got an early shift tomorrow morning, and I really didn't sleep much last night, so I want to get to bed early. I'll have you back at your house by 8:00."

I shake my head.

"Rain check, dude. I'm not feeling it."

"Suit yourself. But if I find some new planet or meet God when I'm down there, I'm not letting you in on it!"

I laugh.

"When's your next day off?"

"Thursday."

"OK. Here's a compromise. If I have the day off too, I'll go with you."

"Yeah! I knew you didn't suck!"

He heaves the baton so high in the air, I can barely see it silhouetted against the sun. I shake my head and walk away.

* * *

"I haven't known the guy for all that long, but I'm pretty sure that he's losing it."

Amy and I are sitting at the same bar in the same exact stools that we sat in the last time we were here. I'm a little alarmed at how duplicative this is, like we're being too boring by going to the same place more than once in the same week. But then I remember that I definitely wore the same shirt more than once this week and also ate the same thing for dinner multiple nights in a row.

There's this general societal consensus that repetition is boring, but I think it's all over-exaggerated. Repetition can also mean that you've achieved a pinnacle in whatever it is that you're repeating. If you eat the same breakfast every day, is that boring or is that genius?

"You consider him a friend, though, right?"

"Yeah." I consider her question for longer than I intend to. "I mean, yeah, of course. A new friend, but definitely a friend."

"So why not just go with him and let him see that this cave is just a hole in the ground?"

"Won't he see that whether or not I go there with him?"

"Fair point. But, you know, it might be nice to have someone there to make sure he doesn't fall and break his leg or something."

"No, I know. That's why I'll go with him. I just didn't feel like it today. Besides, I'm probably the last person who could help him in a situation like that. If he falls down into that cave and breaks his leg, he'd have better luck being dragged out by a baby deer than by me standing at the top with all the camping gear the world has ever made."

"You're that uncoordinated?"

"It's not about coordination...though yes, I'm pretty uncoordinated too. It's about tactical skill in emergency situations. I simply have none of that."

"You never did Boy Scouts or anything like that?"

"I played soccer."

"I guess that takes coordination."

"It does."

"Pretty sure you could play soccer and be in the Scouts too though."

"The Scouts was for nerds."

"My brother played soccer and he was in Scouts."

"Was he black?"

"What?"

"I said, 'Was he a back?' What position did he play?"

She shrugs.

"Honestly, I feel like the dude would be fine going spelunking on his own. Did you know that's a word, by the way? I had to look it up. It sounds totally fake."

"Yeah, that's a word."

"Oh."

The bartender comes over our way and takes our drink order. A song comes on the radio that I haven't heard for a long time.

"Ohh...I forgot about this song! Do you remember it?" I ask. "I don't think I've heard this for like, I don't know, maybe ten years!"

Amy squints and tries to listen, clearly not able to recognize it as immediately as I did. I silently judge her for thinking that squinting will help her hear better. That's not how hearing works.

"It's not ringing a bell."

"I used to love this song. I told myself that it was going to be my wedding song when I grew up and got married."

"You were picking out wedding songs 10 years ago? What kind of teenager were you?"

"First of all, this song is like 20 years old. So I was picking out wedding songs when I was even younger than that. Second of all, yeah. So what? You didn't do the same thing?"

"Nope."

I stand up and push my bar stool out behind me with the back of my legs. I hold my hand out and let it hang, open palmed, about a foot from her face.

"Amy," I whisper, bending down on one knee. "Will you dance to this Bon Jovi song with me?"

She bursts out laughing.

"You wanted your wedding song to be by Bon Jovi?!"

"Come on. It's a ballad. Dance with me."

She takes my hand, and as I pull her toward me, she stands up, her ass barely off the seat of her stool. I pull her body close to mine and step backward toward the non-existent dance floor. It's about seven in the evening, and the bar has maybe a couple of dozen people in it, all milling around and talking aimlessly with each other. I don't think anyone notices us, and even if they do, I don't care.

I spin her around and grab her hips so that she faces me straight on. I pull her body close to mine again, and I'm conscious of feeling her body wrapped up in my arms. Her hips are comfortable, like I'm meant to hold them. They're a little bony, but with the right amount of padding on them so that I don't have to get too concerned that she might have a better physique than me. I can feel her femininity in all the right places.

We dance and sway and laugh as Bon Jovi belts out some lyrics about how long he's going to love a girl. Maybe he just met her a few days before, like me. Maybe he's already falling for her. Or maybe it's just a crush that isn't going to last that long. Either way, he wrote a song that I really thought was going to be meaningful to me for many years to come. At the time that I first heard it, I had no reason to think otherwise. We have no idea how we're going to evolve or what we're really going to want to do with ourselves until we get to that moment in time when it's all happening.

"I could listen to this song on repeat for a full hour and not get sick of singing along to it. I love it *that* much."

"I get it. You're really into this song."

"I am."

The sun's gone, and as I look out the window, I can see the faint crescent of the moon appearing on the horizon over the water. It's a tiny sliver of a crescent, the smallest part of the cycle of the moon that you can see. I had a girlfriend in high school that used to call it "God's thumbnail." I used to laugh, thinking about the idea of God having a hand that looks just like a man's hand.

If God is a creature, he or she probably doesn't have thumbnails. Thumbnails are basically useless. I don't understand why evolution hasn't taken care of them for us and just gotten rid of them already. Unless it's because God really wants them to exist because, well, God has thumbnails too.

Bon Jovi keeps singing because it's a long song and that's all there is to it. When it's over, I lean in and give Amy a deep kiss. She kisses me back. I pull back and look into her eyes. I get lost.

She has two of the most amazing eyes that I've ever seen. I feel like I'm staring into another universe when I look at her. Am I? My mind wanders to Wolf. And the cave. In this moment, I'm realizing a fragment of the reasoning behind his crazy theory. I keep staring into Amy's eyes, and it becomes clearer and clearer.

Maybe a different universe is out there, and we just haven't found it yet. Maybe there are multiple universes, or maybe even millions of universes. Or billions even. Maybe there are individual universes, one for each of us. Maybe we ourselves are a universe. Maybe there's no such thing as being right or wrong because each of us is inherently our own sole existence, our own universe.

"Hello?" Amy asks, waving her hand in front of my face.

"Sorry. Got lost in them eyes."

If I end up dating Amy for years and I ultimately marry her and live with her for the rest of my life, this will be a moment that I'll remember until the very end. And if we end up never seeing each other again after this song, I'll remember it all that time later as well. It's a moment, and there's probably no other adequate way to describe it. I feel it, and I know that she feels it too.

It's a silly moment, in a way, because it was spawned from a dumb song that I thought was going to be meaningful in my life one day. But in actuality, it isn't all that dumb. Because I was right. Maybe this isn't going to be my wedding song, but it does play a part in a moment, a small but meaningful moment that I won't ever forget.

A few drinks later, I settle the bar tab. Amy and I sway out the door, my arm hanging over her shoulder and her cheek resting against mine. I don't know how we both fit out the door this way, but we do. God's thumbnail is bright and almost reflective. As I stare up at it, I think about Wolf and his crazy idea, and I wonder how crazy it really is. Amy looks up at me and smiles, despite what is probably a weird, concerned look on my face.

"That was a good song," she remarks, even though it's been hours since we heard it.

Twelve

"Owww oww owwwwwww!"

That's the sound a wolf makes when it's trying to find the rest of its pack. That's Wolf, right now, trying to see if there's anyone or anything down in this cave.

"Owww oww owwwwwww!"

There, he's doing it again.

"Wolfman," he yells. "You are on the verge of something huge! Owww oww owwwwwww!"

His voice echoes throughout the forest. So much for being discreet. I look down into the cave, and my feet are way too close to the edge. I haven't harnessed myself to anything sturdy, so when I crack a twig under my foot, I nearly shit my pants. I'm gonna fall in this damned hole, I know it.

"Fuck, man. Are you gonna get in there or what?" I ask.

"Yeah, yeah. Don't rush me."

"Pass it to me?"

He obliges and hands me the joint. I take a deep hit. I told him he had to provide the loud if he wanted me to come along with him. And provide he did.

"What are you gonna do down there?"

"I dunno. Talk to things. Talk to myself."

"Yeah, that's totally rational. Lower yourself into a cave so you can talk to yourself."

"And things. Don't you ever talk to things?"

I think about the couch, but I don't bring him up.

"No."

"Yeah, right. How much do you want to bet that you'll be talking to yourself as soon as I'm out of sight?"

"And that is going to be...when?"

It was a hazy afternoon out at the beach when we left earlier in the day. In the forest, all that haze has been replaced by a cool, foggy mist that creeps around the trunks of trees and the sides of rock formations. It's like the forest is a different world, hundreds of miles away from the beach even though it's actually just a couple of miles inland.

Wolf brought a big, deep backpack that he picked up from those Australians at the Farmers Market. In it, he stuffed all the gear that he could fit. He went overboard with the rope. He said he has about a thousand feet of it.

"How deep are you?" he asks the cave.

It doesn't reply.

"Caves can't talk," I remind him.

The water that we saw the first time we were here is gone. I pick up a stick and drop it down into the darkness. I count out loud.

"One."

Nothing.

"Two."

Nothing.

"Three."

Splash. Or, more like, soft splash. I try to calculate the terminal velocity of the stick, but it comes out at something like 400 miles per hour. I might be doing something wrong.

"Alright. If you drop a stick off a cliff, how long would it travel in three seconds?"

"50 or 60 feet?" he guesses.

"60 feet isn't that bad. You can probably even survive that fall if you have to, depending what you've got at the bottom."

"You are probably 60-feet deep," he tells the cave. "In case you're wondering."

"What do you think comprises the cave?" I ask. The joint is definitely kicking in. "Is it just the hole itself? Or is it the rock that surrounds it too, and if so, how much of the rock? Maybe it's all the rock until it turns into dirt. Yeah? Dirt can't be a part of a cave, unless it's at the bottom. Then I think that counts too. What about the land above the cave, is any of that a formal part of the cave as an entity?"

"I don't count the ground above me," the cave says. "Just the hole and the rocks around me."

"Oh, cool!" I yell. "Hey, I didn't realize that you could talk."

The cave pauses.

"I can't."

"Oh."

Wolf starts to unpack his backpack and lay all the rope out on the dirt, length by length, until he has a pile that is almost up to our knees.

"You, my friend, are a lot of rope," he tells the rope.

It doesn't reply.

"Ropey ropey rope."

Still nothing. Maybe he picked out some dead ropes.

R.I.P.

There's a large tree about 40 feet away from the mouth of the cave. It looks like Wolf has decided that it'll be the anchor for his descent. 40 feet on top of the 60 for the depth of the cave is a nice, even 100. Down and up makes it 200. He can do about five lengths of it with the supplies that we have. Not bad.

"You know that I know my way around a rope, right? I know, like, so many lashings."

"Oh...is that right?"

"Yeah. That's what people in the *know* call what you laymen call knots. See, for this, you're going to want to use a Bowline. Or maybe a Yosemite Bowline if you're a pussy. You'll also want to use some figure-of-eights to affix it to the anchor itself. And for me, since I have a number of different pieces of rope, I also have the option of using some Double Fisherman's knots to tie them all together."

"Wow. Can I fuck you right now, or do I have to wait?"

"Jealous," he hisses.

Then he turns and grabs the rope, holding it up in front of his face.

"I bet you would have loved this. You know, before you passed."

The rope still says nothing.

"So there's definitely still water down there. Are those boots waterproof?"

He looks down at his feet.

"Water resistant. Close enough. They'll be just fine if it gets slippery on the lower rocks."

He paces around the edge of the cave.

"What? What are you doing?"

"I'm trying to remember where the water was flowing in from the other day. Do you remember?"

It's dry now. There's no gulch or gulley or anything leading up to it.

"What does it matter?" I ask.

"Dude. Dampened earth is *not* stable. I can't be lowering myself into a cave on the wet side of the rim."

"On the what?" I laugh.

"I need to know which side is the wet side," he continues. "Hey, you still there?" he asks the cave. "Which side did the river come into you from? I mean, not *come* into you. But you know...which side did it enter...ah, you know what I mean. Hmm?"

The cave doesn't say anything.

"Man, is everyone dead around here or what?" he barks.

"Uh, no," says a tree.

I turn around and smile at the valley girl attitude that comes with the reply.

"The tree too!?" I shout.

This forest is pretty dope.

"Do you know which side the water was coming in from?" Wolf asks.

"The north side," the tree groans.

"Thanks!"

Wolf has a compass in his pocket because like a good Boy Scout, he's prepared. He swivels his hips around and locates north, leaning down near the cave's edge and assessing the soil. He makes a face that tells me that the tree is right. He checks on the other sides just to make sure they aren't all damp. Then he stands up and rubs his hands together, smearing dirt into his palms.

"Yeah, man, shit! I love dirt. All up in my palms."

I walk over to the tree and begin tying some knots, trying to help him. It takes a while. There's a lot of rope, and I don't know what I'm doing. He doesn't stop me. After I finish each knot, he drags the rope down to the edge of the cave.

It's all going well until a pinecone falls out of the tree and lands right behind me. I think about what the equivalent human action would be. I think it's something sexual, like the tree just came a little. After all, the pinecone is the mode of procreation for the tree.

So, this dude just came a little. Right behind me. Right when I'm beneath him, tying some rope. I'm a little creeped out, but I try to brush it off with a casual joke.

"Get a little lonely out here?"

"Uh, that doesn't usually happen."

OK. Time to stop talking to the tree. I don't want to know what *usually* happens. I also don't want to be around if another pinecone falls. I'm not looking for a long-term relationship, and I don't think trees are down for a short fling. So we're diametrically opposed just by being who we are. No sense in letting it continue any further. I tie the last knots as fast as I can, and luckily, he keeps his pinecones in his pants.

We now have four equidistant pairs of ropes hanging over the edge of the cave.

"You ready?" I ask.

He reaches into his pack and pulls out a harness and belt. A dozen or so carabineers clank against each other as he straps it around his waist. He grabs one of the waterproof headlamps and tests it out by pointing it down into the cave. The bottom is still too far away for either of us to see, but the range on the headlamp is impressive nonetheless.

He slips on some gloves, which are really just a pair of Harbinger weight gloves, and then he looks around the forest to see if anyone else is around us. Nope. Aside from Wolf, it's just me and that pervert tree. And the dead rope. And the cave that is giving us the silent treatment.

"Here we go, yo, here we go, yo," he sings. "So what's the what's the what's the cave scenario?"

I laugh, but it doesn't deserve my laugh. I regret justifying it. Wolf's clipping in and adjusting the ropes. He has two around his waist, both clipped to the harness, and then one in each hand like a pair of reverse walking sticks. He inches closer to the edge, looking a little nervous.

"Is this crazy?" he asks me.

I don't hesitate.

"Yes."

"Okay, maybe it's a little crazy. But didn't people think that Columbus was crazy?"

"Columbus didn't even do shit. He just got all the credit."

"This is 1492 all over again," he proclaims, before naming off each rope one by one. "You are Nina, because you are pink and feminine just like a la niña. You, you are Pinta, because you're brown like a pinto bean and I actually don't know what Pinta means. You on my waist, you are Santa Maria, my saint and savior. Watch over me. Well, and under me. And then you, the other guy on my waist, you are Frank. Because we ran out of names, Frank."

The tree probably has a name. I don't want to ask.

Wolf places his feet against the edge of the cave and takes a deep breath. The rope is tight, and my knots look like they're not instantly failing, so that's good. He takes his first step down over the edge and into the cave, his butt sticking out over the opening a good few feet before his next step lands alongside the other on the inside of the cave wall.

"Ohhhh mama! Owww oww owwwwwww!"

His voice echoes into the darkness beneath him.

"Shit," he panics. "What if I just woke up a swarm of bats, and they all come flying at my asshole?"

"I don't think that's how echolocation works. It's fine, just keep going. There you go. One foot below the other. Nice and slow."

From up here, the cave has a damp smell, like a basement on a humid day or probably like most other caves. It's got that wet rock smell that isn't necessarily bad but also isn't really that pleasant. As Wolf lowers himself in, foot by foot, I start to look at how wide the mouth of the cave is. It looks plenty wide for there to be light at the bottom.

I get close to the edge, and Wolf is already a good 15 or 20 feet down there. He switches on the headlamp, and I see patches of moss on the walls around him. One foot, then another. It's like a poem about learning how to dance.

"Hey, cave. You still there?" I ask.

It doesn't respond.

Wolf is almost out of sight now, the headlamp the only reason I even know where he is.

"Oh, shit!" he yells.

"What?"

"I just touched the water!"

"Whoa! Really?"

Damn. He's waaaaaay down there. I look at the rope and the knots, and they look fine, I think. I hear soft splashing.

"The water is deep!" he yells. "I'm trying to feel around for a rock or something, but I'm already up to my neck and there's nothing."

"Fuck, man. So what are you gonna do? Take a little cave bath or something?"

"I didn't bring my bath salts!" his voice echoes up at me.

The cave laughs. I look down puzzlingly.

"You're really hit or miss, huh?"

Nothing.

"Fuck! Dude, I forgot to bring goggles!" Wolf yells.

"So?"

"I need them if I'm gonna swim down to the actual bottom!"

"Are they up here?"

"No. I didn't bring them at all."

"OK. So what are you gonna do? Just float around down there or what?"

"Dammit!"

"Just come back another time. It's fine. This cave isn't going anywhere."

Wolf doesn't say anything, but I can hear him rising out of the water and starting his climb out.

"You want me to pull the ropes up?"

"Dude. Why else do you think I dragged your ass out here? Yes! Help me up! I can't climb this whole thing myself!"

I start pulling as best I can, but the rope isn't very thick and it's cutting off the circulation in my fingers. He didn't consider me at all when he chose these supplies, and it shows.

About ten minutes after he started, and with a few tied off breaks along the way, he finally gets his head above ground and drags himself onto his belly and back on solid land. I pull him by the collar like he's a school kid in a fight and I'm the principal. He barrel rolls away from the hole as though it's now too dangerous to even sit next to.

He's panting. Sweat's running down my temples. I really turned up the juice in the last 10 or 15 feet, pulling harder and faster despite the throbbing in my hands. The climb looks like it took a lot out of him, but he's smiling as he breathes heavily into the fog.

A pinecone falls from the tree and bounces on the ground a few feet away from me.

"Goddammit."

Thirteen

"It's not about how much information you bring us. You understand? It's really not."

I have a sheepish look on my face.

"Baaaaaaaaaaaaaaaaaa," I reply.

"What?"

"I said, 'Yes, sir.'"

Tony shakes his head. I can't tell you how many times a conversation in my life has included someone disapprovingly shaking their head. I'm just that kind of a guy. The kind of guy that you sigh and shake your head at.

"You serve a purpose out there. That's true whether you bring in 15 pieces of information in a single day or if you never bring in one."

"Is 15 a reasonable number to bring in? Like in a single day? Is that what those other nerds, I mean, you know...my peers, is that what they're doing?"

"Not the point. The point is that you are providing an immensely valuable service to The Board. Your vigilance is what you are paid for. Your, uh, *efficacy* in obtaining information is secondary to your vigilance."

"I just thought I would have come across something big by now."

He leans across the desk and goes all Gandalf on me. I forget his name and where I am and what color shirt I'm wearing. I don't know what year it is. I don't know what day it is. I don't know nothing, not even grammar. Everything blanks out. The dude is intense.

"That's not the point, Luke. Okay? That's not the point."

He leans back in his chair, and eventually I remember that his name is Tony. I'm still not sure what year it is though.

"Okay."

"You're doing fine. Alright?"

"Alright."

"So, aside from that," he continues, looking down at a small stack of note paper. "How are you adjusting to living here? Making friends? All of that? All good?"

"Yeah, I've got some friends. I met a happy on my first day here, and we've been hanging out a lot, you know, on our days off."

"I see."

"What? No good?"

He laughs.

"No. It's fine. Just don't spend *too* much time with a happy. Hear me? Sometimes it can be a little confusing."

"What do you mean?"

"You know, small town boy like yourself, you come to Malibu and you get hired on as an investigator..."

"But I'm from Carlsbad," I tell him.

He shrugs it off.

"You're content, things are going well, but then you fall in with a crowd of happies. Or shit, maybe just a single happy. Over time, you start to question things. You start to resent the discrepancy between your job and their job. Maybe you start to lose faith in the mission."

"Oh, you don't have to worry about that. I have faith in the mission."

"Is that right?"

"Hundred percent. Wait, so, the mission, it's..." I'm hoping he'll finish my sentence, but he just blanks me and sits there, arms folded. "I just...well, as I said before, I just wish that I was contributing more than I am. But you're saying that it's okay?"

"Don't worry about it," he reassures me. "There are much worse things that you could be doing than *not* providing a lot of information."

"Like what?"

He looks down at his papers and then at his watch.

"Luke, it's been a pleasure. I've gotta run. I have a few more of these that I have to get through today. You good?"

"Actually, I was wondering if you knew anything about that whale that got stranded on the beach the other day. Did it get back to the ocean okay?"

"What whale?" he asks.

"It was a grey whale. Not huge, but it was big enough that you'd have heard about it. You don't know what I'm talking about? It was, like, just a few days ago."

"I didn't hear anything about a whale. On our beach?"

I nod.

"Well, I'm sure it's fine. Those things always have a way of working themselves out the way they're supposed to. You know? Anyway, I really have to go. You good?"

"Yeah, sure. I'm good. Thanks, Tony."

He stands up and walks away. I sit at the desk for a while after he's gone, looking out the window. Why am I the only person that cares about this whale? What is wrong with the people here?

Eventually I push myself up out of the chair and start to walk out. I grab a couple of bananas from the kitchen and stuff them in my backpack before I head toward the door. I'm not sure if the bananas are here for everybody to take or if they're just for certain people. I take them anyway.

The bananas remind me that I have to do a little bit of grocery shopping. Not a lot. Just a little. All of L.A. County just enacted a "No Plastic Bags" policy, and everyone's carrying around these canvas tote bags that you usually just see with the moms at the Farmers Market. I don't have one, so when my turn comes to check out and bag what I'm buying, I have the choice of purchasing a paper bag for 10 cents or a new canvas bag for three bucks.

"Three bucks?" I ask the cashier.

"$2.99. It's a high-quality bag. It's worth it."

"Is it? I could basically buy, what, thirty of these paper bags before it finally starts to save me money?"

"But this bag will last much longer than a paper bag. If you plan on reusing the paper bag, it may only last you three, four more times before it wears out."

"What? Ain't nobody reusing the paper bag. Is that a thing?"

"That's a thing, yeah."

"Hmm. Well, even still. There's no way I'm going to know where this bag is in three or four weeks. I'll lose it. Or puke in it. Or something. It doesn't matter. I'll take the paper bag."

"Maybe next time."

My walk home is dotted with small birds flitting across the horizon, chasing each other, barreling around in the sky. The sun is still low and hasn't burnt off most of the chill from the night before. Little wisps of fog are twirling around above me. When I walk into some shade, I cringe with each step, hoping to avoid a sudden gust of wind or anything that will press that cool air right up against me. I think about the sun and how vital it is to us all.

When I get home, I call Wolf.

"Sup suppers," he greets me.

"I've got a hole for your *up is down* theory."

"Thanks, man. But it doesn't need any holes. It's all good."

I continue on, regardless of what he just said. I'll keep talking even if he hangs up on me. We Balenas call that *persistence*. It's how my dad says that he won over my mom. He just never gave up.

"Explain the sun. What is it? It's not a star; it doesn't provide heat and life to everything on this planet? How does that work in your new the-world-is-inside-out scheme?"

I have a smirk on my face, but as his pause turns into what is starting to feel like a moment of intentional silence, I'm feeling a little bad. It's not like I want to crush his dreams. Maybe it isn't so bad that he thinks this crazy thought. Who is it really hurting anyway?

The silence continues. It's getting awkward. Now it's been about 30 seconds. I might hang up. To hell with the Balena persistence.

"I don't know about you, but I learned about the sun in science classes," he finally responds. "I've never been to the sun. How do I know it's really a star?"

"The sun is not some fake thing. There are stats about it. We know stuff about it. Like, it's fucking huge and it's like 90 million miles away. Why would we make all that up? Why would so many people perpetuate that big of a lie?"

"Why wouldn't they? There's all kinds of reasons to hide something like that."

"Like what?"

"I just don't believe it, man. I just don't believe any of it anymore. I think the cave has something special in it. Maybe not just that cave in particular, but any cave that descends into the earth. Maybe there are certain points in the world where they're closer to some sort of path down and out."

"Yeah, I saw that movie with Brendan Fraser. I know what you're talking about. They find all those dinosaurs and whatnot. That's what you think's going on down there? Come on."

"Encino Man?"

"No, the other Brendan Fraser caveman movie."

"Oh, still no. I don't think there are fucking dinosaurs in the center of the earth. I think the center of the earth might just be above us. The center might be the sun. In fact, that would make a lot of sense, really. You could still have a heat and light source in the middle of your planet if the entire inside of your planet is atmosphere. It would totally work."

"So we're walking on the ceiling? Is that what you're saying? You lost me."

"You lost *me* when you tried to tell me that the sun is real because it has facts associated to it. You know what else has facts associated to it? Every fake thing that's ever not existed."

"Alright, that's fair. I mean, whatever. What are you up to today?"

"Day off. You?"

"I just had a meeting with my boss, but I'm not working again. Wanna meet up?"

"Sure. I'll be over in thirty."

"Just like that?"

"Just like that."

And then, just like that, he's at my house.

"Sup suppers, dude."

"You've got to stop saying that."

"Noted."

He's wearing a grey zip-up hoodie. His hands are tucked into the side pockets, and the fabric's bulging out. His skin has a shine to it that I haven't really seen before. I can't tell if he's just warm or if he's been moisturizing. I don't want to ask in case it's the latter. Dudes don't talk about moisturizing. Besides, I have a terrible moisturizing regimen, and I am not interested in getting a lecture on how I can improve the quality of my skin. I have plenty of ex-girlfriends who told me all about it. Okay, maybe just one. But it's still plenty.

"I keep thinking about the cave. Like, I *smell* it, you know, when I think about it. It's kind of like a mix between dirt and come."

"Uhh, what?"

"I think I'm gonna go back again today. You want to join me?"

I shake my head.

"Count me out for this one. Just don't forget your goggles this time."

"But what if I can't pull myself out?" he whines. "I need you there."

"Tough shit, man. I don't want to go."

"But can you imagine how embarrassing that would that be? I get stuck down in some cave for days and die of starvation down there or something. No one ever finds me. My parents have a funeral with an empty coffin. You make zero new friends in this town. My reserve weed stash never gets smoked."

"Embarrassing is not the word I would use."

"Fine. Dissatisfying."

"Also, I would make other friends. I can make friends. I'm not some weirdo introvert."

"You're not?"

"I'm the one with the girlfriend, aren't I?"

"Whoa whoa," he laughs. "She's your girlfriend now?"

"Well, no, not officially. But you know what I mean. She's more my girlfriend than what you have."

"But I have a story about going down into a deep, scary cave. Do you have that?"

"I don't want that."

"I'm going to go back again later today."

"Alright."

I don't know what else he wants me to say. He can do whatever he wants.

"I'm going back every day until I get to the bottom of the whole fucking thing. I also created a cover for it so that no one else finds it."

"You're really going for it."

"It's just a makeshift cover. I made it out of a big tarp that I had and some sticks and leaves that I threw on top. It's pretty sick. You walk up to it, and you can't even see it."

"What if someone falls in?"

He shrugs.

"Anyway, I might rent some scuba gear and bring it down there with me if the water ends up being more than 10 or 15 feet deep."

"Scuba gear? For a cave?"

"People do that."

"Not when they drop down a hole the way you're doing it. Not alone."

"Then come with me."

"No, I don't want to. It's stupid. You just want to get to the bottom for some ridiculous reason that we both know isn't true. You're just..."

"I'm just what?"

"I don't know."

"I'm just the first motherfucker that's going to discover that the earth is inside out, that's what."

"You say so. I think you're just going to be the first motherfucker to discover that scuba diving in a narrow cave is a terrible idea."

"Maybe I'll just bring a little oxygen tank then. I won't need that much. I've been practicing holding my breath at home, and I've gotten to the point where I can hold it for a full minute without too much strain."

I give him a suspicious look. Then of course I try to do it myself. I take a deep breath and start counting.

"I also did it once while doing jumping jacks," he adds. "Because if I'm swimming down there, that's obviously going to take some energy. I still passed a minute too. But only once."

"Fuck," I gasp. "What was that? 20 seconds?"

"Not even."

"Man, I suck."

"Too many cigarettes, that's why."

"I never smoke cigarettes."

"No, I mean, *I've* smoked too many cigarettes in my life. I used to smoke almost a pack a day. Contrary to what you might think, smoking increases your lung capacity."

"That's not true."

"If you quit, yeah, it is. It's like those guys that train up in the mountains. The lack of oxygen gives you more endurance."

"The more I talk to you, the more I think that you're a moron. Or maybe a genius. I don't know. I can't tell."

"Anyway, maybe I don't need an oxygen tank. Just the goggles. I think I'll go back today and try just by holding my breath."

"You're not worried that someone will see you?"

"With the goggles on? No. My goggle game is on fleek."

"No, you fashionista. Not with the fucking goggles. I mean, what if someone from The Board sees you?"

"Dude, nothing is going to happen. I think the roundabout way in there that we took the other day works just fine. I think they just care about the direct route."

I shrug. It doesn't really make sense, but he's so intent on going back, I give up trying to convince him not to. I don't really care what he does, as long as he doesn't get fucked up or die.

"Hey, wait. So you went in the water the other day, right?"

"Yeah. You saw me. I was soaking wet."

"Are you invincible now? Wolf de Leon?"

He looks at his forearms, like that's where you'd notice it first.

"I dunno. I haven't tried dying yet."

"Well, let me know if you do."

He shakes me off and walks over to the sliding door that's off my balcony.

"By the way," he adds. "I didn't actually have today off. I just didn't show up."

"Damn! Ballsy."

"They had me on that baton shit again! I was like, fuck this. Can you imagine if I'm right?"

"No, I cannot."

"Imagine I'm right, and instead of discovering a whole new dimension of this planet, I'm dwindling away at some meaningless job, twirling a fucking baton around on the beach like a goddamned little girl. Every day that I don't get to the bottom of that cave might just be the biggest waste of my time. The biggest waste of all time!"

I laugh right in his face. I can't help it.

"You're so dramatic! I could say the same thing about work and death. Like, why work somewhere that you don't like if we're all just going to die sooner or later anyway?"

"I agree."

"No, I mean, you can't think that way. It's obviously true, but you have to work to have money. You need money to live. You need to live if you want to, you know, live. So it's a necessary evil."

"That baton can be someone else's necessary evil. I'm sick of it."

"Who would have thought that I'd be defending the job and you'd be the one bailing on it. It must be tough being a happy," I laugh.

"Fuck off."

"You hungry?"

"Yeah, I am actually. Wanna go get some lunch?"

"I was thinking of making food here. I can make you something too."

"You sure?"

"I was just going to make a sandwich."

"Sandwich is good," he affirms.

"I'll make two then. Any dietary, uh, restrictions?"

"No, dude. Whatever you're having, I'll have."

I go to the fridge and take out all the ingredients. I've got a lot. I keep my bread in the fridge despite growing up with such a typical white family that we had a legitimate breadbox on the counter. I don't buy the whole breadbox idea. I know that perishable foods last longer when they're cooler. This is a fact. Besides, I'm going to toast it anyway, so it isn't like I'm going to be biting into a cold piece of bread.

At the store earlier today, I saw this assortment of Italian and Spanish deli meats. They all came in one package that was split right down the middle like they couldn't touch each other. I thought it was kind of funny, so I decided to buy it. On one side it had Capicola, Mortadella, and Prosciutto; and on the other side it had Serrano Ham, Iberico Ham, and some kind of Salami that I've never heard of but that is supposedly from Spain. I also have some Swiss cheese and some French mustard and some good old-fashioned American mayonnaise. These are going to be the United fucking Nations of sandwiches.

"That's a lot of stuff."

"Yeah. I'm into sandwiches. I used to work at a deli. Actually, I worked at two different delis before I moved here."

"So you're some kind of deli meat snob?"

"Dude, look at this thing," I say, waving the cheap plastic container in the air. "You think a snob would buy a prepackaged thing like this?"

"I bet your old deli boss would be ashamed of you."

"Maybe. Though I never saw my boss, at least at the first place. I worked nights. He was always just there during the day."

"How long were you there?"

"Oh, not long. Maybe six, seven months."

Earlier I also took out some lettuce, but it isn't from a European country, so I didn't feel right mentioning it. It's a California spring mix blend. It would be perfect if it had more arugula, but it usually just has like four leaves in the whole bag. The rest of it is just a bunch of little crunchier things like radicchio and radicchio's strange cousins. It does the job, but I know that there's something better out there than this same old mix that I rely on.

Wolf stares at me the whole time I'm putting the sandwiches together, marveling as I spread the mustard on the bread. His jaw drops when I char the bread with a culinary blowtorch.

"What the fuck is that?"

Amateur. Who hasn't seen a culinary blowtorch before? I'm not the most cultured guy out there, and even I own one. Though to be honest, I bought it because I thought it'd be good to have a backup lighter for my bowl in case my main one shit the bed. I don't know what I'm supposed to use it for in the kitchen, so I just burn random things here and there and see if it makes it taste better.

"So the trick is that you always want to have the mustard side of the bread touching the meat. And then on the other side, the mayo should accompany the cheese."

"Why?"

"Well, for one, those pairings taste better. But also, if you're going to add something like pickles, for example..." I turn back to the fridge to get out my container of pickles. Can't believe I almost forgot them. "You're going to want them closer to the mustard since they complement each other so well. And if you make a sandwich with the pickles next to the cheese and you don't eat it right away, the acidity of the pickles will fuck the cheese up. It's a mess."

"Is that right?"

"Total disaster."

"Sad!" Wolf laughs.

"Don't do it. It defies the physics of the sandwich."

I start laying down each slice of meat like it's my newborn son on his first night home from the hospital. Gentle, like I've never done it before, and slow. Very slow. I do this for each piece of meat. It probably takes me five minutes to lay all of it on the two sandwiches. I don't take as much care with the cheese. The cheese is like the second-born son. Now that I know that I won't fuck it up if I'm a little rough with it, I can toss it around a little. I don't have to try as hard. And the pickles? Forget it. They're like a stepchild. I'm tossing the pickles on there with my eyes closed.

Before I put the bread on top, I grind some fresh pepper on top of the cheese. That's not a thing, but I like doing it anyway. It's my own touch. I will sometimes use pink Himalayan sea salt as well, but with all of the salty Italian and Spanish meats, I figure it's already going to have enough sodium to triple my risk of hypertension all on its own. I press the bread down and squish the sandwich into a more compact shape.

"Voila!"

I take a bow.

"Fuck, man. I think you got me hard over this sandwich."

Wolf sits on the couch, and I sit on a chair across from him. We have our plates on our laps, neither of us wanting to take the first bite. It's a weird stalemate for two dudes that ordinarily have no manners or class.

"You can go first," he says.

"I don't need to go first. It's my house. You're the guest. You go first."

"But you made it. You used a fucking blowtorch. You deserve the first bite."

"I used the torch because I was too lazy to turn on my toaster oven. That's all. It's just easier. And anyway, this is stupid. On the count of three?"

We count, and then each of us takes a big, synchronous bite. His eyes roll around in their sockets, and for a moment, I think that maybe he isn't kidding and that he is getting hard over it. It's dangerously close to being an *ohhh* face. I look down at my sandwich and smile. It tastes better than it looks.

"Deli boss...ashamed, my ass..." I mutter, munching and chewing straight through my half-sentences.

"What about the second deli? Where was that?"

"Pretty close to the other one. It's actually where I learned how to make the sandwiches this way. At the first place, I just cut meat. Sometimes I would work in the fish department as well. It was just a grocery store. The second place was more like a little deli restaurant shop kind of thing."

"Well, deli or restaurant, I don't care. This is an awesome fucking sandwich, my man. I had no idea that you had any skills hidden in that big old head of yours. What else can you do?"

"Oh, this is about it. Trust me. Other than knowing how to perfectly cook a tray of Pizza Rolls."

"I'd leave that one off the resume and stick with this."

"Not so fast. I'd argue that no sandwich can defeat a tray of Pizza Rolls."

"Let's agree to disagree."

"Never! Pizza Rolls above all else!"

Wolf thinks I'm joking, but I'm actually dead serious. I'll take a single Pizza Roll over 10 of these sandwiches. I'd take a tray of Pizza Rolls as my last meal on earth if I had the choice. Wolf puts his sandwich down and smiles.

"So, imagine that the way you feel about Pizza Rolls is the way I feel about getting to the bottom of that cave. Imagine that I feel *that* strongly about it. Huh? Can you give me that?"

I think about what he's saying. I'm not the kind of person to not give someone's idea a chance. I really want to think it through before deciding one way or another. He deserves that. Everyone deserves that. I take a few bites of my sandwich and nod as I continue to think.

"I'm going back to that cave and finding out what the hell is in there," he continues. "And I'm not going back to work again until I figure it out. Even if I'm wrong. Shit. Even if I'm wrong, I have to know. I can't *stand* not knowing."

He's so passionate that I just give in. After all, it doesn't matter what I say. He's going to go there and keep trying to figure it out. And in the end, what harm is it anyway?

"Well, send me a postcard when you get to inner space."

His eyes light up.

"Oh, I like that. Inner space!"

"You can have it."

"Yeah?"

"Yeah. I'll give you *that*."

Fourteen

"Star date 47457.1. Luke Balena, reporting for duty."

"Say that again?"

"It's me, Luke," I laugh. "Do you need me to work today?"

The voice on the other end of the line sighs and then hangs up. I turn around and look in through the open door. Amy's sitting on the couch.

"They've been getting less and less friendly," I explain to her. She smiles.

Things are really moving along with us. I have real feelings. I care about her. I think about her when I'm not with her, and not just in a sexual way. I think about her as a person, like as a human being. This is utterly revolutionary to me, but I'm guessing this is what normal people feel like when they like someone.

I'm standing on the balcony off my kitchen, leaning with my back against the railing, facing away from the ocean. I can't exactly see the ocean from my place anyway, so it really doesn't matter which way I look when I'm out here. I turn around and check. Still can't see it. The door behind me slides open, and Amy walks out, slowly wrapping her arms around my waist and pressing her face up against my back.

"You coming in soon?"

"Yeah, I will. How long have I been out here?"

"Long enough."

I can't see her face, but I can tell that she's smiling. I turn around, and she keeps her hands linked together, my body twisting inside of the human hula hoop that she's making with her arms.

"Why are you laughing?" she asks.

Ah, shit. I'm going to ruin the moment if I tell her that I'm laughing because I'm imagining what a human hula hoop would look like and who would actually try to use one for recreation.

"Let's go back inside. I think I've cooled off enough now."

I kiss her on top of her head and take a deep breath. Her hair smells like the kind of shampoo that someone who spends a lot of money on shampoo would use. It's fragrant, yet somewhat understated. It isn't like the Head & Shoulders that I have in my shower. That has all the subtlety of a pack of Jolly Ranchers.

"I can't believe you don't have A/C."

I open the slider and gesture for her to go inside.

"The Board said that with a place this close to the beach, I wasn't going to need it."

"I guess under normal circumstances, you probably wouldn't."

I smile.

"I would prefer that *these* are the normal circumstances."

We're talking about sex. We just went at it for probably longer than I've ever done it in my life. It was close to 20 minutes. That's long for me. I usually don't need more than five minutes, and if the girl needs more than that, I'm willing to just do something else to get her there. I get too tired if I stay at it for too long. Also, I'm usually just too lazy to try that hard for anything.

With Amy, though, I don't want it to end. I came a couple of minutes in, but I stayed hard and decided to just keep going at it. She seemed happy. I was surprised. So when I came the second time and double-checked that she had already come too, I pulled out and rolled onto my back. And that's when I realized how hot I was. I immediately felt all the beads of sweat press against me and soak into the sheets. So I threw on my boxers and walked out to the balcony.

"Maybe you can buy a fan or something?"

"Fans are for sailors."

"What?"

I shake my head. We sit down on the couch, and she curls up against me. I'm still just wearing boxers. I'm too warm to put on anything else. Amy is wearing a t-shirt and some cutoff jean shorts. She looks cute as hell. Meanwhile, I'm just some white-trash-looking loser who somehow has a girl that's way better looking than me, sitting here in my underwear, still a little sweaty, my hair matted on my forehead.

"Want to smoke a little?" I ask.

"Smoke *after* sex?"

"I can't do it before."

"We did last week, didn't we?"

This might be an appropriate time to mention that the advice my father gave me while ice fishing is not universal advice that applies to every situation. Sometimes you have to start telling people about what you're doing, or your life isn't going to make any sense to anyone.

"Usually I get too high to pay attention. I like to just mellow out and let my mind open up when I smoke. Take a break from thinking, all that."

"What are you thinking about during sex?"

"I guess...more sex."

"Yeah, I could see why that would be hard to focus on if you're high."

"Anyway, can I light up if you're not going to?"

"I'm going to! I just thought it was weird that you wanted to do it after. I feel like smoking before sex makes it *so* much better."

"If I can get out of the way of my own head, I agree. But I've had mixed experiences with it, so I usually just wait until after. You know, if it's up to me."

"It's your place. It's up to you."

"Okay," I say, shifting her body away from mine as I stand up. "Then we're smoking."

"Okay."

"Just a little!"

I walk into my bedroom and pull out my bowl and canister from the drawer in my nightstand.

"However much you want," she calls out from the other room.

I pack the bowl with a few buds, and then I lightly press them down before packing a couple more. My fingers are tacky and sticky. I can't stop myself, I have to smell them. I probably like the smell more than I like anything else about it. It's my favorite smell of all time. I don't have a favorite color or a favorite band or a favorite sports team, but I have a favorite smell, and it's fresh bud.

"You want to start, or me?" I ask.

"You'd let me have the first hit?"

"Sure."

"That's so nice!"

"It's not that nice. You can go first."

I pat her on the head like she's my pet. My cute, little pet that I have amazing sex with. Not in a weird, bestiality kind of way. Just in a love-pet type of way.

"It's no big deal."

She looks up at me, and her eyes are twinkling like they're filled with distant stars from a universe that no one has discovered, or some other romantic shit like that.

"I like you. A lot."

Buzzing warmth spreads all over me. At first, I think that I'm getting horny again because I have all these emotions and tingly sensations across my body. But my dick isn't really moving or responsive at all, so I know that's not it. My head is flushed, and my heart is beating faster. I'm hyper-aware of my body. It's giving me a small bout of anxiety.

"I more than like you," I reply.

The fuck? I don't know where that came from. I can't tell if what I just said is smooth or pathetic, but it just came out and now I have to live with it. It hangs out in the air and refuses to disappear, like a fart on an airplane or maybe something that's a little more romantic, given the situation that I'm trying to describe. It's like I'm in the scene in *The Lion King* where the perverted animator snuck in the word *sex* into a cloud of dust. That was a real thing. Someone did that. And he just aired it out there for everyone to see.

I don't know why I can't come up with any nice analogies.

"What's more than like?"

"You know."

She smiles.

"No, I don't know. What's more than like?"

"Okay. I'm going to light this thing up. It's getting too serious in here."

"I thought I got to go first?"

"Do you want to? You can."

"I can?"

"Sure. I don't mind. Here," I say as I hand the bowl over to her.

I hold on to the lighter, and as she pulls the piece up to her pretty, little mouth, I spark it up. The bud singes and lights up with tiny orange embers, and I start to think about how fleeting life can be. Those little crystalline buds were once alive. Now they're spent.

Amy inhales and takes the first hit. She holds in her breath and hands the bowl back to me. She speaks, quiet and restrained, as she starts to exhale.

"Because you love me," she whispers.

I raise my eyebrows as I spark the lighter up again and take in a hit. I hold it in for as long as I can.

"You might be right."

I don't know if I know what love is, but I'm feeling some pretty intense feelings that are hitting me in a rapid-fire succession. Every moment that I spend with her is amplified. The difference between what I have with her and what I've had with other girls in the past is like dog and cat. To hell with night and day.

"Well, I might feel the same way too."

We take a few more hits, and then I set the bowl and lighter down on the coffee table. I lean back and sink into the couch, the same couch that I've been sinking into for years. It's different now that I have someone to sink along with me. I wonder if the couch is going to get jealous.

"Don't worry about it," the couch says.

"Hmm, okay."

Amy tucks her body up against me and curls her knees up toward her chest. She's a tiny, little ball by my side. It doesn't take long for the THC to start to do its thing.

"If you were me and I were you, what would you do?" I ask her.

Or did she ask me?

"I would see what it felt like to masturbate."

"That's a good one."

"What would you do?"

I think about it for a while. There are many ways that one can go with this question. Honest ways, offensive ways, heartfelt ways.

"I think I would go to the women's locker room at an Equinox."

Honest ways wins.

"Touché."

"But after that, I think I would just hang out with me and see what I was like as seen through the eyes of a person other than myself."

"Hang on. If you were transported into *my* body, the second thing you would do is hang out with *yourself?*"

I roll into a fit of giggles, and I can't reply for at least a minute.

"Yeah, I think so. I think so."

"Man, you're like, really into yourself then."

"I'm not really. I just think that it would be cool to know what it's like to hang out with me. Maybe it'd make me be a better person, you know? Like I could learn things about me that were really fucking annoying, and then I can fix them. It's more about self-improvement. It's not about being into myself, I don't think."

"That's sweet."

"Is it?"

She shakes her head.

"I don't know what it is. Are you feeling it?"

"Yeah."

She leans her head against me, or at least I think she does. It might just be my arm feeling it from the time before.

"Can we do it again?" she asks me.

"Smoke? Sure."

"No. Have sex."

"Oh."

I look down at my boxers.

"We can try. But no promises. He might be worn out."

"I bet I can resuscitate him. Bring him back to life."

"Oh yeah?"

She smiles and slides her hand up my leg.

"Oh yeah."

"Oh yeah," the couch repeats.

Shut up, stupid couch. Not now.

In the span of 10 seconds, I go from not even knowing where my dick is to feeling her stroke it gently through my underwear. Blood is emptying from every available part of my body and rushing toward my manhood like a crowd of Walmart shoppers when the doors open on Black Friday.

"I think you might be right."

Her head's leaning against my inner elbow, and I watch in slow motion as her cheek glides down my arm and toward the direction of her active hand. She begins kissing the outside of my shorts, inching slowly across my thigh until she reaches her destination. She presses her lips down against me and kisses me a few more times.

I lean back and stare up at the ceiling, trying to recalibrate and not lose my cool too quickly. I look back down as she untucks my penis from the elastic band of my boxers, her hand delicately guiding it out into the open air. She doesn't look up at me again.

I lean my neck forward as I watch her mouth open slowly, lowering toward the base of my dick. I feel the cool rush of her tongue sliding up until her lips press against the head. I lean back again and wonder what I've done in my life that lets me deserve this. I can't figure it out. Bursts of pleasure scorch through my brain. I flinch and squirm. She keeps going at it.

I stop her before she goes too far, and I lead her into the bedroom. She lies down on the bed, sliding her shorts and underwear off and kicking them toward the door. I get on top of her. I kiss her lips. I kiss her neck. I bite her ear. I don't know what I'm doing. I'm on autopilot. I slide in without even using my hands. It's a miracle. I last maybe two, three minutes at most. When I come, my eyes fill with stars, and I'm about to faint.

God damn. She just does it for me. I don't know what it is. It's probably the newness of it all. New things always feel good. New socks, new underwear, new sex partners. New is always better than not new.

We're lying on top of the covers of my bed, side by side. I'm no longer breathing hard, but my heart is still thumping heavily in my chest. I can feel it all the way down in my toes. It's that post-sex thump-thump-thump heartbeat. It's probably the single greatest sign that your life and your body is doing exactly what it was made to do. When your heart beats that hard, it's like it's your body's way of telling you, *"Hey man, good job!"* If your heart is a motivational figure in your life like mine is.

I don't know what we're going to do for the rest of the day, but I'm pretty sure that we won't have sex again. Four times in a day is not something I think I can pull off, not with a girl. One time I jerked off five times in a day when I had a competition with my friend. But I was 13 then. And I didn't even win the competition either.

* * *

The sun has set, and out my window is a black void with twinkling specks shining here and there. Amy's getting her things together. Her purse, her shoes, her phone, other things that I don't care about.

"Did you drive here?" I ask.

"Yeah."

"Okay, just checking. If you didn't, I was going to offer to give you a ride home."

"Oh, I'm not going home," she replies, leaning down and flipping her hair out of her face as she pulls one of her shoes on.

"You're not?"

"I'm going to my other boyfriend's house."

"Other boyfriend, huh?"

"Yeah. For some more sex. Not getting enough here."

"Here," I say, nodding. "From your..."

She smiles.

"That's right, dude. I just called you my boyfriend. Deal with it."

"Dealing with it. Not a problem. Not a problem at all."

"No?"

"Well, not a problem if you're just kidding about the other boyfriend."

She pulls her other shoe over her heel and walks toward me, the laces scraping along the ground. I look down at her feet. Come on. Safety first!

"Well, I'll break up with him. Okay?"

"Go easy on him."

"I will."

She kisses me on the mouth and then draws her arms around me for a hug. I open the door and lead her outside, the black void following us to the other side of my apartment. It's a very dark night, almost strangely dark. Maybe it's a new moon. Maybe I don't care.

"Goodbye!" I yell out as she walks down the sidewalk.

"Goodbye, boyfriend!" she yells back.

Boyfriend echoes across the walls of the alley behind my apartment. I smile and take in the night air. A cat meows somewhere. I let my breath out in a big, satisfying sigh. Everything feels great. Just great.

I go back to my couch and sink into the cushions, grabbing the remote to the TV like I've done hundreds of times in the past. I turn the TV on and confront the fact that I don't have cable yet. Shit. I stare straight ahead and retrace my day as the silent static flickers across the TV screen.

I walk over to my refrigerator, the haze from my high still lingering in the recesses of my mind. It's the kind of high that I'm not actually aware of but that I suspect is happening nevertheless. The kind that I'm only going to notice tomorrow when I try to think back to what I was doing when I thought I was straight. I open the freezer door, and I feel my eyes smiling first.

"There you are!"

"I've been here the whole time," the couch replies.

"No, not you."

An unopened bag of Pizza Rolls sits alone on the top shelf of the freezer.

"Whaaaa?"

I don't remember buying these. The last thing I can remember about Pizza Rolls is that I haven't been able to find them in any store that I've gone to here. Not in Malibu and not in any of the stupid towns surrounding us. It's really been making me angry, so this bag is actually quite confusing. I take a step back and look around behind me. Then I look back into the freezer. The bag stares back at me.

"Where did you come from?"

The Pizza Rolls don't reply, so I look over at the couch and shrug. The couch doesn't reply either. Fucker.

I stand in front of the freezer with the door wide open, cold clouds of vapor tufting out into the room. Maybe Amy brought them over. Or maybe Wolf did. Or maybe I found them in a store somewhere, but I just don't remember it.

It doesn't matter. They're in my freezer now. Scratch that. They're in my toaster oven now. I sit back down on the couch, and I don't change the channel or turn the TV off. The silent static isn't that bad. Besides, I'm just waiting for the timer to ding while the smell of almost-pizza is filling the air. My quintessential embodiment of peace is on the way.

Fifteen

Today is Tuesday. Or maybe it's Wednesday. I'm having a hard time keeping track of the days. I want to blame it on the absence of reality that is my life right now, but if I'm being honest, I know it's just because I'm too lazy to remember things like this.

The sun is out, and it's probably burning someone on the beach right now. I'm still in bed. Fuck that noise, I don't need a tan. I look under the covers, and I have a serious boner.

"Didn't get enough?" I ask Little Luke.

I don't think that I mentioned this before, but of course I call him Little Luke. Because I am Big Luke, and he is just like a smaller part of me, a littler version. Little Luke. He is not to be confused with Luke Jr., my fictional son. These are two separate entities that do not know about each other.

I throw on some shorts to discourage myself from jerking off before I take a shower. I don't need it. I shouldn't do it. I don't know why he's so charged up right now, but I'm just going to ignore him and hope it goes away. The shorts help a little. It's like putting a blanket on a fire. You'll know soon enough which one is going to out-will the other. I've got to think of a distraction.

I'll poach an egg. I've always liked poached eggs, but I never had the guts to try to make one. I grab a pot from the cupboard and fill it up with water before putting it on my stove. Then I do some searching for life hacks on the Internet. My assumption is that it will end in disaster, like I'll have to throw the pot out and everything. Maybe I'll even burn the apartment down. But the Internet is making me feel better. It seems like it's not actually that hard. After my good showing with the sandwich prep the other day, it's time to see what else I can do.

I look down at my shorts, and I can tell that this isn't enough of a distraction. I need more distractions! I'll play a game. I've got all kinds of stupid games that I play. I really need better hobbies, but this is the kind of shit that I do.

OK. Let's see. I'll do The Race, that's always a fun one. The point is to try to shower as quickly as possible, always racing against some imaginary opponent. Like the commercial break of whatever show I'm watching. Or the countdown of the microwave as it heats up my frozen burrito. I always beat the commercial break. Only one time I beat the burrito. I think there's a lesson in there somewhere.

Right there on the stove is my pot, partially filled with water and just waiting for me to flick the burner on. I look back at the bathroom. The path to the door is clear. I turn around and light the burner, and then I run toward the shower. I slam the water on and it's cold as fuck. Take that, boner! Even if I wanted a warm shower, the water here takes a long time to heat up. Ain't nobody got time for that. Not with a pot of eager water ready to boil over on my stove. No way. This might be the most intense opponent yet. It actually carries a legitimate threat of causing a problem.

Then my phone starts ringing. Shit! No one ever calls me; it's always just texts and messages. It must be important. The phone isn't that far from the shower, so even though I should know better, I jump out and answer it.

"Hello?"

Pools of water are forming around my feet.

"Luke, hi. It's Tony."

"Hey, Tony. What's up? I was just about to call. Am I..."

I look up at the clock. I don't remember what time I'm supposed to call, so I'm hoping he'll give me some assistance.

"No, you're fine. I just wanted to know if you could come in a little earlier today to meet with me at the office."

"Come in earlier so I can leave earlier, that kind of thing?"

"Can you make it here by 12:30?"

"Yeah, I can do that."

"Same place as last time. See you then."

He hangs up the phone. I look over at the stove, and I can see little bubbles forming on the water's edge.

"Shit!"

I run back into the bathroom, slipping along the way and regaining my composure right as I stumble through the door. I imagine falling and injuring myself, my balls flopping around and crashing against the tile floor as I smack my head into the door frame, splitting my head open, bleeding everywhere, killing me dead, instantly, my last thought a run-on sentence. My epitaph would read:

HERE LIES LUKE

HE DIED TRYING TO BEAT A POT OF WATER

IN A RACE

That would be hilarious. Awful, too, considering that my whole life would end with such a laughable event. But I guess there are way worse ways to go. Besides, no one really remembers how you die. Except for those people that die from autoerotic asphyxiation. Everyone always remembers those ones. You know who I'm talking about.

I scrub my body as quickly as I can, almost losing the bar of soap a couple of times. If I drop it, I'm taking it as a sign that I should just stop washing myself. It doesn't happen. I maintain full soap control.

I turn the water off and hastily grab the towel, slamming it against my body in deft, broad strokes like I'm trying to kill a moth with a pillow. I'm not dry, but I know that I don't have enough time to be anything other than done, so I step out into the room and eye the little stream that I trailed between my bathroom and where my phone is sitting on the table.

I look over at the stove, and the water is steadily boiling. I rush to the fridge and grab the carton of eggs, my dick swinging around as I jostle through the room. I believe that one can only jostle when one is naked, and I am as naked as one can get.

"Okay, here we go..."

I'm leaning cautiously over the pot, stirring the water counterclockwise to create a whirlpool effect. I read this in *23 Ways of Poaching an Egg That Only People Who Grew Up in the 90's Would Understand.*

I crack the egg and begin to separate the shell. It's a clean break. Damn it looks good. I drop the egg in the pot unscathed, and then I slam the lid down on top. I don't get how a poached egg actually takes on its eventual shape. It doesn't make sense to me. I just assume that it'll end up looking like a regular fried egg but without the browning on the underside, kind of like one of those fake rubber eggs you get in a kitchen toy set.

But some miracle of food science starts occurring right in front of me. A white membrane forms around the yolk and it envelopes it until I can no longer see any yellow peeking through. I'm staring down at the pot. It's fucking miraculous! How is this happening? I guess that a lot of people have already seen this before, but this is my first time. I didn't know this is how it works. It just turns itself into a poached egg. Actually, I still don't get it, and I'm staring right at it.

The lid on the pot begins to steam up until I can no longer see the egg clearly. I wait exactly five minutes from when I dropped it in there, and then I pull back the lid to unveil my creation.

"Red letter day!"

I throw my hand up above my head in a victory punch, but clumsily, I slam my finger into the vent hood. Shit. As I recoil, I swing my arm down toward my side and clip the edge of the pot's handle with my hand. I mean, I barely hit it. But it's just enough.

Just enough to jolt the pot up a bit. Just enough for a splash of water to bubble its way out. Just enough to burn the fuck out of a little spot on my hip.

"Fuck! Fuck, fuck, ahhhhhh! Fuck, what the ahhhhhhh!"

I'm running around the house, jumping up and down, trying to quash the immediate shock of pain. Little Luke is flopping all over the place. I eventually stop hopping around and take a look at the damage. It isn't that bad. It's just a small patch that's very red.

Thankfully the burn is where it is. Little Luke wouldn't be in the same shape if, instead, he had been the target of that malicious blob of water. I don't need my little hip area for all that much, but I sure as shit need Little Luke. Little Hip has to take one for the team. Then again, I also could have worn clothes or not raced against a boiling pot of water. These are also choices that I could have made.

I look back at the pot. Floating in the water is a beautifully poached egg. I want to take it out, but I'm still not wearing anything, so I grab the towel and wrap it around my abdomen and up to just above my nipples. I look like a shy teenage boy.

I fish the egg out of the pot using a slotted spoon. I'm holding the spoon in one hand while I reach across the kitchen and grab a plate. I take some salt and dust the top of the egg. Little pink crystals sprinkle all around the plate. I press my fork down into the egg, the thick yolk bursting out and looking vaguely sexual. Even though I'm clearly in the middle of a very important life moment, the knot that I had tied to keep the towel on decides to quit on me. The towel begins unraveling and falls to the floor.

"Fine," I moan. "I'll get dressed."

* * *

I walk over to the same building where I met Tony the last time. I still haven't provided any meaningful intel, and even though he gave me that whole rah-rah speech about not worrying about the count and about me doing my diligent duty and all that, I'm still worried that I'm not being as effective as I'm supposed to be. I have it set in my mind as I'm walking that he's going to reprimand me. Or fire me. Or maybe hit me with a clipboard. I deserve all three.

It might be the first time in my life that I actually somewhat care about my performance in anything other than sex. And the craziest thing is that I don't have any frame of reference. I don't know if those nerds are racking up their counts or if they're as futile as me. I don't talk to either of them about it, and even when I do see them, I get the feeling that they won't tell me the truth if I ask anyway. I jog up the stairs to the administration building, and I open the doors. I'm bracing for a clipboard to my nose.

"Luke!"

Tony is across the room in a big leather recliner. It looks strangely out of place in what's an otherwise drab event space. I don't remember seeing it there the last time I was here. Then again, I didn't look in that corner. Maybe it's been here all along.

"Nice chair."

"This old thing?"

I wince.

"So what's up? Is now a good time?"

"Yes. Thanks for coming in. Take a seat."

He motions to his right where there's a little metal chair for me to sit on, like he's been expecting me. I mean, he is expecting me. So this makes sense. I sit down and put my hands on my knees.

"What's going on?"

I'm trying to seem casual and unaffected. If there's one thing that I can probably pull off, it's looking like I'm casual. It's in my blood. Literally. My blood is full of chemicals that make me pretty damn relaxed most of the time.

"First of all, I want you to know that you're not in any kind of trouble. I didn't ask you to come in here because of anything that you've done. Or that you haven't done."

"Okay. Is this about the whale? Is she okay?"

"What whale?" he asks.

I frown.

"Don't get worried and jump to conclusions or anything," he adds. "I don't know what you've heard about us here, but we don't do those things that some people say we do."

"What things?"

"The things you might have heard."

"I have no idea what you're talking about."

"Good!" he exclaims. "Anyway, I've heard that you've been spending a lot of time with a particular person lately. One person in particular. You know what I'm talking about? Is that true? I haven't seen it myself. Like I said, I've just heard it. From people. Here and there."

I smile when I think about her even though he's bringing it up in such a roundabout way. I notice him watching my reaction, so I try my best to shake it off, but I can't. She just makes me so damned happy. Her perfect, little angel face.

"Yeah. It's still kind of new."

"Well, sure. You're new here. That makes sense."

"We met right after I got here. It was on my first day out in the field."

Tony looks down at his clipboard, and I imagine him leaping from the recliner and slamming it over my head. But nobody leaps from a recliner; that's just not what you do. So I'm not actually worried. I'm just actively imagining things.

"It looks like here that you met earlier than that."

I look out the window and off into the distance. I think I can see the faint glimmer of the beach way out there. I squint. I probably look like I'm thinking about what he just said, but I'm really just trying to see if it truly is the beach or if it's just a glare coming from the windshield of a car or something equally as disappointing. I think about the whale, and I fall into a pit of despair.

"Luke?"

I snap out of it. Turns out it was a short pit.

"No. I don't think so. It was my first day in the field."

He shakes his head and taps his clipboard.

"Says here that you met on your first day in training. Says here that multiple sources can confirm this too. After all, it was in one of our facilities. So it's hard to imagine that we didn't have a record of the meeting. Do you agree?"

"We definitely did not meet in training. I'm positive of that. Unless she was...was she here at the same time? I don't think I met her. I mean, if I did, I certainly don't remember it. I'm pretty sure that she's been here for a while longer than me."

He looks up from his clipboard and stares at me with a puzzled face.

"What did you just say?" he asks me.

"I met her on one of my first days in the field. I really don't think I met her during training."

"Who is *her?*"

"Sorry?"

"Who do you think we are talking about right now?"

I pause. Who does *he* think we're talking about?

"The girl that I've been spending time with. The one you mentioned earlier?"

He lets out a booming laugh.

"You've been hitting some tail? Good on you!"

He slaps me on the back, and I jolt forward.

"I...yeah, okay. Yeah. Yeah, I have."

"That's not what I'm talking about. I don't care if you're fucking half of the community out there. As long as they're not squatters or delinquents, you can do whatever you want in that department."

"I also slept with a girl that I met at Air."

"Don't need to know," he smiles. "But good on you."

"Thanks. Yeah."

"I'm talking about your friend, Wolf. You do know Wolf Johnson, is that correct?"

"That's his last name?"

Tony looks down at his clipboard.

"Johnson. Sure. You know him?"

"I know a Wolf. I never actually asked him his last name. That's kind of fucked up, now that I think about it. I've known the guy for maybe a month now, but I only know his first name."

"So you don't know if you know Wolf Johnson?"

"Unless there's another guy here named Wolf, I think we're talking about the same guy."

"There was a Wolfgang here once."

I purse my lips and shrug.

"Okay. So?"

"So you do agree that you know Wolf Johnson and that you have been spending time with him since you arrived here."

"I mean, what a weak last name. What does Johnson even mean? At least my last name has *meaning*. No wonder his parents gave him a cool first name."

"Luke! Do you know Wolf Johnson?"

"Sure. Yeah. I do. He's a happy. You guys give him that awesome baton job a lot. He *loves* it. You should assign it to him some more."

"Well, that's interesting that you say that. Because we would do that. We would give him a full week of baton duty, but he has seemingly gone M.I.A. on us."

"No shit?"

"He hasn't shown up for four days. And he was scheduled all four of those days."

"Maybe he's sick?"

"Luke, look. I like you. You're kind of retarded, but you mean well, I think. You don't really want to get caught up in this, do you? You don't want to cover for your friend and get yourself all wrapped up in his mess. Do you?"

"What mess?"

"When an employee fails to report to his or her assignment, it is a big problem for us. Your friend, Wolf, is violating the terms of our employment agreement."

"So you're going to fire him?"

He laughs.

"Help us out, Luke. You know where he is. We know you know."

"I honestly haven't seen him for a few days."

"When?"

"When did I last see him? Hmm...what day is it today?"

"Wednesday."

"I dunno. It was at least a few days ago. I think the last time I saw him, it was, yeah, it was the first day that he didn't go in. He told me."

"So you knew that he was deliberately conning us?"

"Con? What? No, no. He told me that he didn't want to do the baton thing and that as a protest, he was just going to not show up that day."

"And you think that's okay?"

"He's a big boy. I mean, what does it have to do with me anyway?"

"It's called *aiding and abetting*."

His tone has been getting increasingly serious throughout the conversation, but it doesn't hit me until he makes it sound like I've been doing something criminal.

"Look, I haven't been aiding or abetting anything. He told me a few days ago that he was calling in sick. And then I haven't seen the guy since. I like him. I mean, I don't *want* him to get in trouble or anything. But I sure as hell have nothing to do with him not showing up."

"Can you lead us to him?"

"Sure, I guess. I mean, what happens to him when you get him? Does he get sent to The Hague or something?"

Tony eases up a bit and smiles, but only slightly.

"Don't worry about it. We just need to...*reset* his understanding of why he is here. It's nothing we haven't had to do in the past. Sometimes, people tend to...how do I put it..."

"Stray?"

"Exactly."

"Kind of ironic, isn't it?"

"How so?"

"Wolf. Going stray. Get it?"

"That's not irony."

"It isn't?"

"Can you bring us to him, Luke?"

"Yeah, sure. I mean, like I said, I haven't seen or talked to him in a couple of days, but I can try. Sure, I can try."

"Don't try. Do."

"Okay. You got it."

Tony nods to signify that he's done talking with me. The recliner has full control over his body, and I don't think he's going to get out of it until the lights go out in the building later tonight. And maybe not even then. It looks pretty comfortable, so I don't blame him. I'm sure I could sleep at least a night in a recliner like that.

"Oh, and Luke?"

"Yes?"

"I didn't mean what I said about sleeping with half of the community. You can have girls here and there, but don't take this job as a free ticket to rack up your count. We need you to stay focused. *Discreet*."

"Oh, don't worry. I'm not looking around anymore. I'm a one-woman man."

I smile. It feels good saying it.

"Good for you."

"Yeah. Thanks."

He looks down at his clipboard again.

"Say, what's her name?"

"Her name?"

"Yeah. We're supposed to keep this information here in your file. It's for security reasons. You understand, right?"

"Sure, yeah. Makes sense."

He stares at me. I try to think of a name. Any name.

"Uh, it's...Joanne. Yeah. Her name is Joanne."

He starts scribbling something on the clipboard and doesn't look up at me again.

"Thanks, Luke. Let me know when you've gotten a hold of Wolf. It'd be best if you went looking for him today. Your other shift duties can wait."

"Other duties? I thought I was off today."

"Goodbye, Luke."

I walk outside and breathe hard into the warm air. I felt suffocated back in that room, like I was suddenly asthmatic or dying or maybe just having an anxiety attack over the whole thing.

I'm worried about what might happen if they ever find out that Amy's name isn't Joanne. I don't even know why I lied in the first place. It just didn't feel right. The whole thing was a little too tense. I panicked.

"Wolf fucking Johnson," I mutter.

Sixteen

What a mess. I only came to this town because they invited me. I didn't know that I was going to get to live here, work here, have sex with a beautiful girl three times in one day here. And another beautiful but crazy girl as well. I wasn't expecting any of that. I just wanted to visit and have a little fun.

I came to Malibu to just figure my life out, live while I can still live, do what I can while I can still do it. I wasn't doing anything else with my life, and that invite—it just landed in my mailbox at exactly the right time. But it wasn't any regular invite. It was a chance to come in through the back door, the secret speakeasy version of Malibu that no one knows about. The only problem is, now they're asking me to pay for the next round. And I'm not sure I brought my credit card.

I'm torn over the whole situation. I understand that what's probably best for me is not going to be what's best for Wolf. And while I don't have any explicit reason to think that anything above a reprimand is coming his way, I have a feeling that The Board is apt to make an example of someone every now and then. And a guy named Wolf is probably who you make the example of.

I'm out and about now, eavesdropping on peoples' conversations, trying to pick up something interesting to report back to Tony. Failing as usual. I'm near Amy's neighborhood, so I walk over to her house and ring the doorbell.

"Hey!" she exclaims as she opens the door. "How'd you know I would be here?"

I shrug.

"I'm, uh, working right now. So I figured I'd just swing by while I was out and see if you were in."

"That's so sweet of you."

"It's no big deal. I just wanted to see you if I could. Are you busy?"

She shakes her head.

"No, not at all. Want to come in?"

"I probably shouldn't come in. I don't have *that* much time."

"We can just sit here then," she counters, beckoning toward the steps we're both standing on.

I sit down and prop my elbows up on my knees. She sits next to me. I give her a kiss.

"Did you already finish your shift today?" I ask her. "Or are you going in later?"

"Later I was going to have dinner with you, remember?"

"Really?"

She nods.

"That's right. So you already worked."

"Yeah, *worked*," she air quotes.

"Sorry...I probably wrote the dinner plans down somewhere, but I suck. I'm actually not free tonight."

"Oh. It's OK."

"There's been a lot going on today."

"Like what?"

"Well, for starters, I poached my first egg. Have you ever done that?"

"Poached an egg? No, I haven't."

"It was incredible. I was so proud of it. I've had poached eggs out at restaurants a hundred times, but I never thought about making them at home. It wasn't nearly as hard as I thought it would be."

"Don't you just drop an egg in some boiling water? Also, this is what constitutes *a lot going on* in your life? I can see why you can't make dinner tonight. You've got *eggs* to poach."

Ooh, she's so salty. I like it.

"I burned myself with the water too."

"Oh, now we're getting somewhere with this busy day of yours. An egg and a burn. Let me see it?"

I lift up the side of my shirt. It's red, but it doesn't really look that bad. I wish I hadn't said anything at all. I've probably burned the roof of my mouth worse than I burned myself with that water. But when it happened, it felt serious.

"How about we do breakfast tomorrow instead?"

She nods.

"Sure. That works."

"You want to pick out the place? I don't know any good breakfast places."

"I know a place."

"Cool. So anyway, back to the eggs. I mean, back to my crazy day. I was just going about my morning, doing my thing. Then I get a call from my boss. He asks me to come in."

"Oh, so they finally need you now? What for?"

I look around and scan the people walking on the sidewalk and getting in and out of their parked cars. I lean in close to Amy as a precaution.

"They want me to lead them to Wolf."

She turns her hands up to the sky as if to say, *"Yeah, and?"*

"He hasn't been in to work in four days."

"So they're gonna fire him? Already?"

"That's the thing. I don't know what they're gonna do. I don't know if he'll lose his job. If he'll have to move away. If something worse will happen. I just don't know. Do you know what they do to people that go AWOL?"

"No. It's never crossed my mind, so I've never worried about it."

"I didn't think I was going to have to worry about it either. I mean, I'm a good person. I might do a few bad things here and there, but I'm not like the troublemaker guy. That's not me."

"Is that Wolf?"

I shake my head.

"He's more of a pussy than me."

"So then what's he doing?"

I search the sidewalk for answers, but the sidewalk's all out of answers today.

"I don't know. Exploring that fucking cave like a madman."

"You think he's still doing that?"

"What else could he be doing? He doesn't know anyone else here. He only has this one job, and he hasn't been showing up to it. I can't imagine him spending all of his time doing anything other than trying to snorkel his way to the cosmos or whatever his plan is."

"Oh my God..." Amy gasps. "What if he got stuck down there? It's been how long?"

"Nah. I've been texting him. I've seen that he's read the messages. He's just not replying."

"When was the last time he read one?"

I pull my phone out. I can't even remember what day it is, so I know that there's no way I'll be remembering the timestamp of my last confirmed correspondence with a guy that I'm supposed to throw under the bus.

"Last night. Late last night."

"Okay, well, that's good."

"Yeah, it's great that he's avoiding me."

"I mean, it's good that he's not slowly starving to death down in that cave. Or already dead even."

"He was a Boy Scout. I don't think he's getting stuck down there. I just don't know what he thinks he's actually *doing* down there."

"What if he's right?"

Of all the things for Amy to ask or say, this is probably the worst of them all.

"Come on."

"Look, I'm not crazy. I don't think that hole is a portal to the *real, exterior* universe. Your buddy—who, by the way, I've still never met—he's the crazy one. I'm just saying that for the sake of argument here, one reason he might not be responding to you is because he's floating around in, uh, what did you call it?"

"Inner space."

"I like that. Inner space."

"Wolf likes it too. I should trademark it."

"Maybe he's just floating around in inner space."

"Then maybe I should bring him back down to earth by bringing him in."

"Is that what you want to do though?"

"No. I mean, I don't know. I don't want to be involved at all. At this point, I still haven't brought in any meaningful intelligence. Not even one bit. All of my investigations have amounted to nothing. And it's so far along now that I'm not even sure I would want to find something out. There was a thrill to the idea before, but now it just kind of seems like a nuisance. Like my real job is just to walk around and, I don't know, just *be* there. But having to rat on someone? I don't know if I want any part of that. But I don't know what options I really have."

She smiles and puts her hand on my arm.

"Why *should* you want to do any of that? You're not making any money off this whole thing. What's it to you?"

"Well, sure I am. I take home my paycheck."

"Compare that to what The Board pulls in each week. That's what I'm talking about. That's real money, real incentive. What you're doing? I mean, no offense, Luke...but what you're doing is just making sure that some other people can line their pockets."

"Sure. But how is that different than your job? Or any other job, for that matter?"

"It's not. But I'm not at odds with what I'm supposed to do. I just go out there and, you know..."

"Twirl a baton around on the beach?"

"Look, Luke. This place isn't what it seems like, you know? Not to the normal people out there that are shelling out thousands of dollars to try to get a taste of life here. Not to the people who work for The Board. Not for you. Not for me."

"Right, I know. It's all a big hoax."

"So do you *really* care about bringing someone in? Maybe you can just continue to roam around and not actually *do* your job. And you and I can enjoy ourselves. And maybe Wolf can too, with whatever he's doing. And then we don't have to take this whole Board thing so seriously. After all, if they actually care about you coming up with some dirt, shouldn't they be more on your case about this by now?"

"Yeah, I keep thinking that. But then I wonder if they will eventually get on my case. And that they're just giving me the benefit of the doubt for now because I'm still new here."

"Why don't you just keep walking around, keep *looking*. But, you know...maybe you never *find* Wolf. Maybe you never find a hanger-on. Maybe you're just a bad hire for them. Not a threat. Just not productive."

"What about you? What will you do? How long are you going to continue to be a happy?"

"I don't know. How long does anyone do this? I mean, look. Things are not what they seem like here."

"I know."

"Do you? What do you know?"

I pause and then I sigh.

"Amy, I mean...I get what's going on here. Like, what's really going on. I'm just a guard dog, right? A rent-a-cop. A scarecrow. They wouldn't put a guy like me in charge of actually *doing* something. It kind of sucks to say that, but I'm not that out of touch with reality. I know myself."

"So then what are you conflicted over?"

"I'm conflicted because deep down inside, I was okay with that. I liked it, in a way. So when they start asking me to actually *do* the thing that they're pretending I'm supposed to do, I don't know what to do with that. Do I actually listen to them? Do I go find Wolf and bring him in? Or am I supposed to *find* him the same way that I've *found* all that other information so far?"

"What do you think?"

"Well, that's the problem. I think I forgot how to think."

"You said it before. You don't want to turn Wolf in. You don't really want to turn anyone in."

"Right."

"So don't do it then. Easy?"

"It's just so confusing."

Her grip on my arm loosens, and I feel her hand start to slide away. She has a strange look on her face.

"Would you turn me in?"

"No. No."

"No matter what?"

"Yeah, no matter what. Why would I? That would make no sense. You're really important to me! I wouldn't ever do that to you. I wouldn't do that to us."

"Even if I wasn't supposed to be here?"

"What do you mean, *supposed to be here*? You work here. You're fine."

"Wolf works here. He's not fine."

"Okay, yeah. But you're so under the radar, it's totally fine. Like, I wouldn't even tell them your name today. I said that your name was Joanne. They have no clue. Trust me."

"Wait, what?"

"Your name. They asked me what your name was, and for some reason, I don't even know why, I made up a fake name for you."

"They asked about me? Who asked about me?"

"Yeah. Well, kind of. It was confusing. When he approached me about Wolf..."

"He who?"

"Whoa, calm down. My boss. When my boss approached me about Wolf, I thought he was talking about you. He was vague and saying things like, *we noticed you've been spending a lot of time with someone lately.* I thought they were noticing us being together. But he was really just talking about Wolf."

"So then he asked you for my name? And you said it was Joanne?"

"That was later. I think he just wanted it for my file. But like I said, I didn't give him your real name. I'm sure it's fine."

"How did...okay. Look."

"Look at what?"

"I don't know. This whole thing makes me nervous."

"Nervous? Don't worry about it. Honestly, it was just a passing question, like *what's her name?* And I lied, so it's fine. It's all good. He probably didn't even write it down."

"I don't know. I don't know."

She gets up and starts pacing around on the stoop. Her face crumples into a frown, like a storm cloud forming over whatever a storm cloud forms over.

"What's the matter?"

She looks down at me and crosses her arms.

"I'm not supposed to *be* here, Luke."

"Huh?"

I stand up. If she's standing up, I'm standing up. I don't want to be at a disadvantage on the height front. I'm not that much taller than her, so every inch matters.

"I'm not a happy. I don't work for The Board."

"Then what are you doing here?"

She shrugs. She has a sad but angry look on her face.

"I'm just one of your targets, I guess. I'm the kind of person that you're supposed to be finding and getting rid of."

I'm not incredulous. I'm not even shocked. I don't feel anything.

"How have you not been caught yet?"

"My roommate's a happy. She lets me use her ID when I need to. After a few weeks of being here, she got bored and called me up and asked me if I wanted to come and visit. And then it all kind of happened from there."

"Are you fucking with me right now?"

"I'm sorry, Luke! I wanted to tell you. But I didn't know if I could trust you."

"Oh, you can trust me. You can trust me to turn you in! I can't believe that *you're* going to be my first catch! Of all the people! Oh man!"

Her eyes get very large, and she's frantically searching around like she's looking for a way out. The only way she could escape would be to go back into her apartment. That isn't much of an escape.

"Luke..." she starts, a hesitancy in her voice.

"Amy, relax. I'm just kidding. Okay? I'm just kidding."

It takes a few seconds for her to hear what I'm saying. I think she's still looking for a way to run away from me. Once it registers, she starts slapping my arm, hand over hand.

"Oh, you asshole!" she laughs. "You...you bastard!"

"Hey, wait. Who's the asshole?"

"You are!"

She keeps slapping me.

"I made one joke. You lied to me about who you are. Who's the asshole?"

"Okay, fine. But your joke...oh, God! God, Luke! You scared the shit out of me!"

I extend my arms to give her a slow and earnest hug. She sinks her face into my chest, and I squeeze her tightly, kissing her neck as I press my face against her shoulder.

"I've got you now," I whisper, squeezing my arms even tighter.

She pulls back from me and looks into my eyes.

"Cut it out. I was *so* nervous to tell you. You have no idea."

"Why? It's not really a big deal. I'm not going to say anything."

"You sure you're okay with this? I know what I'm asking you to do goes against what you're supposed to be doing here. I get it. Like, I really get it. You don't have to be okay with this."

I kiss her on her forehead.

"I'm okay with this."

"Really?"

"Like you said before...fuck this place, right?"

"I didn't say that."

"You implied it."

"Okay. Fuck this place."

"There. Now you said it."

We stand still for a few seconds, holding each other's hands and staring at each other's faces. Her expression is not yet calm, but it's on the way to being calm.

"So there's just one more thing."

"Great. Now what?"

"My roommate's name is Amy. She's the real Amy Percy."

"Oh. Oh man. It's...it's like I'm meeting you for the first time! This is crazy! What's your actual name?"

She smiles.

"Don't laugh."

"Oh man. Is it a terrible name? Is it Dorothy? Martha? I can't date a Martha. I just can't."

She doesn't say anything and just stares straight at me.

"Oh, God. It's Martha, isn't it?"

"No, Luke. It's not Martha. Relax."

"Okay, then what is it? What's so funny about it?"

"My name is Joanna."

"Come on."

"Really."

"Come on! Really?"

"That's why when you said that, I just froze up. It was...like, you didn't know, right?"

"Know? How the hell would I know? I just assumed that you were who you said you were. Like any normal person would do. I didn't for a minute think that I might accidentally guess your real name when trying to provide, you know, a fake name. Shit!"

"It's all right. It's all right. I'm sure there's a Joanne or a Joanna that lives around here somewhere. There has to be."

"Right. It's a pretty common name, I guess."

She looks relieved. I'm sure it was a burden to keep that from me. Or from anyone, not just me. I've never had to pretend that I was anyone other than myself. It's probably exhausting.

"Aren't you glad that I am so terrible at my job that I didn't even notice you while you were right under my nose?"

She smiles and squeezes my hands.

"Oh, but I love that about you. It's perfect. You're perfect."

"I'd say the same thing back to you, but I feel like I just met you. What's your name again?"

"Martha."

"Alright. I have no choice but to turn you in. That name is a crime in and of itself."

Seventeen

"What do you think? Is The Board intentionally sending me out when they know that nothing will turn up?"

I pat the couch. It doesn't say anything. I think we're in a fight.

"In a way," I continue, "It actually makes a lot of sense. Maybe the role of someone like me is just to be that intermediary between the *real* investigators and the happies. The kind of person that becomes friends with the happies and then warns them about all the ways that they shouldn't fuck up."

"Why are you talking so much?" the couch finally asks.

"What do you mean?"

"You're talking to yourself, dude."

He has a sarcastic look on his face. But wait.

He doesn't have a face.

"Fuck you, *dude*. I'm talking to you!"

He shakes his non-existent head.

"Whatever."

I pull out my canister and take a look at my remaining weed supply. It's low, but not low enough that I need to hit the dispensary. I can't go there right now. I always end up buying more than I plan on buying. The smell just lures me to do shit that I otherwise wouldn't do.

I put the canister away. I'm not smoking today. It's maybe been a few weeks since I took a day off anyway, so I should probably sit one out. I've been more or less on the daily routine for as long as I can remember. It's a part of who I am. It makes me feel like me. Or at least how I think me is supposed to feel.

I grab my phone and dial Wolf's number, but then I hang up before it gets through a full ring. I have no reason to expect that the Board is monitoring my calls, but then again, there is no reason for me to expect that they aren't either. They seem to monitor a lot of things. I text him instead. I'm not up to date on the latest surveillance capabilities, but I'm thinking that The Board doesn't know how to trace a text.

Where you at? Been a while. Hope you found inner space already so we can hang out

It delivers. I put my phone down and take a quick shower. From time to time, I stop what I'm doing and check to see if he's read my message. He hasn't. Maybe I'll go out to the cave later on today just to make sure he isn't stuck down there or something.

It seems really unlikely, but ever since Amy, I mean, Joanna, put the idea in my head, I've been slightly worried about it. In all likelihood, he's probably just laying low since he knows that he's skipping out on The Board. I send him another message.

Hope there's a lot of herb there too

* * *

I'm practicing saying her name over and over to try to get used to it. I don't want to screw up and call her Amy at breakfast this morning.

"Joanna. Joanna. Joannnnnnnna! Jooooooanna!"

"Joanna!" the couch repeats.

"Exactly. You nailed it."

"Not my first Joanna."

"Really? What do you think of it? Like, as a name?"

The couch shrugs.

(It has arms. It can do this.)

I leave my apartment and walk over to her place. I think I'm here in record time, though I didn't time it and I don't remember when I left, so I don't know for sure. Still, it feels record-breaking to me. I knock on the door and wait for a moment until I hear footsteps descending the staircase inside. The door swings open. My jaw drops.

"What are you doing here!?" I blurt out.

"Me? I live here. What are *you* doing here?"

"You? Live here?"

"Uh, yeah. You could have just text me back. You didn't have to show up out of nowhere."

I look down at my phone. Yeah, I could have text her. But...

"Sorry, I didn't come here to see you."

"You didn't? Come on. What are you doing here then? Delivering the newspaper?"

"I'm...I'm here to see Amy."

"Yeah, well, you're looking at her. Are you on drugs?"

"Joanna. I meant Joanna. And no, I'm not actually. Not today."

"You know Joanna? How?"

"She's my..."

"Your what?"

"Wait. You're Amy Percy?"

"Petty, Percy, sure."

"Jesus. Look, no offense, but is Joanna here?"

She looks over her shoulder and yells out her name. I hear another set of footsteps descending the stairs. I'm half expecting it to not be Joanna, and instead it'll just be some girl named Joanna that I've never seen before, and my Joanna has taken off and left me in the dust. But it is her. Whatever her name actually is.

"Hey! You're early."

"You know him?" Amy asks.

"Yeah, I *know* him. This is the guy that I've been telling you about."

"Him?!"

Joanna takes a half-step back.

"Yeah, *him*. His name is..."

"I know who he is."

"You do?"

Joanna looks at me. I nod.

"Yeah, we've met before."

"No kidding?"

Joanna is smiling and obviously unaware of what she's eventually going to find out. I'm hoping that it won't come out—at least not right now—so when I look at Amy's face and I can tell that she doesn't want it to come out now either, I'm a little relieved. We can control this one. For now.

"Yeah," Amy replies. "This guy tried to buy me a drink at a bar a few weeks ago."

"Oh yeah?"

I nod.

"Yeah. But, correction...I didn't try. I bought the drink."

"But then he didn't give it to me. He just drank it himself."

I shrug.

"I was thirsty."

Amy smiles, but it's a bitchy smile. I think we have a mutual understanding that this isn't going to be good for either of us if we keep talking through how we met. No good will possibly come from this unless one of us thinks that the truth getting aired out is automatically a good thing. I do not think this is the case.

"And," I continue. "I'm thirsty now too. And hungry. You ready?"

Joanna nods.

"You guys have to tell me the rest of this story later!"

Joanna and I walk down the stairs and onto the sidewalk. She's holding my hand as we walk along, down by the water, down by the old main drag.

"So what was that about back there?"

"I had no idea that she was your roommate. I was shocked when she opened the door. Like, shocked."

"Was that the whole story? You guys had some weird interaction at a bar?"

I take a deep breath in and try to hold it as long as I can.

"Yeah, more or less."

"That's it? Why is that so memorable then?"

"Memorable? Who said anything about memorable?"

"You said it shocked you. *Like, shocked you.* What's so shocking about it? It had to be something more memorable than just a failed drink exchange."

I'm heading into dangerous territory. Any lie is going to have to be something I'll have to keep for a long time. Who knows, maybe even forever. And then Amy and I will also have to find a way to talk in private and sync our stories. If I add any new detail right now, Amy is going to have to corroborate it.

This isn't the situation I want to be in. It's usually better to just tell the truth and never get under the lie in the first place. At a minimum, escaping with a generically vague lie is far superior to a specific, pinpointed experience. I have a pretty good idea of what I'm going to say. I'm going over it in my head. I wish the couch were here with me so I could test out some different approaches.

"Luke? Hello?"

"Oh, sorry. I was trying to hold my breath..."

"Luke!"

"OK. Sorry. Yeah, of course. There's more to it than what we said back there."

"How much more?"

"Eh, just a little more. It's no big deal."

"So then why aren't you telling me?"

I slow down my walk and look over at her. She's on the verge of maybe yelling at me. I know what that face looks like. Not from her though; she hasn't yelled at me. Yet. But you don't forget what that face looks like, it doesn't matter the girl. It could be any girl. They all have the same look tucked away in their look reserves. You know what's coming to you if you get that look.

"Well, alright. I didn't want to tell you, but I...I saw her having sex."

"What?"

"With someone. Not with herself. And I didn't mean to. I just happened to see it out of the corner of my eye when I woke up."

"Woke up where? What the hell was going on?"

"She went home and slept with Wolf that night that we met at the bar."

Joanna lets out a huge, almost booming laugh. I didn't even know that a girl could laugh so boomingly. It seems like this activity should be reserved for men. Not to be sexist here, but I just think booming is very unattractive.

"And so you were watching them like a little pervert in the corner?"

"No, no. It wasn't like I was *watching*. I was passed out on the floor. Wolf had brought her back to my place, and I guess he was too lazy to go back to his. So they kind of cozied up on the couch, and that's around when I passed out. And when I woke up later, it was maybe like two or three hours later, there they were. Like, right there. On the couch. Just fucking."

"No kidding?"

"On *my* couch."

"What'd you do?"

"I just pretended to be asleep. I was, like, six or seven feet away from them. I thought it was the best idea."

She gives me a sideways glance, like that awful sarcastic side eye emoji.

"Why did she seem like she didn't like you then?"

"Okay, fine! She saw me see them."

"How?"

"Well, I guess I did a bad job pretending to be asleep."

"Ohh. Awkward."

"So I can't blame her. She knows I saw them going at it. Wolf knows. Now you know. It's a known thing. That might make some girls mad; I could see how that might be. And he never called her again either, so maybe part of her reaction was because of him."

"What position?"

"Huh? Why does that matter?"

"Like was she facing you, or was she underneath him, or was he behind her, or what? What position?"

"Oh...it was some weird Kama Sutra position that I've never seen before. Something where I could see both of their faces and still also see him going, you know, in her."

"Yikes."

"It was exotic. I had never seen anything like it. But yeah, they saw me see them."

"Did they stop?"

"No, they didn't. They kept going."

"What?! No way."

"I think they liked that I was watching. I think it turned them on."

Joanna laughs.

"I doubt that's true."

"She told me after. She told me she liked it when I watched."

"Get outta here!" Joanna shrieks, hitting me on the arm.

"I swear. She was into it. It was really weird. So I just told her that I wasn't interested, and I went into my room and left them alone. And then the next time I saw her was, you know, about ten minutes ago."

I put my hands in my pockets. I think I made a wrong turn somewhere in the conversation.

"Well, that's super awkward. I don't know if I can ever bring it up to her. You know?"

"Yeah, uh...yeah, I wouldn't."

We continue walking to the breakfast spot that she's picked out. I've got to change the subject. I'm burying myself here.

"What kind of food do they have here?"

"You'll see."

"Okay. I trust you. *Joanna*."

She smiles.

"Yeah?"

"Well, that or I just don't really care where I go for breakfast. It's hard to care that much about breakfast if you don't live in Portland."

When we get there, we walk inside, and the smell of syrup and eggs is floating around in the air. God damn, I love maple syrup. It's like a little liquid present from a tree. Think of any other kind of plant out there, and then think about the gifts those plants have given you over the years. I think the maple tree is the most generous tree in the entire tree kingdom. Well, right behind the marijuana plant. That goes without saying. And I guess The Giving Tree should get a little recognition here as well. But then it's the maple tree, hands down.

"Good lord, look at all the different options for eggs!"

"Good lord? I took you to breakfast, not to church."

"Praise the lord for these eggs!" I yell, laughing a little too hard. "Joanna, can I get an Amen for the hash browns?! Hallelujah for the hash browns! I said hallelujah for the hash browns!"

"Luke. Cut it out. People are looking at us."

A hostess comes over to us and smiles a fake hostess smile.

"Praise Jesus for the bacon," I whisper.

She seats us at this little corner table that I think might be the best use of space that I've ever seen. There are two benches that hug along the wall and form a corner that basically renders the space almost useless. But these geniuses—they stuck a little table right at the corner, and now we're here, diagonal from each other. So now it's not just useful. It's magical. It's whimsical. Or maybe it's just a table, I don't know. But I think there's some magic here.

I like how close I'm feeling to Joanna while at the same time also feeling good about the overall efficiency of the space. It must be so satisfying for the person who designed it. Other than the fact that our food can barely fit on the table, it's a perfect, little spot, and I'm so glad that we're seated here. This table has already made my day.

"I prefer almond milk to real milk. Did I ever tell you that?"

I look around.

"No, you never told me that. But that's cool."

"It's creamier. And it's way better for you. It's like a win-win."

"I wonder what's worse for the environment though, a gallon of cow's milk or a gallon of almond milk?"

"For the environment? I'd say the cow's milk. Aren't cows actually terrible for greenhouse gases and water usage and basically all the things that we care about here? Aren't cows like public food enemy number one?"

"I wouldn't go that far. And besides, almonds aren't exactly sitting pretty out there either. They use a ton of water. I read that it takes a gallon of water to grow one almond. One fucking almond! Now imagine how much almond milk you'd get out of one almond."

"Imagine milking that poor, little almond."

I do that little hand motion that people do when they pretend to play the world's tiniest violin.

"Excuse me, Mr. Almond, I'm going to have to milk you now."

"Mr. Almond, I see. The male almond is the one that makes the milk?"

"Almonds are like the seahorses of nut world."

"I didn't know that. That's good to know."

"Next time, we can just skip the milk altogether and make the world a happier planet."

"The whole world except me! I like that almond milk. Even if it comes from a male almond."

We pay for the bill, and as I'm standing up, I catch a glance from a woman at the table next to us. She must have been eavesdropping on our asinine conversation. She's nearly staring me down, not necessarily in a mean way but more in a critical, confused way. I smile at her, and she looks away.

We walk outside, and the sun hits my face. I'm rubbing my belly like I'm a bear that just ate some salmon out of the river. Or maybe just like a slightly out-of-shape guy that ate a big breakfast and then is wondering how big his stomach feels.

"What's up next?" I ask.

Joanna looks over at me as we're walking and then slows to a stop. She fixates on something behind me like the answer is written out in the middle of the street.

"I think there's a guy coming over here."

I look over my shoulder, and sure enough, some guy is walking directly at us. The sun is directly in my eyes, and I can't make him out, but there's no ambiguity about it. He's walking at a medium pace, but he's carrying himself with a lot of intent. I continue to stare ahead at him until he's just a few feet away, hoping he'll divert and walk past. He slows down and stands in front of us.

"Luke!" he barks.

"Oh," I say. "Hey."

It's Tony. I smile. He looks even bigger out in public.

"We need to have a word."

"Okay. Right now?"

"Right now," he repeats.

I brush him off with a laugh.

"Alright, alright. What's up?"

I don't know if he's already impatient or if he just has one of those asshole faces. I never really noticed it before.

"I work for The Board."

"Uh, yeah. Me too. All three of us," I say, as I motion over to Joanna. "So what?"

"That's funny," he says. "For someone that works for The Board, you sure aren't acting like it."

"What do you mean? I called earlier today. You said..."

"I said that you had to find your friend, Wolf. That's what I said!"

"Alright. Yeah. I'm about to. We were just having breakfast."

He turns to Joanna.

"Who are you?"

"She's a happy," I tell him.

Joanna remains silent. She's just holding onto my arm, motionless.

"I didn't ask you," he says. "And I don't recognize you. What's your name?"

"She's a happy," I repeat.

"I said I didn't ask you."

"Joanna," she mumbles.

"We don't have any happies named Joanna," he snarls. "Luke, this is the girl you were telling me about?"

"Yeah. This is my girlfriend. What does this have to do with her? We were just having breakfast."

"She's not a happy!" he yells.

Fuck it.

"OK. Yeah? So? She's not a happy. Big fucking deal. So what? She's not hurting anyone."

"Goddammit, Luke..."

"What? Who cares? Do you really care? She's just staying with a friend for a while. Is that really such a big deal? She can stay with me instead if it matters that much!"

"You are *such* an incredible disappointment. Do you know that? Just absolutely disappointing in every way."

"OK."

"I bet your parents wake up every day and just think to themselves, *Shit, we really made a waste of a human being, didn't we?*"

"I'm pretty sure my parents don't think about me regularly," I counter. "But thanks for trying to bring me down. That's cool."

"Goddammit, Luke. You really are one dumb son-of-a-bitch."

I shrug. I feel like I should stand up for myself, but it's only because Joanna's standing here, watching me get berated by a guy twice my size.

"Tony, look. What's your problem? Hmm? You stormed across the street just to tell me that I'm stupid? Is that it?"

"You were a mistake," he sighs. "Don't you see that? Isn't it obvious by now?"

"How do you mean?"

"You weren't supposed to get that invite. You would *never* get an invite to be a happy here. I, I mean, we, we mailed the invitation to the wrong address. That's it. It was just the wrong address. You weren't ever supposed to even be here."

"A mistake?"

Joanna's wincing. This is probably painful to watch.

"There are no *investigators* here," he continues. "We made that up as soon we realized we had told you too much. It was just supposed to be a temporary thing until we could figure out what to do with you. You weren't supposed to actually *do* anything."

"Really? This whole thing, like, my whole job...it was all fake?"

"Luke," he laughs. "Do you *really* think we would hire you? For *anything?*"

Jesus. That makes a lot of sense now. All those calls into the office that I made every day. The annoyed responses. The lack of shit for me to do when they did tell me to get to work. The overwhelming acceptance of my lack of output. They never even needed me at all. We just stand here for a few moments, not saying anything. I'm a little awestruck.

"But now..." I begin, slowly realizing the advantage I have in the situation. "Now you're stuck with me. And you know that I know things. And I know how to find someone you want. Right? So you're stuck with me. Poor, stupid me. I'm *your* fucking problem now, aren't I?"

His face is a little more relaxed, and he smiles slightly.

"Stuck? With you?" he asks. "We're not *stuck* with anything."

"I don't see what other choice you have. I know too much. I could tell all the residents about what you're doing. I could blow this whole thing right up! I mean, if you give me a reason to. But on the other hand, I could just walk away and pretend that none of this ever happened. Hmm? What do you think of that?"

I smile. It feels good to stand up for myself. But then suddenly, he grabs Joanna's wrist and pulls her close to him.

"We *always* have other choices!" he yells.

I don't even look around. I don't stop to think. I just straight up cold-clock him right in the fucking face. My right hand and his left jawbone. Even his face is big. He reels backwards, and I swing my left arm and hit him in the ribs. Joanna jerks forward, the force of his fall pulling her toward him until his grip on her wrist lets up. I rush forward and knock him down to the ground. I can hear people clamoring around us, but it doesn't stop me.

Something in my brain breaks. I'm raging. No one touches my girl like that. I didn't even know I had this in me, but I just start pummeling his face, one knee jammed into his ribcage and the other steadying me on the ground beside him. Right, left, right, right, right, right, right. I favor the right. I can't even feel it after the first one. Blood is splattering up from his face, but not in a grotesque, Dexter kind of way. Just enough for me to realize how much I'm fucking him up.

I'm getting winded, so I ease up and pull myself up off the ground. His head's lying there in a tiny pool of blood. His eyes are fluttering. His leg's twitching. People are starting to gather around us with their phones out like they do these days. Luckily, Tony is white and I'm not a cop. No one's going to care about this video.

"Let's get out of here," I shout to Joanna.

I grab her by the hand, and we run away from the mess of a man that's lying there in the street. He isn't going to be coming after us; I know that for sure. But I don't know who else might come to find us next. We run all the way back to her apartment and rush inside, locking all the deadbolts on the door behind us and crashing our way up the stairs and into the living room.

Amy's sitting on the couch, wearing a towel on her head and another one around her body. I eye her up and down, and a blurry memory flashes through my brain. It's from the night that she spent at my place. I know what that body looks like under that towel. It's a tight, little body; it's just my type.

Great. Despite everything that just happened in the past few minutes, I'm thinking about sex. With my girlfriend's roommate. She jolts up from the couch and clutches her towel.

"What the...I thought you guys were out for the day!?"

"I got caught!" Joanna shrieks.

"Whoa, whoa. It's all right. He wasn't coming for us. He just wanted Wolf."

"Wolf?" Amy asks. "You have a wolf?"

For a girl that supposedly slept with a guy named Wolf, she is not doing a good job of selling it. Not that she knows she's supposed to be selling it.

"Never mind," I reply. "So this guy, Tony, he's my boss, right? We just finished eating breakfast, and he comes up to me and is like *Luke, blah blah blah.* Then he grabs Joanna's wrist, and I just lost it. I beat the shit out of him."

I look down at my hands, and the blood is running across my knuckles. I don't know if it's mine or his, but it's there, and somehow Amy didn't even see it when we bust into the room.

"What? Fuck!"

"Yeah, we probably have to get out of here."

Joanna runs out of the living room and toward what I can only imagine is her bedroom. This is the first time I've been in her apartment, so for all I know, she's going to the bathroom.

"This is no good, this is no good at all," Amy moans. "They're gonna come for *me*, then they're gonna kick me *out*, or worse yet...who knows? Fuck, man. Just...fuck!"

"Don't worry. We've got some time. I laid him out. He's not going to be telling anyone anything for a little while at least."

"He beat the shit out of the guy!" Joanna yells from the other room. "And he was *huge!*"

Amy raises her eyebrows.

"Didn't think you had that in you."

"Yeah. Me either."

We're both just standing here, looking at each other. My bloody hands. Her towel-wrapped body. I look away.

"But anyway, we can run away or something. You can claim total ignorance, like you have no idea who we are. There's no reason that anyone would ever know that you were lying."

Joanna comes back into the room with a small backpack on her shoulder.

"I don't know. I'll pack the rest of my shit while you go get yours."

"Okay, so...what now?" I ask.

She shrugs.

"Okay. I'll run back to my place and pack a bag as well. And then we can just get the fuck out of here. We can take my car."

"Where are we going?" she panics.

"I don't know. But we can't stay here."

"Alright. But be quick!"

I think about what things I'll have to bring with me. My canister, my bowl. My favorite lighter. Maybe some food. Maybe some deodorant. Everything else can just burn down with the apartment. Not that I'm going to light it on fire or anything. But if it happens after I leave, I won't give two shits.

It's kind of sad, thinking about it. I don't have that many things that matter to me. Just my loud and my girl. And the couch. Fuck. I don't know how I'm going to break it to him.

"We have to get Wolf too."

"Wolf?!" Joanna screams. "You don't even know where he is!"

"I can't leave him behind. They're looking for him too. What kind of friend would I be?"

"What the hell are you guys talking about right now?" Amy asks.

I ignore her. Now is not the time to reveal that we fucked each other. My lie has been intact for the better part of an hour, and I am not about to let it unravel already.

"Where are you going to find him then?"

"You know where. First, we swing by his house. If he's not there, then we swing by the cave. And if I have to pick one place, I'd probably pick the damned cave. And if he's not there, then so be it. Okay?"

Amy flings her arms out to signify that she has no idea what we're talking about. I watch in slow motion as her towel almost falls off her body.

"We go to the cave. We find Wolf. And we get out of here. Okay?"

"Okay."

"You can come too," I say, nodding over to Amy.

"No thanks."

"Are you sure?" Joanna insists. "What if they come after you?"

"If I had to choose between looking for a wolf in a cave and getting *caught*, I'm going with getting caught."

"Not *a* wolf. The *guy*, Wolf. The guy that you slept with."

Joanna looks over at me after she stops talking and mouths an apology.

"What? I never slept with a guy named Wolf! What are you talking about?"

"Denial," I interject. "It's a pretty powerful thing."

I've got to get out of here. This is not going to end well.

"Denial of what?!"

I look over at Joanna and smile, mouthing the word denial back to her as I shake my head.

"I'm gonna go back to my place. Get my things, get my car, and then come back here. I'll call you when I'm on my way. Okay?"

"Okay, be safe! And hurry!"

"Denial of what?!"

"Denial is a river in Egypt!"

I drop the mic and run down the stairs.

Eighteen

Fuck, man. Just fuck. My hands are throbbing like a motherfucker. It's not like I have myself to blame here. I didn't do anything wrong. That was all Tony's fault. You can't just grab a girl by the wrist and assume that no one is going to do anything about it.

I'm jogging back to my place as fast as I can. I won't quite call it running because it isn't all that fast. It's just a brisk jog. My belly is still full from the oversized breakfast I plowed through about thirty minutes ago. It's sloshing around, so I'm taking it slow. I'm not about to get a cramp and fall down in the gutter and get my ass hauled away for assault. Besides, no one chases a slow jogger. I look downright innocent, as long as you don't see my bloody fists. They are somewhat of a giveaway.

I get home and sprint up the stairs, because at this point, no one's going to find me if I get a cramp on some stairs. The door opens with a jolt, and I'm half expecting a masked assassin to be hiding behind it. Instead, it's just my empty-ass apartment. I rush to my bedroom. I find my backpack, a good old Jansport. I'm shoving shit in there like I'm one of those guys in the movies that's trying to escape from someone who's after them. I learned how to pack a bag in exactly this manner from exactly those kinds of movies. *The Fugitive. The Godfather. Ladybugs (Director's Cut).*

I'm tossing clothes across the room onto my bed. I'm flinging open cabinet drawers and rummaging for toiletries, supplies, or anything that seems like it'll be useful while I'm on the lam. I'm splashing heaps of cold water onto my face from the faucet. I'm taking a handful of aspirin while staring at myself in the mirror. I'm flossing. Yes, flossing.

Dental hygiene should never be neglected, and I just finished a large meal that incidentally involved kale. It's important that I not have breakfast remnants in between my teeth before I cash in my one-way ticket out of the city. What if I'm on the road for days? What if I'm hiding out without any running water or a mirror? I'm supposed to be okay with some leftover Eggs Benedict just tagging along for the ride? No, no. I don't think so.

I grab the rest of what I think I might need, and I shove it all down into my backpack. There's still some extra room, so I jam my favorite hoodie down in there as well. It's still morning—late morning—and the sun has risen high enough that it isn't unabashedly crashing through my windows and illuminating the entire room. It's a little dark, and I like it. It's comfortable.

OK. Bag's packed. I think I've got everything. I'm standing in the doorway. Am I missing anything? I've got my loud. I've got some food. That's probably good enough. I don't have much else. The room is bare, except for the couch.

My eyes well up as I stare at the worn-out spots on the cushions. I have so many memories with this couch. I can't just leave it behind here. I've probably spent more time touching this couch than I've spent touching any other person. Maybe more than I've touched every other person combined. I'm not a very touchy guy, but when it comes to my couch, all barriers are down.

"I will remember you..." I sing to the couch.

I'm hoping it'll sing, *"Will you remember me?"* back to me, but it doesn't. It just sits there, looking brown.

"Nothing?"

Above the arm of the couch, it's giving me the cold shoulder. I suppose I'd do the same thing if it were me that was getting stranded.

"I'm sorry," I whisper.

I look at my toaster oven on the far side of the kitchen. My heart is in a freefall. I grab my phone and start texting Joanna. How much time does she *really* think we have before we have to jet? It can't possibly take that long to rent a moving truck. I bet we have time. I sure would like to have my couch and my toaster oven in whatever the next place I end up is going to be.

"Just go," the couch murmurs.

I shake my head and scour the room once more. I don't have any water, but I think I can find water somewhere along the way. It's not like we're going camping. We'll be able to stop somewhere.

"This fucking town," I mutter, slamming the door and double stepping down the stairs to the sidewalk.

I jog over to my car and throw myself into the driver's seat, tossing my backpack over the seat behind me. I hear my canister clink against my bowl, and it makes me involuntarily shudder. All I'm hoping for now as I start up my car is that one of the two didn't break. Or hell, both of them, though that seems less likely. Like most things in life, there's usually one aggressor and one submitter, and when they're both thrown into a bag, one of them is going to break the other.

It isn't too different for people. You put any two people in a situation, and one will break the other one. Maybe not always, but it happens a lot more often than both people breaking at the same time. I'm not even sure what that would look like. I try to imagine what would happen if Joanna and I were thrown into a tough situation. Then I remember that we're in one now.

I rub my jaw as I make a series of right turns down some side streets. I don't feel like I'd be the one to break. In almost any situation, I'm able to keep my cool. And while I feel like I know Joanna pretty well, I don't know her well enough to know how she's going to be when dealing with pressure-filled situations like this one. Is she pacing back and forth in her apartment? Is she chilling out on the couch, waiting for me to knock on the door? Is she already gone?

The whole thing is surreal. I pull up to her house and park way too far away from the curb for it to be considered a respectable parking job. But there's no time for respectable parking! If I can't take my couch with me, I don't give a shit about my tire-to-curb ratio.

I rap on the door to her apartment. It opens slightly, like someone didn't fully close it the last time they thought they closed it. I pause before pushing the door in all the way. Maybe that ninja is here instead, lurking behind the door. Maybe he's waiting for me to walk in so he can, you know, ninja me. I have a sixth sense about these kinds of things. I raise up my bruised fists and tap-kick the door in with my foot. I'm ready to strike, though I know it's going to hurt like a motherfucker to punch someone again.

I creep into the foyer, and then I dart out past the door, grabbing it quickly and slamming it shut. There's no one behind it. Maybe my sixth sense needs to be recalibrated.

"Luke?" Joanna calls out. "Is that you?"

"Yeah!"

Motherfucker. I'm so stupid. I'm obviously the one who left the damned door slightly ajar. What good am I? My girlfriend's in danger, and I can't even close her apartment door all the way shut. Maybe Tony was right. Maybe I am too dumb for anyone to ever trust me with anything.

"Come on up."

"Coming."

When I get upstairs, Amy's still in her towel. This chick apparently doesn't want to get dressed today.

"Laundry day?"

"I just got out of the shower, relax."

There isn't a mirror anywhere that I can see, but I know exactly what my face looks like. It's an over-exaggerated confused face, like I'm so absurdly perplexed by what she had just said that I can't even possibly fathom that it's true. She just got out of the shower when I had gotten here about a half an hour ago. The statute of limitations on towel-wearing is running dangerously short. It might already be fully exhausted. You can't just wear the towel all day. Even the towel knows that. It'll just give up and fall on the floor eventually.

"You get everything?" Joanna asks, causing me to turn my head.

"Yeah. I guess. I got everything I *planned on* getting."

No one asks me what I mean by this. Sometimes you try to bait people for a reaction, and it works. Sometimes a girl wears a towel for a fucking hour and doesn't even flinch when you leave a dangling invitation to ask a follow up. Clearly, neither of them cares about my relationship with the couch.

"Okay. Well," Joanna announces, walking over to Amy and stretching out her arms. "We're getting out of here. I'll call you when we're settled. Okay?"

They hug. I'm staring at the knot on Amy's towel. It's right in the line of fire, all four of their breasts pressing against each other and sandwiching the only thing that's keeping the towel from falling to the ground. I inhale sharply and hold my breath. Joanna's chin is resting on Amy's shoulder and her eyes are pressed tight. It's an oddly emotional hug. And I'm just trying to not get hard while watching it.

"Please do. And don't worry about me, okay? I'm sure it'll be fine. No one is going to suspect a thing."

"Call me if anything comes up though. Like if you need me, call me. Or text. Just let me know if you need us for anything."

That "*us*" is a little concerning to me. I don't have any intentions of helping her out, even if the towel falls straight through the floor and into the garage below us. Even if Joanna finds out that we slept with each other. Even if anything. I barely have enough of an attention span to take care of one girl, and even that is questionable.

They're holding each other for a while, and I can't tell if the knot is getting stronger or weaker because of it. It's possible that it's staying neutral, but like I said before, when there are two things in a situation, there's always one aggressor and one submitter. I wonder which one's going to win in this one, the knot or the force of their hug? One pair of breasts or another?

They pull apart from each other, and the towel stays put. I'm simultaneously disappointed and relieved. Amy turns toward me and adjusts the top of her towel. She flashes a coy, little smile. I think she knows what I'm thinking. I actually think she's stayed in her towel this whole time just to fuck with me. I turn my head and look at the stairs behind me.

"We should go?"

Joanna nods, and Amy does too. So I nod as well. I don't want to be left out.

"Amy, nice to meet you again. Good luck with your laundry."

She shakes her head. I walk forward and grab Joanna's backpack before turning around and jogging down the stairs. I hear her following behind me. When I get to the bottom and see the door, I cringe. Damned sixth sense. I can't believe it failed. I should have warmed it up before I tried using it.

"Did you just stay up there the whole time I was gone?"

"Yeah, why?"

Why? Because I'm secretly hoping that *you* had left the door open.

"Just wondering."

I turn around and face her as we get down to the curb. We're standing behind a fence that creates a little carport where Amy's car is parked. The sidewalk is on the other side of the fence, and as I look into Joanna's eyes, I forget all about everything else that I'm supposed to be thinking about. I lean forward and kiss her. And then I kiss her again. And again. And then I wrap my arms tightly around her and squeeze her back with my hands.

"What was that for?"

I don't have an answer, so I make one up.

"Nothing. I just missed you."

She smiles.

"You're sweet."

We step out of the carport and walk over to the car. I hold her door open as she sits down in the passenger seat. I look up and down the sidewalk before shutting the door. There's no one around us. I walk around the front of the car and hop into my seat, hoping she didn't notice my terrible parking job.

"Alright."

"Alright," she repeats.

"Let's go find my moronic friend and get the fuck out of here."

"Amen!"

I speed off down the road and keep eyeing my rear view mirror, cautious of anyone that seems to be tailing me for longer than a couple of blocks. I know nothing about how to lose a tail, and I don't even know if that is a real thing, but I'm staying aware just in case.

"Is this a secret route or something?"

"I have a sixth sense about traffic. Just trust me."

Then we turn a corner and come face-to-face with a wall of brake lights.

"Fuck me."

"Yeah, you're a regular Bruce Willis."

I laugh.

"He wasn't the one with the sixth sense, you know. It was the kid."

"I actually never saw it. But I generally know what happens."

"Well, either way...your joke was much better than my stupid intuition."

The cars ahead are slowly creeping forward. We're on a small side street that crosses ambitiously across four lanes of traffic and then keeps on going. I can't tell if everyone in the line is going all the way across, but even if it's just one of them, it's going to fuck the rest of us over, as we're all going to have to wait regardless.

"When was the last time you heard from Wolf? Did you try calling him when you went home to get your stuff?"

"I didn't. I just packed as fast as I could."

I fish my phone out of my pocket, and my unfinished message to Joanna is still on the screen. I close out of the message and open my contacts to dial Wolf's number. It rings four or five times and then drops into voicemail. I hang up.

"Nothing. But still. I owe it to him to at least go look."

"I know. I know."

"Let's just go straight to the cave. Forget his apartment."

A car inches up farther ahead, and the whole line contracts like a snake digesting a mouse.

"Should I be worried about him, do you think?"

"You're the one with the sixth sense, Bruce. What's your gut telling you? *I see dead people?*"

"Jesus. No. I think he's just oblivious, or maybe his phone died. But I don't think he's hurt or worse, no. He's got too many of those Boy Scout skills to make a mess of his situation like that. He can take care of himself."

"You keep talking about the Boy Scouts like he was a Marine or something. They don't really teach you *that* much in Boy Scouts."

"He seems to know a lot about that kind stuff."

"I hope so, for his sake."

"You know, maybe he just found the rest of the universe," I remind her.

"Yeah, maybe."

"Maybe in that universe there's a stop sign at every intersection so that we don't have to deal with shit like this. Maybe he's just down there, laughing his ass off at us right now."

She props her arm up on the edge of the window and rests her chin in her hand. She looks so pretty, just sitting there doing nothing at all. Little bursts of emotion are dashing through my heart. A gust of wind blows in through the window, and all I can smell is a nearby jasmine plant in full bloom. The combination of Joanna and that scent makes me want to just die. Everything is so perfect. Except for the traffic. That also makes me want to die, but in a different way.

Eventually, we get across the intersection and continue on toward the trailhead. At the end of a windy, long road, I spot Wolf's car parked alongside the edge of the pavement.

"That's him!" I shout, pointing straight out the window. "I mean, his car. That's his car!"

"You know, isn't it possible that he got caught?"

"Caught how?"

"Like *caught* caught. You know. By your secret housing board illuminati or whatever the hell you guys all are."

"Hey, don't lump me in with them. I am a fugitive on the lam with my woman!"

I always wanted to say some version of that sentence. My life is getting more and more complete by the moment. She laughs and pats me on the knee.

"I know, I know. But honestly, isn't it more likely than anything that someone found him and dragged him off to who knows where and that's why you haven't heard from him for days? His car is practically a giant red flag saying, *Hey, come get me, I'm in here!*"

"But then why would they ask me to go look for him and bring him in?"

"I dunno. Strength in numbers, maybe. May as well have you looking along with them."

"And then when they found him, they just didn't tell me and let me keep thinking he was still out there?"

"Sure. Maybe it's a test. To see if you're still looking."

"I don't know. I don't think they'd test me. I think they knew exactly what I was going to do, and that's why Tony came looking for me." I look down at my hands and at the bruises that his face gave my knuckles. "I think he's out there somewhere. They didn't catch him."

I make a U-turn and park my car right behind his.

"I guess we're about to find out."

"Do you have any weed?" I ask.

She nods. We get out of my car, and I lead Joanna down a path that you can barely see from the side of the road. Its entrance is hidden with thicket and brush and maybe even a spider web or two. She seems like a pretty tough chick, so I'm figuring that she isn't going to sweat a little muck along the way. I try my best to brush back the branches to clear a path for her to follow me, but half of the time, they just snap back at her before she can make it past them.

After about 20 minutes, we're starting to reach an area that feels familiar. I can tell that we're getting close. I scan around for signs that Wolf is nearby or that he had been here recently, but I don't see anything. My soccer skills are not coming in handy at the moment. No one needs me to do a throw-in or kick a corner. A part of me regrets that I had never been in the Boy Scouts. We'd probably be on a beach somewhere if I had, laughing it up and cheersing over our escape.

"Over here!" Joanna yells.

I'm thinking she's right behind me, so when I turn around, I'm a little surprised to see her as far away as she is.

"What is it?"

"A big backpack and a giant gaping hole! Come here!"

I run over to her and look down at the cave. It looks even bigger than I remember it. At the edge of the entrance is a pile of supplies.

"Yeah, that's his stuff. I thought there would be more of it though."

"It doesn't seem like that much, does it?"

"Hmm. Also..."

I look around and spot a folded blue tarp over at the base of a nearby tree.

"Shit. He told me he made a cover to hide the cave so that no one else would find it. Look over there."

I point at the tarp, and Joanna frowns.

"So what does that mean? Is he down there?"

"Wolf!" I yell, my face angling down toward the cave. "Yooooooo! Wolf!"

My voice echoes a deep, guttural echo. It sounds almost robotic. It isn't a pretty echo like when you're climbing a tall mountain and there are waterfalls all around you. I listen intently, but there's no reply, so I yell again.

Suddenly, there's some guy's voice behind us.

"Hello."

I spin around, and there are these two guys just standing there. They're both wearing neon yellow running jackets and some equally neon shorts. They look like they're dressed up for Halloween as a pair of lightning bolts.

"What the hell? Were you here this whole time?" I ask.

"We were just hiking on by when we saw the two of you."

My body tenses up.

"Do you work for The Board?"

They look at each other and shrug.

"The what?"

"Nothing. Never mind."

We're all just standing here for a few moments. Other than the wisp of the wind through the trees around us, it's silent. Joanna eyes them suspiciously.

"So," one of the men begins to ask. "Did I hear you yell out for a wolf? I don't think there are any wild wolves in these forests. They're not native to these parts."

"Native? No, I'm just looking for a friend. His *name* is Wolf."

I can't get over their neon jackets. They're downright ridiculous. I didn't know that a piece of fabric could possibly be so bright.

"And you think he's down in that hole?"

"I mean, I know that he went down there a few days ago, but I haven't heard from him since."

"We're afraid that something might have happened to him," Joanna adds.

"A few days?"

"Yeah. Three days ago."

The man walks over to the edge of the cave and peers down inside.

"I'm afraid to tell you this, but three days down in a cave this size? Your friend might not be alive right now. Have you contacted any authorities?"

"No, not yet. I don't think he's dead. I'm going to go down there and try to find him."

The men look at each other, and one of them frowns. The other one is emotionless. Joanna is staring down at the ground.

"Why do you look for the living among the dead?" the man asks.

"I told you, he's not dead. But thanks for your concern. We're fine here. Nice to meet you."

The men shrug, and I turn my back to them as they walk away.

"What the fuck?" I mouth.

Joanna shakes her head.

"What now?"

I look at the edge of the cave, and my eyes follow a series of ropes that lead from the ground over to a large tree nearby.

"Shit. Look at that. He's definitely down there."

I point at the ropes.

"You don't know that for sure though. They could have left them behind when, you know, *if* they took him away."

"That doesn't sound right to me. If The Board came and found him, I'm sure they would have taken all his gear with them. You know?"

"Yeah. OK. What are you going to do then?"

I stare down the hole and into the darkness beyond what I can make out.

"Fuck me. I'm going down to find him. I have to. Let me take a look in his backpack and see what he's still got up here."

I kneel down beside the bag and unzip it as wide as I can. He has it packed tight and orderly like a good Boy Scout would have packed it. There's some more rope, but I'm pretty sure I won't need any more than what's already hanging down over the edge. There are two headlamps and a pack of batteries to go along with them. A pair of goggles is lying out on the leaves alongside something that looks like a harness. A bunch of flares are bundled up and held together with some thick elastic bands. There's also a small tank of oxygen, a few rolled up newspapers, and an orange.

I hold up the orange and wave it at Joanna.

"Maybe I toss this down there to give him something to eat?"

"How are you always so laid back?"

"I'm not, not right now. I'm scared as hell. I'm just trying to lighten the mood. You know, distract myself. I don't want to go down in this fucking hole. Look at it!"

"So don't? Why do you have to?"

"I don't have to. But if he's down there, he's going to be down there forever, and no one is ever going to find him. If that happened to me, I'd want someone to come looking for me. I don't care how deep the hole is. I want someone looking for me. For my parents' sake. For your sake."

"Yeah...I just don't want you getting hurt!"

"I don't think I can live with my conscience if I don't try to go after him. He asked me to come with him, and I refused. I owe him to at least give it a try."

"I guess."

"Besides, you're here with me. You and I can keep talking to each other all along the way. If something happens to me, you can go get help."

"But we're not even supposed to *be* here, Luke. Who is going to help me?"

I put my hands on both of her shoulders, and I look straight into her eyes.

"You're not going to need to go anywhere. I'll be fine. Okay?"

She wraps her arms around my waist and hugs me.

"It feels like a bad idea."

"Oh, it is a bad idea. But I've got to go looking for him. He would do the same for me!"

She squeezes me tight and then pushes me away from her as if to signal that I'm clear for takeoff. I stand here for a bit. I'm motionless and dumb. I don't know the first thing about descending into a cave by rope. I play around with some of the carabineers that are still attached to his pack, and I begin to fashion a little seat out of the rope and the harness. I don't know if it looks like I know what I'm doing, but I'm completely winging it. Joanna just kneels beside me, nodding and lightly rubbing my back.

When the harness is as strung together as I think I can get it, I wriggle my body into it and tighten all the various places that I can tighten it. I don't know. This feels like a horseshit harness to me. It actually feels just like the one that I wore when we went skydiving. I grab a headlamp and strap it to my head, testing the light a few times as I look down into the cave. It's bright, but I still can't see much more than 20 feet down. The side of the cave appears to angle in slightly. I don't know if that's good or bad. I don't even know what the fuck a carabineer is supposed to do. I just have them clipped to various points on the harness to make me feel better about what I'm doing.

"Don't forget these," Joanna says, handing me the goggles.

"In case I want to go for a swim down there?"

"You never know. Be prepared!"

She holds up three fingers and raises her arm into the sky. I don't know what the hell she's doing, but I smile anyway.

"I'm as prepared as I'll ever be."

I look behind me and down into the cave.

"Fucking Wolf," I mutter.

I edge my way toward the cave, grabbing the rope tight with both hands. Joanna kisses me again, and then she waves me off. I yell out Wolf's name once more just in case. Still no response.

"Here we go."

I start lowering myself down, and I realize right away that it isn't really that hard. It isn't even that scary. I don't know what I was worried about. I'm descending pretty quickly, and the headlamp is providing more than enough light for me to see what I'm doing.

"How's it going?"

"Fine, just fine! It's really not that bad. This harness thing works pretty well."

"So you did it right?"

"Sure."

I lower myself farther and farther, looking beneath me every few feet to see if I can make out the surface of the water at the bottom. Eventually I start to see my light reflecting off something.

"I think I see the bottom!"

"And?"

"No Wolf yet. But let me get down there first."

When I get within a few feet of the water, the stagnant smell of the cave takes over my entire nose and maybe even a part of my mouth. I don't know what I was expecting it would be like, but it smells like a swamp that's taking a shit into another swamp. My right foot touches the water first. I flinch, half expecting it to disintegrate my shoe like it's a tub of acid.

"I'm at the bottom! Can you still hear me?"

"Yeah. I can hear you, no problem at all!"

"That wasn't so bad, right?"

She doesn't say anything. Now is not the time for nonverbal communication.

"Right?"

"Right. Do you see him?"

I look around as I lower my legs into the water. Where I'm hanging, it's probably only six feet wide, and it's making me claustrophobic as fuck. I have to ignore it.

I lower my body farther into the water until I'm submerged up past my waist. I angle my head down. I'm trying to stare under the surface of the water, but the reflection is making it impossible to see anything.

"Hang on!"

I turn off the headlamp and watch as everything around me immediately turns black. I sit still for a moment, allowing my eyes to adjust to the darkness. I've already seen everything that's around me, so I'm not too scared. If anything, the lack of light is making my claustrophobia a little better since I can't actually see how small it is. Way down beneath the surface of the water, I see a small glowing light.

"I think I see something!"

"What is it?"

"I think he's down here! I think he's underwater right now!"

"Alive?"

"Yeah! I see his light, I think. Yeah, I think so! He must be using one of those oxygen tanks!"

"Really?"

I look up at the opening, and all I see is a tiny crescent of sky. Maybe it's the forest's thumbnail. Joanna must be somewhere away from the edge or perhaps on the side that I can't see.

"I guess these goggles are going to come in handy after all."

"You're seriously going to swim down there? Why don't you just wait until he comes up?"

"Nah! I'm really good at holding my breath, and anyway, I want to check it out. It's kind of cool here now that I'm down here."

"Okay, but be careful!"

I look back down, and the light continues to twinkle at me. I strap the goggles over my eyes and look up again toward the crescent above. I see Joanna's faint outline through the blurry, plastic goggles. She must have moved closer to the edge.

"You be careful too! I can see you. You're too close to the edge! Aren't you afraid?"

"Terrified!"

I smile just thinking about her face.

"I love you," I yell out, smiling wide and feeling secure in the pitch darkness around me, like no judgment can come my way since I'm invisible.

"I love you too!"

"Okay, here it goes! I'll be back in a little bit!"

I turn the headlamp back on and take a few deep breaths in through my nose before exhaling hard. Then I take in a deeper breath through my mouth and submerge my head under the water.

I swim and I swim and I swim, globs of murk floating past my head for the first few feet. Then it substantially clears up, and I can see the contours of the walls as I swim farther down, the cool blue light of the LED headlamp casting shadows along the jagged edges of the rocks. The pressure's increasing in my ears, but I keep on swimming. The light's getting closer and closer, and I'm more certain than anything that it's Wolf, staring right back at me. I can feel it. My sixth sense is finally working. I knew it just needed a few warm ups.

Unfortunately, my lung capacity isn't what I thought it'd be. It's time to abort. I have to turn around and head back to the surface. I push my head above the water, and a strand of moss drapes over my goggles.

"Whew!" I yell, sucking in a deep mouthful of air. "That was fun!"

"Is he down there?"

"Yeah, he is. But I didn't get all the way down to him. I had to come back up to breathe."

"Did he see you?"

"He had to have seen me. Hang on."

I take a few deep, hard breaths, inhaling and exhaling as I arch my back. I got this technique from a Hulk Hogan movie. I don't know if it's any good or not.

"Okay! I'm going in again!"

"Alright, but how about this is the last time, okay? Don't forget that we still have to get the hell out of here, remember? I don't like being stranded up here by myself!"

She's got a point. I kind of forgot all about the fact that we're on the run. The excitement of making it down to the bottom made me lose track of everything else that's going on.

"Okay, last time! Love you!"

I take a deep breath, much deeper than my first one, and I shove my head underwater again. This time I'm swimming faster, now knowing how much space remains between Wolf and me. I'm paddling hard and feeling no pressure in my ears, not yet. I can keep swimming for a while. I'm not panicking over the lack of air. Down below and to the right, I can see his headlamp. It's already closer than it was when I had turned around the last time. I keep on paddling, and now the pressure's starting to build in my ears. The light's getting larger and larger. It's really bright. I close my eyes. He's probably doing the same thing as well. These lights are intense.

One of my ears pops. Water surges into my ear canal, and it feels like little wet worms are writhing into my head. Now I'm acutely aware of the capacity of my lungs, and the panic is slowly starting to creep in. I don't have much more time that I can keep swimming before I'm going to have to turn around. The pressure feels like Yokozuna is sitting on a pillow on top of my head.

I paddle deeper. The light's getting closer and closer until it's basically the only thing that I can see. The cave has narrowed down to just a few feet in diameter. I can easily touch every part of the walls around me, but I don't because it freaks me out.

Jesus. The light's so bright that I'm holding my eyes shut as I keep paddling toward it. I don't know what I'm going to do when I get to him. He'd better turn the damned thing off soon, or I might go blind.

Air bubbles start to escape from my mouth. I'm so close that I can't stop now, though I'm getting a little dizzy. Just a little bit further. I keep swimming. Even with my eyes sealed shut, the light is permeating through my eyelids.

Fuck it.

I stop paddling and open my eyes. All I see is light. Shockingly white light, brighter than anything that I've ever seen before. I'm just floating now, staring straight ahead. It's like I'm frozen. The light is numbing, and I can't feel my body. I can't think. I can only stare forward at this startlingly white light that's pouring into every single particle of my retinas. I just keep floating, helpless and without thought.

Something grabs me by the hand and begins to pull me. I recoil slightly at first, but then I quickly give in. I don't have the strength to resist; I used it all to get down here in the first place. Whatever is pulling me is stronger than I am anyway, so I let go.

The light engulfs me. Everything has disappeared, and as my body is pulled down, my hand breaks through the surface of the water. There's cool air on my hand.

The fuck?

My body gets pulled farther and farther until my whole arm is out of the water. Then my head emerges above the water, and I take a huge breath, bigger than I've ever taken in my entire life. It's like I have new lungs. A massive surge of relief rushes through my veins.

I open my eyes, and I see Wolf. He smiles at me and puts his hand on my shoulder.

"You made it."

I look around for a moment before my eyes roll to the back of my head.

Nineteen

I'm getting the feeling back in my toes first. I feel them tingle, like little, tiny spiders are crawling around under my skin. As it spreads up to my feet, the tingling gets stronger. Then my fingers start to regain their feelings. Then my arms, then my legs. Slowly, my body is waking up from what feels like a giant shockwave that paralyzed me. It's like I got hit by a lightning bolt and now here I am, remembering what it's like to be alive.

My eyes flutter open, and I marvel at the exact color of the sky when I first see it. It's an iridescent blue. It shimmers, kind of, in a way. But then I think about what shimmering looks like, and I realize that I'm probably searching for another word. This place, it looks familiar, but it's also like something that I've never seen before. It's a strange combination of foreign and familiar. Is that shimmering? I don't know. My eyelids flick open and shut, and each time I see the sky, I can't believe its intensity. I slowly begin to prop my arms by my sides, and then I push my body upright into a seated position. I look around again.

"You've got to be kidding me," I whisper.

Wolf smiles. I think he might have been smiling the whole time.

"Nope."

We're sitting on a beach. It's one of Malibu's main beaches, and I recognize it almost immediately, or at least I think I do.

"What happened?" I ask.

"I told you."

I wait for him to continue, but he doesn't. He looks over his shoulder and continues smiling as a couple walks by along the foamy line that marks where the tide had just lapped ashore.

"How did I get here?"

"You swam down into the cave," he reminds me, but I already know that.

"Yeah, but how did I get *here?*"

I look around and reaffirm that it's the same beach that I've been coming to since I got to town. It has to be. It has the same contours and positioning between all of the same visible landmarks. There's the replica lighthouse on the deck of that restaurant on the cliff. Off to the side, there's the old pier. And beyond them, I see the dunes and the stupid American flag umbrella that's always planted on the hillside.

"You swam down to come find me. And look," he waves his arms around. "You found me, right?"

"That doesn't make sense."

"I wouldn't worry about sense right now."

He's unusually calm. I push myself to my feet and begin to pace around the area where he's sitting.

"This feels very familiar."

"It should."

"No, I know. Like, this feels like something I know. It feels..."

"Sad?"

He knows. How does he know?

"Yeah. It feels sad. Like I was sad here in this spot before. Not like I'm sad here now, but like there's a memory that's here that just, you know, makes me feel sad."

"That makes sense."

"Does it? What makes sense about it? Why won't you just tell me what's going on?"

"What fun would it be if I just told you?" he asks, smiling. "You made it, Luke. Do you see that? You made it."

"Made what?"

"Well, all of this. But I meant that you made it here."

"Dude. Where is *here*?"

"Think about why you feel sad here. Do you remember? Do you remember what happened here and why this place is important to you? Of all places, why did you end up *here*?"

I look up and down the beach, but I only see the couple walking along the shoreline. Do I know them? I don't think so. They're older. As I stare at them, it makes me feel a little better for some reason, like they've made it a long time through their relationship and this beach is something that they can enjoy together after all those years.

"I'm so confused right now. I was just down in that cave looking for you. I swam toward your headlamp, and it was so fucking bright that I had to close my eyes. It practically blinded me. And now, now I'm here. On the beach where..."

I stop pacing.

"Now you remember," Wolf grins.

"Yeah."

With a nod, he beckons for me to tell him, to say it out loud.

"This is the place where we saw that beached whale."

Wolf springs up and slaps me on the back.

"There you go! And why is that important?"

"Because it made me sad."

"No. *Why* did it make you sad?"

I think about it for a while.

"I dunno. I still feel sad about it. That poor whale."

"Luke, why? Why does that make you sad?"

"She was just lost, you know? She didn't deserve to get stranded on the beach by herself. No one deserves that. She was probably having a good day, just swimming around. And then one wrong move took her down the wrong path..."

Wolf turns his body and scans the ocean. He points at a very specific location.

"Dude, take a look out there."

I stand alongside him, and I try to follow the direction of his finger as best as I can. I don't see anything except the ocean.

"What am I looking at?"

"Look! There!" he shouts.

The forked tail of a whale flips out of the water and reveals itself to us before it sinks back into the sea.

"Is that her?!"

Wolf smiles as he stares off into the ocean.

"How the hell did you know that was going to happen?"

"You made this place, dude. This is *all* you."

"What does that even mean?"

"Everything around you. This is all from you."

"From me how? Am I dreaming? Is this all just some lucid dream? Did we smoke DMT or something?"

"No, we didn't smoke DMT. I didn't have anything to do with this. Other than leading you here, I guess. I did do that. But it really wasn't me; it was you."

"Help me out, man. I'm so lost. Is this...were you right? Is this another universe or something? Your cave wormhole inner space thing was right, or somewhat right? We stumbled upon a vortex that led us to another reality? That's what this is?"

He laughs.

"Sure."

"What do you mean, sure? What the hell is going on?"

"You died, dude."

My heart sinks.

"I what?"

"You died. You died swimming down to come find me."

"Then what is this? This is the afterlife?"

"Sure."

"THIS?!"

"Hey, I died too. Alright?"

"Well, yeah. Obviously."

He laughs.

"Obviously."

"I mean that if you're in the afterlife, then obviously you're dead too."

He shrugs.

"That's not really how it works."

I sit back down. I'm tracing a circle around in the sand. There's no one else on the beach other than us and that couple, and even they are barely in sight anymore. I shake my head, not in disbelief, but more in confusion.

"Then how does it really work? Actually, how do you know all this anyway? Tell me what happened with you when you went down there!"

"I died too."

"Yeah, and?"

"And I'm in my own afterlife."

He's standing over me, and I'm squinting as I stare up at him. His body's blocking out most of the sun, and I'm left staring at a silhouette. His face is shrouded in his own shadow.

"You have your own afterlife?"

He shrugs.

"I didn't make the rules."

"But you do have your own afterlife?"

"Yeah."

"And it's not this one?"

He looks around and smiles.

"No offense, but no. This is not my afterlife."

"So then what are you doing here?" I ask. "How can you be here but not be here?"

"You'll get used to it."

"Dude, how long have you been dead for? You're like the goddamned afterlife expert up in here! Except you don't answer half of my damned questions."

"Why do you think that is?"

I roll my eyes.

"Fuck you. I don't know!"

"I'm here...you know what? You can just think of me as a guide. I'm your guide as you get used to this. I can help answer your questions, or I can point you in the right direction when I can't answer your questions. That sort of stuff."

"Alright. Then please *guide* me to some understanding, guide. Is this heaven?"

"No."

"Okay. Is this hell?"

"No."

"Are you in heaven or hell?"

"No."

"So they don't exist, or...?"

He shrugs.

"It's just an afterlife. You had a life. Your life ended. Now you are after your life."

I stand up and brush the sand off the back of my pants.

"I can't believe I went down that fucking hole to find you, and I just ended up dead! What kind of justice is that? I should have listened to Joanna and not gone down there in the first place. Goddammit!"

"Who's Joanna?"

I forgot that we haven't spoken since I found out her real name.

"Amy with the tight butthole."

"Joanna?"

"Long story. But goddammit! I should have just listened to her, and none of this would have happened!"

"That's not how it works. Just relax. You did what you did, and it got you where it got you. It was what was meant to happen. That's how it all works."

"I was meant to die by drowning in a hole where no one is going to ever find my body? How is that my fate? What did I do to deserve that? I was a good guy. I didn't hurt anybody. Not anybody who didn't deserve it at least."

I look down at my hands, and there's no blood from Tony's face, no bruises or scrapes. Wolf shrugs again.

"I'm sure they found your body."

"That's beside the point. I could be *alive* right now if I had just stayed out of that cave. If *you* stayed out of that cave."

"You wouldn't be alive right now. You did what you did. It's done. In fact, it was always done. It was done before it was done. There was a plan, and that was always the plan. You get it?"

"Does this mean there *is* a God?"

Wolf turns away and mumbles something that I can't quite hear.

"Because if there is a— "

"What's so good about being alive anyway?" he snarls as he spins his body back toward me. "You followed me here. This is what happened! I mean, it's natural to have this reaction. I get it. But, you have to trust me. This is where you're supposed to be right now. This is what was meant for you. And you can't change what's meant for you. It just is what it is."

"Who's here?" I ask.

He sighs.

"This one will take a little bit of adjustment to get used to. Again, I don't make the rules..."

I lean my head back and stare straight up at the sky. It's still that same surreal blue tone, and I let myself get lost in it as I motion for him to lay it on me.

"From the time that you were born until the time that you died, that's the time span."

"Okay."

"Anybody who died during that time span is here."

"Anybody?"

"Yep. If you knew them, if you didn't know them. If they died when you were one day old or if they died an hour before you did."

"That's it? That's the guest list for my after party?"

He laughs.

"I like that. After party! That's a good one."

I smile my first smile since I got here. It feels like learning a new emotion all over again.

"How many people is that? How many people die each year?"

"It's about a billion and a half."

"What? Each year?"

"No, in total. Somewhere around there. It's something like 50 million people that die each year, give or take."

I give him a puzzled look.

"Wikipedia."

"So then where is everybody?" I ask, looking around at the desolate beach.

"A billion people isn't as much as it sounds like when you've got the whole world to play with."

I'm still staring up at the sky, trying to soak it all in.

"My parents aren't here then."

"Right."

"But my grandparents are."

"If they died when you were alive, yeah. They're here somewhere."

"How would I find them?"

"It works like you'd expect."

"I really didn't expect any of this."

"Well, basically, you just walk around a lot, and eventually you find people. It just happens."

"That's weird."

He shrugs.

"You sure are shrugging a lot for someone who's supposed to be my guide. Don't you know anything? What good is a guide if you just shrug all the fucking time?"

"It's not like I applied for this job."

"Well, it's not like I wanted to die swimming after your ass!" I yell. "Why did you have to go down there, man? Why did you have to do this to us?"

I'm mad all over again.

"What happened is what happened. You'll get used to it. Trust me."

"Trust you," I scoff.

"You're not listening to me. I'm not even really *here*. I'm in my own afterlife. I'm just your guide for now."

"Well, you look pretty *here* to me."

"I am. But I'm not. It works like that."

"Yeah, well, I want to be *not here* too."

"Trust me, man. You want to be here. It's great here."

"Fuck you with the *trust me* shit!"

He shrugs. I punch him in the arm, and he smiles.

"It's good to see you again."

It occurs to me only in this moment that by the logic he's describing, he's in my afterlife, but I'm not in his.

"Who was your guide?" I ask.

"Some guy. I didn't even know him."

"Why did I get you?"

"I don't know, man. I really don't. But I'm glad I get to see you. I've just been hanging out with random people for a while."

"How does time work here?"

"There's no such thing."

"Well, I definitely like that. How does eating work?"

"The same as before."

"Who makes the food?"

"I don't know. Probably the same people that made it before."

"Do you still have to go to the bathroom?"

"If you want to."

"Do you have to eat?"

"Only if you want to."

"Can I drive my car?"

"Luke. You can do whatever you want here. It's your afterlife."

"But who runs the gas station? Who drills for the oil? Who fixes my car when it breaks down? Who makes the car in the first place?"

"I don't know."

"Won't we just run out of shit eventually?"

"That's not how it works. Nothing *runs out* here."

"So then how does money work?"

"What's money?" he asks.

"There's no money here?"

He shakes his head.

"You always just have what you want. You don't need money. There's no such thing. There never was."

"What do you mean, *there never was*? I remember money. It existed."

Is it possible that a world could exist without money? That means markets without quantity. That means no abundance and no scarcity. No better or worse. It's the exact opposite of the world that we just left.

"Isn't it ironic that the thing that brought us together in the first place—the same thing that sparked the chain of events that ultimately killed us—it's something that couldn't even exist here?"

"That's not irony," he corrects me.

"Fine, isn't it coincidental then?"

"It's not a coincidence. That was the whole point."

"The whole point of what?"

"The point of you and I getting brought in to work for The Board in the first place. That wasn't a coincidence. It was a lesson."

"I don't think I learned a lesson."

"Look around you. This is the lesson."

I look around, but I just see the beach. It hasn't changed. There isn't a textbook's worth of information scrawled out on the sand.

"No money," I repeat. "So then, how do ugly guys get girls around here?"

"Their personalities," Wolf laughs.

"No way. So basically you have to be good-looking, or you'll never get laid around here? No wonder you like it so much."

"It's not like that."

"Yeah, maybe not in my afterlife. But I'm sure in yours, it's just a nonstop pussy parade."

He shakes his head.

"Nobody has sex here."

"What?! Ever?"

"You actually don't have a dick anymore."

Like any guy in this situation, I immediately grab for it to assure myself that he's just joking, but he isn't.

"Oh, fuck me!"

"Negative."

"Why the hell did they take that away?"

"I don't know."

"So I just don't want to fuck anymore or something?"

"I don't know. Do you want to fuck right now?"

"Well, no. Not right now. But I just got here. And it's just you and me on this beach."

"You'll get used to it."

"Fucking bullshit," I mutter. "How do I take a piss?"

"It all comes out of your ass now."

"Great."

"It's much better. You'll see."

"No sex and no pissing. These are, like, two of my top five favorite things!"

"Well, then I would say that you need to get some new favorite things."

I shake my head and stare off at the thin line between the sky and the ocean. It's so beautiful here that despite all the shock of being dropped into a place that I didn't even think existed, I'm not completely jarred out of my mind. There's a raw beauty in everything around me, and it encourages me in a way that I didn't think was possible. I rub the area where my dick used to be, and it's just a seamless continuation of my pubic area. My encouragement fades away.

"Does the sun still set?"

"If you want it to."

"Jesus."

"I still go by Wolf," he replies with a laugh.

I keep asking him questions, and he keeps patiently answering them to the best of his ability. I don't know what other people's guides are like, but I'm glad that he's mine. As annoyed as I initially was when I was coming to terms with what had happened, I know in my heart that I don't blame him. I didn't have to go looking for him. I did what I did, and I owe my consequences only to myself. There's no reason to blame anyone for your actions other than yourself.

"Is there loud?"

"Hella loud."

I breathe a deep sigh of relief.

"Then I should be fine."

"I'm surprised that wasn't your first question."

"Me too."

"You're a changed man."

"I'll say. I'm a man with no dick."

He laughs.

"That is quite the change."

Another couple is walking along the beach toward us. They're holding hands, and I can hear them laughing as they walk.

"So I'm the last person that got here?"

"The very last one."

"No matter what?"

MIKE AVITABILE

He nods and I frown, staring at the couple as they get closer to us.

"So I'm never going to see Joanna again."

"A billion people," he reminds me. "That's plenty of fish."

"I just told her that I loved her."

"Well, damn."

"Never again?"

"Well, remember...you'll be in her afterlife. You know, whenever she dies."

Thank you, afterlife, for the consolation prize. In a way, I'm happy that at least one of us will get to spend time with the other person. But I selfishly want that person to be me. What good is something that I don't experience? And besides, she might live another 50 years. She'll be so over me by then, she might not even remember who I was.

"So I'm really not in yours?" I ask.

"Nope."

"And you're not really here?"

"I'm here. But I'm also not here."

"Are you going to leave?"

"Nope. Unless you want me to."

"Does the you in your afterlife know about the you here?"

He shrugs.

"I guess this is going to take some getting used to."

"For sure."

"Do you have any bud?"

"Oh, for sure."

We sit down and puff on a joint that he produces from the front pocket of his hoodie. It's a little too convenient, and it tastes a little too pure. Each hit burns exactly how I want it to burn. Each breath I take is laced with exactly what I want it to be laced with. The sun twinkles overhead and provides the perfect amount of light.

"Where do you buy this?"

"You always just have what you want. You don't have to buy anything here."

I stare up at the sky. It's my new favorite color.

"I want the sky to always be this color."

Wolf lays his palms out in front of us and raises them both toward the sky.

"Done."

Twenty

"It was all a dream."

Wolf's shaking his head.

"That's it?"

"Yeah, that's it. What?"

"How can that be anyone's favorite opening line to a song?"

"Dude, first of all, that line is sick. How can you not like it? Second, and probably more importantly, haven't we already had this conversation?"

"Did we?"

"Yeah, I'm pretty sure that it was with you."

"Okay, then that's probably why I brought it up again," he moans. "So you could come up with a better answer than what you had the first time."

"You don't even remember what I said the first time."

"You are 100% correct. I don't. I'm not sure I even remember having the conversation before."

"It's hard to remember what it was like before."

We walk along in silence for a little while. Then he asks me the same question that he's been asking me practically every day since I got here.

"So have you gotten to the point where you actually realize that this is far better than the life you were living?"

I nod, but it's half-hearted, and he sees it. He'll ask me again tomorrow. I know he will. Right now, we're hiking in the forest. It seems like we're always in the forest. I can't get enough of it. I think I might have an obsession. I've been here every day since I arrived.

I hold my arms out and slide my hands across the trunks of the trees that I pass, rubbing the bark slowly and deliberately. My senses are heightened here, accentuated in a way that I didn't expect and that I probably can't explain. The food tastes better. The drinks are more quenching. My sense of touch has heightened to an almost alarming degree. I want to touch everything. Sometimes I just touch peoples' faces. Nobody complains. They just carry on like it's a normal thing for a stranger to touch their faces. I can't help myself. I want to know how everything feels here and how it compares to how things felt back in my old life. My regular life.

Negative feelings no longer exist, not in the way that they used to before. Traditionally negative things like anger or sadness are now exactly comparable to joy and happiness. They're just feelings amidst a slew of other feelings. They're sensations. I don't know how to explain it any other way. When I rub my open palm against the rough bark of an oak tree, I'm not worried about getting a splinter or touching a slug or jamming my finger on a branch. There's no reason to worry because there is no negativity. There is no pain, not really. There are just sensations of varying degrees.

"Well, I do still have a fondness for things that I used to be able to do," I finally respond.

"Like things with your dick?"

"No, other things too."

"Like what?"

I think about it, and then I start laughing.

"Okay, just things with my dick."

"You'll get used to it."

"The thing is, I already *am* used to it. It doesn't actually bother me. I don't even know that it ever did. I understand it and I get it, like, I get why it's unnecessary here. I almost feel like I've always been this way. But then at the same time, I have this existent knowledge that it used to be different. It's like a sense of nostalgia. It's not bad, it's just...you know, nostalgic."

"I know what you mean."

"I just wish there was something that could directly replace it and fill that weird void. Not literally, but like, fill that void that I'm feeling. I wish I had something that is as inherent to being myself as my dick was."

"Damn, man. How great was your dick before?"

"Oh, I'm not saying it was the best. It was all right. But it was *mine*. It made me a man. Like, it definitively meant that I was a man. It was something that I could self-identify with. So not having that is kind of like…it's like I'm missing a part of my identity. I don't know what I am if I'm not a man."

"You're just *you* now."

"But what is that? I'm genderless. So what am I?"

"You," he repeats.

"I'm not explaining myself very well."

"How about this," Wolf begins, leaning against a short tree that bows slightly away from him as his weight presses against it. "Tell me something that you've always wanted."

"Like what? A thing, like an object? Like a Ferrari or something?"

"Sure, if you always wanted a Ferrari."

I shake my head.

"Okay, then maybe think of something that you always wanted to be able to do. Like dunk a basketball or something."

"Super lame. I don't care about basketball."

"That's right. You were a soccer bunny."

"No, I played basketball too. I just mean that I never had this major desire to be able to dunk a ball. Who actually wants that?"

"Short people," he replies.

"Okay. Fair."

"So then think about it. What's something you always wanted to be able to do? Anything, man. Really, anything."

I look around the forest. I'm trying to think of something just to move the conversation along. I'm not the kind of person to have weird, unattainable desires that I keep in a mental list that I can reference and fire off at will. I'm staring up at the trees and looking at how they all converge in on each other as their canopies extend upwards. It's captivating. I can barely form thoughts that I can get out of my mouth. I keep staring up at the trees. It's like they all want to be a part of some small community between all of them. A little bird flies from one tree to another, connecting the dots between the constellation of branches and pinecones.

"I always wanted to fly," I say quietly.

Wolf pushes himself away from the bowing tree and almost snaps it in the process. He walks over to me.

"Dope. I like that."

"Okay. So what?"

He smiles.

"So, fly."

He puts his hands on his hips and stands in front of me, staring straight ahead.

"Huh?"

"Fly. You said you want to fly. So...why don't you fly?"

"Fly how?"

"However you want to."

I'm looking at him like he's crazy because I'm pretty sure that he is. This is the same asshole who thought that at the bottom of a cave was another universe.

"Look," he continues. "I keep telling you this, and I swear, you keep ignoring me. This is *your* afterlife. You can do whatever you want to. Anything you want to do, you can do it."

"I can't fuck," I remind him.

"True. But I know that you don't really *want* to. You wanted to. And you *want to* want to. But you don't actually want to have sex."

It's true. I'm just trying to prove him wrong.

"Well, how do I fly then? Have you done it?"

"No. But I don't really want to."

"What? Why not? Can you imagine what it would be like to be able to just fly around places all by yourself? How fucking amazing!"

"Luke. Just do it."

"Just fly. *Just* fly. Like it's something you can just do."

I force a bellowed laugh to let him know exactly how ridiculous I think he sounds. But Wolf is a real son of a bitch. Without breaking his stare, his body starts to rise up off the ground and into the foggy forest air. He's hovering about eight or ten feet above me. He's staring down at me the entire time.

"Your turn."

I don't know how I'm doing it, but I'm starting to do it too. My feet are slowly lifting off the ground like all the water in my body has been replaced with helium. It's nothing like I thought it would be. My joints are expanding as my body becomes weightless. I'm free of something that I didn't even know I was carrying around with me all my life. I'm someone new. I float up and up, and eventually I'm eye level with Wolf.

"Dude! Look at us! How come everyone isn't doing this?"

"This is your afterlife. They can if you want them to."

I lean to the left, and I start to drift in that direction, getting a hang of how to navigate myself around without any physical friction or inertia like I'm obviously used to. I lean to the right and go back the other way. I move up and I move down and I move up again. I bob and weave and coast around in the air.

"I'm fucking flying!"

I can hear the glee in my own voice. It's like I'm outside of my own body.

"Yeah, buddy! See? See?! Now tell me what's better. Your old life...or this?"

"Wooooooooooooooo-owwwwwww!"

Shit. Look at me! I'm tumbling and turning around in the air. I'm the Baryshnikov of the sky!

"I think the answer is this," he confirms.

"Fuck my dick!"

I'm at least 30 or 40 feet above the ground. I'm whipping through the sky. The width of my smile is breaking all-time Luke Balena records.

"No thanks!"

Now, I know how this sounds. Two stoners hanging out in the forest, flying through the trees like a couple of Peter fucking Pans. Like this isn't downright impossible for a person to do. But that's the thing. We're no longer people. This is no longer the world that we once knew.

In this world, in this afterlife, there are a lot less rules. Hell, there are hardly any rules. It's almost like the purpose of my regular life was solely to train me to expect to accept restriction. And now that I am freed from it, I'm able to appreciate it much more than if I had always been free. So maybe my life was just a training ground, a lesson in appreciation for what was about to come. I just didn't know it at the time. The real meaningful stuff didn't actually begin until now. Until *after* my life had ended.

I don't know if any of this is true. I don't know if there are more afterlifes or after-afterlifes or even things after that. I don't know anything, really. I'm just this dude with no dude parts that can fly and do whatever else I want to do.

I had always heard that people who have everything are still bored and empty. The grass is always greener, that kind of shit. But here, it's all still surprisingly meaningful. It's like I've been invited to a buffet that's filled with all of my favorite foods. No matter where I turn, there's something that I love. And I never get full, and I never have to pay the bill, and I never gain any weight. It's like that. My afterlife is a perfect buffet that was created just for me.

Flying is the shit. This kind of freedom is something that I've always wanted, and now I have it. It's even better than I ever imagined.

I don't even need a reason to be up in the sky. I'm like one of those people who goes running just because they like to run, except I fly around instead. Some days it's all that I do. I coast around over the beach and watch as all the people walking beneath me turn into tiny, little dots that eventually fade away from my vision altogether.

Most of the time, I stay about 20 to 30 feet above the ground. Even though there isn't any limit to how high I can actually go, it's a lot more interesting when I can still hear the sounds that are coming from the people and things on the ground. If I get too high up there, it just gets a little too quiet, and I start to feel like I'm all alone.

A few weeks pass, or maybe it's just minutes. Wolf and I are floating over something interesting-looking. I don't know what it is. A mountain or something. I light up a joint. The sun is sinking into the ocean, and the sky is sparkling with colors that I swear didn't exist until now. We're hovering over the interesting-looking thing, staring off into the melting colors of the sun as the cannabinoids in our blood start to react in our brains.

"Do you realize that we're getting high while getting high?" Wolf asks.

"I do realize this. I also realize that you are an idiot."

"Dude, we're so mathematical. We're high squared."

"You're idiot squared."

"I'm high to the second power."

"I'm a higher power."

"I'm the logarithmic function of high."

"I'm the Hi-thagorean theorem."

"Do you think your Algebra teacher would break her leg here?"

"Algebra 2," I remind him.

Wolf chokes on his last puff from the J and passes it back to me. I hold onto it for a little while, and I get lost in my thoughts. I think about Joanna. I miss her. I'm trying to be pragmatic about my situation and all of the amazing things that I can do here, but ultimately I do still miss her. I know that she can't be here. And I accept that she isn't here. I get it. I really do. I know that I can't change the past—not even in my afterlife—so the only thing that I can do is move forward and try to not think about it. They say that time heals all wounds. I'm wondering if that's true in a place where time is absent altogether.

Sometimes, like now, I get a little too high and forget to forget her. She spills back into my mind, her body dancing rhythmically through my imagination as she lures me into my bedroom. She pulls me on top of her, on top of a heap of disheveled blankets and pillows, on top of her wonderful, little body. She reaches up and runs her hands through my hair. She kisses me softly on the lips and tells me that she loves me. I don't reply. It's easier this way.

I snap out of it. I stare out at the melting sun. I snap back into it. She's hugging me tightly at the top of the cave. She's telling me it's a bad idea. I agree with her. But I go in anyway. I'm staring up at the last glance of her face as the darkness of the musty cave surrounds me. The smell of the wet moss fills my nostrils. I gag. Her face fades out of my sight.

I snap out of it. I stare down at the ocean. Where is the whale? I snap back into it. She's laughing as I read my wine tasting notes. I taste the wine on my lips. I taste her lips as we kiss. She's smiling as I tell her about my first poached egg. She's slipping through the recesses of my mind, and she's fading away with every day that I'm apart from her. I can't remember her face as well as I used to. I can't remember the smell of her hair or the feel of her skin. Her beautiful eyes. I can't remember them, not like I used to. Everything is fading.

I snap out of it. I look over at Wolf, and he's hovering in silence, his eyes closed peacefully. I press the lit end of the joint into the naked flesh of my forearm. My skin hisses. I don't feel anything. I don't snap back. It's easier this way.

* * *

A few more weeks pass, or maybe it's a year. Wolf and I are sitting at a coffee shop that overlooks a small pond.

"Are you sure this isn't heaven?" I ask him.

"What's heaven?"

"I don't know. But this feels like what I thought heaven would be like. It's just so...it's so fucking cool here, you know?"

"I never doubted that you would come around."

"I mean, how can you not?" I ask. "It's amazing. It's simply amazing here. Every day I'm amazed at how fucking fantastic it is. Like, look at this coffee!"

I hold out my mug and stare at it as I bring it to my lips. Wolf does the same.

"It's so good!" I continue. "I've never had coffee this good. Not yesterday, not the day before, not in my old life. And you know what? Tomorrow I'll have even better coffee. And the day after, it'll be even better than that. It's like a giant exponential explosion of amazingness."

"Quite the one-eighty from when you first arrived, huh?"

"Fuck that guy," I laugh. "That wasn't me, that wasn't Luke. That was someone else pretending to be Luke. That guy didn't know what the hell he was talking about."

"You were pretty sad about your girl," he reminds me.

"I still am. She's still here, right here in my heart."

I point at my heart in case he forgot where the heart is located.

"That's sweet."

"But I can also fly. And that is right here as well."

I tap against my chest with my right index finger. Wolf holds out his mug and we cheers. The clink between the mugs is the best sounding clink that I've ever heard.

"I'm gonna go practice my baton for a bit. Want to come watch?"

"Still with that baton. I knew you secretly loved that shit."

He laughs. We both know that in his afterlife, there isn't a baton anywhere in sight. They're probably altogether non-existent, and they will stay that way forever. But in my afterlife, I want him to be into the baton because I think it's funny. So as a result, he is into the baton. I have no sympathy. He's not even really here.

"I'll see you later then?" he asks.

"For sure."

He walks away, and I continue to sit at the table. I'm staring out at the water. Little white flowers are sprinkled throughout a floating sea of green lily pads, all swaying and drifting in tandem with each other. A pair of swans is slowly swimming across the surface of the water. It's a pretty little scene, probably one that Monet would have liked to have painted. Unfortunately for him, he isn't in my afterlife, so he won't get to see it.

An older man approaches my table. He gestures to me as if to say something.

"Hmm?"

"Would you mind if I sit here and enjoy the view of this pond for a little while?"

"Not at all. Be my guest."

I wave my arm across the table as if to invite him into his seat. He slowly sits down and lets out a deep sigh.

"So peaceful here," he remarks.

"Indeed."

I continue to stare out at the pond as I sip my coffee. I can't believe how good it tastes. And it's the perfect temperature too, no matter how long I sit here with it. It's exactly the same the entire time. Exactly how I want it.

"So, how long have you been here?" I ask him.

"A little while. Long enough to enjoy myself, that's for sure."

I ask him the question that I ask every guy that I meet.

"Do you miss it?"

He looks down at his pants and shakes his head.

"Not a day. I lived to be 93 years old. That thing wasn't working for at least the last ten. I say good riddance."

I laugh. He has a point.

"Yeah, I don't miss it either. And mine worked just fine before I got here."

"It's a lot easier when it's gone."

"Amen to that."

I hold out my mug, and he holds out his. When they meet, the clink is better than one that Wolf and I had.

"So what's your name?"

"Jeno."

"I'm Luke. Nice to meet you, Jeno."

"You as well."

We sit in silence for a while, sipping our coffee and staring out at the pond as the two swans glide around through the lilies.

"That's an interesting name, Jeno. What is that? Italian?"

He nods.

"My parents came over from Italy. But I was born in Minnesota."

"Meenah-sow-tah," I repeat, trying to get the accent right.

"I lived there most of my life."

"What brought you out here then? Why aren't you back there?"

"We don't have swans in our ponds this time of year."

"Hmm."

I don't know what time of year it is. I wonder if Jeno knows how time works here.

"I had always heard that this was a nice part of the country to come and visit, so I figured why not? I should make a trip out of it."

"How did you get here?"

"I drove."

"Well, good for you. I'm glad you're here. I love it here. Every day, I just absolutely love it."

"That's good."

A waitress comes by and tops off my coffee. When she reaches over to pour some more for him, he waves her off.

"Too much caffeine," he explains.

A pair of ducks fly in and land on the water, joining the swans and the lilies and the flowers. I sink comfortably into my chair, and the view is too picturesque to even believe. It just keeps getting better and better as the day goes on. Even though Wolf just left, I already have someone else to talk to. In this new life, I like getting to know the new people that I meet. Everyone has a story, and I love to hear about it.

"So what did you do back in your old life? You lived a long time. You must have been up to some good things out there in Minnesota, am I right?"

"I owned and ran a food company."

"A food company? What kind of food?"

"All kinds, really. I started with Chinese food. Canned Chinese food."

"Canned Chinese food? Really?"

"It was really popular when it first came out. This was in the fifties, mind you. It was before everybody cared about organic this and GMO that. Back then, people really just wanted convenience, and our products gave them that. At one point, we accounted for over half of all domestic sales of prepared Chinese foods."

"No shit?"

"It's true. It really helped us move into other business areas that I'd always been interested in. It was a real springboard for the company."

"And this was all you?"

"Founder and President," he states proudly.

"That's amazing. I didn't do anything nearly as interesting as that."

"You were young," he reminds me. "I didn't make my first million until I was in my thirties."

"Your first million? You must have done really well for yourself. People don't just talk about their *first* million unless they made, you know, like a lot of millions."

"I did pretty well for myself, yeah."

"So what other foods did you expand to? Anything I would know of?"

"Well, in the early sixties I sold my Chinese line to a tobacco company for $63 million."

"Shit!"

"No shit. So I took that money, and I invested it in a few things. Frozen foods, mostly. I had been successful with Chinese food, but look at me. Do I look Chinese to you?"

He turns to me and blinks through a pair of thick, black-framed glasses. The waning sun is shining on his pale skin, his short white hair framing his round and friendly face. His hairline has receded, but he doesn't seem to be self-conscious about it.

"No, sir, you do not."

"Nothing against the Chinese. I love 'em. But my passion was to bring Italian comfort foods to the American public. So I took the money from the sale of the Chinese line, and I started working on my new line. And it was even more successful than the Chinese food. Can you believe that?"

"Hey, I love frozen foods. I definitely believe that."

"Later on, I started a magazine that lasted for a little while. I poured a lot of money into that magazine. But it didn't work out. So we moved on."

"Look at you, Renaissance man! What else did you do, record a tenor sax album?"

He laughs.

"Music was never my talent."

"Can't win 'em all, can you?"

"No, you cannot."

The ducks and the swans are all floating in a semi-circle, and I wonder if they know each other or if this is their first time meeting. They seem pretty comfortable considering that they are probably complete strangers. Then again, here I am, chatting it up with the Chinese Chef Boyardee.

"So what would you say was your biggest hit product? Did you do, like, some frozen meatballs or something? That would probably be good. I'd eat that."

He shakes his head.

"There's no question about it. Hands down, the most successful product that I ever created was definitely the Pizza Roll."

"What?"

"The Pizza Roll. You've heard of it, haven't you? God, tell me they didn't stop making it after I died!"

"Heard of it? Oh, I've *heard* of it! Good God, man. You're the inventor of the Pizza Roll?!"

"Jeno Paulucci. That's me."

"That's unbelievable! You've got to be kidding me. You've..."

I look around. Where are the crowds of fans flocking to get his autograph? Where's the paparazzi?

"I take it that you're a fan," he says with a smile.

"A fan?! No, I am *the* biggest fan. Pizza Rolls are my jam! Holy shit! I can't believe this!"

He smiles and nods as he looks out at the pond.

"You have to tell me how you came up with it. I've got to know. I can't believe this! I seriously can't believe this. Do you have time? Can you stay and talk to me?"

"I've got nowhere to be."

"Wow. I mean, I've got to tell you. A little while ago, I learned how to fly. It was amazing. It was something that I had always wanted to do, and now it's something that I can just, you know, *do.*"

I stand up and float around in front of him.

"That's nice."

I land back on the ground and go back to my chair.

"And honestly...and I mean this in full sincerity...sitting here, talking to the inventor of the Pizza Roll? Jesus Christ. Unreal! This is better than flying!"

"That's quite the fan."

"You have no idea. You're practically my hero. I am obsessed with those things. Jeno, tell me that you're never going back to Minnesota. Tell me that you'll stay here and be my friend. You've got to. You've just got to."

He shrugs.

"Sure. It's nice here."

"Oh, it's more than nice. It's the afterlife! It's the fucking best!"

I lean back in my chair, and my cheeks are stretching from the enormity of the smile that's on my face.

"There's got to be something that I can do for you in return."

"In return for what?"

"You know, for hanging out with me. It's an honor. So I'd happily do anything that you want in return. I mean, nothing gay or anything. But anything other than that."

He laughs and stares out at the pond. I can tell that he's thinking.

"Anything," I repeat.

"Well, this might sound a little funny, you know." He lowers his voice. "But I never smoked pot."

"Hang on. You came up with the Pizza Roll, and you never even got *high?*"

He nods.

"You Italian genius! You're a modern day Leonardo da Vinci! But okay. You came to the right place. If there's one thing I know, it's pot."

"Were you a dealer? Is that how you died?"

"What? No. No, no. I was just recreational. I had a job. Well, kind of. I had a girlfriend. I was a straight-up guy."

"What was it then?"

"I just swam down into a cave and drowned. I was trying to find my friend."

"Oh. Good effort."

"Thanks. But yeah, it had nothing to do with the marijuana. It's totally safe. I mean, the fact that you want to try it tells me that you know that it's safe anyway. You probably just never tried it, right? I can see how that would happen. You were busy in the sixties. You didn't have time for that shit."

"Right."

"Well, like I said, you came to the right guy."

"Well, alright then."

"Do you know how to fly?"

He shakes his head. I stand up and start to show him how it works. There really isn't much to show. I just do it a few times, and then I tell him to try doing it. Soon enough, he's floating around and flying like he's been doing it his whole life.

"There you go!" I yell. "You're a damned pro already!"

We fly up and over the pond and out toward the ocean. It's funny to see an older guy flying. Up until this point, I've only seen Wolf do it. But it's all the same. Just a body floating through the air.

I bring us to one of my favorite spots, a little cove that hugs a rocky cliff that juts out into the ocean. We're about 30 feet above the water. The waves are crashing against the rocks, spraying mist that travels up toward us, when a big one hits. We're floating above the churning tide, side by side. I pull out a joint. I light it up and take a deep breath in, the smoke filling my lungs and causing that tingly tickle that every first hit creates. I pass the joint to Jeno, and he takes a hit.

"You want to hold it in as long as you can," I explain, still holding mine in and talking like I've run out of breath.

He holds it for a while, but then he starts to cough, letting it all out. I let mine out too.

"Good job. That was good."

Something amazing is happening right now, but it happens all the time. The sun is putting on a show, slowly progressing through its ritual as it collapses into the sea. Beautiful hues of orange and pink and blue glimmer against puffy, white clouds. I breathe deep and slow, taking it all in. Jeno floats alongside me, silent and smiling.

I wish Joanna were here. She would love the way the sky looks right now. Wherever she is, maybe she's looking at the same sky too, thinking about me like I'm thinking about her. Or maybe we're still together somewhere, holding on to each other in another universe I haven't been to yet. Maybe.

I look out at the ocean beneath us, and my eyes trail off to the horizon. Out in the distance, the arched back of a whale crests the surface of the water. Her tail flips up in the air, waving right at me. I wave back. Then she sinks out of sight, and I smile peacefully, knowing that she's safe and sound again, deep in the belly of the ocean.

The End

Author's Signature Page

Appreciation Page

Without all of you this book would not have been completed.

My Family: My partners in dinner table intrigue, strategy and creative unblocking. xoxo

My Investor: Julie Ford: For someone to believe in a project the way you have with this one is still pretty much in the realms of miraculous to me. Thank you so much.

My Beta Readers: Jessie, Brooke, Katherine and Lorna: Thank you for pushing me when I need it and picking apart the manuscript to make it even more awesome.

My Illustrator: Angel: I believe so much in your work.

My Technical Consultant: Adam: Thank you for making my weapons and fight scenes eerily accurate.

Author's Note to the readers:

Most stories are often told from one maybe two points of view. Some of my chapters have up to four or five points of view. I have not done this to confuse you. Just like reality the truth of anything must be gathered from many points of view.

Disclaimer: There are scenes in this book that are triggers. If you have problems with violence, inferred sex (I don't describe down to the detail), slave trade, child assassins and generally shady behaviour not to mention coups this book is possibly not for you.

Psychic conversations and flashbacks are in italics.

For more information about the Author or the books:

www.buttakittin.wix.com/mysite

Facebook: @elanna11children11

Twitter: @MJWright1976

Wattpad: @Elanna11Children11

Table of Contents

Prologue

{Ethan}

'Your father has flown free.' The callous words from my uncle's lips are supposed to fill me with abject terror. Numbness fills my body automatically deadening the pain such news should evoke. Checking his watch, he dismisses me easily with a wave of his hand. I watch him roll out of the room in his custom-made wheelchair.

Two guards take up posts inside the door of my apartment. Bowing my head, I pretend to appear torn up.

Inside my emotions balance precariously between disbelief and fury. Premature death is an accepted way of life within our family.

Staring down at the brown carpet I know the dynamics of the hierarchy has shifted yet again. My father, Joseph, was the heir to Smythe house. He was not easily manipulated or controlled. His death makes me the new heir.

It is a job I don't want and yet this is the family I was born to someday lead.

Our family mantra has always been 'Protect Charlotte Grace'. I was so young when we started planning for this day. Charli is our weak point. She is an invisible.

We protect her from the cruelty outside the four walls of the family apartment. We protect her from herself when necessary.

The personal detail who surrounded my father like mosquitoes enter the room. Rubbing a hand down my face I stand. Mamma is standing out in the hall.

Her face is streaked with tear tracks. Reading her message in her eyes I continue past her. She has hidden her pain deep inside. She is flawless in her performance. The grieving mate of the late heir.

Mother of the current heir. Not one misstep. Not now. Not ever. Deep inside I know what it has cost her to leave Dad's body to the other Smythe females. She holds her head high. Dipping it slightly. She knows I want to stop and comfort her in a hug.

The new team of bodyguards keeps me moving forward. Children yell the news from street corners. Holding up people desperate for the sales. Desperate to help their parents keep their families together. The solid wall around me keeps me moving. Through the back entrance into Smythe Towers and into the private elevators.

Someone pushes up. When we exit they walk me past our family apartment where Charli is waiting. They crack jokes about being too old to live with females.

We turn many corners before they let me into a new apartment. Fear slides down my back and dissipates almost instantly. I too must be flawless in my performance.

They have put me in a place where they can watch my most minuscule of gestures. Uncle John has put me in a place where no one can hear me scream if death comes swiftly. The first step in his rule of absolute control is always isolation.

He has no idea that I find him predictable. I am Ethan Joseph Smythe. The board has been set. The game is just beginning. I will take this house apart piece by stinking piece before I die.

{**Charli**}

Tears slip down my face unchecked. No one can see them in the dark of my room. Pain surrounds me like a fog. The females who came to tell me fed me the platitudes to make me feel better.

My companion didn't correct them. She is gone for the night. Mamma will come in soon. Ethan. I already know without being told that they have taken Ethan to new quarters.

They think because I don't speak I'm too stupid to understand the world around me. My family knows differently. I speak to them when I need to. I speak to them directly inside their minds.

My reflection stares back at me from the mirror on the table opposite me. I was supposed to be practicing my speech exercises again. I don't see the point anymore. *Daddy was the only one who insisted on it.*

Mamma wants me to be so invisible that I blend in with my surroundings.

If I could control my body's movements, I would. Uncle John was here again today. His excuse was that our therapy room is the best in the entire tower.

Ever since he had that fall at the high council last year he's been watching me more. It's getting creepy. He asks me random questions never expecting answers.

At first, I thought he just liked to hear his own voice. A pattern is establishing. Daddy would have listened to me. Tears flow faster dripping off my chin.

Closing my eyes, I try to reach Ethan. I can't reach him. His mind is preoccupied. I can't break through the wall he's raised. Not without causing him excruciating pain. Last time I did it by accident. Now I know better.

The door opens, and the room is flooded with bright light. Mamma is wearing all white. The Smythe colour for mourning.

She crosses the room and takes a tissue from the box my companion left beside me. I can feel her arms slip around my body as she shudders. Her quiet sobs fill the air. Tears fall unheeded mingling with my own.

Eventually, she straightens up. 'No more tears.' She decrees softly and says, 'Ethan is counting on us.' Wiping her eyes, she then turns to me and deals with mine gently. Her mind is receptive to my mind voice.

'When will we see him again?' I ask holding her eyes with my own hoping that the desperation I feel hasn't bled through to her.

Mamma doesn't answer.

CHAPTER ONE
The Funeral

{Third Person}

Smythe Towers held a certain charm with its curves and clean sharp lines. Instead of standing tall in the domesphere to rival the heights of Mercy house it dominated an entire block of the inner circle.

Four identical buildings with curves created a ripple effect that drew the eye away from the clear walk tubes that connected one building to the next.

History had revealed that it had been built by a Smythe male when the domesphere was only newly built itself. Before Spark city had even been established.

Exuding an aura of lethal calm Ethan Smythe entered the room. The air hung heavy with so many bodies packed closely together to honour a worthy male in a ceremony that had long since lost meaning for most of us. Sweat trickled down the neck of the body in front of me.

Recognising the same thirst in his eyes as I had inside my soul I held myself as still as possible blending into the sea of mourners.

Sitting on the stage I hoped he had only two goals in mind. Avenge his father's death. Keep his family safe at all costs. Pretending to go along with the rituals I studied the room at my leisure from beneath my eye lashes.

Charlotte Grace's attendant waved her hand fan back and forth fanning the golden-haired child. Soft sobs chinked at his armour slightly. His mother dabbing at her eyes with a lace-edged handkerchief.

His stone-cold gaze sweeps around the room. Burning themselves into his memory the small details will be there to be examined later at his leisure. Watching helplessly the words wash over him in continuous waves. Father. Brother. Nephew. Late Heir. Love. Emotion flickers briefly in the depths of his almost black eyes before fading away. Observing the same First Family members I wonder which one of them will be the first to crack.

They all wear white. Pretenders. Nothing more than piranhas feeding off the misery of another. Who would be the first to try to kill him?

Who would befriend his mother to gain inside information?

Who would sit with Charlotte Grace and whisper poison in her ears? Assessing each one coolly I draw my own conclusions of where the danger will come from next.

{Ethan}
His cold demeanour softens slightly when he meets his mother's eyes for a mere millisecond.

They were surrounded by the other First Family females all dignified in their grief. Fake. His mother the only exception. Tears tracking down her cheeks. More brimming in her lovely eyes. She was grieving her mate the way the Brothers of Sabrefield Sanctuary had taught her. With her entire heart.

{Third Person}
Looking past the First Family towards the slaves. He looks directly at us the inmates of the infamous cells from the cells hidden on the two basement levels of the building.

We don't wear white out of respect for the dead. We wear the only clothes we have been given. The barriers are between us and them.

Guards walk a designated pattern. Hands on guns. Sharp words in low voices to keep the inmates quiet in a section of the room that has standing room left only.

Foul promises have quarters cringing away from the aisles. Lewd glances from family members keep us isolated in a world of our own.

The isolation tactics the guards are using cause him to lose focus completely.

{Ethan}

They're afraid of me. Of what this change could mean to their comfortable lives. I've almost got the game figured out. Key pieces elude me. 'Ethan!' Sharp insistent tones cut through the fugue state I've sunk into.

Passing my inattention off as grief I take the microphone from Uncle John's outstretched hand. I wait patiently as he backs his wheelchair out of the way of the podium.

Bowing my head, I feel the pressure in the room weighing down on me. Pressure to say the right words. To show a spirit of unity in the face of immense tragedy.

Keeping the sheep happy has never been so easy. It would be so inspirational not one of my many extended relatives will not dare interfere in the day to day decisions made behind closed doors.

They would never learn about the shoddy finances that kept them in their luxury, the illicit activities or the real estate deals on the outer rim that dealt in more than land rights.

'Today we farewell more than just another heir to this house. We farewell a father.' I focus on Charlotte Grace as she blinks a response. Errant tears run down her face. Her companion shakes her slightly before making a show of wiping it away.

Knowing there is nothing I can do for her from the stage without causing a scene I continue, 'A brother.' Dropping my hand on John's shoulder in a show of solidarity, 'A son.'

My foremother Arcana's steely glare covers the tears forming in her eyes. 'A mate.' I can hear Mother's soft sobbing and choose not to acknowledge it, 'Today we farewell Joseph Smythe in the manner befitting a member of the First Family of this house and today I regretfully accept the position left vacant by his untimely passing. My father will not be forgotten.'

'Keep talking. Uncle John is becoming a problem. He has been overly friendly with me. It makes me uncomfortable.'

My sister's sweet voice whispers in my mind. The barriers I had raised in my mind weren't thick enough.

The information she shared with me left me feeling nauseated.

A layer of detachment envelopes me once more as I retake my seat.

Observing the rest of the proceedings in silence my stomach muscles clench in fury. Twisting my features into the appropriate show of grief I wait for the whole charade to be over with.

Checking my watch, I keep to the shadows in the halls. Waiting for an alarm to be raised once my guards realise I've given them the slip I have no choice but to move quickly.

Keeping the hood up over my head obscuring my features I have no doubts that even now I'm being tracked on the feeds on the antechamber walls in John's private study.

Trust is a commodity to him. Information is valuable. Secrets. Lies.

'Ethan?' Lilianna appeared in the doorway of her private day area.

'It's time.' I wait for understanding to flash on her face before disappearing through the door way leading to Charli's rooms.

She was facing her large picture window overlooking the gardens below.

Standing slightly behind her so she could look at my reflection in the glass she acknowledges my presence with the words, 'You came.' She forces them out through her mouth.

Shaping each one carefully so that I would understand her.

'He's threatened me too. If I don't behave he said he would injure you badly. Force Mamma into another contract. Break us up completely.'

Crouching down in front of the silent blond girl I'd grown up calling sister I wait for her to respond. Charli only spoke to me when warranted lately she'd resorted to a simple yes/no blink system.

Her emerald eyes were steady and focused as she disappeared into her thoughts.

The memory of the day she had joined our family assaulted my senses.

Confused he had not approached her until she had removed his book from his lap.

Gently his father had positioned his arms before watching while she nestled the baby into them.

'This is the new little sister I promised you. Her name is Charlotte Grace.' His mother looked him in the eye and spoke to him seriously like he was a grown-up, 'We are going to call her Charli and you are going to protect her for the rest of her life.

24

This is the most important job I will ever give you.'

He looked down at the tiny scrap of humanity in his arms trying to process the meanings of some of her words she used in what she was asking him to do. 'Ethan, what's your most important job?' His mother asked him softly. 'Protect Charli.' He had replied dutifully.

Twelve years later and they both were still protecting Charlotte Grace from the dark machinations of Smythe Towers. John's passing comment that his sister must be suffering in her silence had rattled him. Charli's observations had been accurate.

John was scheming about something. I hoped she would forgive me for what I had arranged for her. 'You understand what's happening don't you Charli?'

Two blinks followed by two more. Yeah, she got it and she wasn't thrilled.

{Charli}

'I understand more than you know. I don't hate you. Be careful he doesn't hurt you too.'

She wished she could make him hear her words all the time. Long ago she used to be able to make him hear her voice in his head.

He liked to pretend that it had been a game they played between them before their father had died. Charli knew differently. He had grown up almost overnight and she had found his mind blocked, overwhelmed with worry. He had no room for her voice. No room to think about anything other than the new threats coming at them from all sides.

{Ethan}

'Then you understand why you must leave tonight?' I continued softly, 'Uncle John can threaten me all he wants. I need to have you hidden somewhere safe. You will be taken to Mercy House.'

'Isn't there any other way? I'm scared.'

'If there is I haven't found it yet.' I levelled with her.

Noticing how grim my face was Charli stopped protesting. Sad eyes.

'It's too dangerous Charli. No one is safe. Not me. Not you. Not even Mamma.' I pulled her soft travel bag down from the top of her closet and methodically packed it with everything she would need for a week.

I added the personal items I knew she could not live without before zipping it up and hiding it in the bottom of her closet. Returning to her side to reassure her I pressed my lips lightly to her forehead. I could feel her fear thrumming through her body. I needed her calm, 'You have to be brave now. Someone, we both trust will be back later to get you.'

In the distance, the alarm clanged throughout the north tower reverberating at a low pitch through the glass in the windows making them rattle slightly.

Masking my concern, I tossed her a grin before disappearing through her doorway again.

{Charli}

My heart skips a beat. Terror consumes me in the knowledge that Ethan needs to appear on a camera somewhere in his apartment or the corridors would ring with the heavy footsteps of Uncle's males conducting a door to door search.

Closing my eyes, I prayed to all the gods old and new that no one would check my room. Uncle John was growing vicious and I knew Ethan was right when he said that no one was safe anymore.

Forcing my head up took effort and energy I couldn't afford to waste. Mamma had taught me how to be a chameleon and draw the shadows of a room around me like a cloak.

Now was the time to use that knowledge to aid my escape. I could only hope that Mercy House had the room for someone with my extensive needs.

CHAPTER TWO
Jo

{Jo}

Staggering sideways the initial contact felt like a sledge hammer to her temple. Barely able to acknowledge the worn couch beneath her Jo concentrated on the person needing her help. Relying on her senses she reached out with a sliver of her normal intensity. The person was a child.

Gritting her teeth, she tamped down on nausea threatening to embarrass them both.

'I'm hearing you. Turn down the volume little one. Picture a dial and mentally making the sound softer.'

Signalling to her brothers not to touch her she struggled to sit in a semi-upright position. Even using mind speak she liked to afford the other person their privacy.

Touching would add another mind to the conversation. Desperation bled through the emotions spilling over from the end. Jo concentrated on something else to prevent the young female's fear and nerves from disrupting the link.

'My brother is bringing me tonight. Late. Please don't turn us away.' Begging.

Begging was never a good sign. She sent a wave of calm and reassurance back before replying, *'Mercy House doesn't turn anyone away.'*

'We're Smythes.' Jo winced outwardly at the name. Shaking her head briefly her

31

sight slipped forcing her to focus inwards on the conversation.

'You can choose a new name. You will be safe. I promise.'

The equivalent of audible sniffling filled her ears before the connection broke. Rubbing her hand over her face weary with the effort it took to maintain the link she pulled her fingers away sticky with her own blood. Accepting a damp rag gratefully she cleaned herself up before Daire's face swam into view.

'There are two new ones coming in after dark to Mercy House. I couldn't see faces. Brother and sister. Their last name is Smythe.' Jo listened to the unimpressed noise her brothers were making before she added, 'They're going to be important.'

'How important?' Daire didn't waste time by mincing his words. Her brothers allowed her to sit up at her own pace and sip at the glass of water before inundating her with more questions.

Scarlet dots on her arm drew her attention away from the arguing.

Pressing a new rag to her nose with a sigh she focused on stemming the bleed. Violet strands of her hair swirled in disarray around her waist.

The snagged strands tugging at her scalp as she attempted to appear alright for those who cared for her the most. Six male bodies stood before her in a semi-circle of protection.

Five opinions were put forth loudly. An awkward silence fell as they waited for her to reply. Choosing her words carefully she met each set of eyes before venturing her own opinion, 'She's going to need more protection then I can give her.'

Once again, she impressed the truth of her words by meeting each set of eyes lingering on Cerin, 'She's going to need you.'

He shoved his hands into his jeans pockets. His eyes haunted. Waiting for orders. 'You saw something specific?' Daire stopped pacing.

Unwilling to share more information than necessary she gathered her mass of hair and twisted it up into a sloppy bun, 'I'm going to need a bodyguard. One with Cerin's particular skill set.'

CHAPTER THREE
The Escape

{Fane}

The elderly male checked over his shoulder as he entered the hanging gardens. *'Are we being followed?'* His 'hump' asked shifting slightly under his cloak. 'No.' he answered her softly and added, 'You still ok back there?'

'Yes.' She didn't say anything else and he stooped over a little more. Covertly paying extra attention to the cameras half hidden by pendulous flowers in the covered walkway.

He staggered along on a walking stick through the gardens to the opposite exit.

Touching the door handle in front of him he waited patiently for an alarm to trigger. *'Now.'* Charli slipped inside his head.

Boots on the pavement paused at the end of the alley. Opening the door wide enough to admit them they entered Mercy House. He followed the corridor into a large room. Scanning their surroundings for threats, he could sense none.

{Cerin}
Waiting behind the ornate screen hidden deep within the shadows Jo held still. Cerin placed a warning hand on her arm.

The 'elderly' male straightened his back and dropped a duffel on the floor with a soft thud. Sweeping his cloak back he revealed the slender child moulded around his body. Backing up against a chair they worked together until she was seated comfortably.

36

Continuing to shed items the male withdrew sticks he had strapped to his body.

Cerin slid his knife from its scabbard silently.

'Wait.' Jo moved her spare hand to grip his. Shaking her head at his questioning look she turned back to the pair in the foyer. They watched as the male extended each stick and propped them up against the chair.

'I know you're watching us.'

A psychic link snapped into life. Cerin grunted softly in Jo's ear able to hear the words in his head.

{Jo}

Her eyes glowed softly as she replied, *'We want to make sure that your brother poses us no threat with those weapons of his.'*

'You'd already know if he wanted you dead. If he wanted to threaten you he

would not use my crutches to do it.' The amusement was clear in the young voice.

A lethal aura clung to the brother as his jacket swung around his calves.

Adjusting the collar, he raised it slightly shielding his scarred neck from view.

{Cerin}
'Tell him to place his weapons on the floor in front of your feet. This is a sanctuary.' Cerin ordered daring the intruders to cause a fuss as he replied on the private link. He fingered the custom grip of his knife adjusting the positioning. Nothing about the male reassured him.

'You will do the same?' The child requested formally.

'I will do the same.' Cerin agreed as he wiped a droplet of blood away from Jo's ear with his thumb.

Nodding her thanks, she led them forward around the screen into the centre of the room. They stopped a few paces away from the strangers.

Flipping his knife Cerin held it out to Jo hilt first.

Accepting it from him she placed it on the floor between them as a gesture of good faith.

{Fane}
'She needs your protection. I did not come here to start a war.' Fane's eyes flicked between them warily. He slowly withdrew both of his guns and his spare clips.

He placed them on the pile and then continued down to his boot where he had hidden his knife. Balancing it on top of his growing pile Fane stood up. He gave a short nod as he held out his arms. Patting him down thoroughly Cerin spoke, 'He's clean.' Impressed with the male's small arsenal he hid his admiration behind a hard face.

'Why are you here?' Jo asked already knowing the answer. Fane dropped a gentle hand on his sister's shoulder, 'Shake up in the hierarchy at Smythe Towers. John is planning something.

We think he needs Charlotte Grace to pull it off and we don't like the amount of interest she's received from him. The male is power hungry.'

He spoke without any preamble before gesturing to the crutches and her motionless body, 'She needs constant help and care. Can you guarantee her safety and security?'

{Cerin}
'I can.' Cerin spoke with certainty, 'We've run in the same circles before Smythe. You've seen what I can do.' Recognition. Acceptance. Fane nodded, 'Yeah thought I'd seen you before. Take care of my half-sister for me?'

'With my own sister in the room, it should be a piece of cake.' Cerin replied watching Jo lower herself to the same height as the child.

{Jo}

'We will do everything possible to help you adjust to your new home. Most of the females here live and train on the dormitory level. I don't think that they are set up for your specific needs. You can share my apartment.' She said verbally while sending across the link privately, *'What kind of aids do you need besides these crutches?'*

'We will manage. Reassure Fane. He has to go home and tell Mamma he left me with good people.' Charli's wise reply stunned Jo.

Rocking back on her heels she rose and placed her hand on Fane's arm. 'Cerin and I will take care of all her needs personally. You are welcome to come and visit at any hour.

I don't need to tell you to watch your back. I have heard of your Uncle's reputation.'

{Fane}
'Our brother Ethan will be the one visiting her. I'm just the hired muscle. John can never know that she is here. Her life depends upon it.' Fane impressed upon them both the seriousness of the situation. 'She'll be safe with us.' Jo reassured him.

Breathing out in relief he spoke again, 'I can't stay. Other lives that I value are still in danger.' His face revealed nothing until he looked down at the girl in the chair. His features softened while they had a final silent conversation. Cerin watched warily while he strapped his weaponry back in place.

{Jo}
Raising an eyebrow Jo knew he was trying to find a solution to their problem.

Shaking his head almost imperceptibly they observed Fane gather his sister into his arms. As soon as he turned to leave he spoke, 'Send word when he is coming. Charlotte Grace has the same gifts as Lady Mercy. I have some pull on the streets. We can get him between Smythe Towers and Mercy House unseen.'

Fane held out his hand. Grasping his forearm Cerin spoke genuinely, 'Siatifo' Have courage. Fane replied, 'Qortero.' Not fear. Two parts of an ancient warrior's creed. His eyes slid towards his sister once more before disappearing into the shadows that stretched through the open doorway.

'Let's get you upstairs little one.' Jo placed her hand on Charlotte Grace's shoulder. Cerin moved directly into her line of sight and winced internally at the tears flowing silently down her face.

{Cerin}
She would learn that life was different outside Smythe Towers.

Ignoring her tears Cerin said, 'I'm going to carry you in my arms. It is a long way up to the top floor.'

'Thank you.'

Cerin had the impression that her internal voice was stronger than her physical one. He deliberately allowed a thought to surface in the forefront of his mind wondering if like Jo she could connect to those around her and touch their thoughts at her pleasure.

'I can.' She was honest with him. Her green eyes focused on his face.

'There are certain memories that cause me pain. I would prefer you stay out of those.'

He could feel an impression of her silent agreement as he strengthened his mental walls.

{Jo}

'I will have one of the other females bring your belongings upstairs.' Jo interrupted their private mental conversation watching Cerin lifted Charlotte Grace easily into his arms,

'I want you to think about using a different name while you are here. Something you will respond to without hesitation.'

Jo joined Cerin by the huge floor to ceiling camera feeds on the wall once they had settled Charli in her own room. 'Those memories will do you more harm if you hug them too close.' The silence between them stretched out before he finally spoke, 'Maybe what happened was my fault.'

{Cerin}

The past had its hooks deep in his soul. He could feel them there tugging sharply threatening to expose his heart. 'Maybe it's time to forgive yourself.

You can't carry this on your shoulders and look after her.' Refusing to allow him the retreat he wanted Jo forced him to confront his demons.

Refusing to budge even a little Cerin asked, 'You have personal experience I should know about?' 'You will soon enough.' Her words were loaded with pain.

Alone in the next room, Charli shook with exhaustion. She was overwhelmed and terrified. John's methods were brutal even for those he professed to love.

{Ethan}
In the early hours of the following morning Ethan calmly exited the elevator leading to the floor his apartment was on. Solid bodies blocked the door way. Two of John's inner circle waited for him with their arms crossed.

Feigning an air of nonchalance Ethan paused waiting for their message. 'Your sister's gone missing. He wants to see you.' Wordlessly Ethan adjusted the cuffs of his already immaculate suit.

CHAPTER FOUR
Rites of Passage

{John}

He laughed before coldly uttering the word, 'No!' John's gaze swept the office before pausing on his nephew's face. The boy didn't have the good sense to cower before him.

His eyes raked over his appearance noting details as he added, 'Do you take me for a fool? Your sister has disappeared in your absence. Coincidence? I hardly think so. Convenient I would call it.'

Ethan's stoic expression stopped him mid-tirade. His words were making no impact on his nephew.

He had been too heavily influenced by his mother. His eerie blue eyes glowed slightly. He seemed to be waiting for something.

John sat back in his chair watching. Not a hair out of place. No smudges on his suit. Lilianna's days of giving her son advice had come to an end.

She could easily be encouraged into charitable works that would take her outside of the towers for large portions of the day. Without Charlotte Grace, John had lost his leverage over Ethan.

He would need to remain malleable to learn the brutal methods used to run his empire.

Allowing an exasperated sigh to leave his lips John dismissed him with a flick of his fingers.

Waiting until he was alone he picked up the bottle from the sideboard beside him inwardly all the ancient gods and the new. He had no direct bloodline to follow in his place.

Both his children had died in childbirth. The one true love of his existence, Elanna de Montmercy, had walked out on him leaving her daughter in her place.

He had been forced to initiate a naïve fifth into her silken cage while the love of his life disappeared to start over again with someone new.

John took another long pull from the bottle. His life faded away with each breath he drew.

All the power he currently held and all the wealth he had accumulated would soon be in the hands of his brother's child. He slammed his fist on the desk frustrated that there was nothing he could do to prevent it.

Charlotte Grace had been the perfect public face for his brother James to manipulate.

He remembered with cold clarity his unacknowledged daughter. Fiery in her defiance. He couldn't forget the way that her eyes had lit up with amethyst light. They had accused him silently of not being the father she had needed.

He wondered briefly which woman he had sired her with. The female hadn't told him before watching her companions attempt to kill him.

He drummed his fingers while formulating a plan. She had answered to the name Jo.

He wondered briefly what Jo was short for. She had the clothing and mannerisms of someone who had grown up in the rim.

With intensive work, she could be educated and groomed ready to run the empire if his nephew didn't perform as expected within the limited time frame John had assigned him. Charlotte Grace with her soul-searing gaze would make an adequate backup plan.

John finished the bottle enjoying each drop as it rolled across his tongue.

His trackers would all have new assignments in the morning.

Turning off the light on his desk he rolled his wheelchair towards the open door through the darkness. Tomorrow.

Tomorrow he would set in motion events that would shape the future the way he wanted after he was long gone.

{Ethan}
Hiding my disgust behind a parody of a smile I allowed my companions to draw me deeper into the cells. My punishment for my disappearing act was an introduction to the business run from the sub-basement levels.

This was a ritual every Smythe male undertook when he came of age and for me, that time meant now. Strolling through the halls at a leisurely pace they induced me to look over each inhabitant.

Meeting each set of eyes with the same implacable expression I watched hope flare and die repeatedly. I was trapped in this game as much as any of them only they were entrapped completely in my Uncle's web with no way to free themselves at all.

Winding deeper into the darkness the behaviour of the females changed at our approach. Most backed away from their doors. Eyes downcast. Some knelt hands placed open palmed upon their thighs. Heads bowed.

Artificial lighting flickered overhead as they passed through what appeared to be a torture chamber.

'A training chamber.' The cell master pointed out. Seething internally, I blocked out some of the nastier comments and made the right noises along with the rest.

There was almost no trace of humanity left in the hearts of the males surrounding him they seemed to have forgotten where the fine line between control and abuse lay.

Passing under the archway crudely labelled Row X through a narrow doorway big enough only for a single file the air of joviality dissipated.

Deep in the bowels of the building away from any natural light was a single occupied cell in the centre of the room. Assuming it was another 'she' if her neat braid of scarlet hair was anything to go by had her back towards us.

Holding a meditation pose that challenged the laws of physics whilst ignoring the wolf whistles of my companions showed an intense level of concentration. The pursuit of being single-minded even.

Taking my time to peruse her 'room' I ran my eyes lazily over the single bed in the corner made neatly with a patched green silk bed spread.

A brush, mirror and ratted out teddy bear lay at right angles to the pillow in a neat row. Despite appearances, she was something other than what she seemed.

Flipping smoothly from her fingertips to her feet she settled into the familiar posture of supplication. Her show of flexibility had the others groaning audibly. She knew we were there observing her through the plexiglass wall.

She sensed six maybe seven males. Crude comments. Boisterous laughter. High and drunk. The skin on her back crawled in revulsion. 'Pretty isn't she. Not for the likes of us mere mortals. The master is waiting for someone to bid high enough to cover her value.'

The cell master spouted the usual rubbish about her being a precious commodity for the House of Smythe.

'Who determines the worth of a human life?' I examined my nails bored with my current surroundings. 'The master determines everything.' The cell master sounded horrified such a question be posed near such innocent and naïve ears. He too was hiding something about this female.

Out of the corner of my eye, I noticed that she had finally opened hers in a show of simple defiance. Keeping them lowered she studied me from below her thick eyelashes. Keeping my face blank, I allowed her to peruse me at her leisure.

A small smile playing on her lips she slowed down her movements. Dainty.

Graceful. Watching. Waiting always waiting.

Flustered at her deliberate disobedience her keeper spluttered, 'Ember knows better than to cause trouble.

We only get close enough to her cell to place down her rations and remove her trays.' He paused pointedly and waited until she bowed her head completely, 'Such a waste.'

Minx. She raised her ruby eyes to meet ours in a small show of defiance. She had spirit. The world stilled narrowing to the space between heartbeats. Her perfect lips parted slightly. Our eyes locked and held. Rising into a low curtsey she bobbed slightly before turning her back on us and leaving through a door behind her. The snick of the lock engaging reverberated through my senses breaking the spell.

Looking away, disinterested now that the main attraction had disappeared I

murmured an appropriate comment
before turning to leave. Whoever she was
she was a complication I was not prepared
to engage with.

CHAPTER FIVE
Ember

{Ember}

Who said chivalry is dead? What is chivalry supposed to be anyway? Some old code the ancients lived by. Males control my world and every move I make. It's easy to close my eyes. It's easy to take the drugs and just forget.

They don't want us to remember our lives before we arrived in the cells. To remember is to die.

The few fragmented memories that have come back to me - I hold close to my soul. I was snatched from a train in the middle of the night by monsters.

I remember water smashing against rocks at the base of the cliffs. Stairs leading down to a beach. It had pure white sand.

The water was the colour of one of the First Family's sapphire crested rings.

I was stolen as a child. I've been on the master's pills so long they don't work anymore. Memories bleed through my reality in the form of fractured dreams. I remember feeling light. Free. I'm told this is happiness. Every day the weight on my shoulders pushes me under just a little more.

The memories they allow me to keep are painful reminders. Lessons.

Ever since the doctor found my ability he has kept me separate from the others.

Caged. Cosseted like a damn level 5 pampered female. I'm not level 5. Far from it. I'm a nobody. A ghost. Trained to do what the Smythe males can't.

Attract attention. Be friendly enough for secrets to be shared. Death with a single touch.

The dark symphony of multiple screams punctuates the night. Slipping out of bed I huddle in the corner of my bathroom with a ratty remnant of my childhood toy. It is the only place they cannot see me. The only door I have been given permission to lock. The only place I feel slightly safe.

Drawing my knees to my chest I wait out the tiny ray of dawn that my windows afford me. Screams in the night. Sobs in the morning. The unbroken record of life in the cells.

Breathe in. Breathe out. Forget counting sheep. Breathe in. Hope that tonight isn't the night the master calls me back into service. Breathe out. Count to three. When was my last trip to the lab? Breathe in. Focus on the one good memory of my monotonous existence.

I told myself that they would forget all about me. I told myself so many lies to avoid going insane I prayed for someone to help me. Anyone.

She came just after they had separated me from the others. She came under the pretence that the children needed warmer clothing.

She slipped a thin pair of gloves on my hands. The adaptive tech would allow me to mask the raw power in my hands.

Her face had been kind. Eyes fearful. The memories of that night made me shake my head to dispel the cobwebs. Back to counting each breath in and out.

Words filtered through the cells that her mate had flown free. I had liked him. He had been kind.

The Master and his other brother were not. The children of the first family had been at the memorial service.

Charlotte Grace, the golden-haired fairy child had been carried about in the arms of her bodyguard. Ethan, her brother who had calmly made sure made sure that his mother and sister had a rock they could hold onto.

The others had been sighing over his looks in soft whispers. I saw the brief flash of helplessness on his face and in his eyes when all others had bowed their heads for the final blessing. Who would he have to turn to now? Why had he been outside my cage? He was not my immediate problem. The rattling of my cage door had broken through my reverie.

Rising to my feet I run my hands through my hair. Craft 101. Always appear to be something you're not. Keep them guessing.

Keep them interested. They're in the outer cell. A polite knock on the door. 'Time to go to work Ember. Master's waiting.'

CHAPTER SIX
Your's

{Ethan}

'Entrancing isn't she.' John commented from my side. He pointed to the monitor I had been ignoring for the past thirty minutes. My apartment. 'Beautiful distraction.' I kept the tone of my voice neutral.

The female from the cells was in my living room gift wrapped to keep me from looking past the surface of what I was being told.

He handed me a silver key gesturing at her handcuffs, 'We had to restrain her for her own good. She's for you. Go. Enjoy her.'

I took a moment to study the screen further. Handcuffed. Blindfolded. Unwilling. Her struggle to break free from the cuffs obvious in the way she cradled her wrists to her stomach.

Taking my time entering the room another letter in the middle of the dining table caught my eye immediately. Reading the brief contents, I balled it up. Her head swung toward the clanging sound of it hitting the bottom of the bin I kept close by. Narrowing my eyes slightly I assessed her properly.

She was hurt. Hunching forward to protect herself I hazarded the injury was somewhere on her torso. No blood marred the simple green shift dress.

Bruising perhaps I mused as I scanned down her bare arms to her wrists. She'd rubbed herself raw in a futile attempt to free herself from them. Tear stains were still fresh upon her cheeks.

She had frozen in position holding her breath almost as if she feared him.

I moved away from the tiny cameras hidden among the books on my desk. Walking lightly on my feet I positioned myself closer to her.

'Your name?' I injected a hint of dominance into my tone enough to ensure she would give me what I wanted to know immediately.

'I am nameless until you give me something you prefer.' Her tone soft. Light. Almost airy. A direct contrast to the fire I had observed twisting at the core of her nature.

Bending down grazing my lips against her ear in a pretence of affection I asked in a low voice, 'What would you like to be called?' I took the opportunity to run my fingers over her wrists lightly probing for further damage.

She pitched her response soft enough not to be picked up on the audio feeds, 'Liana. Lia.' Taking a moment to process her whispered request my lips curved upwards.

She had not only provided me with a name but the diminutive she preferred as well. Untying the silken bow holding the blindfold to her face I slowly removed it from her face.

My reward a glimpse of her ruby irises before she lowered her eyes. Playing to the cameras. Sliding my fingers into her hair cradling her gently, 'I think I will call you Liana. Lia. A beautiful nickname for a beautiful female.' Tugging slightly, I force her to meet my eyes, 'The bathing chamber is through the door on your left. You will soak until I join you. Am I clear?'

Waiting for me to untangle my hand she obeyed instantly.

'Wait.' Smirking I hold up the small key. She hurried back to my side turning slightly so that I had easy access to the lock. Sucking in her breath sharply she exhaled as I checked both wrists thoroughly now that they were free of the shackles.

Keeping my true feelings in check I nudged her in the direction of the bathroom.

Focusing on a book one of the cleaning staff had left open on the coffee table I allowed her some dignity to hobble stiffly through the doorway opposite.

{Lia}

Black dots still danced in front of my eyes. I narrowed my concentration down to the feeling of the marble countertop on my bare skin. Waiting for the pool to fill I picked up one of the glass bottles off the counter. Removing the lid, I sniffed at the delectable fragrance. Adding a few drops out of the bottle to the swirling water I sighed softly. My bath would have to wait. Business first. Turning the taps off I shrugged out of the new dress someone had put me in.

Staring at my reflection in the mirror my fingertips trailed over my body probing the extent of my injuries. The crippling pain I had suffered had dulled down to a constant ache.

My brow furrowed at the bruises marring my creamy skin in a decorative pattern. Multiple s's imprinted my skin. My mind struggled with the implications.

Surfacing against the side of the pool to soak I methodically worked shampoo through my tresses. Images danced through my mind. No. I had refused this assignment. The Master beat me. The s from his signet ring sinking in. Slipping under the water I took my time before resurfacing on the other side of the pool closest to the patio doors.

Pushing my wet hair out of my eyes a hand shackled my wrist holding it firm. I could play this scenario two different ways.

Choosing to keep my image of a damaged quarter I instantly froze. 'Someone beat you.' His quiet statement sent chills down my spine. Fingers smooth more wet strands of hair away from my ear. His mouth replaces his fingers on my ear demanding answers, 'Why are you really here Lia?'

His intimidation and interrogation skills need work. I close my eyelids showing my defiance.

Coercing me for information would get him nowhere. I had been trained by some of this best. I knew how to be stubborn under immense pressure.

Placing my arm on the edge of the pool his hand circles my neck. Caressing it. Applying unexpected pressure causing pain Ethan doesn't raise his voice. His tone devoid of emotion he warns me, 'Be honest. I don't have time for lies.'

Lies are what I must feed him. I don't answer. Waves of frustration roll off him as his body language changes without warning. Teeth graze my earlobe and then sink into it. Retribution for my silence. He closes off my airway completely.

Gazing at the far wall dispassionately I ignore my body's instinct to panic with the lack of oxygen. He gives me a small shake before releasing the pressure on my airway, 'The truth Lia.'

Dragging much-needed air back into my lungs I swallow apprehensively. He feels the movement.

Stroking my neck with the tip of his forefinger he waits until I've gathered myself.

'The truth will damn us both.' I murmur. My pulse remains steady under his fingertips and I know he's thinking about how easy it would be to crush me. Snuff out my life. His hand tightens into a firmer grip. Trust. I don't trust him anymore then he trusts me. I tell a half-truth my voice emerging as the merest thread of sound, 'I was beaten because I refused this assignment.'

Amusement tinges his words, 'Why you?' He removes his hand from my neck as a show of good faith. 'Why not me?' Pulling my knees to my chest under the foam clouding the water I continue in a monotone voice of my own, 'Don't you know what I am?' After seeing my isolated existence, I was surprised he hadn't dug around in my files.

He had the clearance level to see every pain filled moment. 'What are you?' Ethan injects a hint of menace into his voice. Alone. That's what I am.

Completely and utterly alone with my curse. I can't stop the fear creeping into my voice. 'Death with a single touch.' My voice emerges little louder than a whisper.

A whisper that echoes around the room. He rounds the pool into my line of sight. Hard features. He leans against the opposite wall, 'Explain. Use precise words.' Taking the opportunity to rub my neck lightly I gather the meagre shreds of my courage.

Keeping my eyes firmly fixed on his face I attempt to explain, 'There are many names for what I am. What I can do.' I think for a second before sharing, 'I am a curse of the flame. A hex of the grave. A jinx of anguish. The one most commonly used is a bane of sorrow.' The tremors I have been concealing from him begin sweeping through my entire body. Delayed reaction to the beating.

Surprising me with his kindness he adds extra hot water to the pool. He shouldn't have done that. Peering up through my eyelashes I give up my hidden weapon, 'I have the ability to kill males with a single stroke of my fingers.' Watching with hooded eyes he waits as I work through the swirling thoughts in my mind.

Memories of emotional blow blacks from the past overwhelm me and I concentrate on regulating my breathing to the count in my head. 'How many times?' He asks abruptly and adds, 'You kill on command correct? How many times have you been forced to do it?'

Twice. I look down at the water and speak the number aloud. 'What was your recovery period?' He sounds curious. Just as curious as the mad scientist who serves as the healer for the cells. 'Two days the first time. A week for the second.' Forcing myself to keep breathing I push away the memories of temporary insanity. Words fall from my lips one at a time slightly stilted, 'The foremother I was housed with originally attacked our guard when her sanity was shredded beyond repair.'

He nods thoughtfully. The practised mask he wears snaps back into place easily. He exits into the interior of the apartment.

Releasing a shuddering breath internally I berate myself for saying too much. I curse myself for giving him the truth of me.

Slipping under the water I rinse the stench of death from my nostrils. Taking advantage of the luxury available to humour wrap my body in one towel and my hair in another. Having nothing to wear but the shift dress I woke up in I make the most of my time above stairs by using the lotions and perfumes lined up on the cosmetics table.

{Ethan}

She turns her head. Unasked questions dancing in her eyes. Holding a dress shirt out in front of me I offer it to her, 'I have nothing in your size. When is your deadline?' Deadline. Whose death though? I wonder as she takes her time accepting my shirt wary of a trap.

'Conclave.' Her cryptic word sends ice through my body. Two months. Eight weeks.

Eight weeks to prove my worth and guarantee my survival.

She, however, was a complication. One I had no choice but to deal with immediately.

'If I send you back to the cells tomorrow he will have you killed.' I stated a cold hard irrefutable fact. Lowering her head into her hands Lia replied wearily, 'You are naive if you think that is all that will happen to me. Death is an act of mercy for most of the females who live below.'

Her hair hangs in damp strands down her back as soon as she releases it from the confines of the towel. Rubbing my hand across my face I relay my wishes for her to meet me in the kitchen as soon as she is dressed. My promise of coffee to sweeten the sting of my tone rewards me with a hint of a smile.

Appearing to keep busy by preparing coffee my mind I consider the bare facts. She had been beaten. Badly beaten. I still didn't trust her. Trust was a commodity that had yet to be earned on both sides. The bathing chamber door opens.

She steps out timidly in a strapless dress. Lia has done some weird wrapping thing with it upon closer inspection.

Releasing a low whistle, I catch her quirking an eyebrow in my direction.

Placing both mugs of coffee on the table I wait for her to join me.

Drawing her into my arms for a hug I brush a kiss over her ear and whisper, 'Pretend.'

Her body relaxes against mine instantly moulding herself to me in an overt display of intimacy. 'An army of females will arrive shortly to tend to your needs.' She draws back slightly in silent question.

Smiling at the confusion evident in her eyes I gesture to her outfit, 'While I appreciate this look. You cannot appear in public wearing only my shirts.'

'I am grateful for your generosity.' The standard response she has been taught fell from her lips easily. 'Be honest with me. How do you really feel?' I allow some humour to bleed through my sarcastic comment.

She peers up from beneath her mass of still damp hair, 'If I answer you the wrong way will you hurt me?' She was testing her boundaries. Curious she waits for my reply holding herself perfectly still.

'No.' She had the right to own how she really felt. She considers my single word response from all angles before venturing, 'I have had no right to anything for most of my life. I do not know what it is that you want me to do.'

This must be a version of safe responses covered in the training room instilled in females at a young age that when presented with the opportunity to choose they needed a readjustment period. Drinking my coffee, I knew I needed a new game plan fast. One that included Lia.

The questions remained in my mind. Who was playing who? Could I trust her? She had been sent to distract and kill me in a way that would have severe repercussions on her own psyche. She needed my help whether she wanted it or not.

Decision made I told her, 'I am going to keep you here. You will spend your days with my mother learning to be my consort.'

CHAPTER SEVEN
Consort

{Lia}

Consort. The word hung heavy in the air between us. Could I accept his decree at face value? If he was for real, then my survival was a done deal. Letting my hair swing forward in a waterfall I shielded my face from his view.

I accepted that he wanted to give me a way out. The Master trusted no one.

'He will not believe you wish to keep me exclusively.' My shoulders drooped as I came to the realisation. 'He will.' Gentle fingers tucked the hair back behind my ear dismantling my flimsy barrier, 'I don't share with others. He knows me.' I read the unsaid sentiment in his eyes. John had underestimated Ethan from the beginning.

The pungent scent of caffeine invaded my synapses. Stomach clenching painfully, I struggled to remember the last time I had eaten anything. Correctly interpreting the audible growling emanating from my body Ethan picked up the in-house com system.

Watching him efficiently order food I made myself comfortable against the nearest wall.

Signing off he eyed my choice of seating. 'I don't share with others,' He reiterated before adding, 'and I take care

of what is mine. You're hungry. We'll eat.'
His simple words were reassuring.

Hiding my emotional turmoil with ease I
turned my attention outwards to take in
my surroundings. The apartment had an
aura of overt opulence on a scale I had
never imagined could exist.

Every comfort had been provided for
the heir of the First Family.

Drawn to the comfort of the
overstuffed leather couch I sank down
into the seat automatically snuggling
against the soft back cushion. Feasting
my starving eyes on the colour in the room
I wriggled my toes in the plush carpet in
delight.

He sat in the corner of the room glass of
amber liquid in hand. An amused smirk on
his face. Guilt stabbed at me. Why? Why
did he have to be the new mark? Mood
dropping, I curled up with my feet under

the hem of the improvised dress I was wearing.

{Ethan}

Taking a small mouthful of my drink I rolled it around in my mouth while contemplating the conundrum in my apartment. She acted so out of place within the world that I took for granted.

Everyday items were a source of wonder and excitement for her.

Enjoying the sight of her eccentricity I privately hoped that Mother would take her time rallying her small army of assistants.

This female was an intriguing blend of innocence and assassin. I wondered if she knew how to use her beguiling ways against me. Her mouth quirked up slightly in the corner as she saw me looking. Yeah, she knew exactly what she was doing to me.

Groaning to myself internally I knew she was a complication that I hadn't foreseen. This female had the potential to become my greatest weakness. The staff entered with the food and placed the trays on the table in the corner of the room.

Grateful for the distraction I placed my empty glass down before telling her to come and eat. Lifting the covers off the two trays that the kitchen staff had delivered to reveal two large bowls of soup I waited until she had seated herself before saying, 'I wasn't sure when you were last fed properly, so I got us something light.'

Perusing her face at my leisure I could tell that it hadn't been recently. She had all but frozen at the sight of so much food.

{Lia}

Waiting until he had situated himself opposite to me I picked up my spoon tentatively. 'You don't have to wait for me to tell you to eat Lia.' Tears threatened to spill over at the kindness in his voice. Forcing myself to take small mouthfuls of the soup I concentrated on the impeccable table manners I had been taught.

The light tapping on the door broke my reverie. Somehow, I had managed to eat both bowls of soup. 'One moment.' He answered loudly. Raising my eyes to his face he spoke, 'You will cooperate with everything my mother asks of you.' The underlying message transparent. Don't hurt anyone I care about.

Lilianna Smythe. Confused I kept my mouth closed. I had thought he had meant staff would see to my needs not his mother. Soft voices filled the room.

Too many voices all demanding my attention simultaneously. Touching the side of my head gently Ethan's voice controlled the chaos our dinner had become.

An hour later I stood in the centre of Lilianna's apartment dressed in a dress that reminded me of what I imagined a soft sunset to look like.

Draped in the softest material I had ever worn and groomed to perfection I couldn't help but check how restricted my movement was. Surprised with the range of motion allowed I kept my hands clasped together in front of me. The maids jostled each other for space around me aiding appropriate accessories to complete the look.

A sharp clap sent the maids fluttering out the door leaving me alone with his mother. Her sharp eyes assessed me through glasses that glinted in the light.

'The healer tells me you need time to recover from your accident.' She began her voice light but firm. Accident. That's what we were calling it.

'You have left the cells for a life as a consort to the First Family heir. There are many who will envy your new position. There are some who will plot your downfall. You must remember in this tower there are eyes everywhere.' Her stern words were accompanied by a kind smile. Her thinly veiled warning well received. We could not speak freely in her apartment either.

She was exactly as I remembered. Soft-spoken but direct. 'Your behaviour reflects directly on my son at all times. Your new title is Mistress and you will be addressed accordingly. I believe it will be imperative that we spend a small part of each day on etiquette.'

Recognition flashed in the depths of her eyes as she acknowledged our brief prior connection before warning me that only rest for the next few days would speed my healing.

{Ethan}

Entering the room, I tried hard to reconcile the feminine explosion with the tidy apartment I had left Lia in.

Instantly I recognised the dress she was wearing as an old one of Charli's. 'You have finished with Lia for tonight?' I enquired as I bent and brushed a kiss on my mother's cheek. 'For tonight.' We both turned to face her as Mother added, 'We have much to do before you can present her to the family.' She handed me a container of ointment from the healer, 'Bring her back to me at the beginning of the week and use this.'

Striding confidently through the silent and empty halls she kept herself exactly half a pace behind my shoulder. Beneath her subservient exterior, I knew she was on guard scanning for immediate threats.

A bag of clothing swung beside my legs. More would arrive for her as soon as mother deemed them acceptable.

Glancing covertly around the halls one last time she followed me back into the apartment without a word.

I led her through to the sleeping quarters without stopping. 'This is where you will retire.'

Opening the door to the unused Consort's room I set the bag on the floor before leaning back against the wall to allow her to explore her new space.

{Lia}

Circling the room twice I couldn't believe the vastness of it. Settling in a cream wingback chair beside the bed I thought that my cell would have fitted into the space twice over.

Decorated in the same soft shades of cream and grey as Lillianna's apartment I knew that I would be happy in this colour neutral room. 'Is this all for me?' The hesitant words slipped out before I could stop them.

'You will get used to it.' His voice gruff Ethan pushed himself off the wall and tossed over his shoulder, 'Get some sleep now.' before leaving me with my thoughts. The room was quite pleasant to look at it. In fact, there was not a splash of Sinopia in the entire apartment for which I was truly grateful.

I would have to stop being so impressed with my new surroundings if I were to survive living above stairs.

There was a war brewing in the First Family and I had no intentions of being on the wrong side.

The flashbacks were bleeding into my reality. At first, they were the usual nightmares of monsters snatching her up from her living quarters on the train. Then came the faces. A female with a long thick brunette braid. A boy with a haunted face. A male with a smile that never quite reached his eyes. Nature as far as her mind could comprehend. An unshakable feeling of wrongness. None of it made sense. It never did.

Deep down the constant tiredness and bone-deep aches were never-ending. I wasn't sure how much more I could take without screaming.

I had been forced into this life and I had long since made peace with my choice of staying with Ethan. Massaging my temples, I knew that my time was running out.

Staring out at the sky the dark clouds matched my mood perfectly.

'What did they give you in the cells?' I had bothered him with the constant pacing, 'Was it a needle or a tablet?' 'A green capsule.' My hands were shaking slightly.

Clasping them together to control the issue I walked my path again until I arrived in front of his desk where he was trying to work. 'How long were you on them?'

Ethan put down the file he had been attempting to read. His dark eyes softened as they touched on my deteriorating condition. 'Time has no meaning in the cells. Only routine.

They always medicated us before first meal. They always watched me take it. To refuse is to die.' Twirling a lock of hair around my finger I indicated that this was the kind of conversation we didn't need to be recorded.

{Ethan}

Her extreme agitation concerned me on so many levels.

Leading her into the bathing chamber I watched her make herself comfortable on the padded stool in front of the cosmetics table I had set up for her.

'To remember is to die.' I prompted her not willing to lose the thread of the conversation.

The guards had apprised me of the practice during my tour of the sub-levels. Eyeing her with a shrewd look I informed her quietly, 'You're beginning to remember.'

'Am I?' She asked quietly. We both knew the stakes in the game we were playing.

They would kill us both in a heartbeat. 'I don't know how to interpret what I see. I don't know if they're memories or bad dreams.' Honesty. She needed something tangible she could hang onto. 'I need to read your file.' She opened her mouth and I continued before she could say anything, 'I need to find out what they pumped into you then I can ask Mother's healer to try to reverse it.'

'They called me Ember.' She reminds me in a small voice left eye twitching. She becomes absorbed in her reflection in the mirror.

CHAPTER EIGHT
Her File

{Ethan}

Inserting the skeleton key I had obtained into the lock of the door of my foremother's apartment I slipped through the gap just big enough for my body. I knew drug withdrawal when I saw it. Her odd behaviour had to be something working its way out of her system.

Withdrawing a pair of light gloves from my pocket I paused long enough to listen to the light snores emanating from the bedroom before proceeding to sit down in the heavy office chair.

Accessing Lia's file in the mainframe proved to be challenging. The evidence damning his entire family for all eternity sat on the black and white screen in front of him staring him in the face. Listed neatly on spreadsheets that spanned the course of nearly five centuries were the records for the sub-levels. His family had been trading in females longer than it had been presenting a clean image to the known world.

Reading the unencrypted parts of Lia's file while the rest copied to a portable drive I scrolled through the files looking for the first entry about her.

Child, brunette hair, Oceania origin, refuses to speak. Designation undecided, relegated to c5 until next assessment.

Caging possible there's something about her eyes.

Clicking on the next page I found the next report.

Early assessment young female previously brunette Oceania Origins c5.

The child is exhibiting the outward appearance of the ability known as the bane of sorrow. In my humble opinion, she will be worth more as an asset than as a quarter. Given that she will become dangerous to all males. Transfer to row x is strongly recommended where she can learn to harness her abilities from those of her own kind.

Suppressant r strongly recommended. Dosage: one tablet daily with the first meal.

I kept reading making the conscious effort to resist grinding my teeth together. The clinical nature of the notes reminding me she had been treated little better than a test subject.

Female approximately 12 years old row x cherry red hair and eyes

First mission as an asset. The asset will be instructed to approach the target and touch the skin of his hand as if begging for help.

Debrief: asset appears severely withdrawn and overwhelmed. Given that first kills are always difficult it is my recommendation that she spend time in the isolation cell in row x. Permanent caging.

The asset will make positive contributions to Smythe Towers in return for these privileges.

Asset known as Ember row x

Blood singer. Has performed admirably over the years she has been in the cells.

Mission: infiltrate the new heir.

Find out the location of Charlotte Grace. Report all data collected including anything *regarding Elanna de Montmercy. Terminate target upon receiving the order.*

Methodically cleaning the keyboard of all biological traces, I let myself back out of the apartment.

I knew of only one person I could trust who would be able to decrypt the files.

Slipping into his domain I automatically sidestepped the blade thrown at my head. 'Brother.' Using our standard greeting I held up the drive, 'Need to use a terminal not plugged into the mainframe. Could use some help decrypting some files.'

Fane took the drive from me. Used to our meetings at odd hours he switched on his coffee machine as he passed it. Impressed with his array of weapons on the wall I waited until he announced, 'You can view them now.' Trading places I clicked on the first file. 'Scrub the history when you're done.'

His footsteps faded affording me privacy to view the potentially sensitive material.

Male figures loomed over the small frame of a sobbing child. Together they crowded her back against a table tilted on its end. Restraining her securely they tipped it horizontally. Two machines were rolled in behind her head. They covered the small body in a network of needles, tubes and wires before standing back from her.

His stomach lurched as he watched them fill bags with her blood. Draining her almost to empty and then cycling the collected blood back into her veins.

What were they doing to her? Hoping to find some answers in the second file I opened it. This time Lia appeared to be about the same age as Charli. She now had her signature red hair.

Her mouth held deliberately in a straight line, eyes blank as she was strapped into a chair contraption. James had upgraded his medical equipment. This time she waited woodenly while they cycled her blood through her system. Off to the side, James added chemicals to the blood pouches before hooking them back up.

Lia's eyes flew open. Bone-chilling screams ripped from the depths of her soul echoed around the room. 'Hush Ember. You don't wish to make the Master angry. Take your medicine like a good little female. Pretty little female.' James stroked her face. Instantly the sound of her screams faded. Her mouth was open.

I could see the terror on her face, but her screams had no sound.

'Your new drug works brother.' John's bored voice emitted from the corner of the laboratory. James turned to face him.

His displeasure clear in his voice, 'Of course it does. Did you doubt my brilliance brother?'

'We did not doubt your brilliance.' His father's weary voice emanated from another corner, 'I have concerns about your choice of the test subject.'

The file faded to black.

My mind worked overtime to solve the puzzle in front of me. She had been adamant that they had been giving her tablets with her morning meal. What if the tablets had been a placebo and her compliance had all but been assured through the drugs they had mixed intravenously in her blood?

I hoped the last file could shed some more light on the subject. I could feel Fane's presence before clicking on the last file.

This one could be as recent as six months prior to the length of Lia's hair.

'Ember.'

'Master.' Her voice soft. Her posture non-threatening. she kept her hands clasped behind her.

'It's time for your medicine.' John smiled at her, 'Sit down in the chair.'

Lia sat. She leaned back against the back and rested her arms palms up on the wide armrests. 'I am ready.' She spoke softly.

'I'm not.' I thought silently. Watching her willingly sit through being hooked up in a cocoon of tubes and needles again curdled my stomach.

'This machine acts like a switch for your natural abilities. You will be a bigger asset to us if you can learn to control the after effects of your gift.' John stood before her, 'My brother has been working on a new formula.'

'Thank you, Master.' She responded with the same soft voice.

'What the hell?' I swore softly. She thanked them for hurting her.

She believed that she needed the drug. Pausing the file, I refused to watch the rest of the file. Refused to watch them experiment further on her. A hand landed heavily on my shoulder breaking me out of my anger-induced reverie.

'E. There something you want to tell me?' His brother pointed at the frozen screen, 'Liquid suppressant R. Nastiest shit known to mankind. James masterminded its creation. John's dealing it out strategically through his minions.' Of course. I had heard of it. Used to Fane silently having my back I asked, 'Is there a way to reverse the effects?'

'Weakens the heart.' He almost growled the words at me, 'Complete healing is impossible. Breaking the habit on the other hand...' His voice trailed off.

He peered closer at the image on the screen. 'What is it about her that has you risking your own life?' A note of intrigue hung heavy in the air between us.

Narrowing my eyes, I arrived at an almost inevitable conclusion, 'Why do you know so much about it? Do you know her?'

Fane stabs his fingers at the shadowy circle of figures surrounding the equipment almost just out of shot. 'I. Was. There.' Anger punctuates each word, 'Not everyone above stairs has had it easy. You need to remember that Brother. That female haunts my dreams. They almost broke her on that machine that day.'

{Lia}

Fingers crept along the wall searching for the lock in the darkness. Weak. Exhaustion rolling over me from the constant extensive purging.

Dripping water on the tiles from my wet hair I snagged a fresh towel quickly. Bundling my hair up took more effort than usual. Everything hurt.

Working my way through the silent apartment I retreated to my sleeping quarters. Curling up into a tight ball I prayed for a dreamless night. Sleep swiftly took me into its embrace.

CHAPTER NINE
Surprise Visit

{Third Person}

Mercy House stood blissfully unaware of the two intruders making their way carefully through the exquisite rooftop gardens. Hiding their gear between flowerbeds they took a moment to appreciate the atmosphere.

'These are new.' She commented thoughtfully. 'Have you commed Jo?' He asked her.

Shaking her head in amusement she replied, 'You could have used a cooler code phrase.'

He could hear the laughter barely concealed in her voice. 'We were being pursued at the time.' He defended himself and added, 'Have you told her we're coming?'

Jo's mouth twitched as she glanced upwards at the door to the rooftop. It creaked open triggering a silent alarm on one of the monitors.

Poking his head through the doorway Cerin glanced at the monitor that had started flashing red. 'Stand down. They're guests of mine.' Jo reassured him adding, 'You remember Marianna de Montmercy and her chosen Scott Jackson.'

'Bad timing.' He commented leaving her alone again. Cautious footsteps made their way down the wide circular staircase into the living area. A cloaked figure slowly turned in a circle then pronounced from the depths of the deep hood, 'All clear.'

A slender hand emerged from the depths of a long brown sleeve to gently pull the hood back revealing the pale purple hair of her best friend.

'How's your leg?' A second figure descended from the rooftop into the open area below. 'The usual. We've been moving fast for days pushing it.' Facing him Mari watched Scott scan the room for threats. Finding none, they both relaxed their guard.

'You've come a long way to check up on my leadership skills.' Jo stood outlined in the doorway of the smaller living area. 'We were in town and thought we'd drop in.' Scott answered as the two females met in the middle of the room for a hug. 'Some more warning would have been nice.' Jo admonished them both gently.

Mari removed her cloak and draped it over the back of the nearest chair. At her inquisitive look, Jo continued, 'Cerin is here guarding a young female. She is in danger and he won't hesitate to use his knife.' Jo motioned slightly with her head in their direction.

'I should have sent word that we were coming when we left the farm.' Mari thought as they observed Cerin patiently hold a supporting hand over the young female's and together they raised a cup to her mouth. 'Has she visited our healing centre yet?' Mari asked in an undertone.

'I believe that what Ravenna has is degenerative.' Jo spoke softly as she drew Mari back into the outer living area, 'She came to us under highly unusual circumstances.' Mari's silver eyes met Jo's electric blue ones as they shared a look of mutual understanding.

'It's not like you to be so cryptic.' Jo tried to lighten the mood. 'It was necessary.' Scott spoke as he pulled a leather-bound book from the bag he was carrying.

He crossed the room and placed it in Mari's hands. She cradled it carefully between the palms of her hands.

'We haven't spoken in a long while.' Mari started. 'Since you left here last warm season.' Jo cut in. Mari shot her a quelling look and she subsided, 'Since last warm season.

I've had quite an adjustment period to living in the territories.' Mari looked at Scott and he nodded his encouragement, 'I need to tell you about our journey home.'

Jo led them to a group of chairs with semi-privacy in an alcove off the main living area. She waited till Mari had settled before taking her own seat. 'I know you could pull the story out of my head but please just listen instead.' Mari took her hand.

'The journey home was eventful. After the train could go no further we travelled by wagon over the Black Tips.

The Eighters who control the territory between Spark City and Bordertown took an interest in us.' Mari began.

'You had to fight your way out.' Jo's eyes glowed softly.

'Jo.' Mari raised her eyebrow in warning. Her friend hadn't invaded her private thoughts in a long time.

'Right so they took an interest in you.' Jo grinned back unrepentant.

Mari rolled her eyes before continuing, 'We stumbled into a cave during a whiteout. What we found was heartbreaking. I healed a male of the sickness. We were too late to help his mate.'

'Liam is a seer.' Scott picked up the threads of the story from her, 'He helped me keep Mari safe when she decided to almost obliterate a tribe of Eighters for attempting to take her from me without her permission.'

Jo waggled her fingers at Mari who leaned forward slightly in her seat in response. Jo read Mari's memories of experiencing her abilities unchecked for the first time. The huge toll the overuse had taken on her body. She accessed Mari's memories of Liam. People with abilities had not been chosen at random.

Genetics and the atmosphere were contributing factors just as she had suspected all along.

Why were the Eighters kidnapping the females? How long had they been working with John Smythe?

Jo raised her eyebrows as she accessed the information about the de Montmercy prophecy. She gave Mari a small nod to let her know that she had finished intruding on her private thoughts.

'Tell me about the book.' All traces of her previous levity had fled. Jo felt hot and cold at the same time. 'It explains the history of those who are chosen to have enhanced abilities. Personal accounts from across the five dome cities and assorted territories. There are exercises to help those who have them to learn control.' Mari paused, and her eyes met Scott's, 'It was hoped that this book would help train others who have no access to the learning centres. It would be a shame for such information to fall into the hands of the High Council.'

'Four. Four dome cities.' Jo corrected her softly still trying to process the wealth of information contained in the tome in front of her.

'Five.' Mari replied, 'One broke away from the Union of Souls nearly fifty years ago-it's referred to as the lost colony in the Great Library.'

'Are you going to take your discovery to the High Council?' Jo asked. Her mind buzzing with the information she had just discovered. 'Not yet.' Scott's face tightened in anger, 'The Eighters have infiltrated the building once with us inside. They are as much involved as Smythe Towers. They may also be searching for this chosen one. We need to know more about this prophecy before we approach them again.'

'Are you really putting so much faith in an old folk story from the mountains?' Jo asked struggling to understand. 'I'm not willing to take the chance with Mari's life.' Scott replied.

'You could ask Ethan for help.' Charli's quiet confidence shone through as she mentally connected with them all at once.

'Ravenna.' They heard Cerin admonish her gently out loud.

'I didn't mean to listen in. Sometimes I can't help it.' Charli's apology rang like a sweet bell as her presence receded from the room. Mari's expression changed dramatically as she faced her friend. 'We've all been practising our shielding.' Jo admitted with a small laugh.

They'd had to learn quickly how to establish boundaries with Charli. She refused to communicate on any other level.

Mari's movement caught her attention as she placed the book on the table between them. 'I believe she will benefit from having access to this book. There are many searching for any female with enhanced gifts. She must learn not to broadcast blindly.'

'I do not broadcast blindly.' Charli pointed out to Cerin hurt that anyone could think that.

'You slipped up and showed them what you could do.' He commented and asked, 'Didn't anyone warn you about trusting strangers with your abilities?'

'No.' He could hear the struggle in her mental voice. A tear rolled unbidden down one cheek.

'Choose who you share your gifts with wisely. There are males in this city who exploit those weaker than them.' He wiped the tear away.

'May I join you?' Mari stood in the doorway to what was once her favourite room in the whole building. Cerin blocked Charli from sight. 'It has been a long time my Lady.' He watched warily as she made her way slowly into the room with the aid of her crutch. 'I only wish to talk with

118

Ravenna.' She replied allowing him to read her intentions in her eyes.

He folded his arms across his chest and responded with an insolent grin. 'Not happening my Lady. Lady Mercy said I have to stick to this one like glue.'

Mari dipped her head slightly as she realised that this resistance was because the child didn't know her as well as he did.

'It will give you time to go report in with Dair.' She smiled, 'Your brother can be quite scary when he is worried about those he loves.' He uncrossed his arms and shot her a piercing stare. Mari grinned back at him unrepentant that she had had to play the big brother card.

Grinning back at her Cerin spoke again, 'She needs your help with just about everything.' When he turned to face the blond girl on the couch Mari could see his toughness fade. 'I won't be long.' He made sure that the light cover was tucked in around her small slight body before exiting the room.

'I'm Mari de Montmercy. This used to be my family house.' She cast her silver eyes over the girl's face in front of her.

'I didn't mean to interrupt your conversation.' Charli injected a note of contrition into her mind voice.

'I know. The world outside of the inner circles is full of people who want to take your special gift and use it for themselves. What Cerin told you was true. Would you like to see what I can do?' Mari spoke in a gentle voice.

Charli's eyes flicked in acknowledgement. Mari allowed her hands to be coated with purple energy. 'I can't do this for long or my chosen will be very upset with me.' She explained as she sat down in the wingback chair beside the couch.

Little bursts of purple energy exploded harmlessly below the ceiling. 'Fireworks.' Charli projected the word joyfully at her. 'Fireworks.' Mari echoed with a smile and added, 'I can do more. Want to see?'

'Yes.' The word danced into her mind without hesitation.

She calmly laid her hands gently on the child's exposed skin. After a few minutes, she took them away.

'You were in a lot of pain. I took some of it away from you. It should be easier to breathe now.' She kept her voice light.

'It always hurts to breathe. Why are you helping me?' her voice had turned serious.

'Because I could.' Mari absorbed her energy before continuing, 'There are times when I can do something to help but it is too dangerous.

That's when I hide my gifts and just watch events unfold. Do you understand now?'

'Yes.'

Mari rose to her feet slowly and sat in the overstuffed chair beside the couch. 'The book that I've just given to Lady Mercy will help you. Train you. If there is anything known about your specific abilities the information will be in there.'

CHAPTER TEN
Questions

{Lia}

Frustration plagued me. Irritable and lonely I folded myself into a cross-legged position on the floor of the patio overlooking the second circle. Taking a cleansing breath to centre my thoughts I began my morning stretching. The only difference in my surroundings was I now knew how a fifth felt.

Their cage was self-imposed. A desire of wanting to please their chosen.

Mine had been one of plexiglass. Ethan had not yet returned with any useful information.

Taking another deep breath, I blocked out the rich tapestry surrounding me. Colour, light and true emotions were all new. Below it was ultimately a simpler life. No one else cared if you were hurt. Everyone had their own pain to heal from. Some never did. Plans and intrigue swirled around me. Escape firmly out of my reach. My own dark thoughts threatened to sabotage my meditation.

Picking up the soft snick of the sliding doors opening I huffed silently to myself.

Instantly alert waiting to find out if the intruder was friend or foe I bent my front leg forward to snag the knife I had stashed in my shoe. Warm leather creaked in protest of being sat upon. A china cup clattered against the glass surface of one of the small side tables.

Breathing out through my mouth I counted to four silently before inhaling again just as silently.

Breathing out again in a rush at the fingers drumming on the arm of one of the patio chairs. 'Are you being intentionally noisy?' Calm flooded my frayed nerves as his cologne hit my nostrils. A subtle, clean smell I associated with him. 'Not intentionally no. You may continue.' His light words came out evenly. Sunlight enveloped me as the dome opened for the day. Warming me instantly.

A gentle breeze ruffling the strands of my hair that always escaped my braid.

Sensing that I had his complete and undivided attention I slid my weapon back into my boot before opening my eyes. Uncrossing my legs, I rose gracefully. 'Don't turn around.' He warned me in words low enough to evade the auditory sensors.

Moving onto the next phase of my routine I worked through some flexibility poses before asking, 'Are we being watched?'

We were always being watched. They wanted me to make him think I was naive and innocent. They wanted me to make him forget his duties to the family.

His breathing hitched and changed pattern before he responded, 'We're always on display.'

Moving through a few more stances before he said, 'Very heavy reading your file.'

Wobbling slightly, on one hand, I recovered enough to segue into the next stance. His statement required no response yet. 'It was enlightening.' His tone was measured. I heard him pick up his cup mouth suddenly dry in anticipation I bent over to look at him through my legs.

Raising my eyebrow slightly as he swallowed I challenged him to comment further.

Straightening up to face the city again his next question touched on the same subject my thoughts had been circling around. 'How did you survive being in isolation for so long?' His words came from a place of curiosity.

'The only way I knew how.' I could tell my cryptic reply intrigued him. I had no interest in reliving my poor excuse for a life for someone who could still betray me to the one person I feared the most.

'Your body language is betraying you.' Not wishing to respond any further I turned around and dropped into a deep curtsy waiting to be dismissed from his sight.

{Ethan}

I could tell my last words had disturbed her deeply. She had been kept isolated during the period when she needed people around her the most. If I allowed her to keep running from her past she would never be whole inside again. She was no longer an asset in my eyes and that made her dangerous. Flicking my finger lazily I gave her the signal to rise from the floor.

'Why did you come back?' Once deemed reliable enough to complete solo missions she had been given a single name and a lot of leeway. Her file had been unclear as to why she hadn't run when given the chance. Her orders were always the same. Gain trust. Pretend to enjoy the male's company then kill him.

Surreptitiously she pointed toward the roof of the building across from us.

Light glinted off metal. There was a gun trained on us. If she made any attempt to leave a mark or escape after the deed a bullet would find her. 'Because this is my home.' Her desperate eyes never left mine as she mouthed something for those watching us. Always watching us. She was as much a pet on a long leash as I was.

Lia had thought about escaping. Planned it out in minute detail. Still, she stayed. Her prison had long transcended the four walls of her cell to the scope and imagination of her mind. 'He never fully trusted you outside the building on your own, did he?'

I knew the questions I was asking were explosive but her information was critical, 'Do you have his trust completely now?'

She cocked her head to one side regarding me with large eyes, 'I don't know.' The truth behind her words resonated with me. John would never trust her. Not completely. Not ever. 'You started lessons with my mother already.

She is pleased with your progress and informs me you will be ready to appear with me at a family event together soon.'

Indicating she should proceed me into the cold apartment I followed barely half a pace behind her.

She continued through to the bathing chamber on her own. Water running distracted me from the macabre turn of my thoughts enough to loosen my tie. Reappearing in the doorway she opened her hand palm up displaying 3 bugs. Small listening devices had been planted in the room overnight.

{Lia}

Disappearing for a moment I opened the cistern of the necessary and dropped them without hesitation into the water. Reappearing in the doorway, I smiled prettily for the camera loosening my hair fastening.

Flicking my eyes at the camera directly opposite in the spine of one of the books on the shelves I knew he would understand my silent message.

Swiftly crossing the room, he bent his head crashing his lips down on mine. Dominating the kiss. Bending me to his will he wrapped one arm around my waist holding me upright under his onslaught. Slowly walking me back into the bathing quarters he hooked one dress shoe around the edge of the door and swung it closed behind us.

Pulling back slightly he searched my eyes. 'I think that's all the show he needs for now.' He held me until I was steady on my own legs. Resisting the urge to raise my fingers to my lips I watched him take a half step back from me.

'Your first kiss?' He asked watching me gather myself. 'I didn't get out much before I met you.' I quipped stating the obvious as my breathing evened out.

Chuckling he rubbed a hand over his face. Stubble covered his chin. 'You stayed away.' Stating the obvious I took note of the rumpled state of his clothing.

'It took a while to break the encryption on some of the files. Your story checks out.'

He pulled a portable com out of his pocket and beamed some files up against the cream paint on the bathroom wall. The picture quality is grainy but not damaged enough that I can't make out the video that matches the audio.

'It's imperative that she thinks this is just a nightmare. If you want to earn her loyalty you will have to start small.'

John and James sat at a desk studying a file between them while Joseph lounged comfortably against the edge of it.

'Make the training fun like a game. You've seen my daughter. She learns best by play.' *He suggested.*

'We don't want a soulless killer.' *James's mouth was moving but his expression hid an underlying message. Something sinister.*

Shuddering I clenched my teeth to keep myself silent.

'She needs to keep her emotions for the type of work I have in mind for her.' John weighed in on the conversation and asked, 'How do we negate the after effects?'

'Her abilities end in madness. That much is known. She will have to be trained to use her bare hands as a last resort. A hidden weapon.' James replied thoughtfully.

'I will send my mate to her. She can tame her and make her feel wanted.' Joseph rose from the desk and turned to face his brothers, 'You can't train her like one of the halflings. She will need finesse brother.'

{Ethan}

'So, the nightmares were real?' Her lashes lowered over her eyes. Hiding her true thoughts from me. 'Are real.' I correct her gently and reveal, 'the machine that delivered your 'medicine' was the drugs being pumped directly into your blood stream.'

She's silent as she checks the temperature of the water in the bathing pool before adjusting the taps. Processing the new information rapidly she asks, 'Which drug?'

I allow her to feel the weight of my gaze inciting her to look at me.

I want to look her in the eyes when I deliver the news. Gradually she shifts her attention from her shaking hands to my face. 'They gave you liquid suppressant R. Side effects are cravings, cardiac arrest and death.' She flinches slightly at the word death before pulling herself upright again as if by sheer will alone. 'What do I need to do to survive this poison?' the strength of her question and the quiet conviction in her voice doesn't surprise me in the slightest.

'Keep yourself as calm as possible. I will be meeting with a healer I trust fully later today.'

She nods her understanding of my instructions before shutting the water off completely. Slipping by me she leaves with a whispered, 'Thank you.'

Emerging sometime later I found a note on my desk written in a childish hand.

'It was time for my lesson with your mother. There are more secrets in this building than you could possibly begin to know. The females in the cells love to gossip and sound carries. You should ask your mother about the female who birthed you and the de Montmercy Prophecy. L.'

{Third Person}

Ethan crumpled the note and tossed it into the fire burning in the grate beside him. The female was nothing if not resourceful.

She had not peppered him with questions about his absence. He poured himself a drink and took a small mouthful savouring the flavour of his coffee.

The moment Ethan had said the word 'Consort' Lia had become his responsibility. He sat down in his thinking chair. He had let himself in every night to check on her.

Listening to her stomach purge as part of the withdrawal had been deeply disturbing. Not as disturbing perhaps as finding the blood smeared rags at the bottom of the wash hamper.

Everything had already been stripped away from her. He didn't want her to know that he had seen her rawest moment when she had been huddled over the necessary.

She had been dry heaving with tears streaming down her face. She had a right to keep whatever remained of her dignity.

He turned his attention to the appointment he had set up with his mother later that day. Drumming his fingers on the arm of the chair Ethan took another sip of coffee. The questions he had to ask her would lead him to answers he was not sure he was ready to hear.

'I'm not your birth mother.' The low admission almost tore her heart through her chest. He could see the deep pain he was caused by the conversation he had just initiated.

The world they all lived in was a convoluted one. Leaning forward and he looked her in the eyes, 'You are my Mother.

I still need to know about the female who birthed me and the de Montmercy prophecy. My new consort said something I can't quite forget and it involves those two pieces of information.'

She began tapping her fingers in an agitated manner on the arm of the chair she was sitting in.

Ethan kept a track of it in his peripheral vision while he listened to her voice the words, 'Your father said that her name was Elanna.

It was a political choosing organised between your foremother and the first female of what was then known as de Montmercy house. She ended up choosing your Uncle John. Much of what I know is gossip and rumours. It would not serve our interests to rely on those.'

He watched as she rose gracefully.

Her hand was still tapping a pattern against the skirt of her dress. 'I have my volunteer shift in the healing centre soon. I hope the little information I have given you is adequate.' She bent to brush a kiss on his cheek.

He turned his head slightly for her to whisper, 'Be very careful. Elanna is why your father was murdered.'

He nodded as his brain rapidly converted the information she had slipped to him by appearing agitated by the subject.

He had to give credit to his father. He had set ways for his family to communicate and thrive under the nose of the ever-present watching eyes.

The information his mother had just imparted to him spun him out slightly.

She had told him what he wanted to know and included that he had a sister and two brothers. Marianna de Montmercy had once been trapped in Smythe Towers as his Uncle's chosen. The thought of what could have happened to her twisted his gut badly. The male had a dark side. One he was not eager to meet.

CHAPTER ELEVEN
Closer

{Ethan}

'You're staring at me.' She stated the obvious without raising her head from the book she was reading. 'I'm admiring the view.' I replied feeling the ends of my mouth tipping up into a tired grin.

Lia had taken up almost permanent residence on the floor beside the history portion of my bookshelf during the evenings when I brought work home with me.

She soaked up knowledge faster than most of the top researchers I had heard of. Her love of learning shining as she made up for years spent in limbo.

{Lia}

'Why don't you take a break?' He suggested. Raising my head again I marked my place in the three books I had been cross-referencing at the same time. Smoothing my skirt out I rose from the floor gracefully before accepting the glass of wine he held out to me. Taking my hand without a word he led me through the apartment dimming the lights.

Stopping outside the door at the end of the hall that led to his private quarters he turns to me, 'I would like you to join me tonight when you're ready.'

My voice catches in my throat and I sip the wine to stall for time. 'Yes master.'

The words come out softer than I intend nerves shining through. He's never insisted that I join him in his private chamber before.

'Address me by my given name Lia.' His smile calms my nerves as he tucks a loose strand of hair back over my ear his eyes demanding my trust and compliance.

Keeping a smile plastered on my face I retreat to my own sleeping quarters. Emotions swirl through my body. Fear swamps me. My hands are covered by adaptive tech. The adaptive tech that I have been wearing almost indefinitely since arriving above stairs. If he inadvertently removed them I could not touch him without causing instant heart failure.

Placing my glass on the low table in front of my couch I glanced into the full-length mirror that graced one wall of my bower. My facial expression remained the same.

No extra tell to alert those watching that I no longer thought of him as a target at all.

Raising my hands to my hair I unwound and unravelled my hair so that it hung in waves rippling down my back.

Combing it smooth free of tangles while concentrating on breathing techniques calmed me enough to slip into a semi-translucent nightgown.

Sliding my arms through the matching robe I took another fortifying sip of wine than another until the bottom of the glass was staring back at me.

Leaving it on my low table my bare feet sank deep into the carpet as I traversed the short distance back to the door leading to his room. Hanging slightly ajar it beckoned me to enter. Slipping through the opening I froze unsure.

Backing into the corner of the room I stood waiting for further instruction. Observing the art of being invisible until called upon.

{Ethan}

'Come join me.' Her agitation shows plainly on her face. Holding herself still in the corner she has allowed me to watch her carefully.

The light in the room has been dimmed so that all she can see is my outline in the darkness. Nothing to frighten her.

Not this time. Not any time. Navigating her way across the open space slowly she works her way to my side. Gathering her in my arms I face her away from me.

Melding myself against her back I cradle her gently from behind resting my hands loosely on her stomach. 'You're afraid.' I use my voice as a weapon. Low, soft and as smooth as honey, 'You won't harm me baby.'

Stroking her stomach gently I feel her start to relax against my chest. Becoming pliant as she enjoys my touch. Sliding my hands to the tie of her robe I loosen it so that I can slide it from her body leaving the offending garment pooled on the floor beside us.

{Lia}

I turn around in his arms. Reaching up tangling my hands in the back of his hair I tug his head gently downwards bringing his face closer to me.

Fusing my mouth to his parting my lips in answer to his questing tongue. His arms tighten around me. Holding me against him.

Slowly walking me backwards I feel something hit behind my knees. Sitting down I abruptly break the kiss. A small growl of frustration emanates from him before he grabs the back of my head and joins our mouths again.

Sliding his hands to my shoulders one slides further following the curve of my neck fingers stroking at my pulse point.

{Ethan}

Breaking the kiss, I stretch out on the bed beside her. Eyes glazed she continues to sit there. Tugging her down beside me she sweeps her mass of hair over one shoulder before nestling into my side.

'Tonight, there are no watching eyes. There's just us. This is for us. You have hair the colour of fire.' I wrap an arm around her taking a lock of it in my hand. Playing with it. 'Is that good or bad?' she asks quietly. 'Good.' I replied smiling at her innocence, 'Are you ready for more?' 'More?' She repeats the word. 'Definitely more.' I inform her reaching underneath the bed for the items I had stored there while waiting for her to join me.

{Lia}

Sitting up my heart begins to thud threatening to beat its way out of my chest. He strokes his fingers gently over the inside of my wrist feeling the rapid flutter of my pulse.

'Ssh.' Placing a soft kiss on my temple he brings me back subtly reminding me I can't afford to let my heart rate rise too high without consequences.

'Stand up.' He deliberately keeps his tone dark and steady. Approval at my instant obedience. He checks my pulse again before pulling me closer to him. 'Clasp your hands together in front of you.'

Producing a black satin tie, he works quickly tying it into a loose set of bracelets. Slipping my hands into the holes I watch passively as he wraps the rest of the length of the tie around my wrists.

'Trust me.' He demands producing another tie. His eyes hooded as he searches my face looking for any hint of discomfort. Words failing me I nod slightly.

He slips the second tie through my already bound wrists. Kissing me almost to distraction again he slings the loop of the second tie over a hook in the low ceiling.

{Ethan}

'They want a show.' I murmur in her ear taking a moment to kiss her earlobe and nibble on it before adding, 'This is our time. They will see something they won't think to question.'

Testing her ties, a mischievous smile spreads across her flushed face. Standing back, I admire the view of her hands bound out of the way allowing me access.

Allowing her to enjoy herself without fear of harming me.

Lia stood on her tiptoes, ruby eyes luminous, rosy lips begging to be assaulted with more kisses. Trust evident in her eyes as they follow my hands to my belt buckle.

Taking my time stripping it out of my jeans my fingers hover over the button on my jeans. She gasps softly in anticipation. Laughing. Breaking some of the tension.

'I was wondering when you were going to make a noise sweetheart.'

Undoing the button. Sliding my shirt off my shoulders. Giving her a view of the body she can't touch before pressing myself up against her.

Exploring with my hands learning her form beneath her nightgown. Her soft moans music to my jaded ears.

{Lia}

'Ethan?' His name falls from my lips as I plead for something. Anything. A pressure is building deep inside my body and his every touch is stoking the flames higher.

My body feels both heavy and sweet at the same time. 'I've got you Lia.' He whispers into my ear before prowling around my body again. Admiring it further. Picking me up I wrap both legs around his waist.

We both moan almost in unison. His pleasure stoking the flames ever higher.

{Ethan}

A while later I unloop the tie off the hook, working quickly I finish removing the bindings from Lia's wrists and massage her arms bringing feeling back to them.

Sagging against me cradling her arms against her body she's almost asleep on her feet. 'Stay here with me.' I wrap one arm around her to steady her and pull the quilt back with my free hand.

Scooping her up and transferring her onto the soft sheets she rolls onto her side hair a river of fire against my white sheets.

'Ethan?' her voice questioning heavy laden with her need for sleep. The mattress dips slightly behind her as I join her wrapping an arm around her waist pulling her small body against mine. 'Hmm.' I respond allowing myself a small moment to acknowledge how right this feels. How happy she's making me.

'Can we do that again?' she rolls over to face me eyes shut burrowing deeper into my side. 'Sleep.' Amusement and a strange tenderness flood my body.

'I was afraid.' She admits on the edge of sleep the place where all words are true, 'I was afraid I would hurt you. I don't remember enough about my ability and the little I do know scares the hell out of me.'

'I know.' Stroking the loose strands out of her face I kiss her forehead reassuring her, 'Sleep sweetheart. Tomorrow is a big day for you.' Shutting my own I eyes I enjoy the bliss of holding her in my arms.

CHAPTER TWELVE
Mistaken Identity

{Lia}

The elevator climbed to the fifth floor in the East Tower. Entering through the double doors the restaurant I seated myself at the private table in the corner of the room permanently reserved for the First Family heir. Taking the liberty of scanning my surroundings I pretended to be admiring the decor.

Nodding to no one I pasted a smile on my face blending into the scenery as I had been taught.

Cue the judgement. Sensing the countless looks from multiple directions raising my head I took a small sip of water.

Prickles of danger skittered down my spine. Something or a someone rather was studying me in depth. Pinpointing his location against the far wall I let my eyes drift past him feigning boredom. The collar on his wool trench coat was deliberately left askew.

It topped a casual outfit not usually seen or approved of by the Smythe male dress code. Something about this male made me want to disappear before my waiter arrived. Something about him reminded me of Ethan. Shivering under the intensity of his look I dropped my eyes to the perfectly placed setting in front of me.

{Unknown male}

She knew I was watching her. Her eyes examined the drapes in detail flickering over me before withdrawing. Her meal order caught my attention. Ordered in a well-modulated voice one could almost believe she had been brought up as one of them.

Impressed that she was the only female in the room planning on eating more than a damn lettuce leaf I settled back against the wall blending into the shadows. My job was to watch the little princess. Nothing more nothing less.

Answering a coded message led me to stand around for the next few hours. Cutlery clattering loudly against china drew me out of my memories my head whipping around to where she was seated. Keeping my hands loose I waited to see how the situation would play out before I intervened.

{Lia}

'You do not belong here!' An elderly female's voice shook with outrage.

Looking up from the freshly cooked meal in front of me I found Lady Arcana standing above me leaning on her cane with an imperious air surrounding her.

Arcana Smythe. Ethan's foremother and current First Lady of Smythe Towers was giving me the evil eye. 'My lady?' I questioned racking my brain for the slightest thing I could have done wrong to give offence. 'You have ears girl. You do not belong here. You have overstayed your welcome. You cannot pretend to be something that you are not.' Arcana waved her hand to encompass the dress and accessories I had chosen for the day.

I put down my fork and folded my hands in my lap away from all the sharp, shiny, interesting, everyday weapons on the table, 'I do not pretend anything, my lady. Ethan has made me his consort.

I'm eating here at his request.' It clicked then where she would have found my presence offensive. I was not wearing the identifying cuff of a consort.

A low buzzing filled my ears as panic began to set in. Refusing to bring myself to the Master's attention I watched Arcana march up to the two nearest males observing the altercation.

'Remove this rebellious quarter from my sight immediately.' There was no need for name calling. I refused to be dragged from a public place on the orders of the dragon lady.

Standing I folded the napkin neatly before laying it down beside my barely touched meal. Hands shaking slightly betraying my apprehension I grasped them together in front of me making it obvious to one and all I was being escorted out of the room.

His eyes collided with mine. Fury burning bright. Arching an eyebrow in question I turned and signalled to both males that I was ready. Who was he to me? Why was he furious with the way I was being treated?

{Unknown male}

The two males kept their decorum only until they rounded the corner into another hall. Dragging her along at a faster pace between them they gleefully stripped her jewellery from her ears, neck and hair. Her infuriating refusal to struggle was not slowing her descent back into the hellish cells below.

Scooping her belongings up I followed at a distance stopping only when they paused to check that the halls remained clear of witnesses. 'You will never be one of us.' Producing a wicked looking knife one of the males slid the flat of the blade over her lips. Teasing her with the promise of what was in store for her.

{Lia}

No. NO. NO! Mentally I had begun internally screaming. Slamming me back against the back wall one of the training cells they had thrown me into stunned me slightly. Shaking my head, I listened to the disembodied voice that promised I would never be one of the First Family. I didn't want to be one of them. I wanted to be free of them entirely.

Refusing to give into the fear that threatened to swallow me whole I froze instantly. Ice cold. The blade of the knife left a trail of goose bumps in its wake as it slid down the side of my neck.

The hand wielding it rotated it around inflicting shallow cuts in my skin. Cuts that stung and bled. Wounds that kept me focused and awake. The point of the knife slid down till it shredded the neckline of my favourite dress.

'Be a good rabbit or we'll skin you alive as we remove your finery from you.' A male voice whispered in my ear.

Every cell burned for vengeance. My stomach burbled with the revulsion of the stench of unbrushed teeth.

Forcing myself not to vomit all over their fancy shoes I lowered my eyes in an overt display of submission. The knife blade slid along my collarbone. Jagged pieces of my dress floated to the floor in front of me piece by excruciating piece.

{Unknown male}

Dragging out the torture punctuated with lewd comments still, she did not struggle. Her facade cracked slightly allowing me a glimpse of the fear and fury she was struggling to contain.

'You bloody bitch!' Her head snapped back with the force of a thunderous slap that reverberated around the small space.

'She bit me.' One of the males showed his bloody lip to the other.

He laughed and moved closer to her. She growled low in her throat and bared her teeth in response. Her fight instinct had been triggered. Between the two of them, they managed to wrestle her into a pair of manacles dangling from the wall of the next cell.

{Lia}

Bowing my head momentarily in a fake submission I paused to conceal the tears that had started silently tracking down my throbbing cheek. Probing my teeth, I knew I had been lucky that none had loosened in the attack.

Observing them through my lashes congratulating each other for breaking me I let a maniacal laugh escape my lips. I wasn't broken. I was far from okay, but I wasn't broken.

The clanging door to the cell and the sound of both sets of boots thudding away brought a sense of reprieve.

Closing my eyes completely I counted my breaths in and out until I lost track of how long I had spent hanging against the wall. How long would it be until my mind began to play tricks on me?

Something moved in the shadows beyond the cell. Deciding that my mind had already snapped I closed my eyes again.

{Unknown male}

She slumped against the wall. Removing my trench coat, I approached her with hurried footsteps on the stone floor. Wearily she opened her eyes and studied me. 'Ethan sent me.' I wrapped the coat around her as I released one hand at a time.

'Mistress?' The cell master's voice signalled his approach.

Lia struggled to raise her head. Heard the sharp intake of my breath as she snuggled into the scratchiness of the coat wrapped around her body.

'I've got you mistress.' The cell master released the cell door bowing to me as I strode through opening impatiently.

'No need for the Master to be informed.' I rumbled and asked, 'Did you bring what I require?' Holding a bundle of clothing up he led us deeper into the cells to the dreaded row x. Placing her on the bed in the corner of the cell I motioned the cell master to present her with the clothing. 'Get dressed princess.'

{Lia}

Listening to footsteps once again echo away from the cell I was in I wiped the tears away from my eyes with numb hands. Hastily shaking out the simple dress that had been bundled up I disappeared into my bathing quarters to change.

Hands fumbling through the everyday chore of braiding my hair back into customary neatness I used the twine from the bundle to finish it off.

Slipping back into the cell I curled my bare feet up on the bed under the skirt of my dress. The throbbing of the multitude of cuts prevented me from finding the rest I sorely needed.

{Unknown male}

'Come.' I roused her with a single word. Wrapping my discarded trench coat around her shoulders we walked to the elevator together. Pushing the button, I watched her pull an earring from one of the inside pockets. 'All your bits and bobs are in the left side pockets.' I eyed her cautiously, 'Should I be worried that you're going to faint on me?'

I shook my head still not trusting my voice. 'Not a fainter then. I'm going to need some warning if you need to do something incredibly awkward.' He rubbed his neck clearly uncomfortable. 'What do you class as awkward?' I stumbled through the sentence attempting to appear normal through conversation. 'Crying. Screaming. Female vapours.' He continued, 'It's not usually my department.'

{Lia}

Giving the tall male a sidelong glance out of the corner of my eye I asked, 'What is your department?' Stepping into the elevator I watched the numbers climb ever higher before he smirked his response, 'Killing things that threaten you.'

Who was he? Silent questions filled my mind until the elevator thumped to a stop. Keeping my head down I listened to the doors opening. Ethan's hands guided me out as his voice said, 'I'll take it from here. There'll be a little extra for you this week.'

CHAPTER THIRTEEN
Firebird

{Lia}

'You've been crying.' Gentle fingers probed at my injured cheek checking for damage. He held me close to him soothing us both. He caressed the patch of hair under his fingers, 'I left you alone without protection. This is not your fault. Do you understand me?'

Shaking my head slowly to indicate I disagreed with him I knew it was my fault.

I had ventured into this world under the guise of a mission and attempted to stay there.

John would find out that his grand plan had almost come to a swift halt. The result would be instantaneous and I would be forced to leave Ethan before he even knew what was happening. Forcing air into my lungs I concentrated on my breathing until I had myself under control. Surrounded by Ethan's cadre of personal guards I knew I still had a part to play.

{Ethan}

'I would have preferred to do this in private.' Snapping a jewelled cuff around her wrist I pretended to admire how it sat flush against her skin.

It wasn't tight enough to cause irritation but it screamed everything I despised. It showed she was owned. Guaranteed her rights beyond her position. Meant that no one would question her presence again.

Examining the bracelet with interest she spoke, 'The colour is unusual.' Her voice hesitant. Eyes meeting mine briefly before sliding away again. Hiding her true thoughts. 'It's made from an extremely rare metal.' Tugging on her hand I lead her back inside the apartment.

I had chosen a cuff of a deep rose gold hue. It had a single carnelian set deep in the centre of the cuff and held a hidden message for the rest of the First Family. One I hoped she would not learn of until I was ready to tell her myself.

Playing to our ever-present audience I angle bodies so that the cameras will be able to zoom in on the bracelet. 'You may only remove this when you are bathing.

Do you understand me Lia?' Embodying the role of entitled, self-indulged, pampered prince was becoming easier with each passing day.

{Lia}

'Yes.' I understood. Being mistaken as a quarter playing dress up had nearly cost me my brief sojourn above. He pulled me against him ignoring the stiffness I couldn't seem to shake. Resting his chin on the top of my head, I could almost feel his silent demand that I relax.

A few heartbeats later I murmured, 'What did I do wrong?' We would have to oversell the fact that he believed in my innocence.

'You were there. My foremother would never allow for a break in family protocol. The fault was mine.' Shifting my head into a better position on his chest I made it appear as if I was nuzzling into him searching for a safe place. That I was trying to be brave and fight my fears silently. 'What scared you the most?' His question shocks me out of my downward spiral.

Giving him the obvious answer in a small voice, 'That what they said about me was right.' Pulling me down onto the couch with him as he sat he asked, 'What did they say sweetheart?' 'I belong in the cells.' I answered after a few moments. 'And?' He prompted digging deeper. 'And that I deserved everything that was happening to me.'

{Ethan}

'Why did they hit you?' I asked keeping my voice deceptively calm. 'Apparently, I was insubordinate and had forgotten my place.' She replied with a small smile.

The com in my ear jumped with static before Fane informed me with the true answer, 'They were beginning to get rough with her. She fought back. She left them with permanent limps. It was beautiful to watch.'

Seething with something akin to white-hot rage I forced myself to keep my emotions in check.

Kissing her on the corner of her broken lip I rose to get her an ice pack. Placing it on her swollen features I checked my watch. I didn't want to leave her on her own, but questions would be asked if I didn't reappear on the administration level.

'You have to go.' She never ceased to amaze me. 'I'm reluctant to leave you alone for the rest of the day.' I admitted checking to see that the pack was doing its job. 'Never took you for the sappy kind.' Fane's laughter rang in my ear.

'I never thought to ask if you have a regular schedule.' The sweetness of her statement silenced Fane so I could concentrate. 'Not since my Father passed.'

Tucking loose strands of hair back over her ear I elaborated further, 'It was easier then.

I have so much to learn about running the business and being the head of the family that I can't afford time off.' Pursuing her train of thought Lia asked, 'Do you want me on a schedule?'

Our lives were too unpredictable for a schedule yet the question begged to be asked, 'You would accept me ordering your day for you?' Her good eye glowed, 'Yes. I have never had this much freedom before.'

'Freedom?' They'd taken away her freedom from her a long time ago. Stolen her innocence. Turned her into a killer. They would break the last of her spirit and steal her beautiful soul if I didn't find a way to overthrow John quickly.

{Lia}

'To bathe when I want. To eat what I want. To be warm. To see the sky. Read. To have an opinion.

The right to make choices is a large part of what being free means.' Checking the position of the sun over the dome I knew our time was running short before he had to leave, 'I wasn't brought here to distract you from your work.' John wouldn't hesitate to take me away if he thought I couldn't get the job done.

Pulling me in close again he kissed my forehead gently, 'We'll continue this conversation tonight.' He promised before feathering kisses up my cheekbone to my ear, 'Fane will be watching out for you when I'm not around. He's your unofficial bodyguard.' Our eyes met in mutual understanding before he left me alone in my solitude.

'Bravo.' John's voice sent shivers down my spine, 'Did you really think I would give you my trust so easily firebird?' Laying aside the ice pack I obeyed my instincts to move quickly.

Grabbing the fire poker, I dropped my protesting body into a defensive pose. He stood just inside the patio doors smirking down at me. His blade held loosely at the ready in front of him.

Frustrated that I had allowed him to get so close I allowed the emotion to bleed into my words, 'Why won't you let me complete the job you sent me to do? These distractions are not helping. He will not trust me with the information you seek while he thinks my life is in danger.'

I wanted to add 'especially from maniacs like you.' I didn't dare throw insult after injury.

Blade met poker and the loud sound of metal singing echoed through the apartment. 'You like him. That's good. Falling for your mark will lead to multiple broken hearts unless you learn to be a better actress.' He replied cryptically. What was this? A drop in impromptu brush up lesson?

'Your mother tried to have me broken. Reign her in and maybe he might talk.' Testing the limits of his patience I watched him slightly lower his blade.

An indication that I was to continue speaking my piece, 'Tell her that you approve his choice of consort. What can you tell me about a Fane Smythe?'

'Half-blood of the family. Sent away to further the family's interests elsewhere. When did you two meet?' Blade and poker sang again as I blocked another attack. Eyeing him warily I paced counter clockwise in a loose circle, 'He rescued me from the cells and has been assigned to our detail.' My detail. He swung down at me in a slashing motion which I parried aside easily. We continued circling each other like sharks drawn to blood in the water.

'You will report by the next family gathering.' He decreed and added, 'You will have the information I seek.

Remember your place firebird. This is a job nothing more.' His eyes fell on the cuff on my wrist, 'Pretty bracelet. Maybe I'll let you keep it.' Curtsying deeply so I wouldn't have to keep looking at his smug face I listened to him leave.

{Fane}

'It's safe to move now. He's gone.' Leaning against the counter twirling a blade out of boredom I watched her straighten up before returning the poker to its holder near the fireplace.

She looked toward the open patio door before exiting the room through it. I understood the consuming need for open spaces.

Standing at a slight distance from her I gave her the breathing room she so desperately seemed to need. 'You don't say much.' Lia spoke her thoughts aloud. Cocking my head to the side I waited for her to continue. She was an unusual female.

Her tears had been shed silently while she had worked through a series of stances that built core strength.

Channelling her silent rage into positive results. 'What's there to say?' I replied at length when she didn't speak again, 'You want to chat, go make a friend.'

{Lia}

Funny. 'I was just attempting to do that now.' Turning my head to face him he laughed and replied sardonically, 'I don't do friends. I'm extremely good at silent and menacing. Tends to scare people away.' He shrugged one shoulder.

Stretching out on the recliner I tossed over my shoulder at him, 'About that, feel free to take a break when no one is around. Silent and menacing on your own can get old fast. It isn't as if you can scare yourself away. Takes a real effort to keep a scowl on your face when you don't want to.'

'Who knew the princess in the tower had a sense of humour?' he muttered crossing the patio so that he could still see my face. 'No one.' The truth was blunt, hard to believe but it was the truth. 'I'm sorry I bothered you. I'll go back to being a statue.' If there was one thing I knew it was that anyone who said they preferred to be on their own really wanted someone to care about them.

Ignoring his presence, I flipped over onto my stomach wincing as I probably reopened a few of my cuts again. 'You really don't have anyone else to talk to do you?' His voice sounded closer to me. 'Other than Ethan and Lillianna? No.' Honesty was refreshing to hear in the world of lies and manipulation we existed in.

'We're not getting our nails done together or any other female pampering exercise for that matter.' He decreed lowering himself down into the single chair beside me.

'Why would we?' I opened my good eye shooting him an unrepentant grin, 'I want to know about your weapons collection.' Shaking his head, he leaned back relaxing slightly, 'Nope. Not even. Ethan would have my head if I let you get hurt twice in one day.'

'I'm not made of glass.' I huffed rolling onto my side the absence of adrenaline in my system making me feel sleepy. 'Never said you were.' He stretched his feet out in front of him, 'I've seen what you can do with a fire poker. Don't want to know what you could do with anything more interesting.'

'So no getting our nails done or discussing what weapons you have in your arsenal.' I clarified without batting an eyelash before asking, 'Tea or coffee?' 'Coffee.' His one word answer told me a lot about him.

He followed me inside to the kitchen. Pressing the switch on the coffee machine he offered without prompting, 'Strong and sweet.'

'Dare I ask?' Ethan asked from his office nook. 'Nope.' Fane's face turned to stone instantly as he lent against the wall between us. 'Fane was setting the boundaries of our friendship. Did you know he's got a thing against manicures?' I added another mug to the tray in front of me watching the interaction between both males with interest out of the corner of my eye.

Ethan raised an eyebrow at Fane while trying to keep a straight face, 'What about pedicures?' 'How do you know about those?' Sounding bored Fane studied his nails.

'Females.' Ethan's word encompassed a whole conversation. Fane grunted in reply.

Serving the completed drinks, I placed a mug beside Ethan's hand before handing one to Fane who shot me a grateful look.

CHAPTER FOURTEEN
Dance With The Devil

{Lia}

Looking back over the past week there had been no further incidents. The inhabitants of Smythe Towers had adapted to seeing me interacting with them daily. No one dared accost me in the halls or the restaurant with Fane shadowing my every move.

No longer comfortable with guarding me from a distance he had taken to sharing my table with me.

Hair spread out around me I worked a hairbrush through the knee length mass patiently dispelling the tangles and knots. 'I need your help.' Peering out through the strands Ethan lounged against the door jamb of my sleeping chamber. Finishing my grooming I divided the hair in two and coiled the top half before plaiting the rest.

His slightly haggard appearance made me pay attention. Looking for further clues all I could find were shadows under his eyes. 'You need my help?' I prompted him gently concerned the Master was pushing him too hard.

{Ethan}

'I have business that will take me outside of the Towers today. I need to take Fane with me.

Mother is expecting to meet me for dinner. I was wondering if you would go in my place.'

Running my hands lightly across her bare shoulders I easily found where she was storing her tension and began to massage the area lightly.

Shooting me a grateful smile she replied, 'I would like that.' Brushing her ear with my lips I spoke in a low voice, 'I need to see my sister. She has been too quiet of late.' Blinking her eyes once she raised a hand placing it gently on the side of my face and replied in a soft voice, 'What do you need me to do?' No hesitation.

'Remind me when you stopped calling me master?' he asked for our audience before adding in an undertone, 'Make your report to my uncle.'

{Lia}

Widening my eyes, he covered the hand I had on his face adding slight pressure. Surely, he understood the implications of what he was asking me to do. Turning to face him I pasted a smile on my face replying lightly, 'when you told me to.' What if he didn't believe me? What if he decided I had outlived my usefulness? What if he decided not to send me back?

Tamping down my rising panic I spoke again, 'Your mother said that endearments are also now appropriate. She said for me to ask about the word pooky?'

Amusement danced merrily through the depths of his eyes as he growled, 'you can erase that word from your vocabulary.' Inwardly I winced on his behalf.

{Ethan}

I had no idea where she had found such an emasculating term but the whole conversation was coming in handy as a distraction.

'She had others.' She informed me bursting into laughter at the horrified expression on my face at the thought. She inserted the hook of one of her earrings daring me to comment further with a raised eyebrow. Huffing in defeat I let her know, 'You can call me Ethan.' Adding quietly, 'It's what you should have been calling me all along. Tell him you have gained my trust and a place in my bed only. Do not tell him she's at Mercy House.'

Her eyes met mine in absolute understanding. A small enigmatic smile played across her lips. Drawn to them like a magnet I brushed her lips with mine and laid my forehead against hers.

Much rested upon Lia's ability to conceal information while remaining transparent enough for him to believe her.

{Lia}

The guns were mostly for intimidation. At least this time they had not brought the chains. He had warned me I should expect an interrogation at the very minimum. I was expecting worse. Interrogations were for those who expected some form of rights. Me. I didn't have rights. I was an asset. My treatment depended heavily upon how happy the Master was with me at any given time.

Agreeing to play decoy was probably one of the most stupid things I'd ever done. Reporting to the Master without sharing viable intel would earn me a severe beating.

Turning my attention to my immediate company surrounding me in a loose semi-circle I stepped out of the elevator ready for anything. Using the bulk of their bodies they herded me into a corner. Feeling the solid wall behind me I graced them with a smile.

They were the Master's elite. The males who had trained with me, guarded my cage and listened to my mostly silent sobs in the night. These were the males who could take me down without breaking a sweat if they needed to.

The bruises I had received from them in training had long since faded. The memories of their sadistic pleasure as they caused them had not. With the Suppressant R purged entirely from my system, I remembered each moment with complete clarity.

'Mistress Liana the Master would like to spend time with you today. Will you be able to accommodate him?' the deference they addressed me with was astounding. Seeing it for a complete farce. Nothing more than a charade so that none of the sheep around us would question my removal.

'Yes.' One never said no to the Master and one never made him wait for anything, 'I could go now.'

Placing me in the centre of the group they walked me back into the elevator.

Pressed in on all sides I took deep breaths as I watched the floor numbers rush by. Counting down silently to the one I dreaded above all others. The Master's private office.

Pushing the memories that threatened to assault me of the last time I had stepped foot in the room I concentrated on remaining perfectly calm before crossing over the thresh hold of the antechamber.

Dark wood panelling still decorated the walls. The clock on the wall had the same monotonous ticking sound that I had found annoying my entire life. Composing myself, I took the time to brush an imaginary speck of dust off my skirt to avoid making eye contact with any of the males who had taken up positions around the room.

He kept me waiting silently enforcing his dominance over me. Rumour had it that he kept everyone waiting these days. The Master was preoccupied. Whether it was for business or for pleasure nobody could say for sure.

'Ember, 'He crooned as if we were old friends, 'Or should I call you Mistress Liana now?' Narrowing my eyes slightly I remained silent. He didn't need an answer from me. Speaking up would only spark his temper and earn me a beating more quickly.

Gesturing to someone just out of eyesight he led the way into his inner sanctum. Glancing behind me the elite team were lined up in a solid line across the only exit point. Taking his usual position behind his behemoth of an antique wooden desk John dispersed with the pleasantries, 'You have been my nephew's plaything for nearly two moons now. I'm curious has he been open with you.' Have you discovered the answers I need yet?

No exit. No way out.

Forcing myself to look the Master in the eye I replied honestly, 'He is beginning to be more open with me now that I have proved myself trustworthy.' Knowing he would be listening for a lie my voice dripped with innocence.

'You spend more time with Lillianna then you do with Ethan why is that?' there was a trap somewhere in his smooth question. Sensing movement off to the side of me I fought to remain visibly calm. My intuition was sending up red flags of every shape, size and shade.

Heart sinking, I replied, 'Ethan wishes for me to spend time with his mother so that she can tutor me in etiquette, manners and the history of the First Family. I believe he wishes for me to enjoy her company.' Light reflected off metal.

The glint of a needle not very well hidden. Bastard. Tracking its approach from the corner of my eye I forced myself to stand firm.

'I understand my nephew has cuffed you after a slight debacle with my mother.' John laughed his eyes perusing the cuff on my wrist. His face brightened, 'He thinks to make you more than his consort.' The words had been for the benefit of those surrounding us. Waiting for the signal that I had permission to speak freely despite the company never came. He shook his head slightly at the unspoken question that I allowed to appear on my face. I hated it when he was in the mood to show off before dispensing harsh justice.

Retaining my composure, I ignored the ugly sensations crawling across my skin as someone breached my personal space. Outnumbered. No way out. I'd been fighting the relentless cravings for so long. With a swift jab to my neck suppressant R began flooding back through my system.

Something was different. I'd never had to wrestle the drug so hard before for control of my body. Pretending defeat, I lowered my head complying with the invisible tug on my proverbial leash. 'There now. You have been without for so long. Tell me how your mission with my nephew is going?' His silken tones terrified me. He only had partial control.

I felt his seductive tones trying to persuade me into revealing whatever information he desired to hear.

'I have established a high level of trust with the target sir.' 'And his sister? Has he told you where he has hidden Charlotte Grace?' The silken tone was underpinned with something I could not quite grasp. He stepped out from behind his desk leaving the wheelchair parked with its brakes on.

Of course he had. Defiance flashed across my face before I had a chance to mask my true thoughts. 'Harder to keep your feelings to yourself this time firebird?' He smirked down at me, 'I've given you a dose of the newest formula developed in the last few days especially for you.

Did you really think we didn't know the drugs weren't working? WHERE IS SHE?' he roared snatching me up by my shoulders and shaking me hard, 'That child is the future of Smythe Towers. I did not send you to my nephew out of the goodness of my black heart so you could play house.'

'Safe.' I spat back through gritted teeth know it would only enrage him further. Sinking his fist into my stomach he allowed me to fall to the floor.

Struggling back to my feet I smiled. It was the only warning they would get. Leaning back against the males who had unwittingly grabbed at my arms to restrain me I pushed hard off the ground. Getting a couple of solid kicks into the side of John's head before he stepped out of the way and the elite team surrounded me fully.

I watched him stagger struggling to regain his equilibrium as I spoke coolly, 'My heart is probably blacker than yours. I'm not in a forgiving mood today Master.' I made a point of stressing the honorific he insisted that I use before adding recklessly, 'You want the answer? Beat it out of me.'

'You heard the lady.' John's voice was equally as cold, 'Beat her until you get the answers we're seeking.' Fists began to rain down on her from all directions. Vicious. They were aiming for maximum pain with the least amount of visible damage.

I felt my skin splitting, blood trickling from my ears. Shadows threatened to overtake my consciousness. Feeling my limbs twitching I knew he had given me a reprieve when no more blows fell.

Horror lurked deep in the recesses of my mind memories of warnings of convulsions and worse rising to the surface.

'Where is she?' John crouched down beside my broken bloody form.

He waited for me to spit blood out of my mouth along with a tooth before bending his ear down to my mouth. Thought I'd crack that easily did he. 'Not. In. Your. Wildest. Dreams.' I punctuated every word to get my point across.

Upsetting the Master was the easy part. Trying to determine which of the five images dancing around in front of me was real was a little more difficult. Tossing out a general invitation in their direction I spoke again, 'Another round of beating boys. The boss hates it when his asset won't give up the information.'

John's immaculate dress shoes moved out of my line of sight. Curling into a protective ball to protect my head the pain started again. Fists giving way to boots then as if by silent agreement another reprieve was given. Again, John crouched down beside me, 'Where is she?' Dimly aware of my own response I heard my voice say, 'Mercy House.'

Dismissing my crumpled form, John's shoes turned back towards the desk, 'make sure she's left where Ethan or Fane will find her.'

Rough hands grabbed her arms. Dragging her inert body between them two of John's best bodyguards took her back up in the private elevator.

Dumping her in a pile in front of the apartment they surveyed the mess they had made of her face.

'Looks worse than the time she made him eat carpet.' One commented. 'She shouldn't have pushed him this time.' The other agreed, 'He won't give her the same considerations after this assignment.'

CHAPTER FIFTEEN
Bleeding All Over The Carpet

{Lia}

'Fucking Hell!' A hand touched me gently. Trying to move in protest only made me realise how damaged I was this time. 'Don't move.' Fane's voice ordered in the gentlest tone I'd ever heard him use. Cracking an eye open three of him danced around in my vision.

'Like I can do that right now,' I replied before asking, 'Are you... Are you crying?'

I couldn't be sure. He had an unreadable expression on his face.

'No. I'm dancing around in a fucking pink tutu.' Fane gave me an exasperated look, 'I want names, Lia. I want names so I can go kick asses and kill something. Lots of somethings.' He was furious. Hopefully not at me. Asking with a faint voice I wondered aloud, 'Can it wait until I'm not bleeding all over the carpet?' He stroked some strands of hair out of my face before tapping his portable com, 'Lili, Lia's hurt. Blood everywhere. Get a healer ready and a bed.'

'Uh huh.' He examined the side of my head in the dim light, 'From what I can see they did a real number on her.' Yeah, I could list my injuries for them if they'd listen to the patient. I knew for a fact I had a concussion and some broken bones.

I wasn't going to look pretty for anyone for a while. Zoning out of the one-sided conversation being held above my head I dragged myself into a better sitting position against the wall.

'Lia!' fingers snapping themselves in front me grabbed my attention. Fane's face swam into view.

Realising he had my complete attention he gave me a soft look, 'I'm sorry baby this is really going to hurt.' Snorting and wincing at the same time I gasped out, 'Now I know I look bad. Mr silent and menacing just apologised to me.'

{Fane}

Sweeping her up into my arms and tucking her protectively against my chest I replied, 'Yeah and once I've killed the people responsible then I'll take it back.'

Adjusting her light weight in my arms I noticed she was struggling to remember something. 'I need to tell Ethan something.' Her brow crinkled automatically. She winced again.

She looked no deadlier than a kitten who'd just had a full belly of milk. 'It's important.' She insisted.

Furious with my half-brother I brushed her words off. Striding at a rapid pace through the halls I knew I had to keep her awake and talking to me.

'Baby?' she questioned her mind finally latching on to the term of endearment that slipped out when I wasn't looking. 'Yeah?' I questioned playing along stalling for time praying to everyone and no one that she would still be alive when we got to the South Tower.

'Since when do you call me Baby?' Her words were slightly slurred as she struggled to keep her eyes open. 'Don't close your eyes, Lia.' I warned her. Stopping. Waiting to see that she was going to comply with my order. They flew open revealing the ruby colour I had begun to associate with her.

I could tell her pain levels were rising along with her curiosity.

{Lia}

'Fane?' after calling out to him in a small voice he responded, 'I've always called you baby in my head and princess to your face.' His voice full of worry alerting me to the fact that I was injured worse than I had originally thought. 'Fast Five.' He said. 'What?' Maybe I had heard him incorrectly. 'Fast Five.' He repeated striding along the endless hallways. 'Sorry. I'm the female who has spent her life in a cage. You'll have to explain a little bit more than that.

You won't lose tough guy points. I'm not going to tell anyone.' He laughed. It was a short sharp staccato burst that hurt my eardrums.

'Fast five is a game where people get to know each other. I believe it's a tradition dating back hundreds of years.

You ask me a personal question. I answer. Then I ask you one. We each get five questions.' He explained patiently. Who was this male and what had he done with my intimidating bodyguard?

'What's your favourite colour?' I asked. 'Red.' He answered before shooting back, 'What did the Master want from you?' Studying his face, I decided I could trust him with the honest answer, 'He wanted the intel he sent me to gather in the first place.'

'So, you were a spy?' he persisted. 'Not sure this is how you explained the game but I'll answer anyway. No. I'm not a spy.' Really? A spy? Talk about underestimating my skill set. Thinking fast I asked my next question, 'Why are you alone so much of the time?' I felt his muscles stiffen beneath me.

'People don't understand my line of work. I'm a sweeper. I take the hard jobs.

Do the business and clean up my own messes.' He was just like me. The realisation sent another jolt of adrenaline through my blood system waking me up a little. 'If you're a sweeper I'm a reaper.' I volunteered, 'I get the intel and I get out fast leaving a wake of bodies in my trail.' 'Is that what Ethan is to you?' he asked, 'A job?'

'No.' My answer was short and blunt. 'Am I a job for you?' If I was I'd have to deal with the consequences another day. Once again, his short burst of laughter hurt my ears. 'If you were just a job I'd have left you lying in a pool of blood.' The unfamiliar look of tenderness on his face confused me. 'Ethan put me on your detail. I don't trust many people. He's one of few I'll put my neck on the line for.' He explained before asking, 'Why are you so talkative?'

'Must be the truth serum component to the new version of suppressant R raging through my system.' Squinting up at him I added, 'Or it could be that I like talkative you.' 'You trust me.' He stated at the beginning of a familiar hallway. We were in the right sector of the building now.

{Fane}

'Not really a question there.' She replied. 'Why do you trust me?' I clarified for her confused state of mind. 'Forgive the lack of professionalism.' She attempted to smile up at me, 'You know what I am and what I can do. I don't have to hide anything from you. Hold back in case I hurt you. You make me feel safe. I don't have to always be on guard because I know you'll put anything moderately dangerous down for me.'

Searching for Lili's door amongst the sea of cream doors I didn't respond to her answer. Honestly, I didn't know how to. She had put her complete faith in me and yet she wore my brother's cuff. I decided to ask one last question, 'Did Ethan send you to be a pretty distraction so he could visit his sister?'

'Yes.' She answered her face brightening as she remembered something, 'You need to tell him that the Master beat the information out of me.'

Banging on the right door Lili answered quickly. Moving aside so that I could hand Lia off to the healer he rushed her into the next room to begin his assessment of her condition. Charli was in danger. I couldn't stay until I had passed on Lia's message. Indicating the door with my head to Lili she nodded. Rolling my shoulders, I paused briefly before striding back into the mess that was about to erupt within the family.

Her peculiarities made sense to me. A reaper. Hell, I thought I had issues. Dodging past the cowards choosing to hide rather than face the storm I found a safe place to com Ethan from.

Tapping my earpiece to gain his attention I spoke curtly, 'Thought you'd like to know that I've just delivered Lia to Lili's for her lesson on household healing remedies. Lia is being forced to practise on herself. The fake blood was a little too realistic.'

Willing him to understand the underlying urgency behind my message my brain registered his reply. My body on auto pilot I travelled through the eerie quiet of my surroundings.

Something big was about to kick off. Smythe Towers was going into voluntary lock down. Speeding up I was determined not to be caught on the wrong side of Lili's door when the master locks were automatically activated.

CHAPTER SIXTEEN
The Ants Came Marching Two By Two

{Jo}

A small army of males in black shirts gathered in the foyer. Scurrying around like little ants on the monitor in front of me I watched their organised movements with a detached sense of fascination.

Sensing Cerin I glanced up slightly to see him sling his arm around my waist. His side hug conveying all the words and emotions he couldn't express.

Troubled he asks in a low tone, 'You knew they were coming for Charli, didn't you?'

There were no comforting answers to give him. No glimpses from the minds below showing a favourable outcome for me. 'Yes.' Examining their equipment, I realised they had come prepared to breach the penthouse level. I didn't have time to second guess myself. Any hesitations would be playing directly into their plans and I had multiple lives to save.

Picking up my com I keyed in the direct line to take over the entire building, 'Apologies for disturbing your afternoon but this is an urgent message for all residents. This is not a drill. Get to your evacuation points and follow your leaders. For guests, I urge you to also seek shelter elsewhere. We will refund your admittance fees. We are under attack. Repeat we are under attack.'

{Cerin}

'What should I tell Charli?' I asked drawing my knife. Checking that the edge of the blade was still deadly. I had seen all my sister's facial expressions.

This was her covering the stench of fear with a fake calm. I'd only seen her this way twice before and both times we had escaped a deadly situation by the minutest of margins. Whatever was inbound was worse than bad. She placed her hand on my arm. 'She knows already. Tell her the truth. He's coming for me first only he doesn't quite know it yet.'

Tapping her fingers swiftly over the keyboard she reangled all the cameras throughout the building to cover the doorways and lifts. Entries and exits.

In complete control of her emotions, she spoke again, 'Get her to safety before you have to shed more blood.' 'Jo.' One word was enough to make her look up from her task in front of her, 'Let me help.'

The others would eviscerate me if I didn't try. 'When I tell you to leave. Leave.' She capitulated surrendering to another side hug, 'Go reassure Charli.'

{Charli}

I sensed him approaching from behind. I sat motionless in a deep chair overlooking the front entrance. *'He found me.'* I couldn't help the defeated tone seeping into my mind speech. He inserted his body between myself and the scene below us. 'Yes.' He confirmed verbally, 'He may have found where you've been hiding. He won't find you.' He sounded confident in himself and our surroundings.

'You're not afraid of him?' My eyes latched onto his face searching for answers. *'I don't fear him. I don't respect him. A male who sends others to die in his place is no one. His males must do all the fighting. Secure the perimeter. Make sure it's safe. Once all the work has been done then he will make his appearance.*

Wheel in like some conquering hero.' Cerin pushed dirty blond hair out of his eyes. His tone dismissive. Abrupt.

{Cerin}

I waited until her eyes met mine again before making my request, 'Do you think you can let us know the minute you sense him in the building?' She gave me the mental impression of a nodding head. Eyes wide with worry and concern.

'I'm only going to go slow him down a little.' I couldn't help wanting to dispel the fear from her mind.

'Satifo Qortero.' She gave me a warrior's blessing recognising the true me behind the nursemaid I had been playing. Allowing a cocky grin to spread across my face she dropped her eyes. *'I need you on evacuations.'* Jo slipped into my mind, *'Get the children out into the tunnels. There are some trapped in corridors on one.'*

Sometime later Charli's warning shredded everyone's mental defences, *'Breach. He's inside the building.'* I knew that I had little time to hide Charli before he entered the upper levels of Mercy House. Reaching out to Jo I scooped her out of the comfortable chair I had placed her in close to the door. Fear consumed her normally dancing green eyes. 'Just like we practised.' Speaking into her ear soothingly I felt some of her contracted muscles relax slightly.

Keeping to the blind spots between the cameras I knew Jo had lost control of them when they began swinging back and forth on their stands panning for something. Someone. Entering a hidden passage hidden behind a large painting in one of the basement levels I pulled it shut after me. Masking our psychic signatures Charli hid us from sneak attacks.

{Jo}

Relief flooded through my body. I felt the disconnect when they went dark. Sitting down in the chair behind my desk I swung around to face the windows. He had brought most of the males in his family to take Mercy House and I didn't want to acknowledge them when they found me in the room.

In the space of a few hours, we had gone from being a sanctuary to an anthill. They were using the building across the road. Discovering the zip line on the roof would lead to invasion from above. The garden would bear the brunt of bumbling fool after bumbling fool crushing and bruising the delicate plants.

I was the last resident left in the building.

Eavesdropping unashamedly in the minds around me I analysed the implications of the conversations swirling upwards. They were in the elevators.

Bile rose in my throat as I forced myself to remain seated projecting a sense of calm. Footsteps thudded through the outer offices as the elevator emptied its first load of intruders. Door flying open so forcefully that it cracked loudly against the wall. Flinching at the influx of boots on my polished wood floors I reigned in my swirling fear.

'I've got one. Admin level.' A male voice shouted his com crackling out instant orders to keep me detained. 'Copy that.' The hard voice responded. Still, I waited. I was unwilling to yield even one inch of the small amount of control I still retained to these males. The door to one of the hidden passages cracked by a minuscule.

'Get her to Daire. Do not risk her safety for mine.' Cerin was close. I could feel his strong presence nearby. Charli's voice protested, *'I made him come back for you.'*

'I appreciate it now let Cerin take you to the rest of my brothers.

*They will get word to your brothers.
Your uncle and I have business that must be
taken care of. Go now!'*

The door clicked shut soundlessly. I
listened to the guard's radio crackling and
spluttering with Smythe male chatter.
John was being brought into my home as
if Mari had agreed to a private sale. He's
in the elevator. My heart beats erratically.
His males form up except for the one
standing guard at the threshold of my
office. Feet come together in rhythm.
Words are exchanged. Rubber squeaking
over the tile in the outer office. Coaxing
my face into a semblance of acquired calm
I swing my chair around to face him.

Folding my hands in my lap I stare at a
point just over his shoulder. He waves
away the guards while I peruse the male in
front of me at my leisure. He had retained
use of his upper body after the incident
inside the High Council building last year.

Incident. Such a polite word to use for what I had allowed to happen to him.

Wheels roll to a stop. He greets the guard by name before speaking to me directly, 'I assume you know why we are here.' His confidence would be his downfall. 'Why don't you ask me nicely?' I knew why he was here. He was looking for me. Charlotte Grace had been merely the excuse he used at the High Council to obtain permission to storm in like the spoilt brat that he was.

{John}

'It has been brought to my attention that one of my daughters and my niece have been living here under assumed names. I wish to know where they are so that I can restore them to their rightful place as members of the Smythe family.' I spoke clearly as I catalogued the worth of the furniture in the room. The female in front of me was smothered from head to toe in a grey cloak.

Nothing showed except for her face. 'And the rest of the females who live here in the sanctuary?' Such a pity one so young would be dedicated to the poor and unfortunate.

{Jo}

Adjusting the natural timbres in my voice I hid as much of myself as I possibly could from him until I was ready to expose my identity to him. 'They will join the females in the cells of Smythe Towers. There will always be females hoping for a bed in comfort. My cells stand empty.' John spread his hands palms up as a deliberate gesture to show how harmless he was.

'No.' My single syllable refusal lit a dangerous light in his eyes. I knew I was playing with fire but I refused to allow him to subject these females to any more abuse.

'You would really make me your enemy?' Tipping my head to one side I tugged the foremost thought from his mind with ease. Displaying a small smile on my face I answered it, 'We were not enemies until you Mercy House and its occupants under siege for the second time.'

Grateful no one I cared about was around to hear my hidden secrets. This was the one male everyone considered the 'devil incarnate'.

If he was the devil, then I was his daughter. Gesturing to the seat in front of my desk I invited, 'You might as well make yourself comfortable.' He gripped the wheels of his chair with his palms about to push himself forward when I shook my head, 'No. You may be able to hide your true self from many. You will find that I am not one of the sheep.'

Quirking an eyebrow at me he soundlessly stood up. Watching as he crossed the room to stand in front of me in quick strides I retained my seat with ease. 'You don't give up your control easily do you?' He observed as he folded his long frame onto the dainty chair in front of me. Creaking dangerously, we were both aware this conversation would not last long before it collapsed from under his weight.

'I have told you my request.' He spoke formally still unaware of my identity. 'Yes, however, this is not a truth ceremony and no tea is present that requires me to reply to you.'

I had long since given up wearing the traditional head wrap in favour of simple veils that matched my outfit held fast by pins. Pins that I removed slowly as I continued speaking, 'No more games. You and I have much to discuss before you call me out in front of the High Council.'

Removing the contacts from my eyes and slipping off the veil I knew he recognised me from the swift intake of breath. I was the daughter he had been hunting for. 'You.' He said flatly. His polite affable takeover turning deadly.

'Me.' I replied in my own voice running fingers through my wild violet hair in attempt to tame it as it swirled around my body at its own will. Leaning back, still conscious that he was seated on a stick of furniture he could break in a heartbeat John threatened, 'I will call you out for attempted patricide.'

'Ok.' That was fair. Leaning forward I warned, 'I will counter call you out for breaching the laws of the Mercy House Sanctuary and enslaving females against their will. I have been following your local snatch and grab operation for quite some time.'

He fumbled for hidden weaponry beneath my desk. 'Not here.' I crooned to him as if he were an old friend, 'You wouldn't want Madame Speaker to send you to the territories again for another crime against humanity. There is no coming back from that a second time.'

'Which female did I sire you on?' he demanded seemingly impressed that I knew all his moves. He didn't know? Allowing myself to relax slightly under the onslaught of his intense stare I asked quietly, 'Does it matter?' Assaulted psychically from his loud internal screaming I winced-apparently it did to him.

'You are the rightful heir of Smythe Towers.' His quietly spoken statement hung in the air between us. Leaning back again I sized him up. His calculating air didn't throw me for a second. 'Smythe Towers does not allow the females from the First Family to inherit anything especially anything to do with the family business. Ethan is welcome to the job. I don't want it.'

Smiling genuinely at him I continued in a slightly gentler tone of voice, 'Why would I want to be your heir when I'm already a Queen here?'

{Cerin}

Following the hidden tunnels that led from within the walls through deep under the city, I followed the hidden symbols etched into the walls at intervals to keep us on the right path. Purposely tripping one of the alarms to let my brothers know we were coming I could feel Charli's terror levels rising like waves at the silent flashing red lights. Still, no scream emitted from her mouth. Probing our link, I found her holding the fear in her mind in an unbreakable iron grip. She was aware that I couldn't afford any distractions.

{Charli}

Relieved at my mental state he kept creeping forward through the endless tunnels. We would have time for questions once he had informed the elusive Daire of the situation happening at Mercy House and what we were facing.

Hefting me up over his shoulder so that he could use his hands gave me an upside-down view of the world. On the other side of the door, he was facing was his brothers and safety.

On the other side of the door lay the inquisition of why we would leave one of our own behind.

I blinked warily at the tense male faces the immediately surrounded us. 'Jo?' One demanded in a tight voice without hesitation. Without warning the world turned topsy-turvy and then righted itself again as Cerin deposited me gently onto a couch. Examining the fabric while the voices around me rose and fell in varying tones I came to a decision. It was a comfortable couch which had probably been a nice shade of blue a decade earlier.

Six pairs of eyes put me under a microscope as I connected with them all at the same time, *She has been taken to Smythe Towers awaiting a hearing with the*

225

High Council. He is going to call her out and is planning to ask for a cage match to the death.'

Meaning that they had no legal way to break Jo out of Smythe Towers. Waiting for an introduction while the combined glares intensified I gave Cerin a mental prod, *'Do a female a favour? Tell your brothers my cover name.'*

'This is Ravenna.' He introduced us adding, 'She's an amplified version of Jo.' Pointing at each brother, in turn, he said their names, 'Daire. Zev. Blake. Ed and Reece.' In return, they graced me with an acknowledging nod. 'When will he make his move?' A deep voice rumbled out of the male with the hardest eyes. Daire.

He checked himself after taking an involuntary step towards me. Realising I had not moved anything other than slowly blink my eyes in agreement to something Cerin had said he paused not sure how to approach any further.

'He has not decided.' I knew my mind speech sounded indifferent but I was monitoring a city of people for a more specific answer for him. 'Cerin.' He barked demanding more of an explanation about me.

'Ravenna and I will work as a team Daire. I'm her legs and voice but she can gather intel faster than Reece.' Cerin assured him. Unconvinced he turned to the small circle at his back, 'Reece see what else you can find out. Nobody moves until we get solid leads to work with.'

Weapons were holstered and jokes cracked. The air cleared slightly of tension and I felt as if I could breathe properly again.

CHAPTER SEVENTEEN
Overnight At Smythe Towers

{Ethan}

Raucous laughter echoed around the ceilings in the vaulted room behind me. Raising my head to glance briefly at the live feed from Mercy House a flash of violet hair caught my eye. Isolating the frame, I studied it in detail. Jo.

Lady Mercy herself waited for transport surrounded by the elite team.

Her head remained high despite the restraints binding her wrists.

Fast forwarding through the data there was no identifying glimpse of Charli in the small group of captives they had rounded up from the females who had been too stupid to leave the area immediately.

'Where are you?' I demanded dropping my walls sending out a mental blast hoping she was monitoring for my call.

'Safe.' The one-word reassurance mined through my mental defences right on cue. *'Where?'* Charli couldn't be on her own for long. Grinding my teeth together I had to wait a few moments for her cryptic reply, *'With the rest of Lady Mercy's muscle.'* Not a location. Jo had brothers. Cerin must have taken her back to their safe house. My private com chimed softly in my pocket adding to my frustrations. The entire building was in an uproar.

Yanking the offending item from its resting spot I inserted it quickly into my ear and answered it, 'Yes.'

'Brother.' Fane's voice snapped at me through the earpiece. He continued before I could get a word in, 'Thought you'd like to know that I've just delivered Lia to Lili's for her lesson on household healing remedies. Lia is being forced to practise on herself. The fake blood was a little too realistic.' I spoke quickly, 'Stay with her. Don't let her out of your sight. I'm going to be a while.' Hearing a curt affirmative I switched my com off and tossed it on the desk in front me.

Unease coursed through my veins followed by an empty feeling where my heart should be. Lia was injured badly, and I had been too busy to check on her welfare. Knowing that she would be protected made it infinitely easier for me to survive the next few hours without her.

They would be safe inside the custom-built panic room hidden inside the apartment. It was time to make my move. Chaos and carnage were wreaking havoc inside the hallways.

Striding directly into the fray I gathered those working directly for me as I passed them by providing covering fire so they could join me.

{Fane}

I carried Lia into the safe room through the entrance hidden inside the spare cupboard in Charlotte Grace's room. She still had blood stains on her chin from before we had barged unceremoniously into the apartment. A dark fury of epic proportions threatened to loosen itself from deep within my body. A hand appeared in my vision. Growling I swiped the damp rag from Lilianna and gently cleaned Lia's features myself.

She gently touched my face with the tips of her fingers calming me instantly.

Lili continued to assess Lia from her position. Looking up at me she cajoled, 'She would be more comfortable on the bed in the corner.' 'You need to watch the door and let Lili work. You have my permission to hurt anyone who comes through that door.' She broke through my haze of red snapping me back to reality.

{Lia}

Swallowing my screams agony, I allowed tears to stream silently down my cheeks. White hot pain spread through my limbs as they inadvertently jostled me into a comfortable position on the bed. 'I'm going back to the living area.' Fane withdrew a gun from one of his hidden holsters, 'Don't leave this room for any reason until I say so.' They shared a look of complete understanding above my head. He added darkly, 'We could be in for a long night.'

Rewrapping some of the more persistent wounds Lili averted her face from me. The horror she felt showed up in the stiff lines of her body language as she explored the storage shelves for more medical supplies. Ethan would come as soon as he was able. Fane was spoiling for a fight. I could just see him from the bed.

Leaning against the wall just inside the apartment door with his gun drawn he would fight or he would die.

I wanted to touch him.

Bring him back from that small place inside himself where he took refuge every time he was forced to kill. Feeling broken I succumbed to the realm of sleep.

{Ethan}

Gunfire, screams and silence punctuated the night. John had not returned with more instructions instead I departed immediately with a smaller detail heading into the inner circle.

My ears caught the distinct sound of a gun being cocked a split second before it was shoved against my temple. 'I came to check on her.' Instantly the pressure was gone from my skull. Fane crowded me poking his finger into my chest with each word, 'You took me with you. You took me with you and sent her into the jaws of the beast.'

Merely nodding in agreement, I allowed him to continue his diatribe in a loud whisper, 'You don't deserve her. She was so badly hurt that the healer had to call another healer. If I hadn't happened upon her when I did you'd be writing another funeral speech.' My mother had fallen asleep on her pristine white couch in the main living area with smears of dried blood on her hands and face.

'I know I don't deserve her. You're just pissed because we can't kill him outright.' I pointed out rationally, 'Everything I'm doing Brother including Lia getting hurt is for a reason. I need to you to stay cold. Be ruthless with anyone who tries to get to her.' My voice broke slightly, 'This isn't some game I'm playing with an asset. She's my weak point. She's my heart.'

'Don't keep leaving your heart unprotected Brother because she's my heart too.' Fane advised through gritted teeth before retreating into the shadows. 'When did this happen?' The new turn of events left me feeling pleasantly surprised. Fane reappeared in front of me, 'Come on. I'm set up in your old room.'

Leaning against the wall I waited for him to speak again. 'She's my heart too.' He put it as simply as he could, 'She needs us both. Can you handle that?'

Not willing to go into the fine detail while Lia lay injured in the next room I answered him in measured tones, 'I can.'

'I don't want her touching weapons again.' Fane's voice floated out to me in the darkness, 'We need to end this for her.

She deserves the chance to discover everything she's missed in life.'

'You might not have an option about the weapons.' Raking a hand tiredly through my hair I elaborated for him, 'You've read her records as thoroughly as I have. Not long Brother. It will be over soon.' Pushing off the wall he grabbed my hand as I passed and pulled me into a rough hug. Turning on my heel I took the few steps before I was in Charli's old sleeping chamber.

Lia's still form lay on top of the covers. Her cuff sat on the night table beside her.

Inhaling sharply at the bent form I searched along her bare arm gently with my fingertips. I found her forearm wrapped and splinted.

The bastards had ripped it from her arm, bent it out of shape, forcing it back on and damaging her in the process.

{Lia}

'I'm still alive.' I mumbled. My eyelids struggling to open into slits. When one did I found Ethan crouched down beside me. His expression unreadable. 'It's late.' My voice sounded scratchy to me. 'It's very late.' he confirmed and spoke quietly, 'I needed to see you. Needed to see for myself that you were cared for and safe.' Safe. A word offering false hope to the uninitiated. There was no such thing as safe. Turning my face away from him we sat together in silence.

'Lia?' His fingers probed over my injuries gently investigating the extent of my damage for himself. Praying he didn't turn on a light I felt him touch each bruise.

I was a walking rainbow of technicolour bruising or I would be once my fiercely overprotective bodyguard allowed me to walk the short distance between the bed and the necessary again.

Finger moving over my skin he examined every exposed inch of me. Gently stroking my busted lip, he stopped at my hiss of pain. Grim he turned from me. 'I fought back. 'Swallowing to assuage the pain of my throat I continued in a broken voice, 'I fought back. Laughed in his face each time a fist smashed into my body. Laughed at them when they injected me. Kept my silence when I was convulsing. They worked me over until I couldn't think straight. The next time he asked…the drug forced me to answer him.'

{Ethan}

Fane had warned me she had been hurt. She lay in front of me making her report. Shame swept through me. As necessary as it was this was still the second time she had taken a beating on my behalf. There would be no third. Retribution was coming to each male who had thought to lay hands on her for their Master.

'Want to see something?' I asked distracting her from her dark thoughts.

{Lia}

Flicking a switch above me one by one pinpoints of light appeared on the ceiling until they resembled a replica of the night sky. 'Charli couldn't leave her room without help so I had the sky brought to her.' I knew he would try to salve his guilt with pretty words. Pretty words I wasn't sure I was ready to hear. Everything hurt. No words would make the pain go away.

'No, they won't.' He agreed slightly amused that I was having trouble keeping my thoughts to myself. Settling down on the floor beside me he added, 'I made promises to you that I didn't keep.'

Squeezing his hand with my good one indicating I was listening to him I thought about it. How could he have been in two places at once? Blaming him for his Uncle's actions would help no one. 'That's generous of you Lia. More than I deserve.'

'The best way to fight a war is to win one.' My voice sounded raspy and painful even to my own ears.

'Not at your expense sweetheart. We will beat him but you are not a sacrifice. Not anymore.' He almost fell silent before asking, 'He used the drug?'

'New version.' Enlightening him I continued, 'They added a truth serum component.'

The city lights were growing duller against the lightening sky. It was getting close to morning.

{Ethan}

'You're going to stay here for a few days.' I informed her and rejecting her small noise of protest I stated firmly, 'You are going to stay here until I'm sure you are safe in our home.' Picking her cuff up off the night table I couldn't muffle the curses from escaping. Examining it up close I realised it could be mended.

Lia would heal. Kissing her forehead, I slipped out of her room.

{Lia}

'Why does Ethan see me as more than an asset?' I whispered to Lilianna the next time she came to check on me.

I had dreamt of him putting the mended cuff back on my other wrist. Examining it now I knew it had been no dream.

He had made a point of having it back on my wrist as soon as possible.

'Even though we're First Family, I raised him to have a heart. His father taught him how to conceal it so that no one could use it against him.' Lilianna sat down in the chair beside my day bed, 'I think the better question is why you don't see yourself as more than an asset? Someone who has the right to hope for a future.'

'There is a saying in the cells. Hope hurts. Maybe tomorrow will be better.' Playing with the loose thread in the light throw that was covering me I shrugged a shoulder paying for the careless movement with more pain.

Hope was a luxury. If I began to hope even a little for something tangible I would have more to lose. There would be something someone could use against me.

'I think you should start getting acquainted with hope.' She read the myriad of micro expressions that marched across my face adding confidently, 'You will never go back to the cells again.'

Something tight loosened in my chest. Had he said something to her? How did she know for sure? 'You will not be going back.' She repeated for emphasis struggling to contain all that hadn't been said, 'Rest now.

CHAPTER EIGHTEEN
Overnight At The Brothers' Safe House

{Daire}

Poisoning the pen had been easy. The modifications had been relatively simple. Slipping the small gas-filled capsule into the top half of the pen carefully I placed the finished pen in my pocket.

When John clicked the pen for the nib a small needle would pierce the capsule causing the gas to seep out and invade the system of the intended target.

Once the pens had been switched no one would be any wiser. They were identical in all aspects. Time was slipping through my fingers narrowing the window we had to rescue Jo. If we were going to infiltrate Smythe Towers, it had to be tonight.

Weapons were easy to come by but Jo was irreplaceable. We had banded together out of a common need to survive life on the streets in the rim and over time grew into a family with bonds forged in steel. If anyone thought we were going to let Jo get snatched away from us they had seriously underestimated us.

In the next room, I could hear my brothers checking our weapons and gearing up for the fight to rescue the female who had wormed her way into all our hearts.

'He keeps his pen in his office on the admin level. You can't miss it.

It's the one with all the dark wood past the wall of monitors.

Screams masochistic control freak when you see it. Gave me the chills. Daddy took us down to show us where he worked one day and Uncle John was in there.'

My head snapped up. Her elfin face was facing me, green eyes huge as she slipped into my mind easily again. *'We went back to help her. She told me that this was something she had to face on her own. What you are planning is dangerous.'*

Concern. Worry. For me? Such a slip of a thing and already she had a warped sense of humour. She had been so quiet that I had forgotten she was in the room with me. Covered with one of the old quilts from Jo's bed her white face shone through the shadows.

'You should be asleep.' Speaking in a gruff voice I attempted to hide the emotion that swamped me in a tidal wave of memories. She reminded me of a younger version of my little sister. *Sleep eludes us all tonight.* Her electric green cat eyes glowed with knowledge beyond her tender years as her voice faded from my mind.

Admittedly we weren't trying to be quiet about our plans.

Taking the chair opposite the ratty couch she was laying on I spoke to her, 'We were all lost when we met each other but we knew enough about surviving in the rim to stick together. When we met her, she became the glue that kept us from being pulled in different directions by people who wanted to use us for their own purposes. In some ways, it's because of her that we became the males we are. She made us better and now that she's in danger all the ugly seems to be leaking out again.' I had no idea why I was justifying myself to the child in front of me.

'You can't put your arms around a memory.' Her wise words hit me hard in my gut. We needed to bust Jo out before we lost her for good. 'You know Smythe Towers. Where would he be holding her? Who can we trust to help us from the inside?' One by one my brothers sidled back into the room quietly listening to my one-sided conversation. I could feel the dark coalescing at my back. Ed was furious.

He was struggling not to explode at my order to hurry up and wait.

'He would have put her down in the cells.' A blush formed, embarrassment shining through on her transparent face. *'I'm not supposed to know about them.'* She explained further, *'I know that they are in the sub-basement levels of the towers. The conditions are...'* Her voice petered out as

she struggled to find appropriate words, *'the conditions are dreadful.'*

Her eyes seemed to swirl with unspoken emotions as Cerin repositioned her to sit keeping her upright by wrapping his arm around her shoulders. Nestling her into his side. Glaring at us he dared us to say something. Raising an eyebrow, I chose my unspoken words carefully. *Is there something you need to tell me, little brother?* He shook his head almost imperceptibly. *This is hard for her. Have some patience, will you?*

{Charli}

'If I get word to my brothers and Mamma they might be able to help you.' my words were measured. Fear coloured my thoughts. They had emerged one by one from the dark to form a semi-circle behind Daire.

Each one was equipped with his weapon of choice. Face hard. Eyes cold. They were ready to go to war for their sister.

They were ready to go to war with people I loved over the actions of a self-centred, egotistical male.

Cerin nestled me closer to his warm body. The weight of his arm on my shoulders comforted me in ways I didn't yet understand. 'What if we guaranteed that we would not harm your family and those they care about?' He asked me to voice the question that had crossed everyone's minds.

'Ethan knows you. Fane trusts you. They say they have the female they care for deeply in the same apartment as Mamma. They are the last of my family. Don't let them get hurt in your vendetta to free Jo.' I knew the turmoil I was feeling had been transferred through my words to each one of them.

Leaning forward in his seat Daire was considering my words.

In his mind casualties were a fact of life in the outer rim. He would only bargain for the lives of my loved ones. No others.

Allowing my voice to pinpoint his mind alone my voice whispered to him, *'Fair enough.'*

'Thank you.' He held a hand out for me to shake. If the situation hadn't been so serious I would have laughed verbally myself. I didn't want to scare them away with my poor attempt at speaking normally. *'I have to leave you hanging sorry.'* I apologised to him slightly startled as Cerin leant forward and gripped his brother's hand on my behalf. *'We're a team.'* He reminded me, *'You're the brains. I'm the body.'*

Closing my eyes, I concentrated on reaching out to Ethan. Sensing the brothers getting comfortable the memory of their menace lingered in the air.

Getting no answer from him I tried Fane only to find his mind clouded in a fury so palpable that I could almost taste it. Opening my eyes, I was honest with them, *'This could take a while. Please be patient. My brothers hate when I barge into their minds when they're busy.'*

On my third attempt Ethan answered my cries for attention, *'All hell has broken loose over here. I assume you have questions for me from your bodyguard detail.'* He sounded tired. Strong. Standing firm in his convictions just like Daddy taught us to do. *'They want to know where Jo is and how to get to her.'* I broke their request down into a couple of sentences. *'They're too late.'* He informed me and explained why before telling me to go to sleep.

My eyes ran over the faces counting on me to give them some good news. I had none. If anything, what I would tell them would set them off even further.

Concentrating on Daire I pushed into his mind and told him directly, *'She's not in Smythe Towers. Ethan told me that John turned her over to the High Council almost immediately. There's nothing anyone can do for her. They go to the cage first thing tomorrow.'*

Relaying my news to the others I watched as their facades cracked showing me a room full of lost males all in desperate need of their missing link.

CHAPTER NINETEEN
Death Match

{Ethan}

The summons came in the form of loud hammering on my apartment door interrupting the few hours of sleep I had managed to steal between mending Lia's cuff and settling disputes in the halls after the lockdown had been lifted.

Eyeing my uncle's partially dressed form I knew he was dressing for battle.

He had gathered pieces of clothing from all parts of the known world and was choosing from among them picking over the items lying on his bed. Combat in the cage at the Twilight Colosseum was rare but not completely unheard of. Only one thing would make him take it this far. The unspoken thought danced briefly through my mind.

'Regrets are for males who are weak.' He began imparting his instructions to me while he continued dressing, 'You understand the legacy that will be handed to you. You have it in you to make the necessary decisions for this family's survival.' Picking up a pair of leather gloves he pulled one on as an abstract thought occurred to me. John abhorred getting his hands dirty.

Gripping me by my shoulders he said seriously, 'You are ready. Lead the family to the fight. Sit with them. Be one of them.

Be ready for multiple challenges for leadership. They will begin the moment I pass.' I could see his uncertainty about the outcome of the cage match in his eyes.

I was counting on challenges for leadership.

In fact, I had already planned on open revolts and complete chaos by the end of my first moon at the helm of the business. Turning to face the door I kept my true feelings masked. Betting on the outcome of the match had been encouraged between members of the First Family. Bookies ran from floor to floor giving their odds distracting them nicely from the subtle shift in power taking place behind closed doors.

No one could remember the last time the cage had been used to settle an argument. I had not seen inside the amphitheatre but if the rumours were true the cage was a thing of beauty in every twisted sense of the word. Made of sandstone with a mini dome of stained glass to represent the dome we all lived in. It was also a distraction for the warriors fighting which would be a bonus to the live spectacle not witnessed for many years.

'Form up.' John ordered from our position on the grand staircase. His voice carried to every corner of the room silencing the melee of milling bodies below us.

When they stood in order we took our position at the head of the column. Position depended upon rank. John and his elite team at the front.

My bodyguard detail with me in the centre. Fane, Lia and Mother then the rest of the First Family, halflings, quarters and slaves following along at the rear with more guards. Directing some of my personal guards to stand at intervals on either side of the column would ensure they kept moving even if we fell under attack.

As we left the building I turned my head to see the column filling the streets behind us. Cheering filled my ears as we drew nearer to the rim. John stood up abandoning his wheelchair. Striding ahead of us in rapid strides. No longer hiding behind the lie of being crippled he began smiling and waving to the people lining the sides of the streets with his elite team fanned out loosely surrounding him.

The people of Spark City had obviously been waiting for an excuse to hold a city wide party.

With dome open at its maximum allowance unfiltered sunlight streamed in bathing us all in its merciless heat. Turning my head slightly I caught Lia's eye. She acknowledged me with a slight grimace. Fane cradled her in his arms compensating every time the road became uneven.

A promise of death radiated from the expression on his face warning off any bystanders who wished to reach out and touch her.

Entering through the side entrance of the amphitheatre closest to our designated seating John pulled me aside with an expression on his face almost akin to fondness. Grasping our forearms in a show of solidarity I watched him turn toward the warrior corridors on his own.

His cadre of elite guards helping to guide the family up into the stands and positioning themselves at either end of each row.

Satisfied that everyone was in position I turned climbing onto the dais. Fane nodded once before turning into a living statue barring further entry to the crowds below us.

Under the shade awning, Lia and Mother were sitting in two chairs slightly offset on either side of the empty centre one. Placing a kiss on each of their brows I allowed myself to sit for the first time with nowhere to be and nothing to do.

Gazing around the arena over the crowds I realised every founding family had sent physical representation except for the de Montmercy family.

Their dais remained empty but the seating area behind it was packed to standing room only. More people were climbing the stairs in support of Lady Mercy. Tiny scuffles broke out until two enforcers were obtained to block both stairwells leading into the section.

The raised dais in the centre of the arena was decorated with the emblem of the Union of Souls on the canopies.

Constructed of the same material as the rest of the Colosseum I had no doubt that the High Council and visiting dignitaries would hear every word spoken by the warriors directly in front of them.

White sand packed the arena floor waiting to soak up the blood that was sure to be spilt during the fight.

To my left, John entered the arena. Walking slowly, he raised his hand easily acknowledging the ear-splitting cheers rising from the crowd. Glancing behind me briefly I gleaned small details. Mother supporting Lia to stay seated upright surreptitiously checking the bandages around her midsection. Lia's white face. Fane's thunderous expression. The noise dies down at the appearance of a lone figure entering from the opposite side of the arena.

{Jo}

Defying tradition, my veil flutters to the ground revealing my long violet hair blowing like a banner in the light breeze.

Using the cover of the immediate cheering from the de Montmercy section five hooded figures slip out of the side of one of the stands and surround me.

'You don't have to do this.' Daire speaks empty words knowing as well as I do that there is no backing away from this.

I look down at the light purple jeans and matching form-fitting shirt I had been provided with. The house colours of the de Montmercy. Each of my brothers lower their hoods one after the other.

'Yes. I do.' Keeping it short and simple I explain, 'We all have our secrets and he was one of mine.' My parentage didn't matter. The only family I cared about stood around me willing to fight their way out of an arena full of packed people to save me.

'This isn't a practise match with us. You aim low. You play dirty. Leave your psychic voodoo as your last option.' Zev spoke as he raked his eyes over her assuring himself that she hadn't been physically harmed in the night.

She seemed fine except for the bruising around her wrists. His eyes narrowed as he catalogued the rest of her cuts. His sister seemed to be holding herself together by mere threads. Their eyes met. *'Don't. One day I will tell you. Not now.'* Her voice sounded close to tears in his mind. He grimaced and kicked the sand in frustration.

'He favours his left leg.' Blake pointed out in a hard voice. They couldn't baby her. Not now. Not in this place. 'Remember to keep your centre. Strike to slow him down.' Reece added. 'Then go for the kill shot.' Ed finished in a dark voice.

'Ravenna?' Swiftly gathering up my loose hair I bound it into a low knot at the base of my head so that John couldn't use it against me.

'Cerin has her in the stands. She refused to let us leave without her.' Daire grabbed me with a rough hug. I could tell that the child had gotten under his skin the same way I had long ago.

'Come home to us.' He whispered in my ear. Nodding my promise against his neck he held me until the noise of the crowd invaded the bubble we had created. A lump in my throat had formed refusing to allow me to speak any more words to them. 'It's time.' Releasing me Daire raised his hood. He was the last to melt away into the crowds leaving me on my own.

Continuing my journey into the centre of the arena silence swept through the Colosseum.

Assessing John's strengths and weaknesses as I made my way to him he offered me one more way in a voice devoid of any emotion, 'Last chance Daughter.'

Dropping down into my crouch I informed him coldly, 'I stopped being your daughter a long time ago.' I watched as he grappled with my refusal.

Clearing my mind of his hollow offer we waited for Madame Speaker to approach the edge of the stage. When she did her eyes were blazing full of anger down on John.

Seconds later the anger had softened into indescribable sadness as she acknowledged me. She raised a microphone to her mouth and spoke, 'We have been called upon to witness the outcome of this death match.

This way of settling disputes has not been called upon since before the time of my predecessor.' She paused to allow the significance of the occasion touch each spectator.

'We do not accept crime of any kind within this dome.

Our law stands firm on this principle. Joanna Mercy has been found guilty of attempted patricide. The aggrieved has chosen to fight instead of bringing the matter forward in the usual manner.' Madame Speaker turned to face the crowd behind her, 'This High Council will absolve the victor of all crimes against humanity. You may begin.'

My brothers had taught me well. Training had begun the day we had found each other to survive the brutality of the rim.

I hoped I would be able to keep my promise and walk out of the arena the same way I had entered it-alive. Keeping my head up, my eyes latched firmly on John's face I counted silently to myself. Seven. Seven seconds was all the time he took to launch into his opening attack.

He was good I had to concede but he wasn't great. Telegraphing his moves slightly I allowed my grin to widen slowly as I parried each lethal blow. Timing my movements perfectly. Landing my blows on his kidneys. His liver. His ribs.

Not crowd pleasers but designed to slow him down eventually. The deafening roar of the crowd only added to the atmosphere of confusion.

Spitting blood on the ground from his last punch to my mouth I didn't have time to check for loose teeth before he launched himself at me again with a roar. Narrowing my concentration nothing mattered but surviving him.

{Ethan}

She fought using a style I was completely unfamiliar with. Unable to tear my eyes away from her spinning body I analysed each kick, punch and spinning turn on her hands that turned her whole body into a weapon. 'I hope she wins.' Mother spoke directly into my ear.

Wrenching myself away from the spectacle in front of us she spoke again, 'At least his blood will not be on your hands.' Stroking Lia's arm as she rested against her she looked up at me, 'Nor on hers. There has been enough blood spilled in our family to last three lifetimes.'

'Who is she to us?' I had a sinking feeling that there were many secrets my mother had kept over the course of her life. Much more that she had still yet to divulge to me. Gesturing to the bleeding female in front of us with a feral look in her eyes she said, 'She is the female who will remove our greatest enemy. She will deliver our retribution for the passing of your father.'

Touching Lia's hand, I squeezed it gently Mother's expression remained enigmatic. Turning my head back to the battle in front of me I found John faltering. Stumbling. Eyes wild. Jo was still on her knees covered in her own blood.

{Jo}

'It's time.' Charli's mind voice was gentle as she infiltrated the fogginess clouding my thoughts. Time? Time for what?

'Time for you to use your gift.' She reminded me. Frightened of the outcome I begged her, *'Tell Daire... tell him to check my body for a pulse. I'm not leaving. Tell him I remember what I promised him.'*

Lowering my mental shields, I focused all my energy on John. Stumbling away from me he clutched at his head with both hands. Shaking it. Roaring from the immense agony that was building swiftly inside his mind. Futilely trying to regain his focus he latched onto the fact that my violet eyes had begun to glow. 'You.' He spat, 'You're doing this to me!' Blood trickling down the side of my face turned into a steady stream.

{Charli}

'Help her!' Cerin begged me over our link as we watched her nose start to bleed as well. Her brothers were as lifeless as statues accepting the inevitable scene unfolding in front of them. *'I am!'* My terse reply startled him as did my hands rising in front of my face of their own volition. I didn't care what I looked like to those surrounding me. It was no small matter to keep someone's brain intact and functioning. I trapped her mind in a corner of my own.

{Jo}

John let loose an unearthly wail before he collapsed onto the ground. His body faces down in the sand. 'There's been more than enough blood spilled on earth to buy your entry to bloody hell.' Muttering my final curse on the man deafening silence fell as I rose to my feet.

Unsteady I turned to the dais in front of me unable to make out clear features through the red wash in my vision. My debt to humanity had been paid. He had no pulse left with which to fight. 'You may leave with a clean record.' Madame Speaker informed me. Limping slowly out of the arena I turned the corner into the warrior's corridor leading to freedom and promptly collapsed to the ground.

{Charli}

It was there that we found her cooling body. Forming a circle around her the brothers stood shoulder to shoulder refusing to allow anyone to invade on their private moment alone with their sister. Daire pressed his fingers against her neck. I alone witnessed his steely demeanour slip when he couldn't find one. 'C'mon baby girl.' He shook her slightly. Jo's pulse flared leaving it weak and thready.

'She's still there. Locked inside her mind.' His eyes met mine without a word as I continued to speak to him alone, *'Her body*

is broken. She will need understanding and a lot of rest. She has not passed.'

My focus slipped as Ethan contacted me. Feeling relief at the good news I broadcast it to the brothers, *'Ethan's sending one of our healers to Mercy House. He says that I'm to stay with you for now and he will be in touch when it is safe for me to return to Smythe Towers.'* 'He says a lot this brother of yours.' Reece muttered back to me with a face full of retribution. *'Let your anger go. He is only trying to help.*

Did it not occur to any of you that she's a missing part of our family too?' I blazed back at him before finishing my conversation with Ethan.

{Ethan}

'Tell Mamma I love her.' Charli's plaintive voice floated through my head as one of the elite team almost yanked me off my feet in his haste to rush me back to

Smythe Towers as fast as he could manage.

I had no doubt that their next stunt would be to pull over one of the rickshaw drivers and commandeer their vehicle.

Soundly cursing the entitled fools, I watched as they commandeered not one rickshaw but the entire damn fleet. Idiots! Shaking my head, I knew I had to let Charli slip away so I could deal with the fallout from the bad choices being made in front of me. *'I will. He will keep you safe for me?'* I couldn't help asking the question before beginning to rebuild my psychic defences. *'They all will. Be safe Brother.'* Her voice faded leaving me with a sense of short-lived relief.

CHAPTER TWENTY
Entrapment

{Lia}

Something felt wrong. There was no way the First Family were happy just to let Ethan step into to John's shoes as easily as he had done. Moving restlessly around on the bed silently biting back my curses every time I bumped my sore wrist I finally gave up and took a pain relief tablet that the healer had insisted on me having.

Fane must have passed out on the couch sometime earlier in the night while waiting for me to settle down.

He had been on duty watching over Lili and me for the last seventy-two hours straight. Feeling the drug beginning to work I slowly unwrapped the bandaging around my wrist. Taking off the splints I knew that I was taking a huge chance with it. Possibly setting back my healing by a few weeks. Dressing silently in the dark I thanked all the gods of creation that Lili had finally given into my request for a pair of jeans and light soled shoes. Although if she'd known what I was planning I doubt she would have been so forthcoming.

Carrying the shoes in my hands I tiptoed past Fane sprawled out on the couch out to the patio. Slipping on the shoes I contemplated the climb ahead of me while lacing them up. Wrapping my braid up into a low coil I pinned up tightly before taking a running leap over the patio edge into the space between balconies.

Increasing my speed, I bounced off the walls up the side of the building and around the corner.

Working my way around the towers was quicker than navigating the maze of tunnels inside it.

Landing in a crouch on the patio I had become accustomed to spending my time on I rose quickly silently surveying the darkened interior of the living quarters. Questioning the fact that the patio doors had been left wide open. An invitation? For who? I knew better than to just enter asking a dark room questions. Concealing myself in the shadows I walked through the apartment confidently until I could whisper in Ethan's ear, 'Is it over? Are we safe?'

{Ethan}

'Not quite. You shouldn't be here tonight sweetheart.' Ignoring her quick indrawn breath and the fact she hadn't entered through the exterior door of the apartment meant that she had gone to great lengths to check up on my wellbeing. 'I'm expecting company.' I was getting weary of the fighting that was beginning to become a normal way of life.

Two weeks had passed, and she had managed to outsmart everyone to find a way in. I had no doubt others had been planning the exact same thing.

'You shouldn't be alone when they arrive.' Her soft voice was filled with quiet confidence. She elevated the lights just enough for me to make out her glowing eyes and determined face. 'Screaming like a female will not frighten them away this time.' The words slipped out of my mouth before I had a chance to rephrase them.

{Lia}

Screaming like a female? Levelling him with a look of complete disbelief knowing it would remain largely unseen I huffed my displeasure. I had stopped screaming for help long ago. 'It didn't work last time either.' I assured him once I had gotten over his poor choice of words, 'I will heal from these bruises and cuts. Your mother will not if it costs you your life. Despite all appearances, she is still grieving your father. She cries for him at night when she thinks no one can hear her.'

{Ethan}

Her quiet words slipped through my guard. I contemplated her statement for a few minutes before I realised one thing. Lia was completely right. Studying her outline in the shadows she had begun examining one of her wrists testing its flexibility. I didn't quite understand what we had between us. It was real.

I knew that I was eager to explore it more fully once I could get a few minutes out of the never-ending spotlight.

She alone had come for me. Lia was the only person I craved to have guarding my back in this moment. Containing myself I asked her, 'Stay?' 'I can stay? 'she asked softly seeking clarification when I didn't add any more to the conversation. 'You can stay. Just don't use your hands if you can't see clearly.' I breathed out slowly.

The implications too horrendous for me to imagine. Touching someone would mean her suffering a total loss of control and complete breakdown. Light bathed her face for mere moments. Enough for me to see the confusion and determination shining in her eyes.

She was offering her services. Hearing a noise. I allowed the fury I had been pushing down build up and spread throughout my system.

Lia took silent steps backwards until her knees hit the seat of her favourite armchair. Sitting abruptly, she waited for my signal. Would she hate me for using her as bait? I didn't have time to find out.

{Lia}

Hands wrapped themselves around my neck. 'Pretty Lia. Deadly Lia. Useless Lia.' A male's voice singsonged in my ear, 'Useless Lia. Broken Lia. Dead Lia.' Dead Lia? He cackled squeezing my neck a little. Biting back a scream I struggled to draw a decent breath through the male's iron grip. Moving my fingers to the top of one of my laced-up gloves I began to roll them down over my adaptive ones. I knew who had me in his grasp. Chills still rolling down my spine from his insane laughter I began to pull at the fingertips of one adaptive glove.

'Uh ah.' The voice admonished me, 'Keep your hands still. Where I can see them. Where is your consort tonight?

For one so broken but still so lovely I wouldn't have left you unguarded for even one moment.'

Placing my hands on my knees obediently I weighed my options silently. I couldn't struggle any further without him cutting off my airway completely. He gripped the back of my neck collaring me with his hand while the other one began to roam along my décolletage stroking me softly. 'You may speak.' His voice. I was afraid of his voice. I refused to respond to his command.

{Ethan}

'What makes you think she's alone Uncle?' cold steel pressed itself to the side of the male's head. I watched him peel his fingers off her throat one by one before moving away completely. 'What makes you think I am?' James Smythe the third moved into the centre of the room away from her.

'You are now.' I was blunt, 'In those few minutes I allowed you to mark Lia's pretty neck your sons died.'

Gesturing to where three forms lay slumped on the ground at various points around the room for emphasis.

'You killed them? You?' the incredulous tone in my uncle's voice bored me. They all seemed surprised when I did something remotely interesting. Raising an eyebrow inviting him to try something I stepped neatly in front of Lia shielding her from whatever he had planned next.

He swivelled his head between his sons and me. Shifting his eyes calculating the risks. Telegraphing every thought perfectly. Roaring in frustration he rushed at us. Using his momentum against him I caught him by his arm and planted a hand firmly on his rear sent him spinning straight through the wall into my sleeping quarters.

'Is he?' She pressed her body against mine using me a shield as she peered through the hole in the wall. 'No.' I replied my voice hard. I'd have to put them all in cells until I was ready to deal with more betrayals. When they all woke up they were going to wish they had never broken into my apartment.

Turning around I stroked the side of her neck gently, 'Did he do any more damage?'

{Lia}

'I don't think so.' Probing where his uncle's fingers had been his hand runs along the top of my shoulder. Comforting me. Reassuring himself that I'm alright. 'What is it?' Sensing his conflicted emotions, we lean on each other slightly. 'Go and wait for me in your sleeping chamber. Splint that wrist. When this mess is cleaned up we will talk.' He presses a light kiss on my forehead before sending me to my room.

Tucking my feet up underneath me I quickly took care of my wrist while waiting on my couch. Loud thudding disturbed the calm that had fallen over the apartment. Voices rose and fell. After a while, there was only silence. My doorknob turning has me searching the room for a weapon I can use. Retrieving the sharpened hair pick I had shoved through my hair for decoration I concealed it in the palm of my hand.

'Stand down.' Ethan stood outlined in the doorway holding out his hand for me to take, 'We will not be sleeping here tonight. Come.' Technically I shouldn't haven't even left his mother's apartment. Fane was going to kill me once he realised what I'd done.

Stepping through the living quarter's doorway I was absorbed by a group of large males. Surrounding me.

Gripping Ethan's hand more tightly he took a moment to peruse my face.

Rubbing his thumb over the back of my hand to dispel my anxiety he listened as I asked him in a small voice, 'Where are we going?'

{Ethan}

'To one of the dignitaries' apartments. They are completely vacant. No one will bother us any further tonight.' Pulling her closer to me I swept her up into my arms. 'We should go while the corridors are clear.' Looking down at her once more I asked, 'Ready?' She nodded while I gave the signal to move out.

After a tense trip through the corridors, I put her down on her feet when we were in the new apartment. 'Will they find us here?' She asked softly. 'We'll see.' I replied grimly.

James had amassed a loyal following of his own over the years. Most of whom were the 'shoot first ask questions later' type.

She walked over to the picture window overlooking the city. 'You had something on your mind you wished to talk to me about?' There had been enough sparks flying between us ever since she had arrived in my apartment. 'You came for me.' I said simply. She turned to face me waiting for me to elaborate.

Feelings were easy. Speaking the truth to the one person who had come to matter the most to me-not so much. 'Since the deathmatch, you're the only one who has come to check on me. Everyone else has only wanted something from me.'

{Lia}

'I will always want to know that you're alright.' I replied and added almost as an afterthought, 'If you let me.' He crossed the room in long strides and crowded me up against the pane of glass. 'Do you honestly think I could let you go after all that's passed between us?' the rough quality of his voice had me questioning where he was going with this. 'I can't.' He spoke again, 'I can't let you go back to the cells and I won't let you disappear out of my life without fighting for you. I want you more than I've wanted anything in my entire life.' Pressing his forehead against mine he closed his eyes waiting for me to reject him.

The truth was I didn't want to go. I didn't have the words to express my reply, so I kissed him. My lips touched his lightly at first growing more insistent as they tugged at his tongue begging for entry into his mouth. He threaded his fingers through the back of my hair with one hand to cradle it deepening the kiss further.

{Ethan}

Awareness swept through my body of another person in the room. Watching our every movement. Sneering at our love. Breaking off the kiss I untangled my hand carefully.

Breathing hard I savoured the feeling of her body pliant against mine. Clapping echoed through the large space. 'Romance is not wasted on the young.' I knew she could read regret in my eyes as I caressed her face.

'You honour us with your presence Foremother.' Pressing a finger to her lips warning her to let me do the talking. My expression darkened.

The emotions sweeping through me were unfamiliar and completely terrifying. It was one thing to target me. Targeting the female I love was unforgivable. Keeping Lia shielded from sight behind me I asked casually, 'How did you find us?' 'I have my ways.' The elderly female in front of me stalked closer.

Her gait steady head upright. Aware of the red dot from a sniper's rifle in the centre of my chest I eased my body away from Lia's giving her space to move. To escape a bullet.

Searching through the gloom.
Following the red line back to the scope
that was projecting it.

'You would take over the family by
force?' Keeping her talking might buy Lia
some time to get away. 'I thought your
mother would have forewarned you. I do
not forgive slights easily. You flouted my
authority by rescuing your quarter and
making her your consort. Weapons.' She
demanded perfunctorily, 'I know you carry
guns. All the Smythe males do.'

Moving my hands slowly to do her
bidding I felt Lia place one hand on my
back. She double tapped it gently and
then drew a line diagonally downwards to
the right. The gun I kept stored in the
back of my waistband slid free. Without
further warning, she kicked me in the back
of my right knee forcing me down and out
of the way.

Diving to the left she got off two shots
aiming just above the line of light now

decorating her chest. Hearing multiple thuds, I lifted my head high enough to see that she had rolled onto her back gun still smoking in her hands. Crawling over to her took the gun out of her hand before glancing around again at the carnage. Lia's shot had taken out both threats at once.

{Lia}

'Lia?' He wrapped me in his arms, 'Baby look at me.' The pain pill had worn off and my body had flooded once again with throbbing agony. Taking a calming breath, I focused completely on him my words falling from my mouth hesitantly, 'I expected a blowback. I didn't miss did I?' He kissed the top of my head waiting as my voice grew stronger, 'She was your foremother.' 'Perfect kill shots.' He sounded proud, 'You did what you had to do to get us out of a bad situation.'

I doubted Fane would see it our way. Resting her body against me listening to my heartbeat. I gave her time to ground herself. 'My guards are going to come bursting through the door any moment.' I couldn't help but be amused at the situation we were in. My voice snapped her out of the silent reverie she had fallen into. 'I doubt this isn't something they haven't seen before.' She replied seeing the funny side of it herself.

{Lia}

Grimacing at a sharp stab of pain I rose unsteadily to my feet.

Ethan led me through to the sleeping quarters warning me, 'This is a single apartment.' He sat me on the edge of the bed and removed my shoes for me, 'You've been through enough tonight. Rest. I won't leave you on your own tonight.'

Rustling sounds coming from the living quarters distracted us both. He brushed a strand of hair that had become stuck to my cheek away before kissing my forehead, 'I won't be far away.'

{Ethan}

Entering the room, I surveyed the damage. The spent casings had been retrieved already. Pools of blood remained on the hardwood floor. My bodyguards entered the room weapons drawn expecting to find a hostage situation or worse. Eyeing them sternly I spat, 'It's already all over. Where were you idiots?'

Looking thoroughly chastened they holstered their weapons and looked for further instructions, 'I want two males at the door and another two inside the apartment with us. The bodies have already been disposed of. Someone wake up Fane and apprise him of what's happened tonight then send him to me.'

CHAPTER TWENTY-ONE
Straight Talking

{Charli}

I could feel her link to me curled up in the back corner of my mind. Dormant. Resting. Choosing to believe she was fighting to find her way back to us I had allowed Ed and Reece to move her broken body back to Mercy House. We had splintered without her.

{Cerin}

Split up across the five levels of the building we all worked separately to repair the damage and make the refuge habitable again.

Honestly, I couldn't even remember the last time I had spoken to some of them.

Jo would be so ashamed of the males we had become without her. Fading into the corner becoming one with the shadows I drew my gun silently. Using rubble for cover I watched Cerin stand outlined in the doorway. Pausing by her bed he pulled the light cover-up over her shoulders before kissing her forehead. He took a seat by the bed and began to talk. They all did when they thought I had left the room for an indeterminate amount of time.

At the beginning, I thought that it would disturb the healing process.

After a while, I realised that talking to her had become cathartic for us all. Telling her things we wished she'd known.

Telling her information we didn't want anyone else to know. Holding one-sided conversations and dealing with our problems the way she had always begged us to.

{Daire}

He admitted aloud, 'I can't do this Jo. I told you. I couldn't do it long term. She's getting under my skin and I'm afraid...' His voice faltered before it continued, 'I'm afraid I won't be able to protect her the same way I couldn't protect them.'

Bowing his head into his hands he forces himself to keep speaking through clenched teeth, 'I can still hear them calling for help in my dreams. I see their blood staining the carpet. I smell it. The night terrors are getting worse and I don't know how to shake them.'

He fell silent listening to Jo inhale with a slight wheeze reminding us that she was still there. I had never seen my usually stoic brother display so much emotion at once. I didn't have time for him to fall apart over a mere what if. Charli trusted him and through him us. She was the small bright spot of our days. To hear my brothers tell Jo of something she had told them or some antic she had instigated brought laughter temporarily back into this room.

As much as we needed Jo back we also needed Charli too. Stepping out from behind the rubble I dropped a hand on Cerin's shoulder, 'I'm sorry little brother but you need to deal with your ghosts. They're stopping you from having a future. I don't know where the others are or if they're even still here. For what it's worth Charli needs you now more than ever.'

'Jo told me the same thing the night Charli came to Mercy House. Told me to deal with the past before it dragged me under.' I squeezed his shoulder gently, 'She always knows what she's talking about. Some of the wisest words she told me was to put away the memories that did more damage then made me smile. She was right. Go do whatever it takes to clear your head.'

{Charli}

Respecting his space was harder than normal. His thoughts were closer to the surface. He was clearly in pain and there was nothing I could do. The urge to interrupt him before he as finished his thinking almost overwhelmed me.

Inside his head, he was listing all the reasons why he couldn't keep his promise to my brothers. I waited until he fell quiet. *Have you finished your list yet?'* I couldn't keep the scathing tone from my mind voice.

He had made me feel safe. I couldn't imagine life without him in it. *'You made promises you have no intentions of keeping. Save your excuses. Hand me my crutches and let me go. I'll have someone come for my belongings as soon as I can.'* Emerald fire blazed in my eyes as I looked at him.

{Cerin}

'Charli I...' The rest of my sentence died in my throat as the diminutive blond struggled to her feet in front of me. Her walking gait twisted back and forth as she slowly made her way to where her crutches had been stored almost falling twice. Steely determination set in her features she exited the room without looking back at me once. I felt pride rising inside of me at the sight of her making her way through the hallway.

She had come a long way from being the frightened child begging for the guaranteed safety of her family.

Tracking her easily through the crowds in the food district she was being swept along at a pace she couldn't quite manage to keep up. Determination shone on her face like a beacon drawing me closer manoeuvring my way through the oblivious people until I stood before her. A solid roadblock. Immovable. Forcing the crowd to flow around us. Banging her head against my chest in frustration I heard her amused voice say, *'I didn't order my own crowd blocker.'*

Swinging her up into my arms so that her crutches dangled uselessly from her arms I turned and began walking back towards Mercy House without a word. *'I heard your thoughts. You don't want the responsibility of being my bodyguard.'* She pointed out in a reasonable tone, 'You were broadcasting all day.' 'I've been an idiot.' I replied evenly feeling her muscles relax slightly at my admission, 'Honestly, I'd rather be your friend if it isn't too late.'

'You promise to talk things through with me instead of letting it all build up inside you again?' She asked as the refuge loomed before us, *'I'm more than a brain. I'm a person with feelings and your slight meltdown hurt me.'* 'I know. All the way to the market district by yourself huh? Maybe you should walk more on your own.' Smiling over the top of her head I knew we would be alright.

{Ethan}

Standing behind my uncle's desk absolute loathing for the decor flowing through me I faced my mother. I needed to know what other secrets she had been hiding from me. This was the safest room in the whole tower to discuss sensitive subjects.

There was no surveillance. After the cleaning crew had left the night before I had stretched out beside Lia on top of the bed covers. My gun was hidden within reach should I need it.

The memory of her sleepy smile before curling into my side filled me with warmth.

Narrowing my eyes at my mother. I knew she had a wealth of knowledge at her fingertips when it came to the potential threats from the rest of the family. She needed to share it before someone else got hurt.

'You heard that Lia and I had some unwelcome visitors last night.' There was no gentle way to say what needed to be said, 'You alone understand the politics and power plays in the family. John obviously had plans for Charli. She can't come home until we know she's safe and I want Lia safe in our home.'

{Lilianna}

Sighing deeply, I had hoped this day would never come. The day I would have to tell my son about the prophecy regarding the de Montmercy bloodline. I had foolishly hoped that I could keep both my children from being swept up in the swirling winds of destiny. Ethan's patience had stretched thin over the past few days and Fane's had snapped a while ago. I hoped that the weight of leadership would not crush the male I raised.

'You recall we discussed Elanna de Montmercy. The secrets and lies surrounding this female haven't grown any less deadly over time.' There was more. So much more. He needed to know everything I knew.

Perching on the edge of the seat behind me I regarded him over the top of my glasses, 'There is an ancient prophecy pertaining to the de Montmercy family. When your father mated me, he promised me that you would never be caught up in all of this.' A solitary tear works its way down my face unchecked. 'Why should I care about this prophecy?' He asks stiffly. 'You are a de Montmercy by birth.' The words hang in the air between us, 'You have the blood right to know what I know.'

Sitting down he places both his hands on the desk between us waiting quietly.

It isn't easy for me to tell him something I buried deep long ago. 'When I arrived at Smythe Towers Elanna had already established herself as the First female. Your Uncle was utterly besotted with every breath they took. They all were. Both you and Fane had been relegated to the nursery to be raised with all the other children nobody wanted.

Your Father was trying to pull himself together after Elanna had led him a merry dance before rejecting him.'

'None of this explains any secrets.' He prompts me to continue. The secrets. The lies. The life of a child couldn't be explained in a few sentences. 'As time went by Elanna and John were blessed with a child of their own but the cracks in their mateship were beginning to show. Arguments between them over little things.

John refused to let her manipulate him the way she had done with your Father. One night she told us over dinner about the de Montmercy prophecy. A prophecy so deeply entwined with the foundation laws of our known world.

One that the rulers of the time feared badly enough to bury away deep in a vault beneath the High Council.' Swallowing I looked up at him, 'A female of de Montmercy blood would be the strongest fifth ever born. She would have hair in a colour that none of us had ever seen the likes of before she shook the very foundation of Anna's laws.'

'The prophecy has yet to be fulfilled.' Ethan summarised. 'There is more. The child Elanna and John had was a baby girl. One day she was perfect and the next they were passing off her disappearance as infant death. Only...'

I paused gathering courage for the part that scared me the most, 'only I saw Elanna give the child to a servant. The next day she was gone and her eldest daughter was caged in her place. Such a sweet thing. Shy too. John was cruel to her. She was not his precious Elanna and at every opportunity he made sure we all knew it.'

Ethan held up his hand to stop her. 'I know the next part. John attempted to kill her. He succeeded in killing Elanna and was sent to the territories to answer for his crimes.' Sliding back onto the seat I shook my head, 'That is where the common story is wrong. John may have killed some poor female but it was not Elanna. She had gone into seclusion at what was then de Montmercy Estate.

He was still visiting her daily and they were manipulating everyone into thinking that she had passed. She was alive the last time I saw her and I believe she's out there somewhere still playing her games.'

  {Ethan}

'This child of the prophecy. Is there any chance it might be Charli?' I knew that there was more to her story then what my parents had told me. 'Charlotte Grace is not of Elanna's blood.' My mother stated sadly, 'She's of John's.' Changing subjects, I informed her, 'James and his sons are in the cells. Arcana and her accomplice didn't survive the night.' 'Arcana has passed?' Her face lightens at the thought.

'Yes.' I confirmed. 'Do you think they were working together?' She asks latching onto my train of thought, 'Arcana has always stood for things being a certain way. It makes perfect sense that she would attempt to hold complete control of the Family. James must have had his own agenda though. I've never known him to go against John's orders.'

'Could Arcana have pressured him into it?' Her body language confirms what I had been thinking. 'If I show mercy I will be labelled as soft leaving us wide open to further assassination attempts. If I make an example of him, I will be no better than John for ruling by fear.' I presented my dilemma to her rationally seeking her advice.

'I would call a family gathering. Let them see that you are both unharmed. Let them see James and his sons in chains.' A chilling look crept across my mother's face, 'Let them decide what is going to happen. Give some power back to the people and throw the dogs to the wolves.'

Pressing a button recessed into the desk I made an immediate announcement that would be played over the loudspeaker system, 'Good Afternoon Smythe Towers. This is an announcement for family members, guests, residents below and above. Your presence is required in the meeting room in exactly one hour. Absences will be noted.'

Ending the announcement, I look at my mother, 'Lia is with a detail in 543. You have an hour to prepare her for what she is about to face. I want to present a united family front. Wave a bit of your magic around and make her look spectacular.'

'You would take her as your chosen?' She asks me with a small smile as she prepares to leave. 'We would take her as our mate.' I reply and add, 'Fane has yet to speak to her and she may not feel the same about us once we decipher the puzzle in her mind.'

{Lilianna}

Inclining my head, I acknowledge the complexity of the problems still facing them. I was proud of him. He held true to what he believed in and had continued to do so over the years.

He still displayed an iron determination tempered by both wisdom and compassion.   So much compassion that he was willing to share the one person he treasured the most.

{Ethan}

They were late. Searching through the crowd gathering inside the meeting room I finally spotted Lia pushing her way through the throng to join me. She looked stunning in a dress of deep green that matched my tie and the subtle tones in my mother's outfit as she followed along in Lia's wake. Drawing her into my arms I kissed her briefly before inviting, 'Come and sit with me.' Leading her to the chairs on the dais I made sure she was comfortable before giving the signal for the doors to be closed.

Aware of the heightened emotions swirling around the room I approached the podium with minimal fuss. Foregoing the usual affable greeting I spoke, 'Last night I was subjected to not one but two attempts on my life and the life of my consort.' Waiting until the whispers died away I continued, 'This afternoon you have a choice before you.' The elite team marched James and his sons into the centre of the open space between the podium and first row of seats bound with their wrists behind them.

'What do you want to the penalty for their crimes to be?' I met the crowd's judgmental expressions with complete openness, 'I can report him to the High Council for crimes against humanity.' The room echoed with the roars of outrage and disapproval at this suggestion. Holding my hand up for silence they unhappily obliged too used to obeying John. 'I could deal with them by removing a hand or an eye.'

Drawing my gun, I flicked off the safety and levelled the barrel at James's head, 'I could deal with them the way Arcana attempted to deal with me.'

Placing the gun down on the podium in front of me I knew I had their undivided attention. They were waiting to see what kind of a leader I was going to be based on the decision I would make for them.

'Uncle John's reign of terror is at an end. I will not choose in this matter. Instead, the decision is yours to make. Vote wisely.' I looked down at them my face grave, 'We will cast our votes by a simple method. Raise your hand if you agree with an option after it has been read out. The solution with the most votes will be implemented immediately.' Holstering my gun, I nodded to the new elite team. They all had a part to play in our new semi-democratic society.

{Lia}

Inhaling sharply ignoring Lili's hand on my arm my eyes dart around the room looking for Fane.

I hadn't seen him since he had switched shifts with the new cadre of bodyguards. Ethan flicks his eyes in my direction warning me not to make a scene.

Unanimously they make their decision within mere moments. 'All serious matters will be brought to a vote from now on.' He reminds them before addressing the prisoners in front of him, 'I look forward to your return in five years. Be safe in the territories.' Stepping up to my position half a pace behind his elbow I stared down at them supporting Ethan silently.

CHAPTER TWENTY-TWO
Trust

{Lia}

Pretending to nap I lay on my stomach on the recliner in the low afternoon light of the dome. Ethan spends a large portion of his time in the office trying to get a sense of the scope of John's operation.

I have been making the most of the opportunity to keep reading through the extensive library of books.

Light soled boots moving fast across the tile rouses me enough to raise my head. Fane. He stops a few paces away from where I'm lying. He takes a few deep breaths before asking, 'Don't. You. Trust. Me.' His words are clipped off in a low hard voice. The hem of his trench coat still swirling around his knees.

He's angry with me. I stop as I pull myself up to a standing position. Analysing him I realise that he's not angry at me but furious that I'd snuck out on him. Words aren't going to excuse my actions. How can they? In my desperation to make sure Ethan had someone at his back I hurt Fane. Peeking up at him through my lashes he's focusing on something beyond my face.

He didn't want me for a friend. He was probably right not to. I hurt everyone who gets too close to me. 'I trust...' I try. 'You don't.' He cuts me off glaring in my general direction. I do.

I hate how he's forcing himself to maintain eye contact with me. I trust him enough to insult him by picking up a weapon to defend myself against his unfounded fears.

I try again, 'I trust you Fane.' His eyes zeroed in on the smudges marking the skin on my neck. James's trademark calling card. He reaches out. Fingertips brush the bruising gently before he remembers he's angry with me. His hand falls uselessly to his side.

Swallowing carefully, I wait. Sensing there are more reasons for his anger. 'Don't you dare do that again.' His tone deepens and then softens, 'I don't want to find you beaten within an inch of your life or worse ever again. What the hell were you thinking?'

Cocking my head on one side I take my time perusing his face. He was yelling at me because I had snuck out of the apartment past him.

Because I had almost gotten hurt on his watch. What had I been thinking?

Choosing my words wisely I speak the truth that he needs to hear, 'I was trained to work alone. It didn't occur to me to wake you up after working a 72-hour shift to help me go deal. Nobody had his back. No one.'

Deliberately keeping my tone soft to deflect his temper the words tumble out one after another, 'I couldn't stay safe in a warm bed knowing that he could be... would be hurt like I was. Killed. For what. Power. Keeping order. You and me. We've seen more. Done more. We haven't had the luxury of a sheltered upbringing. This is going to be a rough transition Fane. I've got his back because I know you've got mine.'

My voice fades into obscurity before I can tell him how much I have come to trust him since he became my friend.

Averting my eyes, I stare at his boots wondering if this was the part where they sent me back to the cells. I had never felt so ashamed of wanting to put my skills to good use in all my existence. I had saved Ethan's life. Surely that should count towards something.

'Lia.' There's still no hint of the amusement that usually underscores his words, 'I don't care if I've been watching your pretty backside for three days straight. Next time you wake me and we go together.' His tone resolute.

'You don't trust me?' my voice comes out smaller than normal. This is not the Fane I know. This is a Smythe male. No room for error. No room for movement. All business. Dark. Brooding. He stalks closer to me.

Dark eyes meet mine, 'Don't turn this into something it's not.' 'Right because I'm a delicate female who's lived her entire life in a cage I obviously have no clue what I'm doing in a fight.' Sarcasm drips off my tongue like honey. I think I like sarcasm. It's easy to hide behind.

He's right. I'm dragging out this argument. I want them to recognise that I have skills that they can use. I want them to understand that I won't be caged like the other First Family females. I've been given a taste of freedom that I refuse to give up without an all-out brawl.

'Feisty today aren't you.' His statement grounds me before he continues, 'I've seen you fight. I was there the first time he forced you to use your new gifts.

I was there with you in the cells when Arcana's two idiots subjected you to her wrath. I found in you the halls broken, bleeding and barely alive. Don't ask me to let you keep doing things on your own Lia I don't think my heart could take it.'

Had he been there the first time? That bothers me. A lot. My face feels warm.

He had been there with me through it all. Seen me without all the airs and graces.

'Nobody has ever been kind to me before besides Lily, Ethan and Charli. I'm good at being unapproachable. Until I met you. I trust you Liana.' His voice breaks slightly shocking him as much as it does me, 'I don't trust any other bastard with you.'

'Except for Ethan?' I want clarification. I want to know what it is that's between us. 'Some days not even Ethan.' He admits with a wry smile. Oh. I want to look away. Hide the confusion flooding my features.

My gaze is drawn to the bracelet on my wrist. I wear all the symbols that mark me as Ethan's consort. His large hand encloses over mine. I feel tiny next to him. Delicate.

He pulls me into his arms flush against him so that my head rests against his

chest. 'Baby. I'm not that kind of male.'
His words are unbearably gentle, 'I don't
need to mark my territory. Although it's
getting harder not to clock every male
who looks at you the wrong way. I'm your
bodyguard. He's your consort.'

'It's really that simple?' I ask my
heartbeat picking up pace. Lips brush
across my bruised knuckles before he
chuckles, 'Lia we can make it as simple or
as complicated as we want to. You're ours
and that's all that matters.'

His words echo in my mind 'You're ours
and that's all that matters.' His confidence
is comforting. Snuggling in closer I
respond with the first thing that comes to
mind, 'I've missed you.' 'I know.' His voice
rumbles his hand playing with the end of
my braid. 'Why were you there the first
time?' Him seeing that bothers me.

'All the halflings were there in the
shadows. It was part of our training to
observe what happened in the cells.'

Honesty followed by a real smile, 'I thought you were crazy brave then and I think you are crazy brave now.'

Fane unwraps his arms from around me reluctantly, 'I have to go.' 'I know.' Surprise crosses his face. 'You never left.' My whispered words shock him further. I'm observant. I've seen him when he didn't think I was watching. The illusion he was missing was a key piece for flushing out any remaining traitors to the change of leadership.

'You're good.' I explain without bragging, 'I'm better.' Tipping his mouth up in a half smile he brushes his lips across mine. Fingers trace my lips. 'They're softer than what I imagined.' Boots thudding against the tile from the other end of the patio alert us that the new guards are coming.

Fane raises a finger to his lips before he leaps over the balustrade.

The swirl of his jacket startling me from my kiss induced reverie. Rushing to look over the edge I see him turn mid fall and catch onto another balcony. He grins at me before disappearing into the shadow of the building avoiding the drone.

'Everything alright mistress?' One of the new guards ask. 'I thought I saw a chickadee.' I reply with a smile before returning to the book lying askew on the chair I had been in. Ethan needs to change the guards again if they thought a bird had somehow gotten into the Domesphere.

CHAPTER TWENTY-THREE
Our's

{Ethan}

She was staring at the skyline again. It seemed to intrigue her. So many people. Each living their own lives with their own problems. Sitting down beside her I asked, 'Would you like to go somewhere outside of the four towers?'

Bewilderment flashed across her face before she asked, 'What's the mission?'

Raising my hands in surrender playfully I smiled, 'No catches. No mission. I simply want to take you outside for a while.'

{Lia}

Wrinkling my brow, I simply stared at him still having trouble processing his statement. 'I can go outside again?' I clarified, 'For fun.' 'Yes.' His face was the epitome of patience being stretched to its limit. A giggle slipped out before I burst into full-blown laughter surprising us both. 'I like when you do that.' His mouth tipped up at the corners, 'You good now?' Nodding I checked with him, 'Is there anything you'd like me to wear in particular?' 'Green suits you.' Placing a kiss on my forehead he releases me to go change.

{Ethan}

I took her to the Hanging Gardens to see the trees that were always in bloom.

Leading her through archways riotous in a burst of purples and whites to the walkway of pink petals slowly drifting to the ground.

Stopping beside a park bench I pulled her down onto my lap speaking directly into her ear, 'The first time I came here I asked my mother why there were so many different colours in the world.' 'What did she say next?' she wondered aloud.

'She said that we need different colours just like we need different kinds of people. Some flowers are pretty but only flower for a day, other flowers have thorns for protection and some are deadly. The best kind of flower is one that knows when to put the thorns away and flowers for a long time. One that knows that its deadly leaves are just to keep the bugs away.'

We sat in silence for a while enjoying the serenity of the gardens. The story made sense to me.

They wanted me to be happy without having to watch my own back all the time.

'Your mother is a wise female.' The slope covered in lantern laden trees had captured her attention. The moral of the story had not been lost on her. 'It's beautiful here.' Her ruby eyes caught mine. 'Not as beautiful as my view.' I replied with a slow smile. She blushed before turning back to the gardens surrounding us.

The Hanging Gardens were an integral part of the inner city. Most inhabitants of the inner circles came here to escape the noise of the overpopulated dome. Pointing out the stream that wound its way lazily through the park Lia pointed at the arched walkway in the distance crossing from one side to the other.

{Lia}

'Where does that lead to?' curious to discover where the path went I asked him for more information.

'Let's go find out.' He set me back on my feet before placing my hand in his. In front of me his tough persona had been shed in favour of this relaxed version of Ethan. A new side of his personality reserved for me alone.

Winding our way through the gardens he pointed out the various highlights of each garden room to me. Eventually, we made it out the other side. Instead of taking me back to Smythe Towers Ethan led me to a building within walking distance of this side of the green space.

{Ethan}

'Who lives here?' she asks confusion evident on her face. 'We do.' Opening the door, I wave her through ahead of me, 'I had my own place outside of Smythe Towers and was living here full time before my father died.' She follows me into the elevator and steps out into my penthouse. Eyes darting everywhere.

Taking in the details the same way she did the first time she saw our apartment. Flicking my finger, I watch her unwrap the veil hiding her hair from the rest of the world. Draping it over the back of a chair she made a slow circle of her new surroundings.

{Lia}

'Does it meet your approval my lady?' He asks me playfully as I come to a stop in front of him. Any place he and Fane were would meet with my approval. I didn't care if they took me to a hovel in the outer rim as long as we were together.

'She likes it.' Fane saunters through the kitchen stopping in front of me, 'You're thinking too much.' He declares tugging at the hair clip binding my braid in place.

Fingers bury themselves in my hair unravelling my hairstyle with ease. Digging down gently they proceed to give me a scalp massage. Pressing all the right points relaxing me instantly.

They have me sandwiched between them and it feels right. 'Lia?' Fane turns my name into a question. 'Yes?' I ask. 'Yes, was all I wanted to hear.' He grins before kissing me thoroughly.

'Lia?' Ethan whispers into my ear distracting me from the kiss that's threatening to sweep me away in an avalanche of too many emotions to process at once. 'Hmm....'I reply still slightly dazed. 'Trust us? 'He feathers kisses up the side of my neck.

{Ethan}

'Yes.' Her complete trust in us rocks me for a moment. The dazed look in her eyes shows us that we do the same for her. Fane sweeps her off her feet impatient that I'm wasting too much time.

Following them into one of the sleeping quarters I know instantly that he's put thought into bringing her here. This is the most feminine of all the sleeping chambers. He puts her down gently in the centre of the room.

'Don't take off your gloves.' Fane warns her and adds, 'Anything you don't like you say something immediately.'

'Use the word *red* sweetheart.' I tell her leaning against the wall watching them. Enjoying the expressions on her face. Motioning with one hand Fane leans against the opposite wall satisfied grin on his face as her hands move slowly towards her hair.

She finger combs through it thoroughly destroying the fancy style she had put it up in. Slipping off her shoes one by one her fingers begin to work the intricate fastenings on her dress.

{Fane}

'Stop.' I keep my voice even. Biting her lip, she tilts her head questioning me silently. 'I want this.' I all but growl at her, 'So does he. Do you want us?'

Pushing off the wall I force her to meet my eyes, 'Lia?' Moistening her lip slightly she smiles before pushing my hair out of my eyes, 'I want this.' Eyeballing Ethan over the top of her head we have a silent conversation. She wants us. We do this slowly.

'Baby, 'she shivers at the brush of my lips against her ear, 'Let me help you.' Rubbing strands of her hair between my thumb and forefinger I can feel her frayed nerves almost snapping. Gathering her close I promise, 'We'll do this together. Nice and slow.'

That was the first night she woke us up screaming in her sleep. The nightmares became a steady stream of information. Our days slipped through our fingers as we struggled to deal with our nights. 'What happens in these dreams? What do you see?' I asked her as I pushed damp hair away from her forehead.

If we could only understand the memories from her perspective maybe we would have a chance of tracking down some answers.

She's curled herself into a tight little ball between us. 'It's all mixed up in my head.' She replies in a halting voice still reliving parts of the dream in her mind, 'There's a sad little boy. He's so sad on a happy day. A blond male swings a female with a long brunette braid around in his arms. Demons with blue paint and tattoos on their face. I feel cold. It is cold.'

Ethan tucks a blanket around her shivering frame as she continues, 'Water a shade of blue so bright that it hurts the eyes. Sunsets all gold and pink over a vast ocean. An orange door. Females completely dressed from head to toe in white. A female child with blue hair blowing in the wind.'

{Ethan}

She spoke softly, 'I told you, it doesn't make any sense.' We have the same silent conversation over her head we've been having every night since her screaming started. There must be a solution that will bring her a modicum of peace. 'It will. We will have to treat your memories like a huge puzzle that needs solving. Fane nods agreeing with me. 'I don't even know where to begin.' She admits.

'What makes you think that the sad little boy was sad on a happy day?' Keeping my voice neutral I push her to think about the night terror further instead of giving into her frustrations and retreat into her usual coping mechanism of meditation.

{Lia}

'The male and female have matching tattoos. He feels left out somehow.' I hazard a guess before focusing inwardly on the question, 'He missed his own mother.' Raising my head, I look at them,

'He missed his mother.' Fane hands me the notebook we have been keeping by the bed. Opening it to the next blank page I jot down the dream and some of my lasting impressions from it.

'What you mean by the girl with the blue hair doesn't like me very much. She's pretending to be my friend. I think she's jealous of something.' Ethan asks reading over my shoulder. 'Why would someone pretend to be my friend and be jealous of me at the same time?' I ask in return unable to mask the confusion I'm feeling at this moment.

{Ethan}

'It's human nature. We're taught to use manners, have opinions and feelings. We're also taught what is appropriate to say at any given moment. Your records say that you originally come from Oceanic City.

It is possible you had already entered training and the girl with the blue hair is another female in your group.' I tell her closing the notebook. 'What if I never get my memory back?' she asks softly. Fane meets my eyes before replying, 'You will still be my Lia.'

Two days later...

{Lia}

First class train tickets lay on the table between us where he had slapped them down a few seconds ago. 'We need answers.' Fane pointed out through gritted teeth.

Rubbing my temples in a vain effort to prevent a forming migraine. We needed help to link my broken memories together and the High Council had advised that we approach the Sisters of the Sea for their help. 'If your memories are correct then there should be records of your years in their training facilities.' He added.

We had been having the same conversation for days.

'My memories aren't going to change anything.' I insisted in a soft voice, 'They tell me where I've been, who I used to be not who I am now or who I will be in the future. I may never put all the pieces together and I have to be okay with that.'

'I'm not.' Ethan met my honesty with the words he needed me to hear. Massaging my tight neck, he continued, 'We've stolen the life you could have been living all these years. The drugs he forced you to take every day. The pain he put you through each time you killed for him. I can't erase that. Your memories hold the key to the secrets my family have buried deep. We owe you your life back.'

{Ethan}

She scrunched her forehead before replying, 'I like the life I have now. What if I don't like what I find out?' Continuing her massage, I soothed her, 'You won't be alone.'

Read on for a sneak peek of Anamnesis. Book 3 of the Elanna's Children series.

Anamnesis

{Lia}

The word anamnesis means to remember or to recover lost memories. That's what we intend to do.

Breakthrough the block that's been placed on my fragmented memories to heal me and to help our family survive whatever the world throws at us next.

Catching the train to Oceanic City would prove to only be the beginning of a whole new race against time...

Amusement rippled through me at the antics of my two males double-checking their weaponry bags. 'Really could have used my brass knuckles.' Fane muttered feeling around in his duffle bag. 'Good in a fight.' Ethan agreed absentmindedly checking his favourite pistol. 'Silent.' Fane added before asking, 'Got anything else I can use?

Had to leave half my arsenal in Amvelona when you asked me to come back.'

Spinning one of his throwing knives around in my hands, 'I happen to have a weapon or two.' They both looked up at me in disbelief before narrowing their eyes in slight disapproval.

'Absolutely not.' Fane snagged his blade out of the air examining it carefully, 'My favourite blades too.'

Producing another throwing knife with ease I began a more complicated twirling routine enjoying the incredulous expression marching across both faces.

'How many weapons have you helped yourself to?' Ethan demanded to know before he expertly caught it. 'A few.' Evading them easily laughter bubbled up from deep within.

Stunned momentarily they both pounced on me at the same time.

'Two throwing blades, a knife, a gun with a silencer and a corkscrew.' Ethan looked over the haul before raising an eyebrow, 'Anything else sweetheart?' Examining my nails, I admitted softly, 'My hairpins are all sharpened for maximum effect.

You missed a knife.' The brothers exchanged disbelieving glances before Fane growled, 'Give back the knife. You can keep your hairpins but make with everything else. Now!'

Pouting I withdrew the knife and its scabbard from the waistband of my jeans, 'The corkscrew would've been fun if I'd had to interrogate anyone for information. There's a fine art to torture you know.'

Dropping the offending item into Fane's hand I smiled, 'If you wanted me unarmed all you had to do was let me know.'

He stifled a laugh of his own, 'There's also a fine art to blending in. Females in Oceania don't carry weapons or wear jeans. Go and change into one of your fancier dresses then I'll explain.'

Chuckling as she disappeared into the sleeping quarters he turned to Ethan, 'She's going to keep us on our toes. Bloodthirsty little minx.'

Glossary

Amvelona- A dome city in the south west. Home to the star gazers.

Anna-The woman who successfully changed life for women for the better. Her rules and ideals keep most women safe from harm.

Anna's rules-The way a woman is raised and trained to treat men that they contract with.

Arcana Smythe- Ethan's formidable foremother.

Bordertown-The nearest town two days ride away from the energy harvesting farm Nick and his family live and work on.

Blood singer- A female with the ability to kill a corrupt male with a single stroke of her finger on his bare skin.

Side effects of this gift is being overwhelmed with the blackness of the male's soul.

Brother-A polite way of addressing full and half siblings of the male persuasion.

Caged-Hidden away from the sight of all except for the one man a fifth is mated/contracted to.

Cerin-Charlotte Grace's bodyguard at Mercy House. Next eldest in age to Jo in their family.

Charlotte Grace Smythe- Ethan's younger sister. Trained to be an invisible from birth.

Choosing- announcing to the world that a formal monogamous relationship has formed.

Com-a hand held portable device that is a lot like our smart phones but does so much more.

Consort- An uncontracted female in the position of a mate without the paperwork or the tattoos.

Contract-The legal paperwork that enables a man to have a monogamous relationship (de facto level) with a woman for a period of no less than five years. Male children stay with the father and female children are sent for training to the nearest city.

Daire-D-eye-re-Jo's eldest brother.

Domesphere- The sky area under the dome.

Eighter-a member of the territory of the way of the eight.

Elanna- E-lan-na Mari and Ethan's birthmother.

Elder-a member of the public chosen to help govern the local populace and enforce Anna's rules.

Ethan Smythe- John Smythe's nephew and newly made heir to the Smythe empire.

Family dynamics- Second cousin is a polite way to acknowledge a half sibling on your paternal side. All children on a maternal line are considered full blood siblings.

Fane Smythe- Ethan's half-brother brought back from Amvelona to guard Lia.

Fifth-a female highly prized who is born with all the innate traits that a woman should have and needs no training for the bedroom. Recognized by their purple hair. The lighter the colour the more precious the woman. These women are usually caged during their first contract.

Firebird- John's nickname for Lia.

Half-a sole female in a contracted or mated relationship.

Healer- Hospitals of the present no longer exist in the future.

Medicine is herbal based and all treatment tailored to a person's specific physical makeup.

High council- a ruling council made up of elders from the elite families of the city.

Lia aka Ember-a quarter slave living in the cells in Smythe Towers. Power stone: Carnelian.

Lilianna Smythe- Joseph Smythe's widow. Parent of Ethan and Charlotte Grace.

Joanna Mercy- the foundling whom Mari took into Mercy House at the age of 12 has grown into her personal assistant.

John Smythe- The contract Elanna forces Mari to finish on her behalf.

He treated Mari as property and unsuccessfully tried to murder her. He successfully kills Elanna.

Joseph Smythe- Dead brother of John. Mate to Lilianna. Father of Ethan. Parent of Charlotte Grace.

Mari/Marianna de Montmercy- Mostly known as Mari. Contracts to the Jackson family. Also, known as Lady Mercy and head of Mercy House. Power stone: Sodalite.

Mate/mating-the ultimate commitment within a contract between a male and female that is a lifelong binding tie. Equal to marriage. All subsequent children are raised within this family unit. The female no longer covers her hair in deference to her mated status.

Mating marks-the tattoos a male and female receive at their commitment ceremony as an outward display of the binding promise between them. Each male designs the marks his female will wear for him alone. Mating marks are on display at all formal occasions.

Mercy House-Mari's home and home to many that she has rescued for rehabilitation and training within spark city. It houses a hotel, ballet, fashion house, administration and office level, rehabilitation for battered women, orphanage and Mari's personal home in the penthouse.

Nicholas Jackson-Scott's father and mate to Susanna.

Oceania City-the dome city nearest the biggest body of water to their knowledge. Susanna's daughter Liana lives there.

Passed/Passing- Dead/Dying

Quarter-usually a loose woman found in businesses set up to take care of male needs without contracts.

Reaper-High level assassin. Undercover work usually resulting in death. Doesn't clean up bodies after.

Relaxant R- A drug like Rohypnol. Used in the cells of Smythe Towers.

Rickshaw- A three wheeled passenger cart like vehicle. These are the only vehicles that can be found in use inside the city.

Spark City is run completely on green energy sources.

Scott Jackson-disillusioned son of Nick and Susanna. Lost the will to survive without Rachael when she died.

Shell-Spark City's term for the body of a person who has passed.

Sinopia- orange red brown. The bricks in the cells are this colour.

Smythe Towers- Home to the Smythe family in Spark city.

Spark City-the dome city Mari has resided in since birth. The dome closes out much of real nature.

Spirit woman/spirit fifth-A fifth so powerful in ley line energy that they manifest all the psychic abilities and their hair turns blue with violet strands through it.

Susanna Jackson-Nick's mate and parent to Scott.

Sweeper-Assassin for hire. Quick jobs requiring precision. Leaves no trace of any crime.

The cells- Hidden in a sub level basement of Smythe Towers.

The lost colony- The fifth dome city broke away from the union of souls and has had no contact with the outside world in nearly fifty years.

The rim tenements- Slum like conditions of the outer city circle nearest to the dome wall.

The Sisters of the Sea- The Sisters are the ruling high council of Oceanic city.

The Twilight Colosseum- The place where cage matches are fought in Spark City.

The union of souls- The accords that keep peace between all cities, territories and known nations.

Third-a second female in a male/female relationship. Usually requested by mated couples for the sole purpose of procreation if the first female is unable to have children.

Twice chosen- a choosing between three people. Intimacy in this relationship is a v relationship.

Language

Siatifo-Have Courage
Qotero-Not fear

Two halves of the warrior training motto found on the underground walls of the twilight colosseum which is used for gladiator style games most weekends. Nobody owns the warriors. It is considered an honour to even be accepted into training.

Playlist

The Devil Within-Digital Daggers
Where the Lonely Ones Roam-Digital Daggers
Without You-Ashes Remain
Still Feel You Breathe-Days Of Jupiter
Impossible-Lacey Sturm
The Soldier-Lacey Sturm
Feels Like Forever-Lacey Sturm
Life Screams-Lacey Sturm
Somewhere I Belong-Angel Falls
Angel With a Shotgun-The Cab
Into the Flood-Anaria
Unfinished Memories-Eowyn
The End-Eowyn
Pretty When You Cry-Eowyn
Pieces-Red
What If I Was Nothing-All That Remains
Everything Good-Ashes Remain
Angel-Angels Fall
Dust & Gold-Arrows to Athens
Ghosts In the Water-Arrows to Athens
Chase the Sun-Arrows to Athens
Alive-Arrows to Athens
Ashes of Eden-Breaking Benjamin
Are You Ready-Three Days Grace
Angel's Fall-Breaking Benjamin
Bleed-Days Of Jupiter
If I Break-Red
Here for a Reason-Ashes Remain
Yesterday's Gone-Angels Fall

Something New-Angels Fall
Crime-Arrows to Athens
The Waiting-Arrows to Athens
Chandeliers-Sleeping At Last
We Don't Run-Bon Jovi
Runaways-Sleeping Wolf

EDITING

Broken-Seether feat. Amy Lee
End Game-Taylor Swift, Ed Sheeran
I Did Something Bad-Taylor Swift
Delicate-Taylor Swift
Dancing With Our Hands Tied-Taylor Swift
Call It What You Want-Taylor Swift
Used to Be-Arrows to Athens
I Am a Stone-Demon Hunter
Lonely Together-Avicii feat. Rita Ora
Rewrite the Stars-Zac Efron, Zendaya
Compass-SafetySuit
Be Somebody-Thousand Foot Krutch
Dear John-Julia Sheer
Stummer Schrei-Damien Dawn
Engel-Anna Blue, Damien Dawn
Dein Herz-Damien Dawn
Best Day Of my Life-American Authors
Rule the World-Walk Off the Earth
Bloodstone-Guy Sebastian
Better Days-Boyce Avenue
Courtesy Call-Thousand Foot Krutch
BAMM-Milo Manheim, Meg Donelly, Kylee Russell
Masks-Eowyn

I Don't Want to Be-Tanner Patrick